SAPPHIRE NIGHTS

CRYSTAL MAGIC, BOOK 1

PATRICIA RICE

Sapphire Nights
Patricia Rice

Copyright © 2018 Patricia Rice
Book View Cafe, March 27, 2018
First Publication: 2018

Published by Rice Enterprises, Dana Point, CA, an affiliate of Book View Café Publishing Cooperative
Cover design by Kim Killion
Map design by Melissa Stevens, The Illustrated Author
Book View Café Publishing Cooperative
P.O. Box 1624, Cedar Crest, NM 87008-1624
http://bookviewcafe.com

ISBN 978-1-61138-721-6 ebook
ISBN 978-1-611138-722-3 print

ACKNOWLEDGMENTS

So many, many people keep me sane by contributing their invaluable talents and hard work to making my books happen! Let me acknowledge and humbly thank:

My husband for his unflagging attention to detail through all the various iterations of preparing a book for release,

Kim Killion for the brilliant cover concepts she creates from my insane emails asking for "contemporary romantic magical mystery,"

Melissa Stevens at The Illustrated Author for imagining an entire town from a list of names,

Mindy Klasky and Jennifer Stevenson for reading my rough drafts and not laughing themselves silly,

The whole crew at Book View Café who perform all the tedious repetitive tasks necessary to produce a book—time after time after time,

And most of all—thanks to my wonderful readers who are willing to follow my weird paths just to see what adventure my Muse can invent next!

HILLVALE

$\sim$

The following is a purely directional map, not proportional or representative, but just for the sheer fun of it. Enjoy!

$\sim$

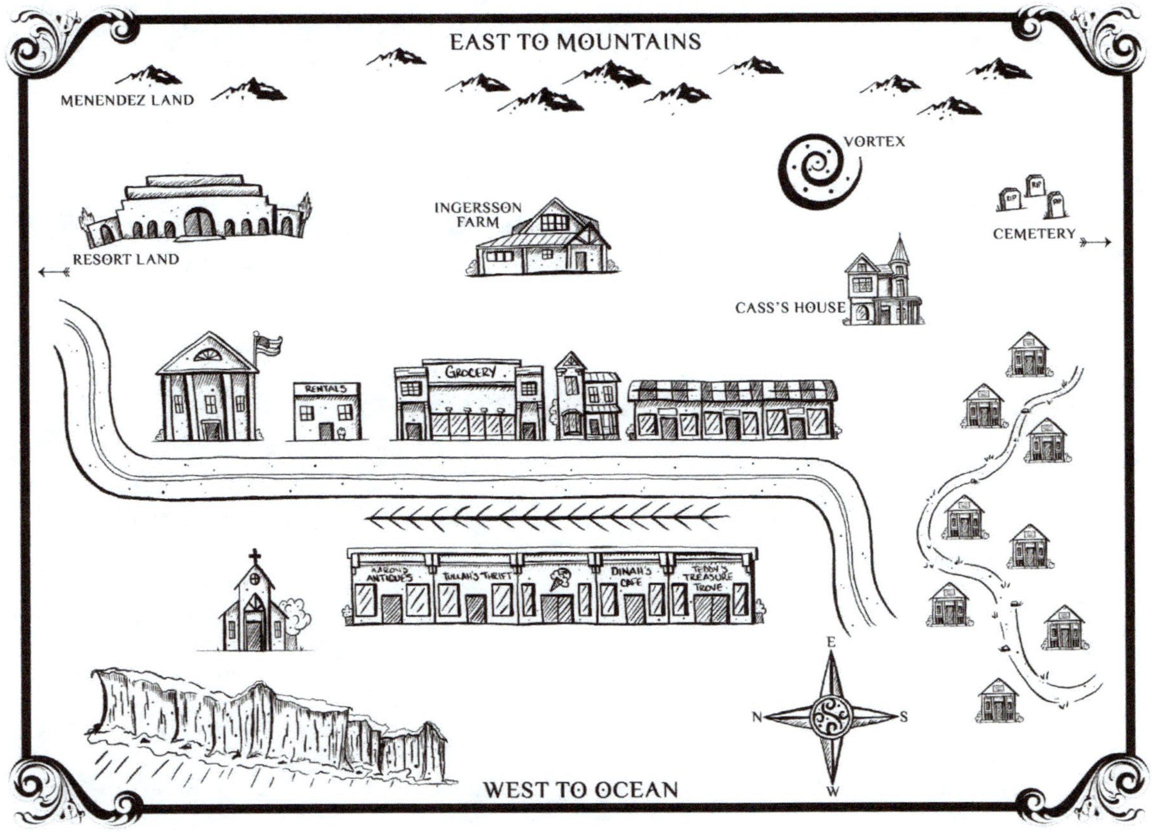

EAST TO MOUNTAINS
MENENDEZ LAND
VORTEX
INGERSSON FARM
CEMETERY
RESORT LAND
CASS'S HOUSE
RENTALS
GROCERY
AARON'S ANTIQUES
TULLAH'S THRIFT
DINAH'S CAFE
TEDDY'S TREASURE TROVE
WEST TO OCEAN
N
E
S
W

CHAPTER 1

DAWN, JUNE 16

THROUGH THE FOGGED WINDSHIELD, A MERE RIBBON OF GRAY PROVIDED the only proof that a road existed where the GPS told her to turn. Would a machine lie? She didn't know. Her head was as foggy as the glass—she couldn't remember her own name. Fear applied her foot to the gas.

Clutching the steering wheel, she mindlessly followed the headlight beams through the thick early morning dreamscape. The robotic voice on her dash was her only guidance. Praying all would be clear soon, she turned at a nearly invisible county highway sign.

The windshield wipers swiped at heavy layers of moisture. The digital clock clicked to 5:30. She'd been driving for hours and had no idea where she was.

The headlight beams picked up an old wooden signpost that might be a welcome sign. She hit the brake, heart pounding, hoping she might recognize the town's name.

HILLVALE
SPIRITUAL HOME OF 325 LIVES AND COUNTLESS GHOSTS

Wisps of vapor drifted through the headlights and around the sign, blocking most of the letters except **COUNTLESS GHOSTS**. An owl hooted in the woods. She shivered.

To drive home the point that she was lost in the wilderness, the GPS went blank and flashed *No Signal*.

She almost wept. When she'd looked at the GPS in the last gas station, an address in Hillvale had been the destination programmed under HOME. She'd pinned all her hopes on that one indication that she wasn't lost.

The only other location programmed in had been the name of the restaurant near Monterey where she'd started out. Those were her only clues. And now she was here and there was nothing, and no means of finding Cemetery Road and what she hoped would be friends and family who could help her.

After a moment of panic, she got angry. Apparently weeping wasn't her style. There *had* to be answers at the end of the road. She clenched her jaw, let her foot off the brake, and continued the climb up the mountain. From the other road signs she'd passed, she knew she was in California. The names of the towns meant nothing to her.

She was praying that at the end of this nightmare, there would be people who could take her in and tell her she'd be all right.

She didn't feel in the least all right. She didn't even know if this was her car.

A deer leaped out of nowhere, and she slammed the brake again. The shock had her breathing hard and starting to shake. She could die out here in the wilderness. Would anyone know or care? She opened the windows, hoping fresh air might steady her nerves.

The breeze was almost warm. What month was this? The damp air fogged up the inside of the windows, and she had to close them again.

She didn't see a sign of human habitation, but at this hour, everyone sensible was still asleep. The car chugged around tight uphill curves. If she could see past the mist, she feared she would find drop-offs to the sea, or maybe the center of the earth. She checked the gas gauge. She could make another thirty or forty miles before running out. All she had was the cash in her pocket. She prayed she'd reach her destination soon.

"I hope this car is mine, Emma," she told the cat in the back seat. As usual, Emma snored. The only way she knew the cat's name was from the tag on her cage. "It brakes and turns on a dime and doesn't eat gas. It's a smart car. Maybe that means I'm a smart person."

There was no radio reception up here. She had only her own voice to listen to. If she'd had music with her, it had disappeared along with her purse and phone. At least she had enough brains left to know what a phone was. And how to drive. So her memory wasn't completely gone.

Finally, the road leveled off. She thought she saw a mailbox and a driveway. A knot formed in her throat. A normal town, please, with normal people and a gas station and a place to buy coffee. A friendly voice would be nice. She desperately needed friendly and normal right now.

The Hillvale welcome sign hadn't inspired hope.

The road widened into what appeared to be a parking lot. A single pole lamp illuminated the shifting haze over painted parking spaces and a concrete walkway. Low buildings lined both sides of the road but no lights gleamed. She supposed the road went on, but she pulled into the lot to peer through the mist at what she assumed was the town. Thick moisture concealed signs telling her what the buildings might be.

She shook the little GPS but *No Signal* was all it displayed. Now was the time to cry. "Emma, we aren't in Kansas anymore," she said, trying for a laugh but not achieving it.

She thought she was quoting an old movie. Was that a sign that her mind was returning?

She could ask directions to the address she'd seen in the GPS, but she'd have to wait until the town opened. Now that she'd arrived, she was trembling badly. Maybe whoever she was didn't cry but went straight to hysterics.

Fog swirled under the one street light. If she wanted to believe in ghosts, she'd see them in the gaping dark holes between the wisps of moisture. A howling dog had her hair standing on end.

She needed coffee. She needed something concrete to pin her to reality. Cats needed to be fed sometime. Did she have cat food in here?

Realizing that in her fugue state, she hadn't looked in the suitcases in the back seat or in the trunk, she climbed out. She must have been drugged. Nothing else made sense. Why wouldn't she have looked before this?

The car was an older model Subaru wagon. Had she known that? The back end popped open to reveal a canvas cover over the cargo area. She unlatched it and studied stacks of unmarked boxes in dismay. She didn't know whether to hope or fear that they were stuffed with cash. Pulling out the first one, she realized it wasn't even taped. Opening the flap revealed a disorderly collection of books—mostly college texts and nothing useful.

She opened a healthy-sized volume on botany, and in the halogen glare of the parking lot light, read *Samantha Moon* and a phone number.

Before she could flip open the others, an ethereal figure emerged from the dark mist into the lamplight. Wearing what appeared to be a Smoky Bear hat—how could she recall that image?—a checked flannel shirt, jeans, and run-down suede boots topped with grubby faux fur, the figure appeared androgynous but not dangerous.

"A bit early for the café," the stranger said in a feminine voice. "But I've got keys. Looking for coffee?"

"I would kill for coffee," she said, then wondered if she might have killed someone. How would she know? She had been hoping someone here could tell her if she had parents, a significant other. . . kids? She didn't think she had kids, but she didn't know why.

"Long drive, huh? I'm Mariah." The stranger approached from across the lot. "I open up for Dinah most days because I'd kill for coffee too."

How did she respond? The polite thing to do was give a name, but all she had was the one in the textbook. "I'm Sam." That felt right enough to continue. "I've been driving all night. Then my GPS died, and now I'm lost. I figured I'd feed Emma first."

One of the boxes contained pet supplies, she discovered in relief. She popped open a can, retrieved a water bottle and bowl, and opened the back door. The cat was an over-large, well-furred marmalade.

Mariah peered in the backseat. "You have Emma? I've been wondering where she'd got to. You saw Cass then?"

How did she respond to that? Admit she had no memory? The first thing a normal person would do was call the police or a doctor, but what if she was a criminal? Who was Cass and why would she give her a cat?

"Last night," was all she—*Sam*—could think to say. She set the food and water on the floor, then let the cat out. Apparently there was already a litter box behind the passenger seat. Someone had thought of everything. It hadn't been her.

"Now you're really interesting me," Mariah said as Sam shut and locked the car door. "And just as a side note, cell phones don't work here either. The Nulls will tell you that it's because we're a valley surrounded by mountains with no cell tower, and the population is too thin to justify satellites." She led the way across the parking lot to a long, low building with big plate glass windows.

"Nulls?"

Mariah plugged a key into a bolt. "Techies, geeks, the unevolved." She flipped a switch inside the door, illuminating a small café with a long counter and half a dozen booths.

It was good to see clearly again. Sam studied the chipped Formica tables and counter, the red cracked vinyl stools, and wondered if she'd traveled back in time.

At least she had a sense of time, that had to be good, right?

Over the counter she caught glimpses of a mural painted between cabinets and behind machinery depicting this same diner in an earlier era—if the clothing on the people was any indication. She studied the faces, hoping to recognize them, but that was foolish. She hadn't been born at a time when women wore leather vests over lacy maxi dresses and tied their long hair back in beaded headbands. For whatever reason, the mural made her feel vaguely uneasy. The painting was faded and covered with decades of grease, as blurred as if concealed by fog.

Mariah set to filling coffee pots with the ease of experience. "Have a seat. The machinery is slow but the coffee is good."

"And there is another theory about the lack of cell phone signals?" Sam had picked up on the nuance, so she wasn't exactly stupid, always good to know. Could she hope that textbooks meant she was educated?

"You don't know about Hillvale?" With the coffee perking, Mariah flung her hat under the counter. The gesture let down lustrous black hair that she expertly braided as she talked. Sam admired her high cheekbones and brown coloring—and glanced at her own hand to verify she was a pathetic white.

Afraid to admit that she didn't even know her own name, Sam shook her head. "I was just given an address on Cemetery Road and told to head north. The town welcome sign was a little spooky on top of that address."

Mariah laughed and took down two plain white mugs. "Since you have her cat, Cassandra must have sent you. She's the only one who lives out by the cemetery."

"You know her?" Sam asked, partially in relief and partially in distraction since she had utterly no clue who had sent her.

"Cassandra is a fixture around here. I don't know why she didn't tell you the Hillvale story. She knows it better than anyone. But last I looked, she wasn't home, so I'll give you a short synopsis. Cream? Sugar?"

Sam didn't know. "Both," she decided, figuring she could try it black, then add what seemed best. So, she knew what went into coffee but didn't know what *she* put into it. Interesting. "Synopsis, please." She hid her dismay that the only person on Cemetery Road wasn't home. Worse yet, this Cass had apparently given her a cat, which indicated she might not be going home anytime soon.

Had she no family? No friends? She really was ready to weep—in disappointment as much as fear. Hope that she was coming home had carried her this far. Now, she had nothing. She swallowed hard on incipient panic.

Mariah filled a sugar container and pulled a box of artificial cream packets from under the counter. "Way back before the highways went in, the late 1800s, I think, there was a ranch and lumber mill up here. But they couldn't keep any help because the place was haunted. That was back in the days when the ladies back East played at spiritualism. Ever heard of Lily Dale?"

If she had, Sam couldn't say. She shrugged.

"Well, the ranch owner's wife was originally from New York, and she had a sister still back there who was one of the Lily Dale spiritualists. The sister got all excited about the ghosts and caught the next train, so to speak."

"I like this story." Sam drew in the rich aroma of the coffee Mariah handed her. "I like it even better with caffeine. Did the sister find ghosts?"

"Oh yeah." Mariah nodded toward the ceiling. "That's my job around here, to catch the ghosts." Without looking the least bit insane, she sipped her coffee.

Sam swung the stool around and studied the ceiling behind her. In each corner was an intricate web of yarn and string decorated with what appeared to be beads and crystals. "Aren't those called dreamcatchers? I don't see any ghosts." She almost felt disappointed as she swung back to Mariah.

The ghostcatcher beamed in approval. "Ghosts are like bad dreams. My nets are modified, of course, and they're empty because they're working. Hasn't been a haunt in here since I hung them."

There was a scam wide enough to swallow a town. "So the sister found ghosts and learned to make ghostcatchers?" she asked, trying to hide her doubt.

"Nothing is *that* simple. She claimed to channel an old Indian, Native American, Ohlone, however you want to categorize him since this tale was written well over a century ago in practically a different language. The spirit told her the ranch house was built over sacred land and the ghosts of his people were rising in protest."

"I'm guessing we've run roads over more graves than anyone can count, but I don't think it's spirits causing wrecks," Sam said, deciding she liked her coffee with sugar but not fake cream.

"Hard to say, but Hillvale is different. I'm sure you've heard about the vortex energy in Sedona. We have that here, only it's opposite. In Sedona, it spirals outward, purportedly providing healing energy, spiritual uplifting, whatever. Have you ever been?"

Sam didn't have a clue. She shook her head negatively anyway. "What would the opposite be? Sucking energy?"

"You need Cass or one of the local psychics to explain. But it apparently gives power to those below, like ghosts. And to those who can channel it, like the various spiritualists who eventually migrated here."

"After the rancher's wife's sister spread the word?" Sam couldn't hide her amusement.

"Why would Cassandra send us another Null?" Mariah cried in

exasperation, raising her cup in mockery. "We're in desperate need of fewer doubters and more believers. Don't let anyone know you're a Null! People have been stoned for less."

Casting aside the commentary as non-serious, Sam insisted, "No, really, what happened after she talked to the Indian ghost?" She'd wanted *normal*. She'd hoped for family. And what she got was a missing witch who believed in ghosts and a town of psychos? It might be time to find a head doctor. She wondered if she had insurance.

"The ranch house burned down over the sacred land. The rancher wisely rebuilt where the town now sits. The sisters started a church of healers. More spiritualists gravitated to the area. We became quite a tourist attraction back in the day when rich city people retreated to the mountains in summer. Then the highway went in, people left, the population dwindled, until the late 60s, when a bunch of hippies formed a commune in the hills you see to the east."

Sam turned to look out the window and could just make out a pink haze rising over those hills.

"We're gradually making it back on the map again," Mariah continued, "but we're still so far off the beaten path that we only make money in summer. So if you're looking for work, I wish you well but minimum wage is about it. Some of the psychics do well, but it takes time to establish a clientele."

"No internet to spread the word?"

Mariah refilled her mug. "Oh yeah, we have cable. Stay here long enough and you'll meet our mayor, Monty Kennedy. His family owns half the mountain north of here. He and his brother had cable run in for the lodge. So far, they haven't actually bought a satellite or cell tower. Give them time."

"I detect a faint sour note," Sam said with amusement as Mariah filled her own cup and opened a pie case with yesterday's leftovers.

"Monty and Kurt are the Null to end all Nulls. Men are so. . . damned logical. To most women, TV waves and internet clouds are magic. To most men, they're easily explainable technology. But give men a whiff of weird they can't account for without cords and wires, and they go bug-eyed."

"That's sexist." Sam's taste buds watered as Mariah slapped a piece of apple pie in front of her. "I'm down to my last few dollars," she admitted. "I can't contribute much to the economy. How much does pie cost up here?"

"It's leftover. It's free. Coffee's on me, a welcome-to-town gift. If Cassandra sent you here, then there has to be a good reason, and I'm eager to hear your story."

Sam tasted the pie and let it melt in her mouth. *This* was normal. She considered her answer as she chewed. "I don't think I'm free to tell my story yet," she said. Not until she knew what it was anyway.

Mariah nodded just as a cheery voice rang out from the back. "Pour me some of that java, dear. I feel a good wind in the air. It's time to fix my beignets."

"Dinah, we've got company. Come meet Sam."

"You finally got a man, Mariah girl?" A tiny African-American cook swaddled in a white cotton apron popped through the swinging doors. Short Afro hair, ruby lips, rings in her ears—and an Adam's apple and no breasts under a flannel shirt much like Mariah's.

Dinah took one look at Sam, cocked a hip, and pouted. "You ain't no Sam. You're as straight as our ghostcatcher here."

That's when the wind blew open the front door and a uniformed officer strode in—limping.

CHAPTER 2

RATHER THAN REPLY TO NOT BEING A *SAM*, SHE STUDIED THE TALL, masculine arrival overpowering the small café. Mariah and Dinah didn't flinch at his entrance. Unlike them, Sam observed the uniformed officer from a perspective of fear—and not just because her eyes were on a level with his broad chest. The mirrored shades tucked between the buttons of his khaki shirt oddly escalated her fear. Had he come in because her car was a stolen vehicle? She bit down on her tongue to keep from freaking out.

Finally daring to lift her chin, Sam looked straight into single-lidded green eyes in a flat-nosed, taut-jawed visage that indicated mixed-race parentage. For some reason, the tightness in her chest lessened. He met their stares with a hardened expression and a nod. Studying his full lower lip, Sam swallowed for different reasons. She was definitely heterosexual. Or terror turned her on.

He took off his official cowboy-style hat, revealing dark hair shaved on the sides. "Good morning, ladies." His laser-beam gaze focused on Sam. "Don't think we've been introduced."

"Sam, this is Deputy Chen Ling Walker. Walker, Sam is staying up at Cass's place. She's brought Emma back, so all is well." Mariah poured a mug of coffee and slid it across the counter. She gestured from Sam to Dinah. "Sam, this is Dinah, the best cook in town. If you're looking for work, she's the place to start."

Dinah held out her hand. It was callused, blunt, and strong. "Sammy here has a blue aura that bodes well, hon. If she's staying, I'm hiring."

Was she staying? It wasn't as if she knew where else to go. "Thank you. Let me sleep for a few hours so I can think straight before I make any major decisions." And pray she'd wake up knowing who she was. Was it possible to hire people without ID?

"That coffee won't help you sleep." The deputy threw his leg over a counter stool one away from hers. "That your Subaru in the lot?"

Oh gulp, here it came. "Good car," she murmured evasively. "Didn't give me a bit of problem even when the deer jumped at it."

"I've been thinking of getting one for the traction in winter, but they're not very tall. You'll have to give me a ride sometime." He drank his coffee and looked at Dinah, adding a note of hope to his voice. "Don't suppose you have any of that pie left over?"

Sam looked guiltily at the last piece on her plate.

"Don't you worry, hon, I brought in a fresh one just for you. Give me a minute to get set up, and I'll be right out." Dinah sashayed out as if she were in full evening regalia.

"Blue aura?" Deputy Walker asked.

Sam mentally thanked him for asking.

"Blue has all the positive connotations of the universe," Mariah said, polishing off her piece of pie. "Clear thinking, healing, calm, intuitive, and in the right shade, clairvoyant."

"You read auras too?" Sam asked, wanting to believe in hocuspocus because she had nothing else to go on. She didn't feel very clairvoyant though. Or calm.

"Nah, I just watch and learn. Pays to keep up with the crazies in this town. Dinah is one of the sane ones, though. I'm sure the good deputy here can tell you all about her past, but it doesn't matter up here. I've got to get back to my route. If you want me to show you Cass's place, I'll ride along with you. That's easier than biking uphill."

Sam would have liked to have heard about Dinah's past, but the knowledge that the deputy checked everyone out scared the bejeebers out of her. Although—if she wasn't a criminal—maybe she could ask him to trace her license plate?

What happened if she couldn't get into Cass's place? Could she leave her car in the driveway and sleep in it?

She savored the last bite of pie, finished her coffee, and stood up. "Good meeting you, deputy."

He saluted her with his mug but didn't bother looking up. Well, so much for that quiver of attraction. She probably looked like dirt. She felt like it anyway.

Mariah shouted at Dinah that they were leaving, then led the way out. To Sam, she said, "We all have our secrets out here. Not all of us keep them. Be careful to whom you talk."

"Like the deputy?" Sam unlocked the car doors, not certain whether it was safe to open the back door to re-cage the cat. Was Emma an escape cat? And how did she know some cats liked to escape?

Mariah solved the Emma problem by opening the passenger side, finding the cat on the front floorboard, then settling down with it in her lap. Emma stretched her marmalade paws and purred. "Walker is a decent guy, but he's here for a reason he's not telling us. There's more to him than meets the eye, so watch out."

Well, so much for asking for a license plate trace. She'd wait for desperation to set in—which could be right after she'd had a few hours of sleep. It belatedly occurred to her that since she had no purse, she had no driver's license or insurance card. *Shit.*

Apparently, she was someone who used foul language. She backed the car out and turned south, as Mariah indicated.

"Does everyone here have something to hide, then?" she asked, wondering if that included Mariah and afraid to find out. She'd like to think she had one friend.

"Nah, the mayor and his family own half the valley. He's been here all his life and is as straight as they come. Boring, arrogant, and a bully, but he doesn't try to hide it. There are a few other people who were born here, not many. Everyone knows the entire past of the locals and some of everyone's future, if you believe in clairvoyance."

"I don't think our fates are carved in stone, so fortune-telling doesn't make sense to me," Sam said, thinking it through as she peered through the fog to find the road. It wasn't as if she knew what her former self thought. If her memory didn't return, she might have to become a whole new person.

"But it might be possible to predict a future based on current paths," Mariah argued. "Let's face it, if a con man keeps on conning, then eventually he'll get caught. That's not hard to predict."

"All right, that makes sense, so the trick would be knowing the person was a conman in the first place." Sam studied the towering redwoods—how did she know they were redwoods?—lining the road. The fog hadn't lifted so much as the sunlight had reached over the mountain. Again, she wondered what month it was.

"And that's the whole basis for fortune-telling," Mariah said in satisfaction, "Knowing your clientele. Cass's drive is right up here, on your right. The cemetery is only a few hundred yards further on."

They hadn't driven far from town. She could easily walk it, if needed—avoiding anything that might require a license. The driveway was distinctively marked by a bright red barn of a mailbox sitting on a rusted hand-held plow post. That didn't look very scary.

"Crazy Daisy built that mailbox," Mariah said as they turned up the rutted, once-graveled drive. "She said Cass's black monstrosity spooked her."

Oh well, live and learn. "Crazy Daisy?" Sam asked politely, searching for some sign of a house amid the trees and overgrown bushes. With excitement, she recognized bay laurel saplings among the redwoods. How did she know these things?

"Daisy is too weird to pry anything sensible out of her. Artistic as heck, though. Creates cool sculptures of twigs and wood and stone, and recycles junk into usable stuff like the mailbox back there. She'd probably be homeless elsewhere, but here, we pay for her talent, if only in food and shelter. It's easier for people who aren't capable of living in normal society to find a place with us. We need all kinds."

A silhouette of a building appeared through the mist, and Sam didn't reply. Cassandra's house was tall, much taller than she'd imagined when she hoped she was coming home. As they approached, she made out a huge Victorian with turrets and wide porches, and if she was seeing correctly, gargoyles on the gutters. "Wow," she murmured.

"Cass calls it a B&B and rents rooms when any of us have guests, but she doesn't advertise. I don't know how she lives out here all alone in this spooky place. She travels a lot, so she leaves me the keys. I'll put you in the guest house. It's more modern and comes with a small kitchen and everything."

"A bed would be good right now," Sam admitted, feeling the stress catching up with her, grateful that Mariah accepted that the invisible Cass wanted her here. "Will Emma be all right in the guest house or does she prefer her own home?"

"Emma is a slug who will do whatever she likes. She's familiar with the territory and comes and goes at her leisure. Don't worry about her. As long as there are food and water available, she's good."

As if in agreement, Emma offered a loud meow. Maybe she knew she was home.

Mariah pointed at a side drive to the back of the house. "Cass had a studio built over the garage."

Sam pulled up to a two-story white-washed stucco garage—a far cry from the painted lady beyond the manzanita and serviceberry hedge. A pot of orange-red geraniums spilled color at the foot of a tiled entryway—a bright spot of light against the gray fog. "This is lovely. Are you sure Cassandra won't mind?"

"Not if she sent you up here with Emma. I'll carry the cat if you want to take your suitcases."

Terracotta tile lined the stairs up to a small balcony overlooking the mountain ridge to the east. Inside the heavy timber front door was an open-floor-plan studio with more tile, artwork, and windows with a panoramic view of trees and scrub tumbling down to the west—presumably toward the sea. Sam gaped at the vast horizon.

"The bed's behind the Mexican blanket over there. It's all simple but functional." Mariah set down the cat, who sniffed the baseboard, intent on tracking down intruders. "I'll bring up the cat stuff if you want to take a look around and settle in."

She needed to investigate her suitcases and boxes. Whatever fugue state had held her all night must be dissipating with dawn. Maybe she had a laptop. As weary as she was, she was even more scared now that she knew she had no family or friends to tell her who she was. Maybe pure terror was blowing out the cobwebs in her brain.

Mariah brought up the cat food and dishes and glanced at the ghostcatchers in the corners. "It looks clear in here. Cass doesn't like having the nets in her house, but she agreed they might be good for guests. I've never found a ghost here though. I think Cass put a spell on the foundation when they were building it."

Sam was so weary, that she almost expressed gratitude for the thoughtfulness of spelling away ghosts. She rubbed her brow, found a small mole-sized bump, and realized that other than a glimpse in a dim rear-view mirror, she didn't even know what she looked like. "Thanks for everything, I really appreciate it. How do I reach you if I have questions?"

"You'll just have to leave a message with Dinah. I'm in and out of there all day, helping when it's busy. There are some basic groceries in the kitchen. You can pick up more at Pasquale's once he opens. Everything is there in the town square. Get some sleep and come on back to town." Mariah slipped out, closing the door behind her.

Sam was alone again. And life was most definitely not normal yet.

She stopped in the bathroom to get rid of the coffee and looked in the mirror over a vanity made from an antique Mexican washstand. Apparently she was a tall thin woman, younger than she felt, with fly-away ash-blond hair, a mole above her left eyebrow, an average nose and mouth, and blue eyes. Her crinkled cloud of hair probably needed a ton of product to control it.

She saw no bruises, bleeding, or knots that might indicate she'd been hit over the head.

Emma curled around her ankles, purring reassuringly. Sam scratched behind the cat's ears and returned to the bedroom and her suitcases. They were battered old hard-sided ones that looked older than she did and could have been picked up in a thrift store. Whoever Samantha Moon was, she wasn't rich.

Inside the first one was a case of toiletries, underwear, pajamas, and a collection of old t-shirts, tank tops, shorts, and jeans. She apparently dressed like an impoverished college student.

Inside the second case was a newer—although not new—navy blazer, no-iron white blouse, and a long gray skirt, all wrapped in plastic to prevent wrinkles. If she was to make a guess, she'd call them job-interview clothes. Underneath was a layer of khakis, leggings, and long-sleeve shirts for cooler weather, plus one broomstick, tie-dye skirt in shades of olive green. She might as well be a time-traveling hippy.

There was no computer or any other piece of technology.

"Well, Emma, we're up a creek now, aren't we?" she asked the cat, who had jumped on the bed to examine her meager wardrobe.

"Hmmmm," Emma purred, before nesting on the plastic-covered clothes.

It would be good to believe the cat had told her she was home. She loved the studio already, but then, she was probably crazy.

Sam removed the suitcases, cat and all, to the floor. A little orange fur wouldn't hurt that motley assortment of apparel. Digging out a ragged gray sweatsuit, she changed out of her jeans and sweater and slid between the sheets.

Maybe she would wake up and all would be right again.

CHAPTER 3

Afternoon, June 16

Hours later, Sam woke abruptly to loud pounding. Sunshine poured through the windows beyond the blanket wall. The urgent thumping on the timber door could have been made by an ax. Panicking, she reached for her phone—and realized it wasn't there, that she didn't have one.

How did one call 911 without a cell phone? Oh, cable, landline. Dragging herself from the lovely feather pillow, she glanced around. An old push-button phone was on the lower shelf of the nightstand.

Emma yowled a warning, leaped from the suitcase, and ran from the room.

Calling 911 would likely bring Deputy Walker.

Grabbing a hair tie out of the toiletry bag she'd left on the dresser, sliding on a cheap pair of rubber flip-flops, Sam slipped into the front room. She tried to peer through the stained glass of the sidelights to the balcony but could only see shadows. The thumping momentarily stopped and a loud bell tolled.

Sam glanced up at the ceiling. Sure enough, a mission bell hung overhead, attached to a rope that probably went outside. It rang again.

She tugged open the heavy door and was rewarded with a sharp rap on her head. Without thinking, she grabbed the offending weapon and yanked it away, then rubbed her head and glared. "Ow, what did you do that for?"

Nearly as tall as Sam, a skeletal woman dressed in a concealing veil and black drapery scowled at her and retrieved her gnarled walking stick. "You didn't answer. I need Cass urgently. Tell me where she is."

"Not here. And hello to you too." Hmmm, this Sam person might be a smartass.

"I *know* she's not here," the—witchy was the best description—woman snarled. "But you must have seen her. Where?"

Since the last address Sam remembered was the one in the GPS, she responded, "Monterey." She was about to slam the door, then remembered she was a stranger here and needed help. Never close the door on someone she might need to ask for help—it seemed a good proverb to live by, whether or not she'd made it up herself.

"Blast and damn," the woman muttered. "She's done it. You'll have to do. Come along."

She was starving. She needed to examine the boxes in the trunk. She needed a computer. Now that she had a phone, she could try the Samantha Moon number in the book.

"I'm hungry. You may come in and tell me what you want me to do." Sam turned to go back to the kitchen, but Witchy Woman grabbed her elbow.

"No time. Without knowing her coordinates, I can't astral project. Lives depend on us."

She dragged Sam out the door and into a. . . golf cart?

Even if she could be heard over the grinding motor, or keep her teeth from chattering from the wild bumps on a bad road without shock absorbers, Sam was too busy hanging on to ask questions. Whoever this wild woman was, she drove like a maniac in a vehicle not intended for speed—or for the gravel lane they swerved onto after they flew through town.

Whose lives depended on them?

With relief, she saw Mariah at the end of the rutted lane. Maybe she'd get answers now.

Staggering out of the cart, into the dusty chaparral well above the town, Sam planted her flip-flops on firm ground and studied the terrain. She noted the natural flora of a dry, west coast plateau but didn't see anyone dying or in danger of doing so.

Refusing to follow the command of a woman who wouldn't show her face, Sam rubbed her temple and strained to recall how she'd ended up in this weird situation—but nothing came to her. She still wasn't even certain her name was Samantha.

Other women appeared over the ridge, walking up some back trail. Sam didn't have a good map in her head of the area yet and wasn't even sure she could find her way back. Reluctantly, she started toward the one known in this landscape—Mariah.

In the process, she almost stumbled over a long fissure in the dry ground. Mariah stood at the far end of it, staring down in. . . horror? Fascination? It was hard to tell from this angle. Sam watched where she walked so she didn't stub her toe on the cracked ground—until she saw the bone.

Instinct kicked in. With appalled fascination, she crouched down to study the brown and corroding ivory with one knobby end protruding. She was pretty certain it was a femur. She had no idea how she knew that—but that was a human body down there. She shuddered when she glimpsed the skull.

WITHOUT A QUALM, WALKER RAN THE SUBARU'S UTAH LICENSE PLATE through the system. He might be taking a sabbatical from his investigative firm and all his agents, but as a cop, he had access to official databases. The car had no stolen vehicle report. Owner information from out of state would take a little longer.

Sam might just be passing through. Tourists kept the town running, after all. But there was something about the way the women had latched on to the newcomer that said she might be more. Hillvale was full of eccentrics. Sam didn't appear to be one of them, but that could be wishful thinking.

Face it, Walker, life is full of weirdness, and you need to get past it.

He pinched his nose and shut up his inner demon. His self-enforced sabbatical from his real life was meant to quiet the craziness and return him to normal. He only had six months of this rural cop stint left to find out what no law enforcement agency had been able to uncover. He meant to leave no stone unturned—and that included listening to weird women.

He steered the county's official four-wheel drive Explorer up the mountain to the Kennedys' ostentatious luxury hotel. Redwood Resort could have been as easily called Timberland, the name of the original ranch. The first floor had a log façade, with log cabins dotting the woods surrounding it. He'd read up on the history. Back in the 70's, environmentalist tree-huggers had nearly burned the place down in protest of the destruction of half a forest and the toxic creosote used to treat the logs.

Walker could see the argument on either side and didn't much care which group was right. The main issue was that the Kennedys and the remnants of that early hippy commune had been at war ever since.

Kurt Kennedy had a security crew to patrol the grounds since the county road stopped at the front door. Still, Walker liked to cruise in, check with Juan, head of security, and keep an eye on things. It was good publicity for the sheriff's department and gave him an opportunity to observe new people.

This small town job was a no-brainer next to the corporate investigation firm he needed to return to.

It still had its moments. Today, the parking lot was spilling over with locals and tourists on foot instead of in cars. He had to stop on the side of the road and stroll the last few hundred feet, studying the crowd for its source. His damaged leg muscles needed stretching anyway.

Crazy Daisy was the center of attention, of course. Her face was unlined and ageless, but her graying dark hair stood out in a tangled nimbus around her head, giving evidence that she wasn't young. She was of average height, probably weighed more than he did, but her flesh hung on her bare arms in folds, as if she'd lost a lot of weight. On any given day she could be garbed in beaded leather or red western attire, but the shedding feather cloak went with her everywhere.

Today, she wore purple and black satin and a ring of flowers in her hair—dead ones. She was busily sprinkling sparkling dust in a design at her feet.

"We are telling you, she will *die*! The prophecy has come true! Look around you, see what you have wrought with your iron and your steel, your destruction of mother earth! The evidence lies right up that mountain," a voice declared in the thunderous tones of an experienced stage actor.

Walker rolled his eyes as the crowd gave way so he could see into the clearing. Daisy seldom spoke in anything except circles and never with such venom, so he knew it wasn't Daisy speaking, but Valdis. Her real name was Valerie Ingersson. But half the people up here invented their own names. Valdis called herself after the Norse goddess of death. Tall, skeletal, usually garbed in flowing black rags, and a veil concealing her face and black hair, she played the part well.

He'd seen her once without all the gear. Her black hair had blond roots, and her chin was marred by an angry scar. Everyone up here had a story.

From the steps of the resort, Kurt Kennedy glared at the show with disapproval. Walker caught his eye and quirked a questioning eyebrow. Kurt nodded without a smile.

Not much older than Walker, the wealthy, uptight resort manager had no sense of humor on a good day, if he ever had good days.

Walker entered the clearing and caught Valdis by her bony elbow. Daisy made an awkward curtsy in her billowing purple skirt. He bowed his head in acknowledgment of her wordless greeting.

Valdis continued screeching, but at him now. "Save the earth goddess or she will die as the other did!"

"I don't think the guests can help," he said, applying the respectful tone he used on his mother when she raged. "Why don't we go some-where quiet and discuss this?" He steered Valdis toward the side of the sprawling lodge and offered his arm to Daisy.

"You have kept your crystals safe?" Daisy asked beneath her friend's shouting. "You are walking a dark path, and you will need them to light the way."

Daisy had built him a clever stone man of wire, rocks, and shiny crystals when he'd first arrived. He kept the sculpture on a windowsill in his Baskerville apartment because he admired both the stones and the art. "Rocky is doing just fine. What's the shouting about?"

"We don't know for certain," Daisy whispered. "But the prophecies have been proven. More deaths will follow."

Sometimes Daisy made good sense, if one weeded out references to paths future and past.

Walker nodded at the security captain opening his office door for them. "Juan, good to see you."

The older, stouter man nodded unsmilingly as he gestured for them to enter. Walker got the impression that Juan disliked Walker's Chinese heritage, or maybe just his educated city background. Since he had more important goals here, Walker ignored any implied slight and used the guard's authority for his own purposes. The resort was private property, after all.

Juan's crew would break up the crowd now that the troublemakers were out of sight. Walker could just leave the two women here and let them calm down, but generally, they didn't create trouble without reason, however weird their purpose might be. So he pushed them inside, where he perched on the edge of the desk and crossed his arms. "All right, ladies, who will die? Is there something I can do?"

Valdis paced jerkily. Daisy drifted off in her own world, staring at a photograph of an owl.

"It is as Cassandra predicted—" With a dramatic gesture pointing up the mountain, Valdis glared. "The earth mother will die unless we act now. Her gatekeeper is already dead." She stalked out, as if expecting him to follow.

"There are four black crows on the gravestone," Crazy Daisy said sadly. "The Morrigan has arrived."

She used a tone that might as well have said "The end is nigh" before following the Norse death goddess.

Since they went up the mountain and not back to the parking lot, Walker debated whether to go after them. *You're a crazy magnet* his inner demon complained. Walker ignored the warning and sent a wordless question to the older man.

"They been gathering up on Menendez land all morning," Juan reported. "Might want to take a look. It could be a ritual sacrifice for all I know. They're off our grounds, so I didn't check it out."

"They?" Walker stood up and led the way out, the shorter man on his heels. He pretty much already knew the answer to his question, but he'd rather avoid surprises.

"The usual bunch," the guard confirmed. "We let them park here when we don't have a lot of guests. Monty says encouraging the locals is good for business."

Walker snorted at the mayor's peacemaking efforts. Monty and Kurt jointly owned the lodge with their mother. He was glad he didn't have to keep the family peace. "What does Kurt say?"

"It's a load of hokum," Juan said in a tone indicating his agreement with his boss.

"Some of the ladies are pretty influential. The mayor could be right." Walker followed the mulch path the resort optimistically called a woodland walk. The uneven ground exacerbated his limp, but he'd deal. Up ahead, he could catch glimpses of the flowing drapery of Valdis and Daisy. He didn't know why all that fabric didn't catch on the prickly pear cactus growing all through here.

Before long, they veered off the mulch path and followed a rockier one. Sand slid from beneath his boots, loosening the stones they walked on. Layers of shale, sandstone, and volcanic rock from the tectonic shifts of the San Andreas fault formed these unstable mountains. In the rainy season, mudslides shifted the geology with enough energy to take out a town.

In place of worrying about mudslides, he probably ought to worry that it had been a relatively dry spring. People weren't as cautious with their campfires here as they were further south in the more arid hills.

He stopped on a rocky outcrop and gazed over a plateau too far north and east for a view of the town below. The area had once been covered in ancient redwoods, but they'd been logged long ago. It was mostly scrub brush now.

The women had formed a ragged circle to his right. To Walker's disappointment, the newcomer was with them. He'd hoped she was just visiting and not one of Cass's coven, although he should have known better. She was sitting cross-legged, leaning against a tree, and studying whatever the hell was happening. Maybe she was an outside observer from some other town's coven.

"There's thirteen," Juan said in disgust as Valdis and Daisy rejoined the group. "Superstitious claptrap."

One of the women waved a smoking weed over the cleared center of the circle, while the others chanted. Were they huddling over hot coals? The day wasn't cold, and he saw no flames, although the ground did seem displaced. Maybe they were raising zombies.

"Think I'll take a look," Walker decided, not liking smoke in the dry scrub. The scene looked off to him, and Valdis and Daisy had talked about the death of a *gatekeeper*. The Lucys were inclined toward superstitious claptrap, as Juan said, but they also displayed a deeper concern and intelligence for the land than the Kennedys and their lot did, for all their money and education.

And Walker had reason to be concerned about mysterious deaths.

Juan shrugged, chugged at the water bottle he carried on his hip, and followed him down the crude path.

The new girl in town—Sam—looked up the instant they hit the plateau. She rose and walked toward them with willowy grace—even in her totally impractical flip-flops. He liked the way her hair flew wild and free around movie star cheekbones. What the hell was she wearing? A sweat suit? With nothing under it? Walker had to force his eyes to focus on her face. He wasn't allowing any more crazy into his life.

As they approached, he could see her forehead carved into worried lines. He expected to hear crows cawing three times any second—and that was his father's Irish superstition coming to haunt him.

"You fall in with the wrong crowd fast," he said gruffly as she came close enough for him to observe the pucker over her aquiline nose.

"They apparently needed thirteen people, and I was all they had. And I'm guessing your attitude is the reason they didn't call you." She said that without an ounce of disapproval, merely turning back the way she came. "But I'm relieved you're here. Val and Daisy said they tried to warn you, but you didn't believe them."

"Val and Daisy talk in riddles. Next time, send someone coherent." His limp easily limited his stride to match her slower one, while he kept his eye on the group ahead.

The women appeared to be keening now, huddled around an open. . . grave?

"I trust there will be no next time," she said in what sounded like alarm. "If this happens often, I'm wearing shoes to bed."

He snorted and glanced down at her dusty toes. "They dragged you out of bed?"

"You think I go hiking like this regularly? There are probably rattlesnakes out here!"

"Only the western rattlesnake survives in this climate. Try not answering the door," he suggested.

She shot him an azure glare that relieved some of his tension as they arrived at the circle of women—which parted to let him pass.

His gut knotted and his relief vanished.

A fissure had opened in the dry earth, revealing a human skull and what appeared to be a leg bone.

He'd been afraid of this, but what was left of his heart split in two.

CHAPTER 4

AFTERNOON, JUNE 16

EFFICIENTLY, DEPUTY WALKER CLEARED VAL'S FRIENDS AWAY FROM WHAT Sam assumed was a grave site. The skull had looked old, but the women were agitated. Call her an unsympathetic wimp, but beyond intellectual curiosity, she didn't really care about long-dead bones. She had an urgent need, not only for food but for the relative sanity of Cass's place and the boxes waiting there. Unfortunately, she was stranded out here with chanting witches and no car.

Old graves were probably scattered all through these parts, so she didn't see any reason to linger. Smudging and chanting wouldn't bring back the dead. When the hunky deputy brushed her off by suggesting she return to the lodge with the surly man in a security uniform, Sam accepted.

The older man helped her over rocky ledges where her feet tended to slip out of the ridiculous beach shoes.

"Did the natives who lived here not bury their dead in the cemetery?" she tried asking once they were back on a reasonable path.

"Natives lived down on the coast, not up here," the guard said. "Only people ornery enough to wrestle with grizzlies settled up here."

Grizzlies? There were grizzlies as well as rattlesnakes? *Western* rattlesnakes, as if the type made any difference.

"Oh, I thought the cemetery was a native burial ground." Or maybe Mariah had said *sacred* ground—and she really hadn't specified the location.

"That's just an old folktale," he said in dismissal. "Gives the locals a reason to keep anyone from building out here. They don't like strangers settling in."

Two sides to every story, she supposed. When they reached a small log cabin marked SECURITY, a tall, solidly built man in a suit, who obviously belonged in a city, waited for them. Dark hair and stubborn jaw accentuated his scowl. He wore a fancy gold watch and what appeared to be an expensive linen shirt open at the throat to reveal a deep tan.

"Where's Walker?" he demanded.

Sam wasn't certain if he was asking her or the man with her.

"Got a situation up there on the Menendez land. Wasn't none of our concern, so I said I'd put in a call to the sheriff's office and escort the lady back down. The witches kidnapped her, and she's got no way of getting home."

"Kidnapped?" the man asked. He unbent enough to look at her. "Sorry, I don't mean to interrogate. I'm Kurt Kennedy, manager of the resort."

Sam held out her hand. "Samantha Moon." She was getting used to saying the name and prayed it was hers. "It wasn't precisely kidnapping. I was half asleep, and they were insistent. Is there a taxi or anything I can take back to town? I don't think I can walk in flip-flops."

She was hoping a taxi wouldn't be expensive. What little money she had was back at Cass's, and she really needed to buy food with it.

Annoyingly, Kennedy glanced over her head at his employee. "What's the situation?"

"Found an old grave. Walker is setting it up like it's a crime scene. Probably just one of the old settlers," the guard said with a shrug.

"Give Walker whatever support he needs, but try to keep the official vehicles to the back lot where they won't upset the guests." Kennedy glanced down at Sam's toes. "I have to go into town to talk to my brother anyway. Why don't I drop you off somewhere? It's the least we can do to show you we're not entirely nuts up here."

"That would be perfect," Sam said in relief. So whoever she was, she trusted total strangers. She took her perceived intelligence down two notches but followed Kennedy anyway. She really didn't have many choices.

She almost hated to pollute Kurt Kennedy's low-slung Mercedes sports car with her sandy flip-flops and ragged sweats. How absurd, she realized a second later. Perhaps, as a student, she'd been uncomfortable about her poverty in the face of wealth. If so, this new Samantha needed to grow up. She ignored the dirty footprint she created on the carpeted floorboard.

"I hope this little incident doesn't mar your visit here," Kurt said as he shifted the car into gear.

She'd like to say starvation was marring her visit, but then he'd feel obligated to feed her. "I'm easily entertained," she said instead.

Apparently, she wasn't attracted to suave rich men wearing expensive watches and aftershave. Maybe she ought to take this opportunity to readjust her thinking—especially since, without a memory, she was looking at a future as a homeless vagrant.

"Walker said you're staying at Cass's?" The question held a note of disapproval.

"I brought her cat back. But I didn't get the key. If you'll drop me off at the café, I'll wait for Mariah." And get food and maybe she ought to take up that job offer.

Would she have a boyfriend or husband worrying about her? Filing a missing person report? The ever-present knot in her middle tightened. She tried to focus on the moment, but the car sped down the winding road, not giving her much opportunity to admire the resort's landscaping.

"I'd like to make up for your rude introduction to our town. Would you be interested in having dinner with me this evening at the lodge? I could clue you in on our neighbors so you won't be kidnapped anymore."

He swung the car into the lot. She hadn't been able to study the town through the fog when she'd first arrived, or as her kidnapper had rattled through later. Now, Sam could see Hillvale was no more than a crumbling mix of ramshackle small buildings lining both sides of the highway, with a parking lot in the middle. Some of the structures had logs like the resort, others were adobe or clapboard. A sagging covered boardwalk connected them. Her driver turned off the ignition, acting as if the question of dinner were already settled.

She looked like a homeless person dragged from under a bridge. Why would this man ask her to dinner? Maybe she ought to find out. Since she had no idea how she would buy dinner otherwise, Sam felt compelled to accept. "What time?" And then she had to wonder what in heck she would wear.

"Will seven work?" He glanced out the windshield. "Looks like Mariah is waiting for you. I'll see you then."

Bossy, she didn't like that. But. . . *free meal*. With a salute, Kurt marched off. Sam crossed the lot to confront Mariah. "How did you get back here so fast?"

Mariah pointed her chin at the mountain looming over the town hall. "Shortcut."

Sam didn't plan to hang around long enough to learn it. "I need keys to get in the house, I think."

"There's a key under the geranium, sorry." Mariah smirked and nodded at the departing resort manager. With the fog lifting, she looked more sturdy and less surreal than earlier. "See you fell in with the rich crowd pretty fast."

"Val's fault. I need food before I talk about it." She let herself into the café.

The café had a few customers scattered among the stools and booths. They all turned to stare. Sam was beyond feeling self-conscious about her attire at this point. So, she was naked beneath her sweats. It wasn't as if she had anything to hide—except her lack of identity. That problem was so huge that anything else was irrelevant.

Dinah greeted them with a wave and slapped coffee down in front of a vacant stool before Sam could choose one. "Breakfast or lunch?"

"My money is still up at Cass's, can I owe you?" Sam doctored the caffeine with sugar and sipped gratefully. She glanced at a newspaper someone had left on the counter. *June*, it was June—another piece of her foundation returned.

"You come work for me, and you get all you can eat," Dinah said. "You're providing free entertainment around here."

"Charmed, I'm sure," Sam said dryly. "Eggs and toast, please, and can I go home and get dressed first? And have the night off? I'm supposed to have dinner with Mr. Kennedy."

Dinah's belly laughed filled the café. For such a small person, she had lungs. Sam felt oddly warmed that her smart mouth was appreciated.

"You have anything besides sweats and jeans to wear to dinner?" Mariah asked, slipping behind the counter to take a tourist's money at the cash register while Dinah returned to the kitchen for eggs.

Sam grimaced in remembrance of the interview outfit in her suitcase. "Business attire. How do they dress up there?"

"Like tourists, mostly, except for some of the older ladies," a plump, orange-haired woman wearing a red peasant blouse and blue tie-dyed skirt said from two stools down. She held out a hand encrusted with rings that matched her hair. "I'm Amber. I do tarot readings across the street. If you're joining Dinah's staff, I'll be happy to give you a complimentary spread to welcome you to town."

"She's good," Mariah called from the register. "Accept her offer."

"Is everyone in this town so bossy?" Sam asked of no one.

"Opinionated," Amber corrected. "It's a small town full of big personalities. It's no place to be shy."

"I'm pretty sure I'm not shy," Sam said, thinking aloud. "I'm just a fish out of water. So business attire will be okay for dinner?"

"The Kennedys wear designer suits like mine," a big, bluff man with so much golden hair it didn't look real intruded on their conversation as he stood and reached for his wallet. "They like their women rich. No one in this pit qualifies." He walked out with the stride of a man confident he owned the world and everyone in it. His suit and watch would probably buy the café.

"Alan Gump from San Francisco," Mariah murmured. "Owns Gump Real Estate. They buy land for corporations. He's not only a Null but an outsider. We don't talk to him."

A tall thin man with stooped shoulders and a faded green blazer ambled out after Gump.

"Xavier Black, Gump's stooge," Mariah added. "He got left in the cemetery too long way back and isn't fit for more than printing out rental contracts for tourists. He has an office here."

"Do we talk to Xavier?" Sam asked in amusement, wondering what *left in the cemetery too long* was a metaphor for.

Mariah shrugged. "Gump is right, though, the town is dying, and we'll never be rich."

Dinah returned with a flaky croissant plus a plate full of steaming scrambled eggs mixed with bits of spinach, tomato, and cheese. "Go see Tullah about clothes," Dinah said. "She runs the thrift store three doors down. Tell her I sent you. She'll find something and you can return it tomorrow. Start work tomorrow at eight and wear whatever makes you comfortable, but you'd better have real shoes."

"I'm never eating anywhere else," Sam said in reverence, closing her eyes and savoring her first mouthful of eggs.

"You ain't eating here again if you chew while you're talking," Dinah admonished.

Maybe whoever or whatever had sent her here had done her a favor. What kind of life could she have had previously if these eccentrics felt like home?

And then she remembered why she couldn't work here.

Sam waited until she'd finished eating, then gestured at Mariah to follow her outside—out of hearing of the other diners. "I have no social security number to give Dinah," she whispered, looking for the thrift store but distracted by the artistically-decorated planters lining the boardwalk. "I don't want to turn her down, but I'm pretty sure she needs ID for her records." Although she didn't know how she knew all this esoteric information and still couldn't remember her name.

"I don't have any either," Mariah said. "Dinah is happy to feed us in exchange for our work. If we work more than we've eaten, she'll pay us in cash. I don't think Dinah has proper permits and whatnot. She has a past in New Orleans that you'll hear about when she trusts you."

Oddly, this evidence of town lawlessness lifted some of her anxiety. She wiggled her shoulders, releasing the tension before examining the planter outside the door. It was decorated in shards of mirrors and mosaic tile and filled with pansies and lobelia. "I feel like I've fallen through the Looking Glass," she admitted. "Can you go with me to pick out a dinner outfit? And should I be nervous about tonight?"

Mariah started down the wooden planks, past an ice cream shop and antique store and more planters, most of them containing struggling flowers. "Kurt is one of the most boringly unimaginative Nulls in town. He'll want to grill you to see if you're one of them or one of us. Beyond that, enjoy the food. It's good."

"And if I'm not either?" Sam asked in puzzlement, wistfully studying an enormous red geranium spilling out of another pot.

"Everyone is one or the other. If you're not one of us, you're a Null," Mariah said, pushing open a glass door that tinkled welcome. "It's not all bad, if so. Val will quit pushing you around and the Kennedys will feed you. But if the Red Queen starts talking backward, run."

Sam laughed, but she wasn't entirely certain it wasn't a genuine warning that she needed to translate. Maybe she was missing the bits necessary to understand what she ought to know.

They found a sprigged pink, green, and white skirt, green tank top, and a white draped jacket that fit. Sam would rather have worn jeans, but Tullah nixed that.

Not as dark as Dinah, but taller and more elegantly dressed, the thrift store owner jangled an armful of gold bracelets as she folded up the outfit. "Put on some heeled sandals and make him look at your legs. It's good for him."

"I only have a pair of black pumps," Sam admitted. "Student wardrobe, I'm afraid." She didn't know that, but the description felt right.

Mariah slapped a pair of strapped, heeled sandals on the desk. "These should be close enough. You really need bronzed goddess shoes to make him crazy, but these will do."

"Yeah, if I'm doing goddess, I want the gold crown and jeweled scepter, please." Sam studied the heels, wondering if she knew how to walk in them.

"This outfit demands a crown of vines and flowers," Tullah said. "We'll find you one of Harvey's carved walking sticks for your scepter."

Sam had a feeling that vines and branches were probably more her style, but if she meant to be a new person, she needed to explore her options first. "I really appreciate this, thank you. Can I do anything for you in return?"

"Depends. Can you sew?"

Sam had no idea. "Sweep floors? Wash dishes?" she suggested tentatively. Surely she could manage those. She glanced out the window to the thrift store's planter, which hadn't been planted yet. Someone had painted it in ocean blue and added seagulls over foaming waves. "What if I fill your planter?"

Tullah brightened. "I never know what to put in them things. They always die anyway."

Now that she'd suggested it, that felt right too. Maybe Samantha Moon had a green thumb? She really needed another look at those textbooks. "Do you think the other owners would mind if I thinned out some of their pots and used the cuttings for yours? I can't buy plants, but I can help everyone weed and water."

"I'll talk to them," Mariah said. "Some are a bit ornery, but if you're volunteering to do pot maintenance, they'll come around. Daisy decorated all the old clay troughs and Monty insisted everyone maintain their own, but not everyone knows how." Mariah pushed open the door. "Thanks, Tullah!"

Sam hefted her packages, waved good-bye, and followed Mariah out. "I think I can do the pots, but I really don't know how long I'll be here."

Mariah planted her hands on her hips. "You'll stay as long as Cass wants. Now go get ready and I'll tell everyone we have a plant goddess in town."

She marched off, leaving Sam to ponder her words. As long as *Cass* wants? She couldn't get in her car and leave?

CHAPTER 5

Evening, June 16

At day's end, Walker limped down the mountain with the sheriff, feeling dusty, sweaty, and grim.

"I can keep the details quiet because I don't have any," Walker said grumpily. "There's no newspaper up here, but gossip flies faster than dust in the wind. They'll know more than I do by morning."

"Coroner is the only one who can give a report," the sheriff said with a shrug. "All the rest is speculation. We'll need to run through our missing person files."

Walker had heard the coroner say *white, male, age late 30s, early 40s.* He knew the file that fit already. He just needed the date of death to confirm it. "I'm going back up after supper. The Lucys will be back, rooting around. There could be more graves up there."

"Can't pay you overtime," the sheriff warned. "You're on your own. It's not likely there are any more bodies unless you have gang wars you're not telling me about."

"As far as I'm aware, they nail each other with insults here, not hammers."

"How about shovels? Pickaxes?" the sheriff inquired. "You got a war of barn tools going on?" The cadaver's head had been split from behind, quite possibly with a barn tool.

If he was a man who wept, Walker would do so now. Only he'd been taught not to show weakness by the man Walker feared was up there. He kept his stoicism. "No barn tool wars that I know, but I've only been here since December. Winter is quiet."

"Doesn't look like this is recent anyway. We'll let you know more when we know it," the sheriff promised, climbing into his car. "The coroner's office gets backed up every time he goes fishing, so I can't say when."

Walker tipped a finger to his forehead, acknowledging the delay. He hated it, but then, he hated the dirty task he'd assigned himself. He had needed time to recuperate, then get his head straight, and the deputy job in this county he'd been meaning to investigate had conveniently opened. Maybe once he adjusted to the loneliness, he'd be able to go home, pick up the pieces. . .

He wasn't ready. Davey's toys still littered the garage. His little bed. . . Walker's insides ground as if he'd swallowed glass.

With jaw clenched against the pain, he continued to the lodge in the dying sunlight, hoping to snag a sandwich so he could go back up the mountain without delay. Reaching the parking lot near the lodge's restaurant door, he watched Kurt's fancy red Mercedes maneuver into a reserved space. Walker waited for the manager to get out so he could hail him but bit his tongue when a pair of shapely legs followed the opening door on the passenger side. Kurt usually didn't bring women up here.

Walker frowned as Cass's guest emerged, standing tall in heels with straps that emphasized her slender ankles and curvaceous calves. She wore a flouncy skirt that hit right below her knee and a top that proved she had cleavage *and* underwear.

The fool female got around—from looney Lucys in the morning to wealthy Nulls in the evening. What in hell was up with that?

In his usual brusque manner, Kurt led the way up the red carpet where an employee hurried to open the door for him.

Feeling like a dirty grub, Walker decided maybe he would go to the kitchen door to beg food. He didn't know why it rubbed him the wrong way that Miss Samantha Moon was already on the hook of one of the richest men in town. He ought to wish her well. He barely even knew her.

But he'd seen the shadows in those big blue eyes and knew the female hid secrets. The fact that a body had been uncovered the minute she entered town—was too coincidental.

Yeah, if he was back in the city, he wouldn't think anything of it. But out here—weird happened. The Lucys would pick up on it soon enough, if they hadn't already.

Walker sighed in exasperation as he turned the corner for the kitchen door and saw the lean figure propped against the timber façade, presumably doing nothing more than whittling at an oak branch. Harvey never claimed to be one of the Lucys, but he always showed up at inopportune times, in places where he shouldn't be.

Dressed in a black t-shirt, tight black jeans, and black boots, with his thick black hair worn in a leather tie at his nape, Harvey was more carrion crow than Goth, biker, or hippy. He lifted his carving knife in greeting as Walker approached.

"Found what you were looking for?" Harvey asked.

That was one of the weird things about this town. Walker had never told anyone what he was looking for or that he was even looking. He scowled in reply. "No one goes looking for skeletons. You got any idea who it is?"

Harvey shrugged. "No one I know," he replied, as if he'd identified the remains and they belonged to a stranger. "Town has its secrets though. Daisy is the one who walks between time. She's your best bet for information."

Where in hell did he begin questioning that line of thinking? "I need facts, not fantasy," Walker said wearily. "Let me know when you have some."

"Facts aren't my specialty, old boy," Harvey said with a faint grin. "I'm just a facilitator." He pried his broad shoulders off the logs and ambled back down the drive.

Walker had some inkling of why a nearly twenty-year-old missing persons case had never been solved.

～

It was difficult to enjoy the delicious dinner while her companion asked questions she couldn't answer, instead of providing the information he'd promised. Sam smiled and sipped her wine, feeling her head spin slightly. Apparently, she wasn't accustomed to alcohol.

"Environmental science, yes," she told him. She'd learned that much in her search of her boxes this afternoon. Samantha Moon had a newly minted master in environmental science from Brigham Young University. Did that mean she was Mormon? If she didn't drink or consume drugs, how did she end up with her mind wiped? She could remember nothing about her university life. Maybe she was running from an enormous student debt.

Kurt cut his steak, speaking as if by rote and not from interest. It was a pity. He was a good-looking, apparently intelligent man. "What does one do with a degree in environmental science?"

Heck if she knew. If she'd had a computer, she could have looked it up. Of course, without passwords, she wouldn't get far. She'd searched the notebooks and texts from the car and hadn't found anything useful yet. "Teach, plan—I have a minor in landscape management, so I can design parks with an interest in ecological preservation."

She'd skimmed enough of the texts to garner a few familiar keywords to fling around. Had she come out here in pursuit of employment? If so, she hadn't found any paper trail. She needed her email.

"So you're taking a sabbatical between school and work?" he asked.

That's what she'd led him to believe anyway. "Cass offered an opportunity I couldn't refuse. These mountains are so beautiful! And so isolated. I hadn't realized cell phones wouldn't work and that Cass would have no computer."

He gestured over his shoulder. "Use our business office if you need to keep in touch. We keep computers and printers for the guests. I'll tell the front desk to give you a key card to get in."

Hope bloomed. Here was reward for her patience. "Thank you! That's so generous of you. Is there anything I can do in return? I haven't had a chance to admire your landscaping yet. Perhaps I could look around, make suggestions?" At least knowing her major offered a hint of why she knew about plants and landscaping.

"Knock yourself out," he said, finishing his wine and looking for a waiter—not as if he needed wine but as if he checked on the efficiency of his employees.

Carrying on a conversation with an empty head was tough. Sam admired a painting nearly hidden by tall plants. "I saw a mural in the diner that resembles an earlier version of the one on your wall. The same artist?"

Kennedy wrinkled his brow as if trying to remember and turned to see what she was looking at. He shrugged and watched the waiter fill his glass. "There used to be an artists' colony here. The whole town is littered with pieces like that. I suppose someday, we need to find out if any of those artists became famous. Although with our luck, it would probably be as an art fraud."

Sam widened her eyes at the disparagement, but before she could ask questions, he pulled his beeping phone from his pocket and frowned at the screen. "I have a situation I need to handle. Stay and enjoy your dessert. I'll be back to take you home in a bit."

Shit, shit, shit, she wanted that key card. "I could wait in the business office," she suggested quickly.

He nodded in approval. "Good idea. I'll speak to Derrick on the way out. He'll have a card waiting."

He strode off without a look back. So much for making an impression. She'd even shampooed and used a ton of product to tame her hair into something better than a haystack, and he still didn't notice.

Oh well, she had access to a computer. Too excited to bother with dessert, she finished her meal and hurried to the front desk, wondering what kind of *situation* required his attention.

The desk clerk didn't seem concerned, so the place wasn't on fire at least. He handed her the key, gave her directions, and picked up a ringing phone.

She hoped she'd know how to use the computer the way she knew how to use a fork and drive a car. Apparently, she had a strong unconscious memory.

The business office was dark and empty. She unlocked the door, flipped a light switch, and settled into a desk chair in front of a monitor.

The hotel's computer password and username were printed on a sheet of instructions. Taking a deep breath, she logged in, opened a search engine, and typed in the phone number she'd found in her textbooks.

Brigham Young University came up.

She'd written down the *campus phone* in her textbook, not her own? What kind of person did that?

One without her own phone? Was she that poor or that invisible?

HOURS LATER, A RAP ON THE WINDOW OF THE BUSINESS OFFICE SHOOK SAM out of her computer search. What time was it? She glanced at the computer clock—going on ten. She turned around and saw a dirty, disheveled Deputy Walker leaning against the glass. At least her alliterative depiction didn't include *dangerous*. Beneath his whisker-stubble, his face looked drawn and exhausted, which made him slightly more approachable.

Had Kurt sent a police officer to take her home? Rude.

Feeling better that Samantha Moon didn't seem to have any missing person or "This person is armed and dangerous" warnings on the internet, she unlocked the door and joined the deputy in the hall. "Are you on duty twenty-four hours?" she asked, more sympathetically than she'd intended.

He shrugged. "They save me a room here for nights when I'm running late. Kurt's mother just arrived, and they're having a family wrangle. I can run you home if you like."

Charming. She'd been deserted for his mother. A ticket to wealth seemed even less appealing than earlier.

"I'm thinking of storing bicycles all over town," she said crisply, stalking for the nearest exit. The swish of the skirt against her legs felt odd and sexy. Non-student Sam seemed to like skirts.

She could feel the deputy looking, which made her feel a tad better about being so callously abandoned.

"Getaway vehicles? How about roller blades?" he suggested. "Easier to store. Although either of them in that outfit and without helmets and knee pads is asking for trouble."

She was tired, frightened, and horribly alone. That was the only excuse she had for the vain thrill that he'd noticed what she wore. "So I need to store my Superwoman costume in telephone booths with the bikes? Maybe I'll just take up hitchhiking."

"Don't recommend it. Small towns come with crazies too." He opened the door of his tall SUV and assisted her in.

Her hand felt swamped by his rough grip. At the same time, she was reassured by his strength. Hormones played havoc with her swirling emotions. Why on earth did this a scruffy cop strike sparks when the wealthy resort owner didn't?

She stared at her hands as he climbed in rather than study the profile of the man who might one day lock her up. "Are you free to talk about the grave we saw today?" That was better than—*can the police tell that I don't have an identity?*

"Not really," he admitted. "Not without a coroner's confirmation. But it's not one of the settlers as the Kennedys will try to make you believe."

"So the body is bad news to keep from the tourists?"

"You catch on quick. But it's old news and shouldn't cause too much of a stir, unless the Lucys go loco. I don't suppose you can offer any influence there?" His tone didn't sound negative, just discouraged.

"Lucys?" The fog was rolling in again, and she couldn't see his expression in the dashboard light.

He slumped in his seat and steered with one hand. "The local psychics, witches, whatever. I understand the early spiritualists called themselves the Lucent Ladies. It kind of devolved from there."

"Understandable," she acknowledged dryly. "So the normals got called Nulls in retaliation. No, I don't have a bit of influence there. The best I can do is sneak you a pie at Dinah's when I start working there."

"That will put you in command central. Try to keep them calm. Feed them lots of Dinah's pie." Amusement tinged his voice, until they arrived at the town square. The parking lot was full and all the café's lights were on, and he turned grim again. "I don't suppose that means she's serving hot beignets."

"Probably not?" she guessed. It appeared to be standing room only inside the small café.

"Mind if we stop? I can understand you'd rather go home, but I either need to go in there and calm the Lucys or run back up and stand guard over that grave."

"I need to keep walking shoes in my superwoman booth," she said. "Let's stop. I'd rather not be dragged out of bed again."

"I kinda like the gladiator shoes you have on," he said, parking the truck. "At least they're not the kind with the spiky heel."

Delighted that he'd noticed, Sam swung her gladiator wedge at him as he came around to help her down.

"Don't tempt a hungry man," he countered, causing her a visceral thrill as his green gaze took in her leg. "It's been a damned long day, pardon my language."

Damn if that hungry look wasn't a little bit dangerous, but he caught her hand instead of her ankle. "Your mother brought you up right," she said, hopping down. "Did you grow up around here?"

"Hardly." Returning to taciturn, Walker put his wide hand on the small of her back and steered her toward the café. Golden light streamed through the gray fog, and the aroma of coffee spilled out when he opened the door.

The crowd noise died down at their entrance.

Mariah waved from her perch on the counter. "Kitchen's closed but you're welcome to volunteer for the séance. Cass isn't here to lead it, but Tullah said she'd try."

"You need to learn not to bring the fuzz," a male voice called from the corner of the room. Wearing all black, with his hair tied back in a leather thong, seated on a stool and bending over a guitar, the musician looked up long enough to wink.

"I bring a pretty lady and all I get is insults?" her escort asked without rancor. "Shall we leave?"

"Harvey, pipe down," Mariah scolded. "We're trying to help the deputy. Tullah, you make the choices. How many of us do you need?"

"May I ask who you're trying to contact?" Sam asked, surprising herself.

"The spirit polluting the vortex, of course," Val said from the shadows of the room. "We must send him across the veil so he does no more harm."

"She means she wants to know who the body belongs to," Mariah translated. "None of us has been here long enough to know of anyone gone missing in recent times. He's not a settler, is he?" she asked directly of Walker.

"That's for the coroner to say," he replied in a low rumble that reached the entire audience. "If you don't need us, I think I'll take the lady home. You'll scare her back down the mountain with all this hocus-pocus."

"But she's the reason we're here," Daisy protested. "If we don't consult the spirit and find a murderer, Samantha will die."

CHAPTER 6

Late evening, June 16

Mariah unlocked the front door of Cass's Victorian mansion and the chosen ones spilled inside. Electric candle sconces flickered on in the foyer as they entered. Lights that lit themselves were just one more horror to add to this thriller film Sam had fallen into.

Shaken by Daisy's ridiculous proclamation that there was a murderer on the loose and she might die, Sam threw a longing look toward her guest cottage, but she would never sleep now.

Walker had abandoned her to the Lucys, saying he had to guard the gravesite or one of the lunatics would be digging around, looking for more bones. She feared he was right. The people who hadn't come with the chosen thirteen had quickly departed for their cars and bicycles, and at least half of them had headed up the hill. She didn't envy him his job.

Not that she envied her position either. Mariah patted her on the shoulder, then led the others past two enormous dark parlors into a dining room decorated with gold 70's flocked wallpaper and hung with a crystal chandelier. Sam appreciated that the chandelier didn't light automagically as they entered, but several sconces on the wall did. She'd watched this time but hadn't seen anyone flip a switch. Motion detectors, perhaps? The room was too dim to watch everyone at once.

No draperies adorned the floor-to-ceiling windows, but the fog pushing against the glass was curtain enough. Sam could make out a variety of paintings along the wall but couldn't discern their subjects. Oddly, some seemed to be frames with no art, and there were blank places where it looked as if pieces had once hung. But the shadows prevented closer inspection.

Mariah pressed Sam down in a chair at the head of a long table while the others flitted about, seeking positions between her and Tullah, who took the other end.

Did feeling weird mean that she'd never attended a séance?

"Join hands," Tullah ordered in the same perfectly matter-of-fact voice she'd used when telling Sam to wear the sprigged skirt. "It's late, and our guest is tired, so let's keep this quick and focused."

The marmalade cat leaped to Sam's lap, then climbed to the table. She curled up in the center. Mariah had said the cat had escape hatches. Good thing, if so, because Sam sure hadn't been around much to look after her.

Mariah held her right hand. Susan, a grandmotherly woman with a cheerful smile and a head full of curls, took Sam's left.

The lights went out. Since everyone was at the table, holding hands, there had to be a switch on the floor. Sam had a feeling this wasn't the first time the ladies had held a séance here.

"Spirit of the vortex, speak," Tullah commanded in a low, reassuring tone. "Tell us who you are."

Sam felt ridiculous. She concentrated on the warmth of the two hands she held. That the hands of strangers held comfort worried her a little. Had she been a lonely student? Had she had lovers?

"He is here," Susan said suddenly. Her hand now felt cool and moist. "He senses our guest."

Well, now there was a great opening for a scam. Excite the newcomer, get her invested in the outcome, then start making demands. Or was that just scientific skepticism?

"Name yourself, spirit," Tullah inserted into the following silence.

The cat stretched and walked down the table to one of the women to whom Sam hadn't been introduced. Buxom, with graying auburn hair, she wore tangles of gold and garnet beads. Emma batted her head against the woman's chin.

"He's not clear," the beaded lady said in a low contralto. "He's been gone too long."

A rustle of disappointment whispered around the room. Sam felt Susan's palm grow clammier. Mariah squeezed her other hand as if to reassure.

"Evil," Tullah said in a guttural tone unlike her own. "He speaks of evil."

"Tullah has a spirit guide," Mariah whispered in explanation.

"Evil must be cleansed," the spirit guide said.

"How?" Mariah asked.

Startled by this sensible question to an insensible speech, Sam almost released her grip. Both Mariah and Susan tightened theirs. An almost visible ripple of excitement circled the table.

"Fire and serpents," the guttural voice responded sadly. "Fire cleanses." A hesitation, followed by a sharper, less dolorous tone —"Tell his son to beware."

The sconces abruptly flickered back on, and the women dropped Sam's hands. Susan surreptitiously wiped hers on her skirt, and Mariah frowned.

"Well, that wasn't helpful," Valdis said in disdain. "We really need Cass. She can translate even the most reluctant spirit."

"That was more than enough for me." Deciding a master of environmental science would be firm and decisive in the face of lunacy, Sam stood and scooped up Emma. "Even I know that fire up here would be devastating."

"We'll have to wait for police to learn the spirit's identity before we can find and warn his son," Mariah said worriedly. "Tullah, are you all right?"

The thrift store owner raised her palm. "Nothing a good whiskey won't help. See our guest home. We already know that evil walks our town, and we need to look out for each other."

Holding a purring Emma, Sam didn't feel the fear she was probably supposed to feel. "If evil is real, then there are plenty of other places in this world that need to be burned," she said as they walked past flickering sconces to the front door. "I thought *serpents* were supposed to be evil."

"And I thought the devil thrived on fire," Mariah agreed cheerfully. "Séances are seldom useful. And Val is right, Cass's are better, but I'm pretty sure she adds her own spin to the spirit's words."

Relieved that she wasn't the only skeptic, Sam set Emma down when they reached the door at the top of the stairs to the studio. She rummaged in her purse and retrieved the ring with her car keys and an unidentified locker-type key, along with the studio key she'd added to it. Hiding keys under geranium pots negated the purpose of a lock in her opinion. Emma sniffed at the flowers on the tiny balcony as Sam unlocked the door. "Do you have a ride home? It seems a little ridiculous to walk each other back and forth."

"I know these paths better than evil does," Mariah said with a chuckle. "There's a shortcut by the rose bed, leads past my place and into town. Safer than walking the road."

"I'll watch from up here." Sam gestured at the stucco wall above the roses. "Holler if you meet evil."

"I'll blink my front door light when I'm home. That's what I do for Cass."

Sam was doubtful that she could see much through the rising fog, but a wind kept it to wispy drifts. She waited until she saw the light blink down the hill, then reached inside and flicked the front door light switch.

"Come along, Emma. Did you eat everything I left you? Do you need more? I wish this Cass person had left care instructions."

The studio seemed like a quiet, sensible safe haven as Sam entered, flipping on normal lights. She pushed boxes up against the wall to clear floor space. Had she left those books out? Scooping them up, she deposited them in a partially empty box.

It wasn't until she entered the bed area behind the blanket and saw her interview suit crumpled on the floor that she realized someone had violated her space.

∾

Early morning, June 17

THE LAST TIME WALKER HAD TAKEN TIME OFF HAD BEEN FOR THE HOSPITAL and funeral. That had been over a year ago. But officially, today was his day off, and this time, he was taking it. He showered and shaved at the lodge. He kept his very own Superman stash in an employee locker so he had jeans and a flannel shirt. He actually grinned when he took out his wrinkled clothes, remembering the newcomer's sardonic comment from the night before.

He hadn't felt like smiling in a very long time. He would never smile again if he allowed another flaky female under his skin. So he needed to steer clear of Sam if she was a Lucy. The jury was still out on that.

He'd diverted the crazies from the crime scene by warning them that he'd seen a cougar and her cubs prowling the grave site. So he'd managed a decent night's sleep and was now prepared to be entertained hearing about the séance.

The people who knew him waved as he entered the café. The tourists didn't look up from devouring Dinah's scrumptious breakfast. The food almost made up for not having cell service. If he'd wanted a setting out of time and place to recover, this was a good one.

Samantha glanced up from filling a coffee cup and smiled, but dark shadows still circled her sad eyes. The therapist had told him he had a strong need to protect derived from his teen years of being his abandoned mother's crutch. He was trying hard not to go looking for the helpless and needy anymore, but damned if he could avoid those big blue eyes sparkling like sapphire crystals when she glanced at him.

He took a stool at the counter and nodded at the coffee pot she lifted in his direction. This morning she'd tied her hair back and covered it with a ridiculous ball cap with *Dinah's* written above the bill. The orange didn't clash with her blue denim shirt, but it stood out.

"Did the spirits talk?" he asked after inhaling the first half of his caffeine.

"I think the consensus was that we should burn evil or maybe just the serpents. Does this mean we should burn the person who ransacked the studio last night?" She kept her voice low enough that only he could hear.

He froze in mid-sip, then lowered the cup. "Anything taken?"

"I don't have anything worth taking. Someone just wanted to know who I was." Her whisper was almost accusatory.

"Not me. I can look you up in a database anytime I need to. Do you want me to take a look around? Help change the locks?"

"I'm a guest. I can't change locks. But thanks for asking." She plastered on a big smile and spoke more loudly. "Pie or do you want something more healthy?" Her voice wasn't precisely sultry, but the practical question held a pleasant musical note that was better than her earlier fear.

He played along. There wasn't much he could do about a B&E with no damage. It cost money to run fingerprints and the county didn't have much. "I'm off duty. I have time for healthy. I trust the Lucys don't mean to burn down the lodge to stomp out evil?"

She refilled cups up and down the counter while she talked. "They consider the lodge evil?"

"Vile interloper polluting the environment," he answered solemnly.

"Money is the root of all evil," Harvey added, sliding onto the empty stool beside him. "Greed corrupts."

"Tourists put food on the table," Dinah said, emerging from the kitchen to slap an enormous omelet in front of Walker. "Don't condemn what you ain't got. Poached for you?" She glanced at Harvey.

"As always, dear, with a bottle of your devil sauce," he shouted after her as she strode back to the kitchen.

"Evil." Walker pointed at Harvey.

"Go f. . ." Harvey grimaced and watched Sam smiling, chatting, and pouring juice for a child. "Where the hell did she come from? Do you know?"

"Utah." Walker bit into his heavenly omelet and ignored Harvey's frustration. Swearing did seem inappropriate around the ethereal Miss Moon.

"Salt Lake City is the only excuse for that air of angelic innocence. Botticelli would have loved her. Hey, Sam, could I have some of that juice?"

Sam picked up an empty glass and set it in front of Harvey. "I don't believe we've been introduced. Did I see you playing a guitar last night?"

"He's a wandering minstrel," Walker told her. "Sam, meet Harvey the Loafer. Harvey, this is Samantha the Moon Goddess."

"Someone got up feeling perky this morning." She filled Harvey's glass, then refilled Walker's cup with the coffee carafe in her other hand.

"I get to go into Baskerville today, restock my kitchen, and do the laundry," Walker explained. "Fun day ahead. Can I get you anything while I'm down there?"

He watched her brow furrow and a cloud of uncertainty cross her face. The woman had secrets. He intended to spend a little of his time ferreting them out. He figured the missing person file would be on his desk, but he already knew what he'd find in that, and it wasn't Sam.

"Nothing that I know of," she replied, before hurrying off to take someone's money at the cash register.

"Look for Cass," Harvey said urgently, just as Dinah appeared with his egg.

Dinah set the plate down and looked as grim as her perpetually cheerful red lips could manage. "Cass is in trouble," she agreed. "Look where Sam was last."

Well, hell, so much for his day off.

CHAPTER 7

Afternoon, June 17

AFTER THE LUNCH RUSH, DINAH COUNTED THE CASH DRAWER, PEELED OFF several bills, and handed them to Sam. "You're a powerful draw, hon. Reckon you earned your wages today. Go have some fun, smell some flowers."

Sam had been questioned by every local who'd stopped by the counter. She felt as if she'd *earned her wages* just fending off questions about her past. She'd finessed queries about the skeleton so she said nearly nothing and drew the conversation back to the person asking. That performance alone was worthy of actor's pay.

Relieved that she had a little more cash to get by on until her brain started working again, Sam shoved the bills into her pocket. "I need to plant Tullah's flower pot. Do you mind if I dig out some of those alyssum volunteers you have in yours?"

"No idea what an alyssum is. Mariah planted that thing. Take what you like. Go over and see Amber, get your cards read, see if she'll give you some of her pretty flowers." She nodded at the planter across the street spilling over with lobelia, geraniums, salvia, and marigolds.

Sam would rather not have her cards read, but if that was what she needed to do to dig around in that planter, she'd bite the bullet. She was itching to pinch back the geraniums and salvia and thin out the marigolds. The purple lobelia was too gorgeous to touch.

In last night's computer session she'd learned she couldn't do much of anything about her lack of driver's license without her birth certificate or other government identification. She didn't even know what state she'd been born in. So if she wanted to use the computer again, she'd either have to borrow a bike or risk driving without a license.

Early afternoon and the sun was shining brilliantly as she crossed the street. Tourists poked around in the shops, but there was no line waiting beneath the squat wooden building with a Tarot Reader sign. A bell rang overhead as she entered. The shop was lined with candles, boxes of aromatherapy bottles, herbs, crystals, and other accouterments of the trade. Sam didn't know what her previous persona had thought about woo-woo tricks, but she suspected a person with a scientific background wouldn't approve. Having no memory certainly opened up one's mind.

She stopped to admire an abstract oil painting in bold blacks and reds. Delicate line drawings of human figures disappeared into the inferno of color. Dante's vision of hell?

"I'll be right out," a feminine voice sing-songed from the back.

"It's just me—Sam. Dinah told me I should stop by and take you up on that tarot reading. If you're busy, I can come another time."

"I'm just dusting. Come on back! This time of day is always slow."

Amber was a striking woman in her early thirties. She wore her orange-red hair covered in a turban that left ringlets hanging around her ears. Sam suspected she wore the off-shoulder, ribbon-bedecked white gypsy blouse and colorful skirts because her round figure looked good in them, not just because of her profession. Maybe one led to the other.

"I'll fix us some tea. Dinah probably half-worked you to death. You need to be off your feet a while. Have you ever had your tarot read?" Amber bustled about, pulling tea leaves from a cabinet, filling an electric kettle, cleaning old leaves out of a colorful teapot.

"No, can't say that I remember it," Sam said. She thought it might be bad karma to lie.

"Well, it's not an exact science. It's all about interpretation. The really good readers like me have a psychic connection with the cards and the client. But a lot of it also relies on you and what questions you have in your mind when we cut the cards. So think about what you'd like to know."

"What I'd like to know?" Sam drifted over to a counter where boxes of beautifully illustrated cards were displayed. The list of what she'd like to know was endless.

"Most people ask about their love lives or their financial situation. The cards are specific to the person. We can't predict world peace or anything universal. Some of the cards will produce a general prediction of the future, if you'd like that." She poured the boiling water over the leaves.

"Could we ask about Cassandra?" Sam didn't want anyone looking into her personal business. She was terrified of what they'd see. Not that she expected anything from pieces of painted cardboard, but the idea made her twitchy.

"We could, in relation to you, perhaps. That works better. Want to choose a deck?"

"They're all so beautiful. The artwork is exquisite." Sam admired the various decks Amber had scattered over a tablecloth. "This set is grim though." She pointed to one with haunted houses and eerie moons and witches on broomsticks. The style seemed similar to the artwork in the front room.

"That one was designed by one of the original Lucent Ladies. There are only a few decks still in existence. I'm not sure if she was mocking Halloween or if her mind was just bent that way." Amber set teacups and saucers on the table, then spread the deck expertly. "Her skeleton drawing is almost lifelike. I've always wondered if she had a model to work from."

Sam shuddered, remembering the skull she'd seen uncovered yesterday. "Let's not use that deck. How about this floral one? I've come to ask you if I can work in your planter and thin out a few marigolds for Tullah's planter, so that seems apt."

Amber picked up the floral deck, flipped through it, and studied Sam. "Yes, your vibrations are in synch with the earth cards, interesting. Do you work in agriculture?"

"Environmental science," Sam said, almost proudly, because this was the only thing she knew about herself. Maybe.

"Interesting that you chose this deck. It's another one handed down from the Lucent Ladies and is more interpretative than the usual Italian spread. Sit there." Amber pointed at one of the straight chairs adorned with white slipcovers. She poured the tea without offering cream or lemon.

"We'll just start with a simple spread today. How would you like me to phrase your question? Where is Cassandra? Is Cass all right?" Amber settled into a similar chair on the other side of the table.

"When will she come home? Can I ask that?"

"We can't get dates, just what happened in the past that's influencing the moment and what will come of it, but we can focus on that question. Cut the deck into three stacks, please."

She probably ought to be asking what would become of *her*, but that might depend on when Cass would return and throw her out. Sam cut the pretty deck as directed. Amber's ring-covered fingers lifted each pile as if they were precious gems, and spread three cards from each stack in three rows, face down.

"The bottom row is your past." She gestured at the line closest to her and flipped the first card. "A tightly bound sheaf of wheat could have many meanings. There's an almost magical effect to the tie binding them, and the wheat stalks are very young." She held up her palms and closed her eyes. "For you, I think it means that you were tightly controlled by family, circumstances, energies over which you had no power."

She flipped the next card, one with crushed leaves and a single untouched blossom. Sam wasn't entirely certain what kind of flower it represented but it was pink and not completely unfurled.

"Tragedy, I think. Did you lose your parents early?" Amber asked with concern.

Sam couldn't answer. She simply stared at the crushed plants. She prayed that didn't represent her real past.

Amber didn't wait for her to answer but flipped the next card and exclaimed softly. "Freedom, but the flowers are still just buds. You are reaching outside of your tight world but you've not fully blossomed, and the leaves are starting to wither, as if they've been without water or nourishment too long. That's probably your college years. College can be pretty dry terrain if all you do is study. I don't use this deck often, so you're really influencing my reading with your presence."

Since the only thing Sam knew about herself was that she'd recently been a student, perhaps Amber *could* read minds a little. Considering the bleak picture she painted of her past, Sam hoped she was just good at guessing. She stayed silent, not feeding her any information.

Amber started on the middle row, flipping the card on the right. "This line is your present." She exclaimed softly again, running her fingers over the gnarled old woman standing over what appeared to be a garden bed. "The High Priestess, that has to be Cass, casting a spell. . . over seedlings? Over the earth. Bringing you here?"

Amber flipped the next card, not waiting for any response, although Sam felt the tug of truth. She was turning as mad as the people of the town. Maybe it was something in the water.

"Fire," Amber whispered in horror, gazing at a card showing a charred landscape with only a small orange poppy unfurling its pretty bloom. "Scorched earth, change, wiping out the old to make room for the new. This could be a disaster, or it could be a controlled burn, but it's in your present, not the future. So perhaps it represents leaving the old behind and starting fresh?"

"That's what it feels like," Sam said with a little more confidence. She was definitely starting with a scorched brain.

Amber breathed a little easier and flipped the next card. Instead of flowers, two eccentrically garbed people faced each other. "Ah, the Earth Goddess! That's you and the Magician. He must help you fight Judgment—that could be any obstacle in your path. This is a card of power and control. There are forces tugging at you right now. The magician could even be Cass, if she's working on you in some manner."

That part made utterly no sense, so Sam stayed silent.

"Now, the future." Amber flipped one of the three remaining cards and frowned at a large oak surrounded by agricultural images. "This card should interpret similarly to the World card. If this is your future. . . I may be wrong in interpreting the High Priestess, unless we think of you as the future one. This doesn't seem to answer your question about Cass. It seems to be a spread about you and Hillvale. I'm seeing this scarecrow as Deputy Walker. In this deck, the scarecrow is the same as a knight errant. It could reflect his obsessive need to know everything happening here. He already knows Cass, but he's still searching for more."

"Does that mean he's worried about her?" Sam asked, not understanding.

"No, this line is your future. It means he'll worry about *you*. Turn the next card."

Sam flipped the middle card and admired the tall sunflowers spilling around a fence. It made her even twitchier to think the deputy might someday worry about her, but she could only handle the present right now. The deputy would have to do what deputies did.

"More change," Amber said, a frown forming above her nose. "Cass is opposed to change, but you might be the harbinger of change. The two of you are in opposition somehow, not enemies but on different sides. Turn the last one."

The final card showed funeral lilies and a casket. Sam felt a strong urge to flee. "Someone is going to die?"

"No, the card doesn't necessarily mean death. Or if it does, it can be the death of a concept, death of wealth."

"Or dead flowers," Sam said with relief. "I hope I don't kill your planter."

Amber deliberately set her mouth to a smile. "Of course. I'm being too serious today. I hope they discover that skeleton was just some lost hiker from decades ago. We should think about making the world better with flowers."

"None of this explains where Cass is," Sam reminded her.

They both looked at the casket, until Amber scooped up the cards and shuffled them.

CHAPTER 8

THE NEXT DAY WALKER DROVE UP THE MOUNTAIN IN THE EARLY MORNING fog on his usual rounds. He'd spent part of his day off trying to satisfy his curiosity about the new girl in town. Another few hours had been spent at the office, checking out Jane Does who might be Cass. Without an official request, he couldn't do more.

It hadn't taken long to verify what he already knew about the skeleton case. The coroner had estimated the corpse had been buried approximately fifteen to twenty years ago. The only missing person reported on that mountain in that range of time was Roger Walker, his father. Hikers occasionally went missing and so had some of the hippies who had last been seen at the commune, but the timing, age, and sex of those didn't match the coroner's guesstimate.

He'd found what he'd taken this job for, but that wasn't enough. His mother had clung to hope for years, then remarried when he was in college, after having his father declared officially dead. Walker had never believed the man he'd idolized had willingly deserted him. Now he needed to know why his father had been killed with a blow to the head all those years ago.

Walker had shown his father's missing person's report to the sheriff, who had labeled the case as homicide and sent forensics up, but they both knew there would be little to find after all these years.

The case rested on the people of Hillvale, the ones who had lived here eighteen years ago, when his father had last been seen here. Cass was one of those people, and now she was missing too.

Driving into town, Walker knew he should continue his route up to the lodge. He could ask questions of the Kennedys, who'd owned property up here all their lives. Or walk up to the crime scene, see if the locals had behaved.

But he pulled into the parking lot instead. Samantha Moon probably would have been six or seven years old when his father disappeared. She knew nothing. But he stopped anyway.

As he entered, pulling off his sunglasses, she smiled at him, and his pulse raced. So maybe it was more than police instinct pulling him in here. He liked that she seemed to see *him* and not his genetics. Even in this day and age, bigotry ran rampant—one of the reasons he'd taken over his father's company instead of entering the police force after college, he understood now. He had believed that hiding his mixed race behind a desk allowed him to accomplish more than in the streets.

He was six years and a lifetime of experience older than Sam, so he had no business acting on hormones. That didn't make his physical reaction to her go away.

There were still shadows under her eyes, but she didn't seem quite as wan and hesitant as she had upon arrival. She was a striking woman, and he wasn't dead yet, so of course he was interested.

She set a mug down and filled it to the brim. "Pie or breakfast?"

"Pie is fine. I ate before I left. Did everyone behave while I was gone?"

"They held a death ritual last night." She reached into the pie case to give him the last leftover. "They had to do it in the lodge parking lot because resort security blocked the path. I understand words were exchanged."

Dinah popped out from the kitchen and slapped what appeared to be a cheese biscuit in front of him. "Taste this. Tell me what you think. And leave Sam alone. She don't know nothin' about nothin' and people been running her ragged with foolishness."

Walker hid his grin behind his coffee cup. "I reckon Sam's old enough not to need a mother hen clucking after her." He imitated Dinah's accent. It slipped back to its origins when she got excited.

Sam walked off to take a customer's cash. At this hour, there weren't many people to overhear them.

"You been lookin' into Sam the way you nosed into everyone else?" Dinah demanded, unfazed by his mockery.

"You said you were worried about Cass. Sam seems to be the last person who saw her. What else do you want me to do?" Walker bit into the biscuit. It nearly melted in his mouth.

His appreciation must have shown because Dinah looked satisfied. Sam returned and broke off a piece of the biscuit to taste it.

"Those things are priceless. I could arrest you for felony theft," he warned guarding what remained with his arm.

"Then you'd never have another because Dinah wouldn't have time to make them if I'm not here," Sam said without concern. "Were you saying you were investigating me?"

"Sharp ears." Walker sipped his coffee while he decided how to play this without offending the two women waiting expectantly. "Okay, I ran your plate. It's no big deal. Your sticker will expire in July, so if you're staying in California, you'll want to get to the DMV before then and transfer the title."

She frowned a little. "How do I do that?"

"You'll need your Utah title and sales receipt, but first, you need to have an address. So wait until you're settled in. There's no rush. Your old address expired a few years back, so you won't receive any other reminders."

She nodded, still frowning. "What do you mean, my old address expired?"

"You didn't update it when you moved a few years ago." He'd looked into that, too, but he wasn't certain how much to tell her before she dumped coffee over him. Since she was obviously not a career criminal, he had no right to be nosing around more.

"You're forgiven if all you're doing is helping out," Dinah said with dignity, before returning to her cave.

"That's not all you looked at, is it?" Sam asked in a low voice. "You exude guilt. They told you to find Cass, so you looked up everything you could legally find."

She didn't seem ready to pour coffee over him. He shrugged. "You graduated with a master, as you said. There's no record of a more recent address. I'm guessing you left university housing to move in with someone. Since that has nothing to do with Cass, it's none of my business."

"Damn right," she said with hostility. "But you checked out my parents, too, didn't you?"

He resisted tugging at his collar. "I'm investigating an eighteen-year-old missing person case. You're not old enough to know anything, but you know Cass. So I had to wonder how and guess it was through your parents, who may have lived here before you were born."

She crossed her arms and tapped her toe—definitely hostile body language. "And?"

"And, I'm sorry. I didn't realize your parents were dead until I found the news story on the plane crash. It must have been while you were just starting university. That had to have been rough. If they had any connection to Cass, you'll have to tell me."

She'd gone pale and her toe stopped tapping. She looked as if she was trying to hold herself together by her elbows.

"I don't remember any of it," she whispered.

HER PARENTS WERE DEAD. SHAKING AND TRYING TO HIDE IT, SAM abandoned the deputy to help a customer who'd just entered.

She couldn't believe she'd told the nosy police officer her problem, but she was tired of faking it, tired of being alone, and desperate to know who she was. *And she had no family.* He would have told her if she had a husband and a married name. Now she knew she had no one, no one looking for her, no one to go home to, and apparently no home. It was a harsh blow, and she fought back the tears she despised.

In just a cursory search, the deputy had found out more than she could ever hope to.

While she took orders, Walker finished his coffee, left cash on the counter, and put on his hat. "I'll talk to you after the morning rush," he called, as if women told him all the time that they had no memory.

She could run away, get in the car, and go back to Utah where someone presumably knew her. But they'd probably put her in a mental institution. She probably *belonged* in an institution.

"That cop giving you trouble?" one of the morning regulars asked. Tall, thin, straggly gray hair thinning on top, faded green blazer. . . Xavier. She remembered the man who followed the loud real estate guy around—except Grumpy Gump had gone back to the city.

"No, he's just doing what cops do. More coffee?" Sam held up the pot.

He nodded a little eagerly. "Saw you with Mr. Kennedy. You looking for a place to stay?"

Real estate, she recalled, Xavier rented real estate. "I probably won't be staying long, thanks."

His face drooped, and she felt sorry for him but forgot about him while she waited on others. He was gone next time she looked, disappeared, like one of the town ghosts.

Mariah arrived a little while later, black braid and feathers swinging, to check her ghost traps and help with the morning rush.

"The spirits aren't happy," she told Sam as they passed behind the counter. "I should probably check Cass's traps. I put some in where she wouldn't notice. Will you be up there later today? I'll check yours too."

"You have a key," Sam pointed out, unhappy that everyone knew more about her than she did. Had Mariah searched her belongings? How many other people had keys? Anyone could have made a copy while it was hiding under a flower pot!

Mariah raised her eyebrows. "I wouldn't walk in without your permission. I try not to at Cass's, but she's been gone over a week. I don't know what else to do."

"Sorry. The deputy was here and he's been invading my privacy and got me jumpy. What happened last night?"

"Mrs. Kennedy happened. She had a tantrum and ordered security to throw everyone out of the parking lot. Not everyone is fit enough to walk up through the woods, but a few of us tried. There's yellow tape all over the place. There weren't enough of us to surround the police boundaries to do a proper exorcism. Cass would have made it happen, but on our own, we failed. Now that section will stay as polluted as the rest."

She hurried off to help a customer, and they didn't have a chance to talk again until mid-morning.

"What precisely were you hoping to accomplish with an exorcism?" Sam asked as Mariah stopped to sip tea.

"Ward off evil, mostly," Mariah explained. "It's not as if there's a spirit handbook."

Sam fretted about the fire image in her tarot cards—after the séance spirit had said fire cleansed *evil*. It sounded a lot like someone was setting the stage for arson. Apparently, whoever she was had a suspicious mind.

"Did you ask the other merchants if I can putter in their planters?" Sam changed the subject to one more pleasant.

"They all said root away to your heart's content. It's not as if we have a nursery up here to keep the pots looking good. We've threatened to order the mayor to provide plants if he wants the wretched things kept up. The rich are used to picking up phones and hiring everyone to do everything." Mariah's long black braid bobbed with righteous indignation.

"Socialism, I like it," Sam said, her lip twitching in amusement at her friend's passion.

They returned to work. The tourist trade might be declining, but Dinah's was the only eatery in town. She wouldn't go out of business even in winter. It was well after lunch before Sam could escape. The planters called to her. She was glad everyone thought it was okay for her to play in their dirt.

She stopped to remove some faded yellow pansies from the antique store's planter. She loved their cheerful little faces but pansies were an annual, and these had passed their prime. She hated to compost them —even if she had a compost pile, which she didn't. So she tucked them into a shady corner beside the store and watered them down, just to see if she could keep them going to brighten a dull corner.

With that thought in mind, she decided to wander up the cemetery hill first. Old lots often had perennials that came up even after the house was long gone. They only bloomed a short time, so they were better used around foundations and bare lots than in planters, but if no one objected, they'd add color to dusty streets and odd corners.

As she climbed, she found wild plots of milkvetch and yarrow and what was probably wild columbine. They weren't showy, but they were a nice start. Maybe some native grasses to add soft feathery seeds. Watering would be a problem. She dug around in the soil to see how hard it was and marked her findings to come back and separate later. The earth here smelled and felt rich, but she didn't know what she'd find in town.

Cass's grounds were large and shaded by old pines. She'd have to ask permission before digging up anything there, so she walked on past to the cemetery.

She studied the graveyard before going in. The entry was marked by an old wrought iron arch that must once have held a sign, but any other fencing had disappeared over the years, probably melted for other purposes. Wandering in to investigate a wild rose, she noticed the newer gravestones seemed sound. A huge expensive vault bore the Kennedy name. Most of the older stones had fallen or disappeared into the weeds over the years. The plots were overgrown with grasses, but not the thistles and trees that would have sprouted after years of neglect. Someone occasionally came through and cleaned up.

She found what appeared to be spent daffodils and lilies and even one old tea rose among the weeds. Those were a good start. If they'd survived all these years, they'd be hardy. She needed to poke around Cass's place and find a spade and clippers.

The earth here felt more alive than back in town. Perhaps because she was less distracted? Soaking up the refreshing vibrations and the warmth of the sun, Sam returned to the road and followed a path past the cemetery to higher ground. Before she got far, the deputy's car pulled off the end of the road. He got out wearing his annoying reflective sunglasses.

She waited for him to catch up, again noting his limp. Had he been injured in the line of duty? Or could it be an old football injury that had prevented him from passing the physicals for a major police force, leaving him side-lined here in rural nowhere? She didn't know him well enough to ask.

Why was she about to trust him with what she didn't know? If he had discovered she had no criminal record, did it matter? Could she hope he was discreet? She didn't want an entire town full of busybody witches clucking over her.

As she realized what she was thinking, she chuckled and managed to greet Walker with a smile. "I just realized I've come to accept that this town is full of witches."

He laughed. He had a deep-chested laugh, which made her like him a lot better.

"Spiritualists," he corrected, tucking his glasses between the buttons of his shirt. She almost sighed in relief once she was able to see his jade-green eyes. Despite his eye color and carved cheekbones, he looked more flat-featured without the glasses, which was why he probably wore them. For some reason, she trusted his vaguely foreign appearance more than the stiff sunglasses-wearing police officer guise.

"Some of them may be Wiccan," he said, "but that's a religion, not a magic service. Where were you going?"

"I'm looking for plants I can bring into town."

"Do you mind if I walk with you? Do you need a strong back for digging?" He fell into step as she continued up her chosen path.

"Possibly, eventually. Right now, this is an observational expedition. You've come looking for me for a reason," she said without accusation, uncertain how—or if—to start this conversation.

"You can't tell me you don't remember the death of your parents and walk away without my wondering." He didn't seem perturbed but scuffled the dirt around a rock as if to see if it could be moved.

"That's just the tip of a very large iceberg. I'm not certain if it's a good idea to reveal more, but I'm approaching desperate. How much can I trust you to keep what I say quiet?"

He pondered. "If we're talking criminal activity, then I have to report it. If it's personal, then I already carry more secrets than anyone knows. I can add another."

She'd suspected that. He was more than an underpaid rural deputy. An intelligent man of confident authority should be sheriff or mayor by now, if power was his career path. She ought to be afraid of what he concealed, but anxiety made for sleepless nights.

"I have no memory of *me*," she said, testing his ability to understand.

He considered that for a minute as they climbed. "You have memories of other people?"

"The ones I've just met. I don't remember my parents, so I assume I won't remember anyone from my past. I am currently living very much in the present."

"But you remember how to drive and what plants are what and the basics of everyday life like etiquette and how money works." He stated that as if it were fact, which it was.

"Exactly. I don't remember if I take cream or sugar in *my* coffee, or even if I drink coffee, but I remember coffee. I keep waiting for something to jog my memory free, but it's been gone since the night I arrived in a fugue state that semi-lifted when I entered the town."

"That sounds like something one of the witches would say," he said in disgust. "I hope that doesn't mean you're expecting me to accept that if Cass is found dead, that you don't remember murdering her?"

She glared at him. "Thanks for that. That's not a possibility I've considered until now. All I mean is that I arrived the morning before last after following directions from a GPS, and when I got here, I abruptly woke up and realized I had no driver's license, no phone, no purse, no nothing to tell me who I am—except textbooks with a name in them and a certificate of graduation."

He whistled. "You need to see a doctor. You could have been mugged. A concussion is nothing to mess around with."

"I don't have a concussion," she said irritably. "No bumps, no bruises. No explanation. And who steals my purse and ID and not my car? Then programs in directions?"

"Admittedly, that's odd, unless it was a new GPS and you added it yourself. Maybe you were drugged. We could have toxicology reports run. Were there any other addresses in the GPS?"

Sam took a seat on a boulder on the outskirts of what appeared to be a natural amphitheater, with rock ledges forming seats in a circle around a depressed area. She dug her fingernails into her palms and tried to form a reply. "I have no insurance that I know of. I imagine blood tests cost more money than I have. Unless you want to charge me with DUI, I'm not seeing that happening. And there was one other address in the GPS for a restaurant down in Monterey. That appears to be where I began this insane journey."

"Give me the name and I'll start there." He pulled out his phone and jotted down what she told him. "But I still think you need a blood test. You might have a tumor."

"Oh goody, one more thing to worry about." She sat in morose silence, absorbing the heat of the rock. Realizing she had no family left her heart as empty as her head.

"C'mon, you have to know that medical science is the best path, unless you want the witches to read your past and future."

That was exactly what they'd been doing, Sam realized, shoving her unruly hair back. And she'd let them, because her instincts required a connection to real live people. "I just have this superstitious notion that I'm meant to be up here for some reason, as if I can prevent something that's about to happen. I know, that makes no sense."

"Finding the skeleton reinforced that feeling. It's not valid. You didn't find it. The others did."

She shouldn't be irritated by his logic. She simply wanted. . . more. "I know. I apparently know enough psychology to understand I'm grasping at straws. But part of it is also feeling vulnerable. How can I go to a doctor with no insurance, no money, and no ID?" She glanced up at him with a glimmer of hope. "If you found my old address, would that be enough to ask the DMV to replace my driver's license? Can you find my social security number?"

His stern visage offered no expression. "You would need to be a suspect in a crime for me to access your personal history. And DMVs require a birth certificate, a passport, or the equivalent these days before they'll issue a license. Name and address alone won't do it."

"Then charge me with a crime," she said angrily. "I can't go on like this."

"I'll find a free clinic. If you'll go with me and have blood tests done, I'll ask the sheriff if special circumstances warrant entering the database. It's not likely to have anything much, but the DMV should have your social security number if you have one. That's enough to get me your birth date and your full credit record."

"Tell me the name of my parents," she said. "Maybe their names will jog my memory."

"This is just basic search engine stuff. You can look yourself up online or go into the university enrollment database."

"Not without a computer," she pointed out. "If I had one, it's gone too. I can't keep driving up to the lodge if I have no license." She grimaced. Now he knew for sure she was breaking the law if she got into the car.

"Point taken, sorry. Their names were Jade and Wolf Moon. Ring any bells?"

She played the names in her head, searching for familiarity. But she'd probably called them Mom and Dad. "Nothing, not even the weirdness of their names," she replied with a sigh. "Can you research them more? They're dead. It's not as if it's an invasion of privacy. They're not exactly common names, are they?"

"That's a thought," he agreed. "What if something in your subconscious about your parents is drawing you here? I can dig around into their background."

She frowned skeptically. "Weird names do not necessarily mean they come from a weird town."

He pondered possibilities and frowned as he did so. "They sound like hippy names, but the commune was two generations ago. Your parents might have been born here, but the commune was gone by the time you were born. And if they returned as adults, someone in town would have remembered you or them."

"That's for sure. I was hoping *someone* here would know me, but the whole town must pass through the café and no one recognizes me. But now that I have names, I can kind of ask around, so thanks for that. At least I know I'm not an alien from another planet. What about the skeleton? Has it been there long enough to be related to the commune?"

He tightened his jaw and narrowed his eyes into his inscrutable expression. "The commune was gone thirty or forty years ago, and the skeleton hasn't been there that long, so no. Mostly, I need to question people who lived here eighteen years ago."

Wondering why his mood had changed, Sam watched a dust trail coming up the road. Someone was driving too fast. "And maybe you could ask if they remember my parents? This town is the only connection I have besides the university." She didn't let excitement build. There were too many unanswered questions and speculation was useless. "What about some of the people my age or a little older?

Could their grandparents have lived up here? I mean, what else would draw young people up here?"

"The excellent company?" he asked, lightening up. "You have a point. The vortex is a draw, but we're not famous like Sedona. Want to help me nose around looking for old-timers?"

"Might be better asking questions than answering them for a change," she said with a grimace. "Where is this vortex?" She watched a white Escalade pull up at Cass's house.

"You're sitting right above it." Walker gestured at the basin at the foot of the amphitheater. "Guess that means you're not psychically in touch with the earth spirits or whatever nonsense they profess."

Guess that made her a Null. She felt good out here, *grounded*, but not spiritually evolved in any way. They both watched the Escalade. "Who's that stopping at Cass's?"

"Carmel Kennedy. She's been on the warpath ever since she arrived the other night. I just steer clear. Monty and Kurt are the ones who suffer. She owns the biggest share of the resort and almost all the land around town, so they're at her mercy."

"They could find employment elsewhere," Sam said callously. The passenger remained in the car while the driver loped up to Cass's door, knocked, then pulled the old ringer. The chauffeur wore black and gold livery—quite a retreat to days gone by. "I hope her driver is paid well to wear that outfit."

"Francois insisted on it is what I heard. He likes the military look. I wonder what they want with Cass? I'd heard there was a feud between her and Carmel."

Sam broke off a grass stem and chewed on it. "My mind reading skills say she is furious about your skeleton, and she wants to blame it on Cass and demand she clean it up. Or take the fall."

Walker snorted. "Good instincts. I understand the grave has been a major part of the ongoing *discussions* at the lodge."

They watched as the driver returned to the car, backed out, and drove up to the cemetery. He stopped at the arch, and a tall woman with Viking shoulders got out. She wore a casual loose beige tunic and trousers that Sam could tell from this distance were raw silk. The color complemented Carmel's tawny, sleek hair. Sam pulled at a strand of her own childish white-blond haystack. She would never look that sophisticated.

"Do you believe in evil?" Sam asked as the figure below picked her way up the partial gravel path to the enormous monument to the Kennedys.

The driver opened his window and a plume of smoke filtered out.

"What makes you ask that?"

"Answering a question with a question is evasive. If that driver sets the mountain on fire with his cigarette, does that make *tobacco* evil? Or the driver?"

"I guess it's the concept of evil that needs defining. Do I believe in the devil? No. Do I believe some people completely lack moral fiber and soul? Yes. And fire in these woods is a natural occurrence. Forests require fire to start new trees. You should know that."

"I do, but I worry about all the people here. They could lose everything."

"And again, I ask what prompted this conversation?"

"You won't appreciate the answer." Telling him a spirit and tarot cards warned of evil and fire would only make him question her sanity more. "So should we search for a free clinic?"

She got up and dusted off her jeans as Mrs. Kennedy emerged from the tomb, tucking something into her purse. "Did she just take something from a grave?"

"Don't rush to judgment. It might just be her flashlight. Or maybe she uses it as a vault for her jewels. Anything in there is hers anyway." Walker stood and checked his phone. "Time for me to get back to work. I'll let you know when I find a clinic."

"And anything else you uncover about me?"

"Of course, if you'll begin those discreet inquiries into who's lived here for the past twenty years and who might be related to people from that time."

"I can be a detective," she said teasingly. "I have a notion that environmental science is a waste up here."

The car below pulled away, and they strolled down the hill.

"Not a complete waste. If the Kennedys keep buying up property to build condos and a spa, the town might need you for an environmental impact study."

He said it with a laugh, But Sam felt a cold chill down her spine. Was this the reason she'd been steered up here?

CHAPTER 9

Afternoon, June 18

As Walker drove his route, he used his radio and Bluetooth to make calls. Just because he was 99% positive he'd proved his father had died on this mountain didn't mean he could shirk his official duties to investigate his personal concerns. He made his usual stops, talked to the people along the route he was there to protect, and drew satisfaction from the basic task. These past years, he'd distanced himself too much from his original purpose in pursuing a career in justice. This job was a good reminder, although it offered a few too many opportunities to brood about what he'd lost and how he would move forward. Having Sam's case to work on was a relief.

Once he was off duty, Walker pulled into the sheriff's office in Baskerville. He checked his desk for the coroner's report, but it still wasn't ready.

Sheriff Brown came in and caught Walker's scowl. "The body's been up there for twenty years or so. Coroner figures another few days won't hold us up. He's got a fresh victim to work on."

"I'd be good with that except this skeleton is stirring up the locals. They're only at the finger-pointing stage now, but you know how quickly that escalates." Especially with the Lucys chanting and beating the bushes.

"That's what we have you for, de-escalation. Don't see how your amnesia victim fits in, though." Brown threw a stack of papers on his desk.

"You'd have to understand how superstition and gossip work in a place like Hillvale. Half the town believes in ghosts. Some of them are trying to hold exorcisms. And the Kennedys are out to sweep the whole scene out of sight. And for reasons beyond my understanding, Miss Moon is in the thick of it."

"Well Jennifer has the clinic lined up, like you asked. And she's done some basic research on the family. We can't place them in Hillvale, but the Moons are originally from 'Frisco, not Utah. You might be onto something."

"That's a start, thanks. I'm going to treat Miss Moon as a missing person and run her through the database, along with Cassandra Tolliver. Two people in town have filed a missing person report on her." —After he'd persuaded Harvey and Dinah that he couldn't search without one. Legalities tended to elude the village inhabitants. "Weird to have two essentially missing persons in one small town."

"Plus the skeleton, if he's your father as you suspect. He went missing too. Not that any of this connects as far as I see."

The sheriff hurried off, leaving Walker to commune with his computer. It wasn't as if he had a life after work. Once upon a time he thought he had—but that illusion had ended badly. He straightened his aching leg, kneading the muscle as he typed one-handed.

He dug into Samantha's history first, since it would be the shortest and easiest. As he'd told her, she was pristine clean. She didn't even have traffic tickets. Her driver's license photo matched her appearance, so she was definitely the Samantha Moon in her textbook. Amazingly, she'd sought a TSA Pre-check recently, so she had fingerprints on file. Had she planned on doing a lot of traveling? On what money?

The address she'd given to the TSA was different from the one on her license. He looked it up—just graduate student housing. He sent a message to the Provo police department asking them to question the residents, but unless she was in danger or a murder suspect, they wouldn't act quickly.

He could send one of his investigative firm's agents, but the downside of working corporate-level research was that they were accustomed to paid travel expenses and billable hours. As CEO, he could order them to do as told, if he had a good reason. But he was supposed to be taking a sabbatical.

Sam's credit bureau report showed one credit card with little activity. Her only employment history was at the university. With date and place of birth, she could apply for her birth certificate. Then she could get a new social security card and driver's license.

Sam was only six years younger than he but her sheltered life escalated the difference.

He sent all the information to his research assistant back in LA.

Walker noted recent credit inquiries. Often, employers would check the bureaus when they were considering a new hire. Sam must have driven to California for a reason. For a recent grad, a job made the most sense. Of course, not enough employers did due diligence, so these could be dead ends. He wouldn't make inquiries until he'd shown them to Sam.

Since he'd positively identified Sam, he didn't have a good excuse to investigate her parents, so he started on Cass. Cassandra *Kennedy* Tolliver—Walker's eyebrows rose over that—had been born sixty-seven years ago. She'd lived in San Francisco in her early years. She'd gone to Berkeley, and her address after that varied between Hillvale and Berkeley. Cass was practically the stereotype of the hippies who'd inhabited the commune over forty years ago—except for that Kennedy part. With that name, she could have been living with family at the resort.

He'd have his assistant do a genealogy search to see how Cass was related to the current Kennedys. He noted she moved into the house on Cemetery Road when she was in her early twenties, but no mortgage or deed was filed. That indicated no ownership transfer— a family trust, perhaps. At the time, she appeared to be working for a charitable foundation as director. If she was a Kennedy, then her wealthy family had enough connections that they could have found the job and given her the house. Or they could have funded the charity for all he knew.

She married Tolliver when she was twenty-three, and he died not long after she moved into the house, when she was barely twenty-five, so she wasn't living at the commune. They appeared to have one child —which was a surprise to him. None of this was helping him find her —unless he wanted to blame the Kennedys for Cass's disappearance. She had a history of being a thorn in their collective sides—but if she was family, it was hard to imagine they'd hurt her.

He found no credit cards in her name. She had no known employment these days, so there were no workplace inquiries. She kept a bank account at one of the private banks the wealthy used, so he had to assume she'd come into money at some point.

She had no frigging driver's license. How had she left the mountain? Broomstick?

Without even a driver's license photo to use, Walker had little to enter on a missing person bulletin, but he sent one out, then called the Monterey police to have them start questioning at the restaurant listed in Sam's GPS.

He'd have to look for Cass's son next.

A little after eleven, a report of shots fired in Hillvale dragged Walker from his desk. If the Nulls started shooting at the Lucys, he'd need to permanently rent a room at the lodge.

LATE EVENING, JUNE 18

SAM WOKE TO AN ODD HOWLING MOAN THAT HALTED WHEN SHE SAT UP, AS if she'd startled an owl into silence. Rubbing her sleepy eyes, she glanced at the clock—it wasn't even midnight.

The mountain air was chilly at night. She slept in heavy socks and sweats. Pulling on a cardigan she'd been using as a robe, she abandoned her bed. A cup of warm milk might relax her shattered nerves and put her back to sleep.

She wished she had a computer. A mindless game always helped. . .

Wait, what? She remembered playing mindless computer games?

Now she really wouldn't sleep.

Emma woke up from her bed in the suitcase and came out to curl around Sam's ankles. The cat's dish was empty.

Sam had bought a few basic fresh groceries with the money Dinah had given her. She poured a little milk into Emma's water dish as a treat, then heated more in a saucepan. Looking out the studio's enormous windows, she rubbed her elbows. What else might she remember if she tried hard enough? Or was *trying* the problem? Did she need to be startled into remembering?

It would be far more useful if she could remember why she was in California than the fact that she used computer games to go to sleep.

While Emma happily lapped her treat, Sam watched a light bob up the shortcut path from town. Mariah lived down there, but she was up at the crack of dawn and had to be asleep at this hour. So who was coming up the path?

Car beams flashed on the road on the other side of the bushes, heading in the direction of the cemetery. Who would go to the cemetery at *midnight*?

She ought to drink her milk and go to bed. But she was too on edge. Living with uncertainty was not conducive to sleep, and this mystery wasn't helping.

She pulled on her furry boots and a coat, filled a travel mug with warm milk, and let herself out on the balcony. The car lights had gone out. The flashlight was still approaching. Did she need a weapon? She snorted. As if she knew how to use one.

So, sneaky does it. She'd already found several flashlights scattered around the studio, presumably for power outages. She tested the one in deck storage and it worked. The concrete steps didn't creak. With light off, she quietly slipped down them.

The person on the path wasn't as surreptitious. They walked right up past the rose bed with their flashlight still on. Heart pounding, Sam waited in the shadows of the wall. There were only two houses out here, the studio and Cass's place. The person would have to walk right past her to reach the mansion.

Did she make herself known or follow them?

The light hesitated at her driveway. The figure was tall and lean and quite possibly male, judging by shoulder width. The silhouette of long hair tied at the nape made her doubt her assessment until she remembered Harvey, the guitarist at the diner. A car door slamming up by the cemetery caused him to flick off his light.

The evening fog was rolling in, but she could see enough to follow him as he walked down the drive to the road. She had absolutely no reason to be suspicious, except that was apparently what she did. Was that telling her something from her past?

He didn't try to hide as he strolled toward the cemetery. She was probably out of her gourd to even bother keeping up with him. But her head was empty and needed filling, apparently.

He grew more cautious as he approached the cemetery. The car had turned off its beams and engine. The night was still. The wisps of fog could easily be mistaken for spectral figures forming and dissipating. An eerie creak caused her to bite her tongue and freeze, before she realized what it might be—the door to the Kennedy vault.

How many people had keys to the vault?

Harvey—if it was he—halted. His shadow nearly blended in with that of a fairly young pine. A moment later, a car swung back to the road. It turned on its beams at the curve leading downhill toward town. Sam didn't know one car from another but this was a large SUV in a light color, like the one Carmel Kennedy had used earlier that day.

She waited until the hidden man started back down the road, swinging his flashlight beam. He wasn't really trying to hide—except from the car. Interesting, but not enough to raise even her suspicion. After all, she was doing the same exact thing—being nosy.

She needed to get a life—if only she could remember where she'd left it.

WALKER CRUISED INTO HILLVALE A LITTLE OVER HALF AN HOUR AFTER THE shots-fired report. The deputy on duty had been writing up a bar fight in Baskerville and had been relieved when Walker had agreed to take the call. He had used his flashers and the safest speed possible on that narrow road, but the town was isolated. They couldn't expect an instant response. If they'd had to wait on the assigned officer, it could have been another hour or more.

Dinah's café was closed and dark, as were all the other shops. He found Valdis and several of her sycophants waiting at the base of the road leading to the lodge. They huddled around a small campfire and gazed up at him expectantly when he climbed out. Had he been in the city, he would call it a homeless encampment, but they had homes when they weren't fomenting trouble.

"Did security shoot at you for trespassing?" he asked.

"Menendez land isn't theirs," Val said snottily. "We have permission to use that land. But we heard shouts and gunfire as we came down the path. They came from up near the resort. Has anyone filed a report?"

"Just you. Has anyone come down from the resort since you heard the shots?"

They were nicely located on the only car access to the lodge, so they would see anyone making a vehicle escape.

"The big white Escalade Carmel uses," Val said in satisfaction. "It went out right after we heard the shots and came back not long after. The engine will probably be cold by the time you get up there though."

Spoken like a true mystery aficionado. He wouldn't have pegged Val as one.

"Go home. If I need you, I'll let you know," Walker said curtly, returning to his car.

That they were camping out here, reporting unusual occurrences probably meant that the Lucys were up to something.

Since the women might be slightly deranged but were generally not vindictive, he didn't worry about them. He drove on up to the lodge, watching for any unusual activity. Most of the guests were sound asleep in their beds, if the darkened windows were any indication.

Xavier Black and Alan Gump from the real estate development company emerged from the restaurant and headed for Alan's BMW. Late for a dinner, but they were probably having a business meeting with Kurt. Gump had a long drive back to the city, but Black lived locally. They didn't appear to be carrying guns, and he'd rather not speak with guests.

But out of curiosity, Walker pulled into the private parking lot the Kennedys used. The Escalade was there. The hood wasn't warm, but there was no condensation on the windows. He looked at Kurt's Mercedes next to it—the fog had formed a thin layer of moisture across the windshield. Carmel or her driver had been out, but that was mean-ingless. For all he knew, they might have been in San Francisco and had just returned.

The light was on in Lance's studio. Carmel's artistic brother kept odd hours and tended to leave the light burning night and day. The man barely knew how to feed himself. Walker doubted he'd be out shooting guns. Disturbing him would mean enduring a tour of his gallery while he mumbled through whatever was in his head. Lance wasn't much better than a Lucy except that he seldom went anywhere.

Walker drove around back to the security office. Alonzo was the evening shift officer in charge. He got off the phone as soon as Walker entered.

"What brings you out here at this hour?" Alonzo asked, rightfully curious.

"Report of shots fired," Walker said without expression, waiting for a reaction.

Alonzo shrugged. "Bernard thought he saw a cougar near the dumpsters. We've told him not to disturb the guests, but he's young and stupid."

"Mind if I take a look around anyway? Just to show I'm doing my job?"

"Sure, knock yourself out. I'll take my break and get some coffee. I'll let Bernard know you're out there so he doesn't try to shoot you too."

"Generous of you," Walker said wryly.

Cats and bears in the garbage were nothing new. The Lucys knew that. It was illegal as hell to shoot at them in a residential area, but people out here hunted. That's what they did and there wasn't any stopping them. So why did the Lucys want him here?

He strolled around to the dumpsters, but there wasn't enough light to check for tracks in the woods. The pavement showed no dusty paw prints, but that didn't mean much. He didn't find any shell casings either, but Bernard might have been smart enough to pick those up.

Circling the sprawling lodge, he found Bernard sneaking a cigarette by the glass-enclosed swimming pool. "Do you think you wounded the cat?" Walker asked, admiring the expanse of glistening blue water in an area surrounded by parched and dry.

Bernard looked startled, then shrugged. "Nah, just scared him off."

Bernard was a lousy liar. He puffed his cigarette to hide his nervousness.

"You shouldn't be using firearms around here. Just keep guests away from the cat and call the game warden. A wounded lion can cause a lot of trouble, and if she has a litter, someone is bound to report it. Don't lose your job over an animal."

The kid didn't look happy about the reprimand, but he nodded. "Sorry to bring you out for nothing."

"It's okay. I'll just crash here for the night. Let me know if the cat comes back." Not satisfied, Walker continued his survey of the guest cabins further up the hill, but all the lights were out.

An owl screeched deeper in the woods. He shuddered and headed back to the lodge. Instinct told him something was off, but this was private property. He could only push so far with no evidence of criminal activity.

CHAPTER 10

EARLY MORNING, JUNE 19

"How did you find out about Hillvale?" Sam asked Dinah the next morning on the fourth day of her new life. She wiped down the counter as her employer re-filled the pastry shelves. "Is the area well known in circles I don't belong to?"

Dinah laughed. "The whole point of Hillvale is that no one knows of it except those wealthy enough to stay at the resort. You tell someone you're packing up and leaving for New Orleans, they know right where to find you. You tell them you're going to Hillvale, and it could be anywhere."

"That's going to change," the big blond guy in the tailored suit at the end of the counter corrected.

Grumpy Gump, the real estate mogul. Dinah elbowed her, and Sam remembered no one talked to him. But she needed information.

"Why is that?" Sam asked, taking money from a customer at the register.

"When you have a lot of wealthy people congregating, like in Vail or Jackson Hole, people hear about it. Once we get the condos built and the ski lift in, we're going to be the next Vail." Golden Boy wiped his mouth with a napkin.

Dinah snorted and slammed back into the kitchen. Sam could see why. A ski lift in this tranquil town?

"I've lived a sheltered life," she said, closing the register. "Explain why I should know about Vail if I'm not a skier?"

"If you want to make money, you go where the money is," he said as if to a simpleton.

"Ah, and the people who currently live here do so because they *don't* want to make money. They want quiet lives to be themselves in an area they can afford. Got it." Sam smiled and abandoned the real estate mogul to wait on a customer.

He glared, left his money on the counter, and slammed out the door.

She wasn't very good at this interrogation bit. She hadn't learned a thing this morning but managed to irritate a rich customer. She almost looked up in relief when Walker blew in, looking crisp in a fresh uniform, his dark hair recently washed and slicked back.

"Any chance you can get away for an hour or two?" he asked gruffly, studying the breakfast crowd.

Dinah immediately reappeared. "Why you ask?"

Obviously understanding that every ear in the place listened, he leaned on the counter and replied in a low voice. "Because Val has turned banshee, and I need a translator."

Dinah looked somber and yanked at Sam's apron strings. "Go, girl. Mariah will come in to take your place."

"Why can't Mariah translate? I don't know Val," Sam protested.

"'Cause, just 'cause. Go."

"I think I'm here to be the town stooge," Sam grumbled as she followed the deputy out. "Everyone knows more than I do. Explain why Mariah can't do this. What am I supposed to translate? Do I know a foreign language?"

"Mariah sent me to get you." Walker opened the door of his official vehicle and let her in the passenger seat. "My psychic guessing powers say the Lucys need you for reasons only they understand. Maybe you're some kind of trigger that makes them logical."

Sam almost laughed. "That's not happening. What do you mean about Val turning banshee?"

"She's way above Menendez land wailing like a wounded catamount. Her usual tribe is refusing to climb past the skeleton site and demanding that I fetch you. You are the only rational person any of us know, apparently."

"Charmed, I'm sure." Sam watched the cultivated landscape of the resort pass by. Once they drove through the lodge's parking lot, Walker turned up a gravel road that deteriorated to ruts.

"Old timber road. The Menendez family may own land up here, but they've never built any other entry. They've apparently claimed some right of way that the Kennedys have paved over. Rather than argue, both families share access. It's not as if any of them comes up here more than twice a year."

"So, applying my psychic guessing powers, the Menendez family probably does own the right of way or the Kennedys would have put up gates and locks. I wonder if I'm really this cynical or if not knowing who I am has changed me?"

Walker shot her an admiring glance that tingled her spine and heated her cheeks. Sam glanced out the window so he couldn't see.

"If you're smart now, you were smart before. And I don't think you learned about people in a couple of days at a café. You may be feeling comfortable mouthing off here where no one knows you, but that's the best I can offer."

"Stripped of my façade, I've become my real self?" she asked with a laugh, until Walker stopped the car and bent to look out the windshield.

She did the same. Up on a rock formation taller than the vehicle was a familiar scarecrow draped in black rags. Someone needed to buy Val some new clothes. Might be hard to replace the long black veil though.

Her mournful operatic cry had silenced even the crows.

"I trust I'm not supposed to translate wailing?" Sam asked dubiously.

"When the Lucys told me she was up here, I tried talking with her. She rattled on about crows and gravestones and the past returning to haunt us." Walker looked more concerned than angry at Val's descent into madness. They both knew she could speak normally when she chose.

"I doubt I can translate symbolism either. Why don't you go back down and pick up whichever Lucys are most lucid? If they don't want to make that climb up to Val, I can. I'll see what I can get, then come back down and maybe they can translate."

"Tried that," Walker said gloomily. "They refuse to walk on evil. You want to start with translating that?"

"Not touching it," Sam said fervently. "I haven't defined evil yet either. So okay, that's why Mariah isn't up here. The Lucys find something about this area evil and are fearful of polluting their so-called powers with it. I can almost understand that."

"That's more than I can do. Want me to help you up there?"

"I have no idea. Unless I led a really secluded life, though, I'm guessing I spent a good amount of time scrambling around rocks. What else is there to do in Utah?" Sam got out without waiting for Walker to open the door. "I don't like snakes," she added, watching for slithery creatures in the rocks. Apparently primal fears were more memorable than whether she took cream in her coffee.

As she located footholds in the craggy boulders, Walker got out to keep an eye on her. She hoped his radio signal worked so he could call an ambulance if needed. She was wearing well-padded athletic shoes, but they weren't boots by any means.

She didn't feel comfortable on this side of the valley, not the way she did over by the cemetery. The morning fog still lingered, making it damp and cool. And the earth. . . just didn't feel as welcoming. There was a sharp—oily?—quality that made her think of clammy caves and old bones. Was that weird? Maybe not, if the Lucys sensed it.

Val's keening lessened as Sam climbed. She could almost talk over the racket once she got close.

"Are you in pain?" Sam asked, taking a seat on a flat rock near Val's feet.

"The universe cries in pain at the injustice," Val keened in a wail that at least contained words.

"That's not news. What injustice brought you up here today?" The rock was cold, and uneasiness quivered in her middle. She didn't much like this setting. At this early hour, a chilly wind blew in from the coast, lifting the hair off the back of her neck.

"They kill, they kill without punishment! They litter the mountain with bodies, and the gods cry out for justice. Look at the crows—five! First there were four, now there are five! The mountain weeps."

"So, the new crow means someone died out here last night?" Sam asked, using her wildly imaginative psychic power of guessing.

"Evil seeks evil," Val said mournfully.

"Is the evil nearby?" So much for psychic guessing. She was starting to feel as if she were the insane person, sitting here tempting snakes while talking to a banshee.

Sam glanced down at Walker. He leaned against the hood of the car, arms crossed, keeping a sharp eye on them. She hoped he wasn't expecting Val to attack her.

Val pointed a long bony finger. "There. They dumped him there. The animals have already found him."

Sam's blood curdled. She followed the direction of Val's finger, but she saw nothing but rocks and scrub trees. No animals, no body, not even crows. Another skeleton?

"Did they do it last night?" she asked cautiously. For all she knew, Val could be remembering her childhood.

"That's when the spirit rose," Val said with a definite nod. "You heard him. We all heard him. He howled his anguish."

Remembering the cry that had woken her, Sam really got spooked. "Did you see what happened?"

"The world sees," Val cried, gesturing dramatically at their surroundings. "The stars, the moon, the birds in the trees—they all know when a life is taken. He must be mourned and his spirit laid to rest."

If Sam was *translating* correctly, someone had died last night and been dumped up here in these rocks.

She hastily scrambled down off her perch, to the safety of Deputy Walker—who was already striding toward her, ready to catch her if she fell.

CHAPTER 11

EARLY MORNING, JUNE 19

WALKER HELD OUT HIS ARMS TO CATCH THE NORDIC BEAUTY DESCENDING the rocks so hastily that her platinum hair flew in a breeze of her own making. She practically fell into him, and he held her like that, letting her catch her breath—enjoying the fresh scent and firm curves of a woman for the first time in over a year.

He was too male not to notice how well her tattered jeans fit her hips and the way her loose shirt clung to her breasts—while they anticipated death. Nice, Walker, real nice.

Warily, reluctantly, he set her back. He wasn't ready for anything resembling a relationship, and someone as young as Sam had commitment written all over her.

"I think you may need cadaver dogs. Is that what they call them?" she asked, brushing nervously at wisps of hair escaping her disheveled pony-tail.

She sounded normal, but she was pale as death and breathing erratically. Walker wanted to crush her against him and return her to the laughing know-it-all she'd been while driving up here, but he was on duty, and she was off limits.

"There's another body?" he asked grimly.

"You asked me to translate." She marched back to the truck, her shoulders stiff.

He was translating her body language as *rattled*. This place would do that to you.

"Can you tell me exactly what she said to make you think there's a corpse?" He opened the passenger door, caught her elbow, and helped her in. She shivered, as if with cold. Or fear.

She waited until he climbed behind the wheel to reply. "Aside from evil, spirits, and crows, she pointed at the tumble of rocks on the far side of the clearing and distinctly said *There. They dumped him there. The animals have already found him.*"

"I saw her pointing, but it could have been at the horizon for all I knew." He muttered a word he didn't want her to hear, but she flinched anyway. He needed to remember she had sharp ears. "I'll take you wherever you want to go, then radio for help. Can you keep this quiet until I get a cadaver team up here?"

"I won't say anything, but the Lucys know already," she said, sounding as grim as he did. "And you can take me to the lodge. I want to use the computer, and you may need me to *translate* later. Want to ask me where I was last night?"

"Not up here, I hope!" A thousand scenarios flashed through his mind. He knew what crazy was. He'd lived with crazy. He was really bad at differentiating between mentally ill crazy and Lucy crazy.

"I was in my bed, listening to a spirit howl, according to Val. And afterward, I watched a car a lot like Carmel's—maybe it was a ghost car—driving up to the cemetery just the way we saw it do earlier. And I saw a man who might have been Harvey watching from the woods. I'm ready to join Val's exorcism. She may be right and evil walks the night."

He was relieved that she wasn't taking any of this seriously. "Nah, that's just Harvey hunting for branches for his walking sticks. He's a vampire who sleeps most of the day." Walker tried to sound humorous but it came out hollow.

"Oh good, vampires and witches. Any werewolves I should know about?" She slumped in the seat and shoved loose strands of pale hair out of her face.

"Want me to describe the Nulls?" This time, he did manage amusement. "We've got sexual predators, embezzlers, and looks like possibly, a murderer. I'll take the witches anytime."

That got a laugh out of her. "I trust the predator is old and gray and not about to start stalking women?"

"Ask Dinah," he said curtly. "Although if she's seeing auras now, I'm not sure she qualifies as a Null. Maybe it's this town that makes us crazy."

"Dinah as a sexual predator?" She sat silent and contemplated that. "At what age did they slap that label on her? When she looked like a little boy and was exploring why she felt like a little girl?"

"She's black and it was New Orleans. I didn't read the case, but psychic guessing will get you there, yeah. Our laws are about as primitive as our medicine sometimes."

"She's happy here, where people only care that she bakes a mean biscuit. I'm glad she found a way out."

"It's good to know you don't judge people because they're different. You need that here." Given the harassment he'd suffered as a kid for his not-quite-Caucasian features, he appreciated her ability to see past the surface. Walker pulled up to the back of the lodge. "I need to warn Kurt we'll be filling this lot with cars again. He won't be happy."

She sat there, staring at the lodge. "Call the sheriff first, get people up here. Val may very well be right about evil. And if it exists, this is the place closest to where the bodies are. It didn't feel right up there."

She got out and walked away as Walker punched the call on his radio. The lodge didn't *feel* right? The dispatcher responded before he could go after her.

SAM PULLED THE KEY CARD OUT OF HER BACK POCKET. HAD IT ONLY BEEN yesterday that she'd learned the names of her parents? So many things had happened. . . and she'd had no way to combat her anxiety and curiosity and get to the lodge until now.

Before she could slip in the side door where Walker had left her, a lanky, graying blond man ambled out of a small cabin near the lodge kitchen. He bore a strong resemblance to Carmel in the broad, bony shoulders, sharp nose and cheekbones. She'd heard about Carmel's artist brother. Splashes of paint on his shabby gray clothes identified him.

If she ran into him in the dark, she'd almost believe in ghosts, though. From the little she'd seen, Carmel was brimming with color and temperament. It was hard to believe the two were related.

Sam stopped to greet him, but he didn't seem to notice her existence. He opened the kitchen door and wandered inside. Shrugging, Sam took the side hall back to the empty business office. The aroma of coffee and bacon emanated from the restaurant, so she assumed most of the guests were eating. Taking a seat at the computer, she logged in and put her parents' name into the search engine.

She didn't find much. Her father had been a pilot. The plane had gone down in a winter storm over the mountains just after she started at the university, as Walker had said. The Utah paper called them local artists who showed their work in galleries in major cities.

Having just seen Lance, the Kennedy artist, she wondered if he'd known her parents—but she had no way of connecting them to Hillvale except her strange position.

She searched under her parents' names as artists and found one or two newspaper articles from San Francisco and Los Angeles. The news photos of their artwork weren't good, and she got no sense of familiarity from them. She'd have to drive down to the galleries. . . After she got a license.

Had they left a will? A house? An executor?

Digging deeper, she found one grainy photo of the two of them together. She stared in disbelief.

Wolf Moon was as Native American as his name—thick black straight hair pulled back from a wide dark brow. Sharp nose, powerful jaw, grim mouth.

And Jade. . . Jade Moon was at least part Asian. Delicate bone structure, elongated eyes, petite nose, smiling warmly.

Sam felt a distinct tug at that smile, but *nothing in this photo looked like her image in the mirror*. How had Walker concluded that they were her parents? She dug her fingers into her own pale haystack of hair and gazed in admiration at her parents' silken black locks.

If she'd been adopted, she supposed their names would be the ones she would use as her parents on a university application. She wouldn't know any other.

Feeling totally spooked now, she decided she ought to know as much about Deputy Walker as he did about her. That decision tilted her world back upright.

She dug down, looking for a Chen Ling Walker with a police background and an age of roughly early thirties. She uncovered a small article from about a year ago, in the *LA Times*, about a Chen Ling Walker who'd been shot attempting to save his young son from his suicidal wife. There were no follow-up stories. Someone had hushed it up or there would have been big headlines on a story this juicy.

Sam stared at the article, her stomach roiling. It merely listed this Walker as CEO of a Los Angeles security company. The wife had a history of mental illness. No specifics. The son had only been a toddler. He'd died. Her heart ached for a man she didn't know. Or did she?

Walker limped—from a gunshot wound? There weren't too many Chen Ling Walkers in the world. Could this really be him? If so, she wished she hadn't looked. How did one survive that level of anguish?

But why would the CEO of anything be working as an underpaid deputy in the middle of nowhere?

She poked around and couldn't find anything more likely. Maybe he was related to this other person, and it was a family name. Or maybe he really was just that invisible—no public recognition for anything. She didn't have the ability to search credit records and government databases the way he did.

She had just put her own name into the search engine when the glass office door blew open on a whirlwind. Sam looked up, startled, as Ms. Viking Shoulders swooped in. Carmel Kennedy practically glowed California gold—including amber eyes that weren't warm as she glared at Sam.

"Who are you and what are you doing here?"

"Good morning," Sam said brightly. "And you are?"

She was definitely smart-mouthed. Wouldn't a poor student be obedient and terrified?

Carmel obviously thought so. Her glare grew colder. "I own this place and you are not one of my guests."

"What gave that away? The tattered jeans? The muddy Nikes?

Sorry I didn't wear my diamonds to climb the hill." Really, if she'd talked like this all her life, someone should have shot her—except she didn't talk like this at the diner. "May I help you? The other computer should work, if you need it. The facilities here are excellent."

"Only guests are allowed access to this office. I will have to ask you to leave," the ogre demanded frostily.

The more Carmel irritated, the more Sam dug in. Weird. She really ought to be intimidated.

"Kurt considers me a guest," she said with her biggest smile. The resort manager would no doubt kill her, but she was quite done with being treated like an insect. "If he asks me to leave, I will happily do so."

Fortunately, before Golden Girl exploded, a familiar male voice spoke from behind her.

"Samantha? We're going to need your help with Val. Good morning, Mrs. Kennedy. Kurt said we could use the back lot again, if that's all right with you."

Deputy Walker waited in the corridor, unable to enter the office without bodily removing the resort owner. Although he wasn't a bulky man, he stood taller and broader than Carmel. Despite his polite words, his authoritative baritone said it wasn't a request. This was not the deference of an underpaid deputy.

"I am talking to the DA about this repeated invasion of private property," Mrs. Kennedy said in a low voice that resembled a hiss. "I will not tolerate these locals harassing us."

"Then find a way to keep people from burying bodies up there, and my job is done." He backed up and gestured for her to depart.

Oh crap, they really had found another body. Did she want to go with him? No, she wanted to flee this mountain and never come back —if only she knew where to go.

Only because Walker looked sympathetic as she stood up did she agree to accompany him. If he'd been one of those glaring, belligerent cops, she'd have. . . Behaved as she had with Carmel? If so, it was probably a good thing she hadn't encountered police before or she would have a record for Walker to find.

"Kurt told me I'm to ignore his mother's temper, so I do," Walker said, taking her elbow and escorting her toward a back entrance. "It sounds as if he gave you the same advice."

"Was I awful? Kurt didn't advise me of anything. I really don't know where that came from. I'm a mousy looking person, driving a mousy little car, but I dare roar at lions?" She was still a little shaken by her behavior.

"Mousy?" he asked incredulously, staring at her as he opened the side door and let her out. "If I were to describe you, it would be lionesque. Your roar suits you perfectly."

"I don't feel like a lion," she grumbled. "Maybe a battered alley cat. What have you found and do I really have to go up there again?"

"You don't have to see the body," he said, with a hint of sympathy. "We've positively identified him. We know the last time he was seen. But Val won't leave. And her tribe is starting to gather." He gestured at the women congregating in the corner of the lot nearest the road.

"So maybe I can stay here and encourage them to stay here?" Sam asked with hope. "Or I can talk with them and ask what it will take to bring Val down?"

"That works," he said in relief. "Thank you. I know it's nuts asking a complete stranger to deal with the locals, but I think that's what's needed. Everyone knows everyone too well around here, and they push each other's buttons. You're fresh meat."

Sam laughed. "If Carmel had her way, I'd be roadkill. Why on earth would she care if I used the hotel's computer?"

"My guess is that she's a controlling bitch. I'm sure the Lucys will give you more colorful alternatives. If you need any help, let Alonzo in the security office know."

He started to walk toward his car, but Sam caught his arm, almost startling herself with the familiarity of the gesture. He wore a short-sleeved shirt and his brown arm was hard and muscular. She dropped it the instant he turned.

"Can you tell me who you found? And can I tell the Lucys?"

"We haven't notified his next of kin. He's local, so the Lucys will know soon enough. Sorry, that's all I can offer."

She let him go. The uneasiness had returned. Her legs seemed to be trembling, as if the ground moved beneath her feet. Maybe they were having an earthquake. But no one else appeared concerned. Maybe they had quakes here so often, no one noticed.

Shakily, she walked over to join the women. She identified Tullah from the thrift store, Amber the Tarot Reader, Crazy Daisy, and Mariah. The others had been in the café, and she recognized their faces, if not their names. The only male today looked like a university professor with a closely-cut goatee and well-barbered chestnut hair.

He bowed slightly at her approach. "You are the forest sprite who has added lushness to my garden pot, thank you. I don't believe we've been introduced. I'm Aaron." His accent was vaguely British.

"Of Aaron's Antiques," Sam said, recognizing his name from the sign. "Pleased to meet you."

Wearing her long black hair in multiple braids tied with feathers and beads similar to her ghost-catcher nets, Mariah spoke up. "The spirit is caught here. He's furious and arousing the other spirits. My nets can only stop so much before all hell. . . and that could be literal. . . breaks loose. We need to pass him on. Val is trying, but she can't do it by herself. We need safe ground for a ceremony."

"What is safe ground?" Sam asked, thinking of landslides and earthquakes and wondering why they'd worry about those.

Mariah gestured toward town. "The vortex is still safe, and the land beyond it, but that's two miles away. We usually use the hill above the resort but the cops won't let us up there. We need somewhere unpolluted by evil and accessible for as many of our group as possible."

All the women had dressed for hiking, but some were elderly and frail. Some of the more portly members were already seeking places to sit. The trail required athleticism, and the Lucys didn't qualify. Sam got that part. "Unpolluted?" she asked. "How do we determine what's polluted?"

"If you can't tell, you can't help," Mariah said with a sigh. "I'd hoped Cass had sent you for a reason."

For all Sam knew, she'd killed Cass and stolen her cat.

"I've only just arrived," Sam said, trying to sound reasonable. She wanted these people to be her friends. She desperately needed their support. "I've not had enough time to explore."

"She's right, Mariah," Tullah said. Even in boots and khaki, she managed to look like an African queen. "It takes time to learn the energy of a new place. What about trying her with one of Harvey's sticks?"

"I have one with me," Amber called, getting up from the rock where she'd perched. She carried a polished redwood branch. A carved seahorse head with a crystalline eye formed the handle.

"Good thought." Mariah brightened and tested the stick by circling it in the air, perpendicular to her body. "We should ask him to make one for Sam."

"I can't pay him," Sam protested, taking the lovely walking staff when Mariah handed it to her.

The seahorse perfectly fit her hand, and the energy flowing through the wood felt happy and positive. She coveted this stick. Which was crazy, right?

"He negotiates." Mariel waved away the protest. "How does that feel? Lift it toward me, see what happens."

Sam pointed the stout flat tip in Mariah's direction. The stick seemed to quiver on its own, then circle and nod. It felt *happy* in her hand. "Positive?" she answered tentatively. Did sticks normally *feel* like anything? Like cream in her coffee, she couldn't remember.

"Good. Let's give this a try. We know the ley lines are polluted from the ridge and south toward the vortex. Let's spread out and try going downhill *away* from the lodge. Don't take any dangerous routes that we can't all follow. Ideally, we'll find ground flat enough to gather. Ready?"

With the tactical skill of a general, Mariah divided up her army and sent them out to search for *safe* ground.

"I'll take this more polluted upper section," she told Sam as the others traipsed off. "We can hope to find safe spaces between the lines. Stay to my left, just far enough that we can see and hear each other. I'm sorry I expected you to jump into this with both feet. We're kind of desperate and had hopes Cass had found someone skilled."

"That wouldn't be me. I don't even know what skills you expect."

"Listening is a good one," Mariah admitted while her gaze tracked the path of her army marching downhill. "Did Walker tell you anything we should know?"

"Only that the victim is local. He says you'll know soon enough."

Sam had a horrible thought. "He would have said something if it were Cass, wouldn't he? Is anyone else missing?"

Mariah looked troubled. "If it happened last night, I think one of us would have known that Cass was back. And it's too soon for anyone to report a missing person. Whoever it was created enough disturbance that he was found before he was declared lost."

Sam nodded. "OK, lead on. Let's see what I can do."

Even though she was doing as Walker had directed—keeping the Lucys occupied, she felt like an idiot. She was a *scientist*. Walking through the woods, holding a walking stick in front of her, waiting for it to take a nose dive like a divining rod was just too ridiculous. At least she knew what a divining rod was, even if she'd always believed they found water, not *safe* ground. Although maybe if there was water below, it carried off evil pollution? Alice, meet Wonderland.

As they searched, Mariah carried on a running dialogue about the old mill that had once occupied the area, the sisters who had lived in the cabin marked by fallen logs, and the village well that had once been up here and lost in an earthquake.

Sam tried to take in the concept of all these people living here over the centuries—while she held onto a staff with a mind of its own. It dipped and jiggled and shook back and forth like an old man saying *no, no, no* as they slowly proceeded downhill. The blasted thing practically talked.

She was trying to find the peace she'd found on the other side of the valley, but mostly, she felt edgy and scared. Did a killer live on this mountain? Could he be watching them now? She'd be a lot happier if Walker told her someone had died in a bear fight.

The staff dipped so forcefully, she almost fell. At the same time, she felt her fears lifting. Positive energy soaked through her shoes, and all the muscles she hadn't known were tense, relaxed. She took a deep breath. Even the air smelled cleaner.

With no memory, she had no preconceived notions to fall back on, so the sensation didn't strike her as weird or out of the ordinary. Maybe everyone felt safe on some ground more than others. Would that be in her textbooks?

"Mariah," she called, afraid to sound too certain. "Is this what you're looking for?"

"Did you find it?" Amber called from the left. A crashing of under-brush and old leaves followed.

Mariah arrived on silent feet just as Amber stumbled over a log and caught herself on a tree trunk. Both women looked around expectantly at the tall grass and saplings.

"It feels right," they agreed simultaneously.

"It's not too hard to reach," Amber said, gazing skeptically back up the hill they'd descended.

"It's flat and wide enough and the walking stick approves," Sam added, hoping this would draw Val out of the hills.

"I think this is where the old church was." Mariah turned around to study the trees. "That was back in the day when even the spiritualists still believed in good and evil. They would have blessed this land when they consecrated the church."

Amber beamed proudly at Sam. "Your cards said you would were the Earth Mother. Let's bring this meeting to order."

Earth Mother? Sam felt more like Class Clown, even more so when the Lucys began arriving without any particular command for them to do so. Convenient, when cell phones didn't work. She needed to learn psychic communication.

Maybe desperation had made her a little nuts.

"Daisy, will you be able to reach Val from here?" Mariah asked as the numbers filled the small clearing.

"Val is already here," Daisy replied, settling on a rock. "She is watching for Cass. The buzzards are circling. It is almost time to dispel them."

Sam glanced questioningly at Mariah, who shrugged. "She's time walking, seeing a different circle in a different time where Val is present. But she can communicate from anywhere, so let her be."

That was one step past crazy into Twilight Zone. Sam wanted to run back to the lodge and the familiarity of technology, but she feared she was letting down her new friends if she did.

Desperation had apparently given her a ridiculous niggling hope that maybe woo-woo could return her memory if modern science couldn't. That thought fled when she saw her new friends lighting dry tree branches in a makeshift rock basin they'd created.

"You can't have fires up here," she cried. "One spark could set this tinder into disaster!"

"We're careful. We've cleared it down to dirt around the cauldron." Mariah removed dried leaves from a pouch on her belt and blew them toward the small flame dancing in the rock bowl of dirt. The flames danced higher.

Each woman had her own pouch and her own smoldering branch, but they all chanted the same words. Smoke circled the clearing, smudging the air in the same manner as the fog had earlier.

Visions of soaring flames rushing through the woods, engulfing the timber-clad lodge and its occupants froze her in panic.

The scent of sage and incense swirled. She swayed dizzily, but her feet were rooted to the ground. The ground. . . she let the energy flow upward, clearing her head. The staff in her hand bobbed excitedly.

The owl shrieked again. A swirling wind swept through the clearing, casting flames higher. The chant rose. Mariah flung more ashes on the flames. And a circle of white light nearly blinded the clearing.

Sam screamed, grabbed her head, and dropped to the ground.

CHAPTER 12

Afternoon, June 19

Walker had started downhill the minute he'd seen smoke rising behind the lodge. From his vantage point, he could see the crazy coven in a clearing far below.

He watched as, surrounded by the Lucys, Samantha raised a stick. In the flash of an instant, the circle exploded in an inferno of light.

Save him from the effing crazies! Walker broke into a run. Arson was no laughing matter. Just when he thought—

Sam collapsed, screaming, while smoke rose around her. Her cry escalated his heart rate to terror mode.

He leaped over fallen trunks and skidded through debris, descending the hill at a breakneck pace. Resort personnel ran toward the clearing with buckets and hoses, but he could only see Sam crumpled in the weeds. He barely noticed the women stomping out smoldering branches and chanting what sounded like *Blessed Be*. It was his own damned fault for letting a mentally impaired female loose with the looneys. Sam's lack of memory was definitely an impairment if she didn't know better than to set fires.

He stumbled into the clearing, out of breath and furious.

The women finished stomping on their smoking sticks and throwing dirt on their fire. Lodge security shouted curses and dumped buckets of water on hot rocks, exploding them in steam. Walker could see Carmel Kennedy and her chauffeur marching in this direction, steaming hotter than the rocks.

His duty was to keep the townspeople from killing each other, but right now, the victim he'd sent into this brawl was his primary concern.

He scooped up Samantha and felt her wriggle. Good. She was alive. Now he was damned well taking her down for medical help, as he should have done in the first place.

"I'm fine, put me down," she sputtered, wriggling to get free. "I was just a little overcome with smoke."

"Yeah, most people shriek and wave wands when they have smoke inhalation, right." He marched on, taking the shortest unmarked path to the parking lot. Stones and rubble rolled beneath his boots, but he didn't release his grip.

"Not a wand," she muttered, pounding his shoulders. "Just one of Harvey's walking sticks. I kept the Lucys busy, didn't I?"

"You let them nearly set the mountain on fire! That is not what I meant about keeping them busy. What the *hell* did they explode on that fire? The place lit up like a ten-thousand-megawatt magnesium flare."

"For all I know, it *was* magnesium." She shoved hard, nearly toppling them both. "I do not need medical assistance."

"Pretend you do so I can get us both out of here. The sheriff has his homicide team up there and doesn't need me. I'm supposed to be covering my rounds or giving assistance to the locals. You're the local. I'm assisting. We're getting off this mountain now, before Carmel rains fire and brimstone on our heads."

Even as he said it, he saw Kurt Kennedy crossing the parking lot and Aaron Townsend jogging up the trail, headed his way.

"We can take Miss Moon down to the ER," Kurt said with concern. "This happened on resort property, and I'd like to see that she's unhurt."

"I'm unhurt," Samantha shouted. "And I'm not going anywhere with potential murderers."

Kurt's dark eyebrows shot up. Aaron looked amused. Walker kept walking.

"She's impaired," Walker said grumpily. "The Lucys probably put pot on the fire."

"We did not," Aaron protested. "We released the spirit of the man who passed this mortal coil last night. Miss Moon was not prepared for the impact. And I wish everyone would desist from calling us Lucys. I am not female, nor is Harvey."

"We could call you Looneys," Kurt offered, following Walker across the gravel lot.

Aaron was a big man, larger than Kurt. If they squared off. . .

Samantha yanked one of Walker's fingers and pulled it back almost far enough to break it. In retaliation, he dropped her. She had to grab his arm to steady herself once she was on her feet again, but she had everyone's attention. "I am not going anywhere with any of you. I'm going back to town to play in dirt."

"Not with emergency vehicles flying up that drive, you're not." Walker caught her arm and kept marching her to his Ford. "I'll take you down."

"I can go with one of the others." She tried to shake him off, but he wasn't allowing that finger trick again.

"We offered rides," Kurt reminded them. He crossed his arms and watched Walker open his door and fling Sam in. "Are you arresting her?"

"Maybe. I'm thinking about it." He slammed the door. When she opened it again, he removed his cuffs from his belt. "You stay put or I'll lock you in."

"You wouldn't dare." Her eyes were a challenging, long-lashed azure, and Walker could almost feel her ire cutting out his heart.

"I don't respond to zanies anymore," he told her. "Stay there or I'll haul you in with cuffs." He glared at Aaron and Kurt, who were looking belligerent. "She needs help. Stay out of this."

"Zanies, nice," she repeated in a fulminating tone that might well lead to an explosion.

Walker checked to see that his gun was still in place.

Mariah popped up like an evil genie, her hair braided with trinkets, making her look more like a lunatic than any of the Lucys. "Find out about Cass," she commanded. "That was her with us just now."

Even Sam stopped protesting to stare.

Mariah shrugged. "If you can't tell, I can't explain. Just go. She shouldn't be on the astral plane this long."

Walker climbed in, shoved his sunglasses on, and turned the ignition. "Are you sure you want to stay with the Looney Tunes?"

Sam remained silent long enough for him to send the car rolling down the drive and away from their audience.

"I understood what she meant," she finally said in a small voice.

"About the astral plane?" He almost ground his teeth. His late wife had always sounded perfectly rational when she'd talked about the voices in her head. He'd never known when Tess was referring to characters in the novels she wrote or the demons that controlled her.

"No, I know nothing of astral planes. But I felt another presence that wasn't me, unless I really am crazy. I need to dig some plants, do something constructive."

"You need grounding," he almost said in relief. People who realized they were thinking crazy weren't really crazy, were they?

She smiled weakly. "Right. Grounding. But I remember what Cass looks like now."

He almost slammed the brake. Instead, he drove straight through town, aiming for the main highway. "Describe her."

"Tall and thin, like me. Classic roman nose, no makeup, blue eyes, silver hair pulled back tightly from Katharine Hepburn cheekbones." She fell silent, as if waiting for his approval.

It was only as he recognized the description that he realized what she was really waiting for. "*She resembles you.* That's why the Lucys took to you."

"You said she's in her sixties. She couldn't be my mother unless she had me in her forties." Her voice trembled.

"What do you mean, your *mother*? Your mother is Jade Moon. Her name is on all your records." He'd been hoping against hope that she was sane and it was the town that was nuts, but none of this computed.

"You didn't look up my parents, did you?" She gazed out at the passing landscape. "You'd understand if you'd seen their photos."

"My phone should start working when we pass the gas station." He handed it to her. "Call up the images you saw."

She poked at icons as if she knew what she was doing. "Jade appears Asian, Wolf, Native American. Neither of them looks anything like me. And they must have looked horribly out of place in Provo. I researched the town where I grew up too. It couldn't be any more white if it had been bleached."

"Maybe they were Mormons," he argued, even knowing that was grasping straws.

He pulled into the gas station and took the phone when she passed it to him. The couple staring back at him possessed none of Sam's classic—blond—beauty. They were handsome in their own way, but he could see what she was saying. Her mother looked more like him than Sam. He scrolled down, read the article, then handed the phone back to her and returned to driving.

So chances were good that Sam had never been who she was raised to be.

"What else are you remembering?" She'd been raised by a Chinese mother, as he had. What did that signify? Jia Walker had more superstitions than a house full of cranks, but she was completely, totally sane —almost painfully so.

Sam shook her head. Her hair was falling from the combs she'd used to hold it off her nape. Had Cass's hair once had streaks of gold and ash?

"Nothing, really. There are just these vague. . . shadows. I may be remembering the restaurant where I met her. I'm not certain. But my life before, nothing. Maybe I need the Lucys to chant over me." She said that grimly.

He glanced over to be certain she wasn't looking as if she'd like to jump out of the car. His late wife had led him to be wary of hysterical females. Sam seemed weary but calm, so he brought the conversation around to a subject that almost made sense. "Thank you for keeping the Lucys off my back and bringing Val down. She was giving us all the willies. Was that a signal fire that had her scrambling off that rock?"

"You don't want to know," she assured him. "But I'd take matches and lighters away from the lot of them if I could."

"I'll agree with that, but even if I catch them on a no-fire day, all I can do is slap a penalty on them." Remembering that flash of light, he resolved to investigate the ashes, but first things first. "Val has probably spread the word of the body's identity in her death goddess role, but she doesn't know the details. If I tell you what I know, can you keep quiet?"

He didn't know why he would trust anything she said, but he liked it when Sam was paying attention. Her powers of observation were as keen as her hearing.

"Like you, I know how to keep my mouth shut."

He nodded approval. "We found Juan up there, the resort's security manager. He'd been mauled by a cougar. He was last seen at the lodge bar, so I don't know how he got out there. We're treating it as suspicious. How did Val know he was there? We need to nail where everyone was last night."

"As far as I know, except for Harvey, we were all in bed, listening to his spirit howl," she said, sounding as unhappy as he felt. "Did he have a family?"

"No wife or kids. He's a long-time local. His parents live down the mountain. They've been notified. I hate that part of the job."

"I don't even want to imagine it," she said in a troubled voice. "But as far as the Lucys are concerned, Juan now rests in a better place and his spirit won't haunt us. Let's find a normal topic. Who are you and what are you doing up here?"

"Wow, that took a nasty turn." Walker ran a hand through his hair. One thing led to another, and he really didn't want to open up his life to anyone.

"I ran a search on you, you know. I like knowing I can trust the people to whom I've bared my soul." Her voice was distant and stiff.

Shit. Of course she had. "You didn't find much," he said with assurance. "My firm is paid well to keep personal information out of the news when it's of no importance to anyone but the people involved."

"Yeah, if you're the Chen Ling Walker from LA, your *firm* did a good job," she said with a wry intonation that he deserved. "I don't want to pry into your family situation, but it would be good to know why a CEO is working a deputy's job. Is that part of your business?"

Shit, he was bad at explaining, and she had every right to be ticked at his keeping secrets when she was an open book.

"I took time off," he said, weighing his words. "My father started the company. He performed fraud investigations, had an accounting and a criminal justice degree. He disappeared on a case eighteen years ago. At the time, his office was ransacked. The files he was working on were destroyed, the computer hard drives smashed. Back then, cloud computing wasn't easily available. Even flash drives were pretty high-tech, so he backed up his files on paper. Recent files, he carried on memory sticks, which he carried with him. Needless to say, none of the files were found."

She uttered a sympathetic noise and patted his thigh—the sore one. If she thought that would make him feel better, she was mistaken. He got hard. Therapists had told him that it was far easier to get physical than explore the emotion. More pleasant, too.

"I'm sorry. I didn't know. You don't have to talk about it if it's painful."

Yeah, this itch could become a real pain if he didn't satisfy it—especially since he wasn't satisfying it with any more lunatics. Walker forced his dirty mind back to a subject guaranteed to cure what ailed him. "The only clue we had was a phone call. Dad called my mother every night that he was away. The last one came from Hillvale. He was staying at the lodge. The police questioned everyone in the blamed town. You know enough to understand how far they got."

"Even the Kennedys didn't cooperate?" she asked in surprise.

Recalling his research on his father's disappearance eased the tightness in his pants. "Eighteen years ago, Kurt and Monty were kids in school. Carmel had just lost her husband to a sudden illness. She was trying to cope with his estate and the business and claimed to know nothing about the guests. They verified my father had checked in. His car wasn't there. They found it in San Francisco a week later."

"You think the skeleton belongs to your father," she said in horror.

"Almost certain. Just waiting for the tests." He could feel her stare nailing him, but he kept his eyes on the road.

"Was Val there then? Did she wail his fate?"

He was relieved she skipped over the sympathies and platitudes. He could handle no nonsense, practical questions, even if they were about insane subjects. "As far as I'm aware, Val didn't arrive in Hill-vale until about five years ago. We're still trying to find out who lived in Hillvale back then—Juan did, he's lived here all his life, but he swore he knew nothing."

"And now he's dead. That's suspicious," she said, as if thinking to herself. "All I know is that Mariah, Tullah, Amber, and Dinah arrived over the last few years, well after your father's disappearance, but the Kennedys, including Carmel's brother, have been here forever. I haven't got further than that. The older people keep to themselves and don't talk to me much. Cass really is your ticket, isn't she?" She slumped lower in the seat as they drove into town.

"Yeah. I've got the cops and my firm working on her, but she's disappeared into thin air. We don't even know how she gets off the mountain." He pulled into a run-down shopping center. "Clinic is here. They're expecting you, but I'll go in and show them my badge so they don't ask for details. Then while they're drawing blood, I'll run over to the taco shop and pick up food." He nodded at the restaurant.

"You're not hauling me to the hospital?" she asked warily.

"Not as long as you remain sane." He got out before he weakened beneath the light of those gorgeous eyes.

While he was off the mountain, he'd make a few phone calls. By now, his firm ought to have a good list of the town occupants at the last census before his father's death.

PULLING HER DENIM JACKET ON OVER THE BANDAGE TAPED TO HER ARM, Sam left the clinic to find Walker waiting for her with a heavenly-smelling white bag. He handed her a big cup of sweet horchata.

"I think you're supposed to eat sugar after you've given blood." He was already tearing into a giant burrito while leaning against his cruiser.

He was wearing his mirrored sunglasses, concealing his expression, she noted grumpily.

"I have no idea about sugar, but the horchata is good." She drank deeply, then dug into the bag, producing a deliciously greasy pork burrito. "I don't know what I'm accustomed to eating, but I recognize good Mexican. And I know when someone is concealing his thoughts. The Chinese inscrutability thing doesn't work so well when you have your father's eyes, right?"

He bent a scowl on her. "Is that something you remember?"

"Heck if I know." She leaned against the car next to him. The closeness seemed odd but also. . . comforting, even if she ought to be mad at him. They'd both gone a little insane back at the resort. There was something about that lodge. . . that unleashed her inner demons, apparently. "In that photo, Jade's eyes appeared flat-lidded to me, not inscrutable. She used fake lashes and eye makeup for definition."

He snorted, took off his shades, and tucked them in the V of his shirt. "So did my mother. She still did inscrutable well, when she wanted. Other times, she'd take my head off with her sharp tongue, so enigmatic doesn't go far."

She laughed, relaxing enough to enjoy her lunch. She was still tense about Cass and Walker's earlier fury, but they'd both been shaken. Maybe they could work past it.

In between bites, he caught her up on what lay ahead. "I'll take you over to have your fingerprints run through the database when we're done here. Once I prove your ID, I'll give you the data you need to file for a new license and birth certificate. The office has sent an address-forward request to your last known address. It might be good to see if you've established a mail drop."

They were practically rubbing elbows. After this morning's encounter, she was hyper-aware of his proximity. He'd scooped her off the ground as if she'd been no more than a sack of potting soil. But she had no clue how to act on tingles of awareness, especially when dealing with an older man with way too much authority. "I'm guessing I need a non-public computer to file for the birth certificate," she said dubiously.

It would be good to intellectually *know* that she was Samantha Moon, but in truth, she simply didn't feel like anybody. Although if she resembled Cass—there had to be a connection.

"Finish up the burrito, and we'll see if we can expedite the fingerprints. Once you're free to use the data, you can use my laptop. I don't generally carry it with me since I have the official one. I have an apartment here in Baskerville, we can pick it up later."

"I looked up Utah drivers' license replacement. I can't do it from here," she said glumly. "And without a Utah license, I can't get a California one without an address and taking the driver's test again. Officialdom is complicated."

"One thing at a time, grasshopper," he said in amusement. "Maybe we'll find your missing purse before all that happens. And if you were moving here, you'd have to go through the system anyway. You're just feeling overwhelmed."

"There's the understatement of a lifetime. Okay, let's get on with this. I wish I had some way of looking for Cass. I can't help feeling she's the answer to everything."

"Yeah, I know." He handed her a paper napkin and began wiping the grease off his fingers with another. "We'll see if there are any reports waiting when we get there."

Sam caught herself staring at Walker's fingers and had to jerk back to the moment. He'd carried her down a damned mountain, kicking and screaming. For a CEO, he was pumped. Had she ever had a lover like that?

She couldn't remember ever having a lover at all, but her body knew what it wanted.

Wiping her hands, she got back in the car and apprehensively waited for her visit to a sheriff's office. Walker's threat to lock her up rang loud in her head, but he was behaving reasonably for a change. How long did it take to get back blood work? He couldn't arrest her if she had drugs still in her system, could he?

They didn't have far to drive before Walker pulled the car into a lot filled with official vehicles. She'd thought this was a rural area, but the building looming over the lot was a sprawling concrete monstrosity. Maybe they had a lot of criminals in the mountains.

"I was hoping we could see the ocean from here," she said in disappointment.

He turned off the car and looked at her with curiosity. "Why do you say that?"

She wrinkled her brow in puzzlement. "I'm not sure. If I grew up near Provo, then I probably never saw the ocean. Maybe that's the reason I drove this way once I graduated."

"So maybe this is some wisp of your memory creeping up?"

"A wish can be a memory? Maybe. I don't know the geography here. I just assumed a road going west would take me to the ocean, I guess."

"We're not far from the coast. I'm supposed to be on duty, so I can't take you right now. Maybe later."

She took his hand without protest as he helped her out of the SUV. She'd calmed down since the incident on the mountain. She still resented that he'd turned into macho man and threatened her, but maybe she'd frightened him as much as she'd frightened herself.

She dropped his hand once they were inside. She followed him through cold-tiled corridors, past busy offices, until they reached a portion of the building where people greeted him with waves and watched her with idle curiosity.

A young Hispanic woman in uniform rushed toward them, carrying a sheaf of paperwork, as soon as they entered the door marked Sheriff's Department. "They've found her," she called, waving the papers.

Walker stopped to take them away. "Found who?"

"Cassandra Tolliver. From the description you gave, she's the Jane Doe down at Community Hospital in Monterey."

CHAPTER 13

Late afternoon, June 19

With the announcement that Cass had been found, Walker picked up another file full of papers from his desk and handed the lot to Sam. "Let's get your fingerprints done."

Once he had prints, he passed the file on to the secretary to match against government data. Then he caught Sam's elbow and steered her out of the building and toward his official car. "Now we can go see the ocean."

He was more eager than she to get his hands on Cass. Trying to read the file as she walked, Sam slowed him down, waving the papers at him in protest. "You're taking *me* to see Cassandra? What about the others who really know her? Should we let them know?"

"How? Call? I'm not driving back up there. What are the chances that any of the Lucys stay connected to their computers or landlines?"

"Probably not good," she admitted. "But I can't say for certain that the person in my head is actually Cassandra."

"If you recognize her as the person you met at the restaurant, we're on the way to solving two mysteries. I'm willing to take the chance." If Cass could bring him closer to his father's murderer, he was all over it.

She slid into the passenger seat and began flipping through his file folder as well as the papers the secretary had handed him. "Coroner's report on the skeleton." She handed him a brown folder.

Walker grabbed it before he started the car. "A blow to the back of the head. If it's my father, that's the only way they could have done it —from behind, and even then, it's suspicious. They may have drugged him first. He never drank to excess. They don't have the DNA back yet, but everything else fits him."

He slapped the folder back in her lap and turned the key in the ignition. The sheriff wouldn't appreciate him leaving the county without permission, so he'd just forget to let him know. At this point, they could fire him, and he'd still be good.

"They don't have a medical reason for Cass's coma," Sam said worriedly, apparently reading the hospital report. "She had no identification on her when a maid found her in a hotel room."

"Did she have a car? Was there any luggage in the room that might be yours?"

She shot him a puzzled glance. "Why would she have my things? From what I've heard, she's hardly a purse snatcher."

"Because this case is weird from top to bottom and *someone* has your purse. If you remember seeing Cass in Monterey, it's the next natural step."

"You think I drugged her?"

"Given your squeaky clean record, if anything, Cass drugged herself. She has a history with drugs, you don't." His mind was running full throttle. "Does the report say they checked the parking lot at the hotel where she was found?"

"They did a cursory check but haven't invested time in running every plate," she said, reading through the report.

He radioed in a request for another sweep of the parking lot and told the Monterey police that he was bringing in someone to ID their Jane Doe. But *he* knew what Cass looked like. Taking Sam was just a meaningless gesture of hope that something would jog her memory.

There was no fast way to traverse narrow county roads to the coast. Due to the rugged terrain, the major state highway ran parallel to the Santa Cruz mountains and the Pacific, through rolling valleys of grape vines and nothingness. Walker tried to imagine the woman beside him traveling this road at night, in a fugue state—as she called it—with no knowledge of the geography or facilities. *Mindless* might be the best way of traversing this route.

They pulled over once to refuel and refresh. Sam spent most of the drive with her head buried in his files on his father and Cass. He had a lot of research in there. She only spoke when she had questions. He took radio calls from the office. When the sheriff's assistant called to say Sam's fingerprints matched her TSA file, he pumped his fist in the air. Sam slapped his hand in acknowledgment and went back to reading.

Even though they'd verified her identity, she still had no memory of who *Samantha Moon* was. Got it. At least she wasn't waving sticks and chanting. The scientist doing research was more relaxing.

It was dinnertime before they made the outskirts of Monterey. If he'd been in his hybrid i8, he'd have cut the time considerably. In an official vehicle, he had no excuse to turn on the emergency signals and break the limits.

"Need food?" he asked, glancing her way at the first red-light inter-section they hit.

She looked at him as if he were the crazy person. "Cass first."

"A lady with her priorities straight, right. I'll take you to eat on the ocean later."

That earned him a beatific smile. He'd chew tacks to earn that smile again.

He needed to get a grip. It was probably just the adrenaline rush.

Walker pulled into the hospital parking lot and helped Sam out of the SUV. She tugged nervously at her hair, pulling it back up in combs and buttoning her jeans jacket over her dirty shirt. He could tell her she'd look like a regal princess even if she wore rags, but that probably wasn't appropriate.

He flashed his badge, and they were directed up to the ICU. While Walker checked in at the desk, Sam strode straight to a window as if she knew where she was going. The patient inside looked like all the other patients being watched—swaddled in blankets, pale, shrunken, and surrounded by beeping equipment.

The nurse followed him over to the window—Sam had picked the right one without inquiring.

"Can you recognize her from here?" the nurse asked.

It didn't look much like Cass. Her silver hair spilled over the pillowcase in a tumble she never allowed. Her face was pulled so taut it looked like thin paper over raw bone. Her snapping frosty blue eyes were closed. Her lips had nearly disappeared.

"That's her," Sam said in a whisper. "That's Cass. That's my grandmother."

WITHOUT WAITING FOR PERMISSION, SAM PUSHED OPEN THE HOSPITAL room door. She could *feel* the connection with the woman in the bed.

The nurse hurried after her, complaining about contamination. Acting on pure instinct or a call deeper than that, Sam picked up Cass's bony hand.

Her eyelids moved.

Sam squeezed her hand tighter. "Let go now, Cass. I'm back. We need you."

She had no idea why she said that. She had no idea why she'd called Cass her grandmother because even with her fuzzy head she knew that wasn't quite right. But there was an essential *essence* that bonded them. She could feel Cass's stirring within her own head, feel Cass's brain bubbling with activity.

The bony hand stirred. Sam stroked it. "Cass, please, let go. Come back."

Walker's big male presence in his official uniform hovered uncomfortably. He must think she was crazed. Maybe she was. But she couldn't stop. She stroked, she whispered, and the woman beneath her hands gained color and movement.

The nurse checked monitors and hurried off, presumably to find a doctor. Walker, miraculously, stayed silent, not interrupting their internal communication.

"Water," Sam murmured. When Walker handed it to her, she offered the glass to Cass, as if the patient had been the one asking for it.

Thin lips closed around the straw and sipped weakly. Sam nearly collapsed on the floor. Walker shoved a chair beneath her so she didn't have to drop Cass's hand.

Her brain felt empty, floating, as if a weight had been lifted.

"Samantha," the woman on the bed whispered. "Sorry."

A young doctor rushed in, followed by the nurse. He demanded they leave while he took vital signs.

Feeling completely drained, Sam squeezed the frail hand in hers. "I'm here. Come back now, please."

The doctor repeated his demand that they leave and Walker dragged her out. "You look like a ghost. We need to get food in you."

"Give me a minute." She slumped to the hall floor and rested her head against her knees. It wasn't exactly a classic non-fainting mode, but it was the best she could do without a chair. Her head spun, and she didn't feel as if she had the strength to remain sitting.

A nurse brought crackers and soda. Sam dutifully nibbled and sipped.

Walker offered his hand. "Let me at least take you to the waiting room where there are chairs."

"No, I'm good. I need to be here." Close to Cass, close to whatever was happening between them.

Lowering his dignity, he slid down beside her. "Can you tell me what's wrong?"

"No, because it makes no sense. I'm a scientist. I *know* this. I may know more about plant anatomy than human, but I know what's happening isn't. . . I don't even have a word for it. Cass is inside my head. I need to get her back into her own. Did they find drugs in her system?"

"Nothing for which they're equipped to test," he admitted, sounding wary. "What do you mean, she's in your head? Do you hear voices?"

Oddly, he clenched his fists, as if a cold wind blew between them.

But she was too shocked to do more than explore her own dilemma. "No. No, it's like. . . the part of my brain that is me has been cut off by a wall, and the wall is coming down, only it's not that solid and feels like Cass. How does hypnosis work?"

That silenced him. Sam took deep breaths, finding it easier now. She was afraid to stand and see what they were doing to Cass. Her head ached in a vague sort of way, as if numbness was wearing off from a root canal. There was a hollow but it didn't hurt.

"The hippies experimented with hallucinogenic drugs and hypnosis back in the day," Walker said haltingly. "I need to do more research. If you met Cass in the restaurant and she gave you something. . ."

"Why?" Sam asked. "Why would she do that?"

"We'll have to ask her." He stood as the doctor left the room. "How is she?"

"Coming around. If she's more coherent in the morning, we'll take her to a private room. Visiting hours are all day. Why don't you come back after she's had a good night's sleep?"

"May I see her again?" Sam asked, accepting Walker's hand and standing. "I need to let her know I'll be back."

"You've helped, but don't take too long." The doctor strode off, leaving the nurse to let them back in again.

Sam hurried back to take Cass's hand. Her veins were blue beneath her pale skin, but her face had color again. After squeezing her hand reassuringly, Sam rolled up Cass's silver hair, pressed it against her skull, then fastened one of her own combs in it. "I'll be back in the morning. We need to talk, please. There's too much I don't understand."

Cass's eyes flew open for a brief moment. "Samantha," she said in what sounded like satisfaction. "Welcome home."

She appeared to drift into a normal sleep. Without giving it any thought, Sam slid her hand into Walker's, clinging to it as a lifeline as he led her out of the hospital.

"We'll go to the wharf. It's easier than finding somewhere fancy at this hour." Without asking questions, he helped her into the car.

Grateful for his understanding, Sam meditated on the empty place in her head and the memories slowly infusing it. Not until they were walking on the wharf, smelling the salty air, watching the waves, did she finally breathe freely again. "The ocean is so. . . *immense*."

"Puts things in perspective, doesn't it? Sit here, just take it in, and I'll be back with food." His voice was warm chocolate reassuring.

Sam sensed an emptiness when he left, but she still experienced a *connection* with him, like a filament of invisible essence, as she had with Cass. Rather than examine that weirdness, she admired the brilliant blue shades of the ocean lapping beyond the wharf. The noise and colors of the people and shops lining the old pier fell into the background as she concentrated on the battering wind and the crying gulls. She let these new sensations wipe the slate clean, let her body relax, and began the blessed process of refilling her memory and becoming herself again.

Walker returned with a bread bowl of chowder and bags of fried seafood and slaw. "It's tourist food, but decent."

"I've never had fried food," she said, and her heart felt lighter at the recollection. *Samantha Moon had returned.*

He dropped down on the bench beside her, sprawling his long legs across the planks and digging into his soup before he halted in mid-bite to stare at her. "You remembered that? Of all the things to remember, it's fried food?"

"Lack thereof," she corrected with a smile. "All organic, all the time, and lots of tofu. We had goats and chickens for milk and eggs. I never saw the inside of a Walmart until a friend took me when I was sixteen."

His eyes narrowed warily. His five o'clock shadow made him look tough, but at least he wasn't wearing his damned shades.

"I learned to curse at college," she added, digging into the chowder.

He all but inhaled half his soup before speaking again. "How much do you remember?"

"You're thinking this was all a hoax, aren't you?" She opened a brown bag and pinched off a bite of fried fish. Remarkably, she didn't resent his assumption. Knowing who she was made everything sane again. Joy ballooned inside her. One took moments of happiness and reveled in them as they happened, she'd been taught.

She would get angry later, but her empty head required peace to fill it.

"I'm thinking you're as looney as the rest of the Lucys if you want me to believe that finding Cass magically returned your memory." He reached into the bag, produced a fish sandwich, dumped slaw on it, and ripped off a huge bite, obviously not as happy as she.

"That's fair," she acknowledged. "I have no idea how she did it.

The night we met, Cass explained that Jade and Wolf had been paid to keep me away from her and her family and anything to do with Hillvale. It's a complicated history. I'm not sure how much of it I buy either."

The fried fish melted on her tongue. She didn't want to pollute it with cabbage. She poked around and found shrimp and sampled that next.

He tugged his cell phone from his pocket, hit a number, and said, "Sofia, did you run the genealogy on Cassandra Tolliver?"

Sam wriggled with happiness. She knew problems still existed in Hillvale, but for right now, she was a recent college graduate with a master's degree and her whole life ahead of her, and she was about to find out about her birth family. And she was sitting next to a powerful man who could summon information with a phone call. She was pretty certain Sofia wasn't in the sheriff's office.

"I'll check my account, thanks." He clicked off, hunted through his phone icons, pressed one, and opened up a list of files.

"Cass took my backpack. That's where all my valuables are." Sam watched with interest as he opened what looked like a family tree. He had to scroll back and forth to follow the lines on the little screen.

"We need my laptop to read this," he said, as if reading her mind. "But if I start at the top, it looks like Cass is related to the Kennedys through her father. He was married twice, to her mother first when they were young, and to Geoff's mother after his first wife's death."

"Geoff?" For cheap thrills, she peered over his muscled shoulder while nibbling her way through fried shrimp.

"Geoffrey Kennedy was Carmel's husband, father of Kurt and Monty. I knew that much. He died from a sudden illness just before my father disappeared."

"Ah, I remember that. So that makes Cass their what? Half aunt? Do they know that?"

"I didn't know enough to ask." He scrolled through some more, then hit a contact number. "I think we'd be better off asking Cass to explain in the morning, if she's up to it. We need to find a place to stay for the night. I'm off duty at this point, but I'll have to let the sheriff know I'll be late coming in tomorrow."

Sam munched her way through the food while he called both his offices. She tried recalling meeting police officers or even businessmen, but the gallery owners her adopted parents occasionally entertained were the best she could summon. Her university professors occasionally wore suits, but there was nothing particularly authoritative about scientists and teachers. Even in his uniform, Walker exuded command —the kind that got things done.

Which was why she was surprised at his frustration in arguing with what she had assumed to be his secretary.

"Then take the f. . . frigging suite," he all but shouted, obviously substituting a mild swear word as if talking to his mother. "I'm not driving back up the highway at this hour." He grimaced, ran his hand through his short hair, and listened to the voice on the other end. "Fine then, call it my case and bill it to me. It's not as if the d. . . darned suite will break us."

He waited a moment, nodded, muttered, "Good, got it, thanks," and clicked off.

Taking a deep breath, he visibly calmed his temper and reached for a fry. "I inherited my secretary from my father. She thinks we're still building the business and counting every penny. She runs a tight ship and I can't complain, but sometimes. . ."

She hid her smile at his frustration. She liked that this powerful man treated his elderly secretary with respect.

He munched the fry, checked that the bags were empty, and stood up. "There's some kind of festival in town. All the hotels are booked solid. The only opening is a suite at the resort back up the road. I hope you don't mind."

He didn't sound as if he cared if she did. He was already stalking toward the car. Taking her time, Sam strolled after him. Powerful men needed people who reminded them they didn't rule the world.

Her parents had raised her to be independent, although the extremely narrow environment they'd raised her in hadn't fostered independence. Interesting.

Walker turned around and realized she lagged behind. He waited for her at the end of the pier. "Did you want to see more of the coast? We can walk toward the cannery."

She brightened. "Is there a place where we can have wine and watch the sunset?"

"It will be packed at this hour," he warned, but he took her hand and led her down the street.

She'd tell him later that she knew where her backpack was and what was in it.

CHAPTER 14

Edgy, Walker drank only one beer while Sam sipped white wine and admired the sunset. In jeans and jacket, she wasn't dressed provocatively, but he was so aware of her that it was all he could do to keep from grabbing her hair and hauling her off to his cave.

Memories were tumbling out of her, and the story was fascinating, like a giant puzzle he needed to piece together. He ordered her another chardonnay.

"I was so *sheltered*," she admitted with a gesture of self-deprecation. "It never occurred to me to wonder where the money came from. I knew my parents were established artists and assumed the income was theirs. When I turned sixteen, Wolf bought me the Subaru, nothing fancy. He said he didn't want me driving icy roads in anything less than a four-wheel drive, and I just accepted that we had money for new cars. When it came time for college, I received a full scholarship at Brigham, so I never asked about the other costs of school."

"Why environmental science?" He wanted another beer, but one thing led to another, and he was keeping his head on tight this time around. He wouldn't let his caretaker neurosis mess with his head again, especially with a woman who was a mystery even to herself.

Sam shrugged. She'd removed her jacket and her slim shoulders lifted her breasts against her loose shirt in a way that had him sucking an empty bottle.

"I've always grown plants. I took care of the vegetable gardens and the flowers and it was just something I did. It kept me grounded, as you said earlier." She paused, as if considering how much to tell him. "I knew agriculture wasn't for me. I didn't want a farm. But science. . . that offered possibilities. My parents were all for it."

He waited while she gathered her thoughts. She had long, slender fingers and despite the work she'd been doing these past days, her nails were neat and well-shaped. His mind drifted to how they would feel. . .

"And then they were dead," she said flatly, even though grief shadowed her eyes. "One day I was planning on going home for Thanksgiving, and the next, I had no one to go home to. They had filled my life so completely that I hadn't realized I had no life without them."

He remembered the day his dad disappeared, but at the time, he had hope he'd turn up. It wasn't the same finality she'd suffered. "Painful memories. I can see where you might want to shut them out."

"*Cass* was responsible for shutting down my memory," she said without equivocation. "I loved my parents, and I know they loved me, even if I was adopted and didn't think or look like them. I *never* tried to shut out their memory, even after I learned that they didn't tell me the whole truth."

"Which is?" He could listen to her all evening, which was probably safer than going back to the suite.

"It took me a while." She sipped her wine as she worked through her thoughts. "After they died, a lawyer called to say he was the executor of their estate and that he'd keep providing for my student housing and allowance as always. He suggested I sell the farm, though, because the artwork had a finite inventory and the income from it would eventually dry up.

"I was too grief-stricken to ask more." She looked regretfully at the almost empty glass. "Are you sure you want to hear all this?"

"It's the best bedtime story I've ever heard. What did you do with the farm?"

"I couldn't bear to give it up, at first, but then I realized I couldn't bear to live out there all alone either. So I had the lawyer sell it to an elderly neighbor who had adult children who wanted to live nearby. I thought my parents would approve of that. It was only at that point that I started questioning where my allowance came from."

"You said it was in a trust?"

She nodded. "The Samantha Moon Trust and it had been established shortly after my birth, which finally made me wonder about my birth parents. I knew I was adopted and had never cared to know more."

"But you were suddenly without family and started looking around." Everything she was saying was sensible. But somewhere, the crazy came in. "How did you do that and still keep up your studies?"

"Not well," she admitted. "The Mormons have one of the biggest genealogy databases in the world, and I simply didn't have time to sort through it. After I realized Jade and Wolf had been born in San Francisco, I wondered if maybe I had been too, so I checked California adoption records and discovered I was born to Zachary and Susannah Tolliver. But I couldn't find anything in the database for either of them. That's when I gave up and hired a professional."

"A professional genealogy researcher? I wish I'd known you'd done that. I could have saved Sofia the trouble of digging." Although would he have taken Sam's word? He ran his hand up and down his empty bottle—until she abruptly stood up and almost fell.

"We need to read your laptop to see what your secretary found out about *Cass*." She steadied herself on the table. "I know Cass raised my birth father as her own, because she told me so, but she didn't give me the whole story."

Standing, Walker laid down cash for the bill and grasped her elbow to lead her out. "You're not used to alcohol."

She laughed. "Mormons, remember? Only one of my friends drank, and we didn't have money for anything except cheap beer. No matter how I tried, I never fit with the crowd anyway. By the time I graduated, I desperately missed my parents and their more liberal views. I hoped to find others like them."

Others? As in other artists? People with brown skin? Walker wanted to know more, but he had to stick to the case. "So you somehow found Cass in California?"

"The genealogist did. She traced census reports and addresses and thought Cass might be a relation because of the Tolliver name and her location. She could only find a mail-drop for her in San Francisco. I was prepared to start knocking on doors if necessary, but Cass finally responded to my letter."

"And she agreed to meet you in the restaurant in Monterey?" Walker helped her into the Explorer and hurried around to the driver's side to hear the rest of the story.

"I told her I'd never seen the ocean. I don't know why she didn't suggest San Francisco. Maybe it's too big a city for me to drive in?"

"Probably, or too big for Cass to handle anymore. She pretty much lives in Hillvale these days, although I guess her occasional disappearances are to whatever she has going in San Francisco."

"Anyway, she sent me the GPS as a graduation gift when I told her I would be driving out. I was so terrified of leaving all I knew that the GPS was like someone holding my hand."

"And it never occurred to you that Cass might be a fraud trying to con you out of your trust fund?"

She shrugged, and her loose pullover slid off one shoulder, revealing skin pale as moonlight. "I'm sheltered but not stupid. The trust fund was well invested, and my parents didn't draw on it often. It isn't enormous, just enough so that I can survive if I don't live luxuriously. I was trying to get up the nerve to travel on my own—I even got my TSA pre-check card—so I took care not to overspend. I never carry anything but my credit card with a small limit."

"What did Cass tell you when you showed up?" He steered the SUV up a narrow road to the hilltop resort.

"She told me that she'd raised my father since he was an infant and gave him her husband's name, so Zachary Tolliver was his legal name, and I could look at her as my grandmother." In the moonlight, her pale features wrinkled with concern. "She said my real grandmother was part of the psychedelic drugs era, became a heroin addict, and my father was born with fetal drug addiction, which made him a difficult and sickly child."

"And Zachary's real father?" Walker parked the Explorer in an obscure part of the luxury hotel's lot, away from the Jags and BMWs. No sense in disturbing the clientele with an official vehicle.

"My grandfather didn't marry the heroin addict. According to Cass, my grandmother died of an overdose within a year of her son's birth, and my grandfather didn't want anything to do with his sickly child. But he provided a trust fund for Zachary's support."

"This isn't going to end well, is it?" He got out his case with the laptop and punched his reservation into his phone, gaining the code for their room. By the time they reached the front door, he had their e-key and steered her toward the elevators.

She halted at the elaborate bouquet in the main lobby. "Some of those are from Australia," she said in wonder, reaching out to touch what looked like a prickly purple thorn. "Do they grow them here?"

"Clueless. The only plant I've ever grown is weed, and I don't mean the garden variety. And it died." Walker finally dragged her away, but now he realized she'd never been in a fancy hotel. He was dealing with a virtual newborn.

"Were you experimenting with smoking or growing?" she asked as they entered the elevators.

Not totally a newborn then, if she knew what pot was. Of course she did, she took botany classes and lived with artists. "Both. That was back in college when I was young and stupid."

"And now you're thinking I'm just out of college and equally young and stupid." She yanked her elbow from his grip.

Shame that, he'd been enjoying the flesh-to-flesh contact. "No, a little naïve, perhaps, but not stupid by a long shot."

She pondered that as the elevator opened directly into the suite. Even he was a little impressed by the grandeur. Sofia had warned him that this would suck his pocket dry.

Sam gawked in silence.

Walker removed his holster, then perused the sleeping situation. Two equally grandiose bedrooms joined by an enormous sitting/dining area. If he were really lucky, it had a well-stocked bar. He found the refrigerator and the bar and poured himself another beer. It was going to be a long night if he had to stay up and watch Sam sway around the room, caressing flower arrangements and tinkling the keys on the grand piano. He wanted to yank the combs out of her hair and let it fall down her back.

"More wine?" he asked, offering up a full-size bottle. "Or champagne?"

"Champagne? I've never had champagne." She sauntered over to examine the bottle. "I can't drink all that. Maybe some other time."

He unwrapped the cork and popped it. "It's not every day you find long-lost family *and* your memory. How much more did Cass tell you?" He must be as insane as the Lucys to believe this crap, but it all fit with what he already knew. He found a glass in the bar and poured the bubbly under a bright light so she could admire the fizz. She was a cute drunk, and he needed her to continue the story to keep from pouncing on her.

Sam gave him another of those devastating smiles that went straight to his groin. Taking the glass, she sipped cautiously. "It tickles."

"It's really dry, so it may be an acquired taste. You don't have to drink it if you don't like it." It was the hundred-dollar a bottle stuff, but as he'd said, it was worth celebrating this temporary reprieve from real life. Tomorrow, they'd head back up the mountain to lunacy.

One day at a time was all he was doing these days.

"I probably shouldn't acquire the taste, but I'm willing to try anything once." She sipped some more before returning to his question. "Cass kept things from me. I remember getting frustrated when I asked who *my* mother was and why she gave me up for adoption. She told me Zack died the same way his mother had, by overdose. But she didn't say my mother was dead too. And she didn't mention what happened to Zach's father, my real grandfather."

He seated her on the couch so she didn't wobble—and so he could sit beside her and drink in her scent as he opened up his laptop. "Let's see what Sofia turned up."

"Do you think any of this affects your father's death?" she asked, watching over his shoulder.

"We already know Cass is related to the Kennedys, who own half the town. My father was researching some kind of fraud case when he went up there. I'm pretty sure he wouldn't be looking into drug addicts. His business was more corporate than that." He connected with his personal hotspot instead of the hotel Wi-Fi. "If you're what. . . twenty-four?"

She nodded.

"Then chances are good that if your birth father lived with Cass, he was connected to people who were still living in Hillvale a few years after you were born—when my father arrived. If Cass is a Kennedy. . ." He scrolled through the family tree file Sofia had created on Cass. "Bingo." He turned the screen around where she could see it.

She studied all the crisscrossing lines. "Complicated family. My heroine-addict grandmother doesn't seem to be related to Cass. She put no father's name on Zach's birth certificate. So why did Cass and her husband adopt him?"

Walker clicked a link so she could read the data easier. "Sofia has access to databases your genealogist doesn't. Geoffrey Kennedy ran a DNA test on Zach before he set up the trust fund."

She clicked back to trace the family line. "*Geoffrey Kennedy* was my grandfather? I went on a date with my *uncle*?"

CHAPTER 15

Late evening, June 19

Sam took the laptop away to study the screen. Her head spun from the champagne, but she could comprehend the lines well enough. Geoffrey Kennedy, late husband of Carmel, father of Montague, Hillvale mayor, and Kurt Kennedy, resort manager, was her *grandfather*?

"Are Montgomery and Kurt Kennedy my half-uncles? Do *they* know that?" she asked tentatively. "I've never had a family. I don't know how the relationships work."

"Looks like Zachary, your father, would have been their older half-brother, so yeah, I guess you can go with half-uncle," he acknowledged, still studying the screen. "Looks like your grandfather had Kurt and Monty late in life. They were only five or six when Zach died, so it's possible they know nothing about him."

Sam shuddered, realizing her *uncles* ran the town—and may never have known about her existence. She stared wordlessly at the screen, trying to absorb the hot mess that was her real, very mixed-up birth family. Jade and Wolf were much easier to handle in comparison. Now that she had a memory again, she had a longing for the sanity of the university and the office waiting for her back there.

Walker took the laptop back and scrolled around. "Even better, Cass and Geoffrey seem to be half-siblings, so I guess Cass is. . ." He scrunched up his nose to figure it out. "She'd be Zach's half-aunt and your great-aunt. She essentially raised her nephew because Geoffrey wouldn't claim him."

"I remember her telling me that she was *like* a grandmother to me. I guess, since she raised my father, that was truth of a sort too." She curled up against his side to study the screen, but her head couldn't take in much more.

"Cass sent you up to Hillvale for a reason. And given your relationship to Kurt and Monty, I'm guessing it's not one Carmel will be happy about."

"I still can't recall how Cass sent me up there. If I'm remembering right, I think I refused to go. I didn't want any part of a family that didn't want me." That hurt as much now as it had since she was a kid and learned what *adopted* meant. "Geoffrey Kennedy or my birth parents essentially *paid* Wolf and Jade to keep me away."

"Don't be so hasty to jump to conclusions. We still don't have all the data on your mother. Where did she hook up with Zack? In Hillvale? Frisco? Did she know the Lucys? The Kennedys? Did they pay her to leave too?"

"Is she even alive?" Forgetting about Walker's search for people who might have met his father, she spun the laptop screen again. "Susannah Ingersson Kennedy. Zack *married* my mother."

"He also used his birth father's name and not Tolliver, which is why your genealogist was running into difficulty," Walker pointed out, as if that might be significant.

"That's rude. I'm Samantha *Moon* because my parents adopted me. I don't want to be a Kennedy or whatever. My birth parents gave me up. Why would my father cut out Cass's married name if she raised him as a Tolliver?"

"To taunt his father and his father's new family would be my guess. Looks like he wasn't more than twenty when he married. That's not always a real bright age, especially for a troubled addict. Since Cass was a Kennedy before she married, he wasn't completely disrespecting her."

She wrinkled her nose. "But when I was born, they used Tolliver on my birth certificate. None of this makes sense, unless they deliberately wanted to confuse me."

"I don't have answers," Walker said with a shrug. "Cass can tell us more tomorrow. But look at the *Ingersson*."

"Why does that sound familiar?" Were there still holes in her memory?

"Valdis," he replied curtly. "Her real name is *Valerie Ingersson*, and her real hair color is blond, just like yours."

Sam snapped the laptop shut. "That's it. I can't take any more. I'm related to a witch, a death goddess, and the owners of half the town. I never had any idea that family could be such a headache."

Walker dropped the computer on the coffee table and hugged her at the same time.

She knew he only meant to comfort her, but she needed more than that. She needed out of her head and back to basic human touch. Walker smelled of delicious masculine musk and the remnants of after-shave, and he'd opened the top button of his shirt so she could just. . .

Glimpsing a tattoo on the brown skin beneath the V of his shirt, she leaned over and kissed it.

He grabbed her hair and pulled her head up so he could meet her eyes. "I want you too much to turn down your offer, Sam," he warned. "You are no longer a missing person and no longer my case."

"I hope that means something significant." Thrilled that they were on the same page, she unbuttoned the next button to see the tattoo. It was a Chinese symbol she couldn't interpret.

"It means I may regret this in the morning, but at least I won't feel guilty preying on a victim." He bent to capture her mouth.

Selfishly deciding to believe that his comment about regret was his problem and not hers, Sam climbed across his thighs. Alcohol had a lovely effect on inhibitions, but she would have done this without the champagne. As if starved, she devoured Walker's mouth. He had flex-ible lips that plied hers with expertise, authoritative, demanding, and as hungry as hers. She absorbed his male scent, the rough texture of his jaw, and his strength. She wriggled downward until she could feel his hard thighs and the long ridge lengthening beneath her bottom.

"Your duty is to serve and protect?" she asked teasingly, coming up for air. "I'm not a victim, you know. I've been taking care of myself these past six years."

"You and your trust fund in your ivory tower," he corrected. But then he ran his hand under her shirt and released her bra and everything was all right.

"Broaden my world," she murmured some minutes later when he lifted her and carried her toward the bedroom.

"No promises," he muttered back. "One night, that's all this is."

"One night is all I need," she taunted, tugging his shirt from his pants as he laid her on the largest bed she'd ever seen. "Drive my family out of my head."

Walker was all gorgeous male. The purple tattoo emphasized his admirable pecs. Another cryptic tattoo circled his muscled biceps and stretched when he leaned over her. He was tougher than her grad student boyfriends, a man who had lived a real life, not the sheltered one of academia.

A man who knew luxury suites supplied condoms and had the sense to grab one.

She needed to absorb some of his toughness and experience if she was to survive this next phase. She needed to know she could withstand that toughness.

But the kisses he used to arouse her were tender, so tender she nearly cried at the need welling up inside her. And the need was more than physical. Alone and adrift, she clung to him as a sturdy mast in the storm. And when they joined, he set her free.

MORNING, JUNE 20

"FRUIT IS NOT BREAKFAST," WALKER SCOLDED AS HIS TOUSLED BEDMATE placed her order with room service the next day. "Fruit is dessert."

"Fresh fruit is nirvana," she countered, almost drooling over the picture on the desk menu. "Fresh fruit is nectar of the gods. Manly men can crunch baby chickens and three kinds of grease on an empty stomach. This goddess can't."

She *looked* like a veritable goddess with all that moonlight hair tumbling into her sunlit face and down her robe. Last night, she'd awakened him in ways that must have been magic. He'd been dead inside for too long. He wasn't entirely certain he wanted to return to the living, but her delight was not only irresistible but ego-inflating.

"Goddess, huh?" He lifted her against him. "Mystical, mythical, or comic book?"

"Tarot card." She wrapped her fine legs around his hips and kissed his neck. "Does that count?"

"Works for me." And he carried her back to bed to fill in time before room service arrived. A year was a damned long time to go without sex. He had a lot to catch up on, and Sam was no shy virgin. She was a natural earth goddess. He didn't need to worry she would take their encounter seriously. Maybe sex without considering commitment and babies could keep him going. He blessed the hotel's box of condoms—or his secretary's wisdom in ordering them.

They'd showered and dressed by the time breakfast arrived. Walker had sent yesterday's clothes to be express laundered. That had earned him extra hugs and kisses. At least Sam knew how to do appreciation. Must have been that small-town upbringing.

Watching her salivate over berries, yogurt, and honey tickled him more than anything in his life lately. He'd have to watch himself once they returned to the real world, but for now, maybe his cynical soul needed a fresh perspective.

After he finished his three kinds of grease, and she'd practically licked her bowl, they used hotel toothbrushes and checked out. Walker grabbed the champagne bottle on the way. It might not be bubbly, but it was his, and a good memory for the lonely nights ahead.

"So first thing we do after we pick up my backpack is ask Cass who lived in Hillvale twenty years ago?" Sam asked as they drove back to the restaurant where she had first met Cass. "She may still not be strong, so let's line up the important things first."

"I want to know how in hell she put a hex on you for days while she lay in a coma," he grumbled, pulling into the storage facility next door to the restaurant.

A cloud crossed Sam's usually sunny face, but she held back her feelings and shrugged. "She'll just say drugs. Focus. Have you ever asked her if she knew your father?"

She punched her birthday into the keyboard, and the gates opened. She produced the key on her key chain with the locker number on it, and he drove down the aisle until he found it.

"I didn't know he was here for sure until this past week, so no. I've kept his name on the down low while I snooped."

"Snooping while learning about everyone, letting them trust you—you're sneaky but good." She climbed out, distancing herself literally as well as verbally.

Walker thought he should be good with distance—he'd been the one to impose the limits. He kept a professional eye on their surroundings as Sam applied the key to the designated box lock and twisted. They both sighed in relief when it opened, revealing a backpack. She rummaged around inside the pack until she found a small leather cash purse and opened it. Smiling triumphantly, she climbed back in with her treasures and waved her driver's license and credit card at him. "I'm real again."

"That relieves you of cartoon goddess status then. You'll have to be normal like the rest of us." Forcing her back into his mental closed case file, he drove out of the storage unit and headed for the hospital.

Cass had planned this whole damned expedition, right down to a restaurant and hotel near storage lockers and a *hospital*. He ought to strangle the old lady.

As they circled the hospital parking lot looking for a space, Sam stiffened. Walker hit the brake and followed her gaze. "Effing shit."

He eased the car down the next aisle and over to a construction dumpster where a tall, slender, gray-haired female wrapped in shawls waited. Cass let herself in the back door of the SUV before he could even turn off the engine. "Home, Jeeves," she ordered.

"What are you doing out of bed?" Sam asked with what sounded like horror. "Did the doctors say you could go?"

"They want to run a battery of tests and bill Medicare a fortune. I'm fine. Let's go. We have work to do."

Walker didn't let up on the brake. He glanced at Sam. Her fingers were balled into fists. Remembering how she'd nearly broken his finger in her fury, he waited to see if he needed to intervene.

"That's all you have to say to me?" Sam demanded, still sounding horrified. "You medicate me, send me into the void, leave me helpless —and all you can do is *order us to take you home*? Do I get an apology? An explanation? Or do we need to haul you back into the hospital and tell them you're insane?"

Walker winced. But he stayed out of it. It wasn't his head the old witch had played with. In his rearview mirror, he saw Cass lift her bony chin and glare out the window.

"You were bent on returning to your narrow world, rejecting us without a valid reason," Cass replied sharply. "You needed to meet us with open eyes, using that observational mind of yours and not childish emotion. And now that you've had time to study Hillvale, do you still want to walk away?"

"*That* justifies whatever you did to me?" Sam cried, although some of her fury had deflated. Walker suspected she'd already recognized why the old woman had done what she had.

How Cass had done it was another mystery entirely.

"Hillvale is special," Cass said quietly. "We could change the world, if the world doesn't destroy us first. I was willing to die if it meant you would return to help us."

Shit, the old lady had hit Sam's sympathy buttons. Sam frowned in thought. He really didn't want to fight the old woman and carry her back inside. But he didn't want her dropping dead on him either.

"I'm fine. Let's go," Cass said with a wave of her thin hand. "They could be up there bulldozing the vortex if we don't go back now."

"Bulldozing the vortex? Is that what this is all about?" Sam asked, nodding at him in an unspoken command.

Walker took it as an okay to move on. The hospital would already have Cass's information. He'd have his secretary double check to make certain they knew she was okay and that they didn't need more. He was all for interrogating the crazy old bat all the way back to town.

"Are you prepared to tell me what you did to Sam?" he asked before leaving the lot. "Otherwise, I'm hauling you back inside."

"Drugs, dear. It's all in knowing your pharmaceuticals. Well, and a little hypnosis, perhaps. Did that work?"

Walker checked his rearview mirror. Cass had a too academic, sophisticated air to look like an innocent old lady, no matter how she tried. He knew she lied, at least partially. She'd probably used mushrooms, all right, but the Lucys did weird inexplicable things. He needed to figure out how before they did it again.

"You scared the heck out of me," Sam said angrily. "Do you have any idea what it's like to not know who you are?"

"My friends took care of you, didn't they? They only had to look at you to know who you are. That's the reason Susannah insisted you be sent away. The girl is paranoid."

Diverted, Sam's anger turned to interest. "You know my mother?"

Walker recognized the old lady's tactic. Cass had no intention of accepting responsibility for these last days of horror. And since he wasn't even certain a crime had been committed, he grudgingly accepted her change of subject only because it was one Sam needed to hear.

"So Sam's mother is still alive?" He had already done the math and knew her father had been dead and her mother had moved on before his father had gone to Hillvale, but he knew Sam's curiosity burned.

"As far as I'm aware," Cass said airily. "Susannah ran the opposite direction to Jade. She could be in China by now. They were good friends."

"My birth mother is *alive*?" Sam almost shouted. Walker was afraid to glance over to see her expression.

"Happily remarried and mother of three, last I heard, which has been a while," Cass admitted, apparently oblivious to her effect on Sam.

"Cassandra," Walker said warningly. "Sam is just learning all this. There's no need to hit her over the head with a baseball bat."

Sam gave an ungraceful snort but didn't argue.

"It's all old news, dear," Cass replied with a wave of her bony hand. "The important part is that we have you back. You'll complete the circle, and we can begin turning things around."

"No," Sam said quietly. "The important part is that my mother thought it necessary to send me far away from Hillvale to an environment exactly opposite of the one I was born in. And then she ran the reverse direction. That doesn't sound as if I belong in Hillvale or that she wants me there. Do my uncles even know I exist?"

Silence from the back seat was damning. The Kennedys knew

nothing of Sam. Walker could almost feel her pain as Sam took up where Cass's silence left off.

"I'm damned tired of not belonging," she said. "But first, we need to know more about the skeleton buried on the mountain. How much do you know about that?"

Walker wanted to pump his fist and cheer. Cass was an intimidating old hag, almost as bad as Carmel, but she had met her match in Sam.

He would have preferred to have had this conversation where he could study Cass's body language, but an occasional glance in his mirror would have to suffice. He had to take this brief interval of captivity before Cass disappeared inside her weird mansion again.

"A skeleton?" Cass sounded alarmed, but a glance in the mirror showed sadness. "We knew the vortex was drawing on negativity, but a skeleton?"

Sam left the opening to him.

"Do you remember a Michael Walker from almost eighteen years ago? He would have been staying at the lodge and asking questions around town." Walker knew how ludicrous the question sounded. Cass had no reason to know about resort guests. But she was his only connection to that period.

"The year Geoff died, I vaguely remember the sheriff asking after a missing tourist. But we had no reason to believe the tourist had died in Hillvale." She sat there sadly, gathering her thoughts. "It must have been his spirit who spoke to us on Zack's birthday a year or so later. He didn't give his name. We were trying to contact Zack, to see if he was in a happier place."

Walker gritted his teeth. He handed his phone to Sam so she could look up the genealogy he'd downloaded. She poked through it, apparently understanding his need to confirm dates.

"What did the spirit say?" Sam asked as she scrolled.

"Mostly, the stranger wanted to express love for his family, but he was too furious to be clear. And we were too afraid to listen. We were expecting Zach's gentle presence, and this one was just too forceful. We could try again, I suppose."

"We tried that. Tullah claims he is too far out of reach to speak to us, but her spirit guide warned of evil and fire and said to tell his son to beware." Sam sent him a guilty look. "I didn't know she meant you."

Walker wanted to rage about the non-validity of spirit guides and voodoo and schizophrenic voices, but Sam and Cass were the public he was currently serving, not a family he had to fix. He bit his tongue and played along. "It sounds like Tullah knows something. Was she here eighteen years ago?" He might not believe in spirits, but he'd learned there was a kernel of truth behind every mystery the Lucys produced.

"No, Tullah joined us a year or more after Katrina wiped out her home. She's the one who told Dinah the café was available. Natural disasters bring out the best and worst in people, and Dinah had been having a hard time in New Orleans."

Walker was afraid the old woman was wearing out and starting to ramble, but all information was useful. "Who else was there back then?"

Cass hesitated. He had no way of knowing if she was gathering memories or choosing her lies. A little of both, he suspected. "Daisy, of course. She walked through time and found us when she ran away from home. Susan McQueen was part of the commune. She was at the séance, but she doesn't participate much in the town otherwise. Marta Josephine was probably there. She's been with us since she left Berkley."

"What about Valdis?" Sam asked.

"Valdis and your mother are sisters, dear. Their parents owned the commune's farm, and they grew up in Hillvale. But Valdis left for college, and Susannah left after Zach died. Valdis only recently returned after some tragedy she won't tell us about."

"Harvey and Aaron?" Walker asked impatiently. He couldn't imagine any of those unworldly women hitting his father over the head. Harvey, the long-haired musician, and fastidious Aaron, the antique dealer, were probably too young, but he had to try.

"Oh, Harvey is a friend of Monty's. He's not been around long. I'm not certain what brought Aaron up, but it was long after that particular séance. He doesn't participate in them anyway."

"So the circle consisted of you, Daisy, Susan, and Marta?" Sam asked. She appeared to be typing notes into his phone.

"Yes, that sounds about right. It probably would have been better if we could have had some men, if the spirit was male, but we didn't."

Walker seriously doubted that four irrational women had any idea of what happened to his father. But he had only straws to grasp, so he tried to keep them sorted. "Once you knew there was a spirit floating around, did you even attempt to figure out why?"

"Evil has inhabited the land around the resort for as long as we know," Cass said as pragmatically as if she claimed the lodge had termites. "We avoid going there. All we could do was try to reach out for the spirit and lay him to rest. If Tullah couldn't reach him, then we may have at least partially succeeded."

"Valdis goes up on the mountain," Sam pointed out.

"Valdis walks with death. She must learn to be strong. But this is why we need you, Sam. The evil must be eradicated before any more are hurt. Daisy sees disaster in the future if we don't act."

Cass was so insistent, that Walker would almost have listened— had she said an arsonist was on the loose or tree beetles were destroying the pines. But evil and spirits did not compute. Maybe they were metaphors.

Before the old lady could lay a guilt trip on Sam, Walker intervened. "You drugged Sam and sent her blindly up an unfamiliar mountain into the arms of strangers. I'm thinking she's better off going far, far away, maybe looking for her mother to get the real story."

In the mirror, he read a flicker of panic on Cass's face. Good. Mushrooms had been a damned dangerous trick.

"He's right, Cass," Sam said. "It was a horrifying experience. If I have no guarantee that it won't happen again, I can't stay in Hillvale."

"You needed to see it with clear eyes," Cass repeated, almost angrily. "Your mother sent you to be brainwashed by the most deadly Nulls she could imagine. You would never have opened your eyes to possibilities if I hadn't interfered. Did you feel the earth? Could you not sense what was happening? Can you understand that Mariah and the others aren't freaks?"

Sam waited so long to reply that Walker almost missed his turn in anticipation of her answer. When it came, it wasn't the one he wanted.

"Misguided, perhaps, but not freaks," Sam said so quietly he almost didn't hear her. "There's a difference in the earth energy between one side of the vortex and the other."

WALKER HAD GONE SILENT AFTER SAM'S ADMISSION ABOUT FEELING EARTH energy. She didn't blame him. She's always been aware of good and bad energies. It helped her know where to plant. She had just never known other people didn't feel the same—like seeing colors others didn't.

Letting Walker work it out for himself, Sam continued adding names to his phone as she dragged them out of Cass. Casting aside her whirling emotions, she focused on the here and now, aware of a subtle connection to her great-aunt beneath what was said aloud. If she believed that link—Cass was not telling all she knew.

Given what she already understood about the wily woman, Sam was inclined to believe this odd bond. To Cass, Walker was an outsider. In Cass's mind, that kept him off the need-to-know list.

But in many ways—despite her hereditary status—Sam was also an outsider. She knew how that felt too well, and her shoulders twitched in discomfort. But in this case, maybe being an outsider was a good thing.

Once Cass insisted she didn't know any other names for Walker's list, Sam turned to face her and remonstrated, "You brought me to Hillvale for a reason, Cass. If you want me to be objective about the town's problems, you have to tell the truth."

"You are young," she said with a weary wave of dismissal. "When you reach my age, you realize there are layers of truth, and the world consists of shades of gray. I tell you what I know, not what I suspect."

Unexpectedly, Walker agreed with her. "I don't want speculation. Like Sam, I need to be objective. If you didn't know my father, I believe you. He would have appeared to be any regular tourist. The question becomes—do you have any idea why a fraud investigator would have been in Hillvale?"

Sam raised her eyebrows at Cass's silence. Walker slowed down to check the rearview mirror. But Cass was alert—and pensive.

"Eighteen years is almost a generation ago, dear," she said at last.

"We can't bring your father back. But we *can* release the evil energy if we stir things up. We have enough trouble without adding to it."

Can, not may. Sam shuddered. If she believed Cass. . . "The evil has already been stirred," Sam corrected, before Walker could object. "The security manager at the resort was killed a couple of days ago."

"*Juan?* Oh, that's dreadful." Cass gave a heartfelt sigh. "His poor mother. She had fourteen children. She was so proud of her son when he took the job at the resort. I didn't have the heart to warn her that he would be surrounded by evil."

"He was here eighteen years ago?" Walker asked immediately.

"Yes. Many of the lodge employees have been," she conceded. "I don't know most of them. I really didn't know Juan that well. Juan's parents moved down the mountain when the bank foreclosed on their little house."

Cass waved a dismissive hand at Sam's look. "I know, give me a minute. My memory isn't what it used to be." She sat silent, watching out the window as she gathered her thoughts. "The foreclosures started around twenty years ago. That's about the time that Geoff began talking ski resorts and development and started buying up land his neighbors lost."

Sam heard her bitterness. "Why did everyone start losing their homes?"

"The usual reasons—recession, the mill closing, a rockslide took out the road for nearly a year so tourists couldn't get in, an avalanche of bad luck."

"It happens," Walker said curtly, keeping his eyes on the narrow switchback up the mountain. "California real estate is a shell game. Mortgage companies, developers, real estate agents promise the American dream. People overextend their finances to buy a piece of that dream in the belief that they're on the way up in the world. First economic downturn, they're out on the street. The rich developers sweep in, buy the foreclosed land for peanuts, build a new development, and resell at higher prices to the next fool."

"Capitalism, dearest," Cass said with a smile. "The biggest wolf wins."

"And the sheep get eaten," Walker countered. "If that's the evil you're battling, it's pretty much worldwide."

"Which doesn't make it less evil, but no, this evil is innate. It feeds on souls."

Before Sam could question this insane conclusion, Walker cursed. She turned back to glance out the windshield. Smoke billowed high above the trees.

The mountain was on fire.

CHAPTER 16

MORNING, JUNE 20

"OH DEAR," CASS MURMURED. "IS IT THE SOLSTICE ALREADY?"

Walker turned on his radio and hit the gas. "What the hell is that supposed to mean?" he demanded as he took the curves at breakneck speed, siren screaming.

"Nulls once burned bonfires to ward off evil—like witches—on summer's eve. The cards warned hostilities would commence on the solstice." Cass peered out the window.

"I think that's tomorrow," Walker said after reporting the fire to the office. "And any fool burning in this drought needs to be horse-whipped."

Meeting a line of cars exiting Hillvale, Walker flashed his lights and used the siren. They eased to one side so he could reach the parking lot. A line of traffic still streamed down from the resort. On a weekend, the lodge was packed—it was like watching money flow down the drain.

The chatter on the radio indicated the fire had been reported and emergency services were heading up, but Hillvale was a long way from anywhere.

"You ladies need to get out here," Walker ordered, eyeing the lick of flame through the pines on the ridge.

"Does the resort have any earth movers?" Sam asked, not unbuckling.

"Monty does. He parks them in the town lot." Cass did unbuckle, but only so she could open the door and hail Mariah. "Tell Monty to move the mountain," she called.

Mariah signaled understanding and trotted off.

"Get out, Cass," Walker said between clenched teeth. "I don't have time to fight you."

The old witch leaned over and patted him on the shoulder. "You're not a fireman, dear. Direct traffic, keep Sam safe, and we'll do the rest. We're prepared for this."

He only bit his tongue because she climbed out to join the rest of her coven gathering in the lot, carrying shovels and hoes. His blood pressure probably soared thirty points.

"Sam—" he said warningly.

"They're going to cut a line between town and the fire. That fire is aimed for Hillvale, not the lodge," she said acerbically. "Someone is literally and metaphorically trying to burn them out."

That was craziness. And she believed it? He cursed again, turned the sirens back on, and began forcing traffic to the side of the road so he could reach the lodge. After years of sitting behind a desk, he indulged in the visceral satisfaction of active command again.

Except he couldn't force the insane woman beside him to follow his orders.

While he maneuvered past hulking SUVs driven by terrified tourists, she leaned over to gaze up the mountain. "Looks as if it started on Menendez land. I don't remember any tall trees there. I thought it had been logged."

"Pines all around it." Pines that would shoot sparks all over the mountain if the wind picked up.

"Water hoses won't reach that far. How do they fight fire up there?"

He shut the sirens as he hit the parking lot where lodge guests still spilled from the building, carrying suitcases and children.

Children. They had effing damned children in the path of that fire.

He watched a curly-haired toddler no older than Davy had been and his lungs ran out of air.

Focus, Walker. Resist the urge to grab the children and run. "Water trucks," he said curtly. "Planes. They're on the way. Clearing brush is the best thing we can do."

He slammed out of the car, fighting his protective instincts. He couldn't take care of Sam, and he sure as hell couldn't take care of a hotel filled with people. But he had a job to do.

Walker watched warily as Sam let herself out the other side. Her elegantly boned face was so much like Cass's it was eerie, now that he'd seen them together. Both women were poised in the face of danger. Sam's stillness was almost terrifying, akin to a cougar that smells danger and freezes before leaping.

"It's fueled on evil," she murmured. "I can feel it flowing through the ground. Cass is right. Someone deliberately set that fire."

Shit, back to crazy again. "Stay here. Don't move or I put you in handcuffs."

Lazy, lanky Harvey, the long-haired musician and wood-carver, hurried across the lot to add to Walker's escalating fury and anxiety.

SAM WAS AWARE THAT—AFTER ALL HE'D DONE FOR HER—SHE'D TICKED Walker off, but the primal elements flowing through her were stronger than any need to please him. She felt as connected to the land as she did to Cass. She could feel the *stress*. It was an odd feeling, stronger than the ones she'd used for planting.

Walker's stress was of a different sort. He'd donned his concealing sunglasses, and his expression was one of control so rigid that a muscle ticked in his jaw. He was watching the people pouring from the lodge with their belongings as if he wanted to make them all disappear.

A baby cried, a child shouted. He flinched, and his fists curled as Harvey approached.

The musician provided a welcome distraction. Harvey's height gave him a lean look, but his black t-shirt revealed sinew and muscle. For a musician, he took athletics seriously, it appeared.

He held out one of his carved staffs to Sam. This one was a blond wood, slender, the tree branch's original knobs and curves adding an almost feminine quality to it. The handle had been carved to resemble an antique sailing ship prow—a woman's face with crystal blue eyes and hair streaming in the wind. Sam instinctively reached for it before he spoke.

"Protect the earth," Harvey commanded.

Beside her, Walker nearly growled. Harvey loped off to help Carmel's brother haul his paintings to a battered Land Rover. The stout real estate mogul Grumpy Gump was already loading stacks of small canvases into the vehicle. For the first time, Sam noted gray shooting through the mogul's thick blond hair.

Kurt and Carmel Kennedy were there, assisting their guests in their departures.

Sam's staff twitched. She had no idea what that meant, but after being trapped and helpless these last days, she needed her *self* back. She glared at Walker. "Handcuff me, and you can arrest me for assaulting a police officer."

"That would be a reverse policy. I mean it, Sam. Don't be part of the problem," he ordered.

"I think we're *all* part of the problem, but that fire up there is manmade. I can feel the malice burning." Torn between intellectual obedience and the innate sensation of *knowing* how the earth felt, Sam's two heritages battled for control.

Even as she spoke, one of the resort's uniformed security guards raced down the hillside, shouting, "It's a cross! The crazies are burning a cross!"

"No, they're not." At that deliberate slur, Sam chose sides and started toward the path into the woods. "The Lucys are in town, blocking evil with bulldozers."

She said it for Walker's benefit, not the guard, who was too far away. Walker grabbed her elbow and swung her around.

"That part, I almost understand," he said. "But you can't put out the fire. Stay here and keep the Kennedys in line or they'll be rounding up your friends and shooting them."

Startled, she studied his expression, but wearing his mirrored sunglasses, he played his inscrutable card. Last night, in his arms, she'd thought she understood him. Today, not so much.

Remembering Carmel at the graveyard at midnight, she had to consider his conclusion, but she shook her head in disagreement.

"The Kennedys may be a negative force, but they're not the *wrongness* seeping through this soil. I'll hold them off with my new stick," she suggested facetiously, yanking her arm out of his grasp.

Last night had been a moment out of time, one she'd never have again, she feared. He was the Null voice of sanity and authority, and she was just a crazy Lucy, apparently. She stalked off toward the lodge.

She discovered the walking stick had a belt that she could strap around her arm or waist or anywhere that suited her. She fit it to her waist and hefted a toddler wandering after his father, who was bogged down in bags of toys and coolers.

"People are more important than things," she warned the mother racing up to fling diaper bags in the back of their van. Sam handed her the kid. "Get out now, before the fire spreads."

Both parents glanced in alarm at the flames licking down the hillside. Thank all the stars, the wind wasn't blowing hard, but it would take only one gust. . . Following Sam's advice, they fastened the kid in his seat and climbed in without going back for suitcases.

Turning around, Sam came face to face with Carmel. The older woman looked as if she'd like to spit in her face. "Out," the older woman said in a threatening tone. "Get out of town *now*."

"And hello to you, too, step-grandma," Sam said. "I'll invite you to tea sometime, but right now, you have a bigger problem we should address first."

That wasn't like the old her to talk like that. She now knew she was normally cautious and determined, hunting for niches where she might fit in. She wasn't comfortable with this new aggressiveness, but maybe she should learn.

Carmel looked so stunned, Sam couldn't regret the wild freedom surging through her. Turning her back on the lodge, she threw caution to the winds and jogged over to where Harvey strode up the path toward the exorcism clearing.

Behind her, the Nulls were being sensible. Walker was directing traffic. Her *Uncle* Kurt was helping the last few straggling guests. She could hear fire engines screaming up the road, and a plane flying over the mountain.

She refused to watch helplessly if there was any small part she could play in saving a town that had taken her in. But she didn't have bulldozers or even a hoe. All she had was a pulsating stick and the Lucys' foolish superstition. If she wished to be an objective, open-minded scientist, shouldn't she at least experiment?

She unclipped the carved staff and held it in her hand, not like a dowsing rod this time, but as a walking stick. It seemed to amplify the vibrations she'd sensed when she'd climbed out of the car.

"What the hell am I supposed to be doing?" Sam asked as she caught up with Harvey.

"Find the source of the fuel?" He lifted his thick black eyebrows in question as she approached.

"We find a source of *malice*? That could be the entire damned world," she said, biting back her fear that they were all crazy. But she'd found the old church grounds earlier. . .

"Is that what this energy is? Malice? Sounds about right. It's all a learning process," he said with a shrug, proceeding onward now that she'd caught up with him.

"Swell. We won't learn anything if we burn to death." The acrid stench of wood smoke filtered down on the breeze, but the fire was still a few miles away.

"Fitting end for witches, I suppose," he said fatalistically, hiking on.

She should follow Walker's sensible advice and get the hell out of here. But she didn't—because she could *feel* what Harvey was talking about. Her scientific observational skills required tracing the source of this energy, if only to prove its existence.

"There are no such things as witches," she protested. "We may have a sensitivity to faults in the earth or uncannily strong senses of smell for pollution, but magic isn't real."

"Magic explains the inexplicable," he said, covering ground in long loping strides. "I suppose one could substitute God, but too many nebulous variables attach to that concept. I try not to offend more people than I already do."

He was luring her with his voice, she knew. She followed easily, keeping her eye on the distant flames. "I just offended Carmel, again. I apparently offend her by existing. So I'm guessing whatever magic voodoo you think we do isn't the only reason people find us offensive."

"I carve wood," he stated flatly. "I imbue no magic into it. Tell me these vibrations are the magic of my carving."

She held the rod out and watched it quiver. "I've never felt wood vibrate before, but people have been using dowsing rods for centuries. Aren't they supposed to be forked?"

"I'm hunting energy, not water or gold," he said irritably.

"Fine then, I'll experiment and try to keep an open mind." Energy dowsing sounded better than hunting for malice.

He didn't bother acknowledging her attempt to understand. Harvey had a bit of a chip on his shoulder, she suspected.

Sam tried to sense a path with the staff, but the energy it amplified was widespread. She swung around in a circle, holding out the rod, but one side wasn't stronger than the other. She glanced up the hill. The stench of wet charred wood was heavy. The plane had dropped its chemical load between the fire and the lodge, leaving flames to lick downhill in the other direction—toward town and the bulldozers. She didn't sense danger, yet.

She created a distance between herself and Harvey, spreading their range. The ground was relatively clear of brambles, but she kept an eye out for fleeing critters—like snakes.

"Did you find Cass?" Harvey poked through the dead leaves with his black staff.

So much had happened that she'd forgotten they hadn't had time to share the news. "We left her down in Hillvale, bossing everyone around."

"Long story best told over a fire with a bottle of wine?" he suggested.

"A whole barrel of whiskey might be required. Cass has to live here. I'll leave her to tell the tale, or the part she considers suitable."

"Yeah, she keeps secrets. You and Walker an item?" He was ahead of her as he asked that, so she couldn't read his expression.

She didn't know how she felt about that, or the intriguing man asking her. She wasn't in a place yet that let her think about relationships. Last night had been necessary for both of them, but they were worlds apart. "Not sure. He helped me and Cass, but he's here for his own reasons."

"Aren't we all?" He glanced toward the fire line creeping closer despite the chemical retardant. "May be time to get out."

Sam felt a tug on her staff. She halted and tried to sense the energy flow. Was this how she had chosen the best areas to plant back on the farm—without the need of a stick? Neighbors had claimed she had a green thumb, but she'd assumed it had more to do with paying attention as to when to plant, water, and fertilize. Choosing the ground for planting had involved sun and the chemical composition of the soil and she'd let instinct guide her.

"I don't know enough," she said in frustration, swinging her stick over the area that had drawn her.

"There's underground water around here somewhere," Harvey reminded her. "That's the reason for the well." He dug his stick into the ground as if hoping it would create a magical fountain.

"Water, oil, evil, who knows what we're sensing? I had no classes in earth vibrations and what they mean." But the urge to slam her stick into the ground next to Harvey's was strong.

Their sticks vibrated hard enough to disturb the ground. To her shock, a few drops of water trickled out, leaving a shiny streak over the rock beneath their joined sticks.

"Does that mean you're leaving Hillvale?" Harvey asked, twisting harder, as if he wished to flood the valley.

"I'm not certain I ever knew who I was or where I belong." There was part of her dilemma. Was she the Samantha who wanted to escape her stultifying environment? Or the Sam who wanted a family? Or some weird Sam she didn't know but who liked walking sticks and found *water*?

Instead of fleeing for safety, she excitedly twirled her staff deeper. Jade had taught her feng shui. If one could feel *chi*, it might feel like this. "This is more than water."

"It's flowing from the direction of the Menendez land." Harvey gazed eagerly toward the heavy smoke above.

From his expression, she judged he was more interested in water than *chi*. Everyone here had a damned agenda.

Threads of fire caught on dead pine debris on the hill above them. Tiny lava flows of sparks aimed straight for the lodge.

"We should have brought shovels, not sticks." Ripping her staff from the ground, Sam ran for the parking lot, in a path parallel to the fire line. She knew the wind could change and spread it in any direction. What was she doing here anyway? Had Cass made her stupid?

A snake slithered across a rock ahead, and she froze, trying not to scream. Animals ran from fire. They had more sense than she did.

"Samantha!" The warning came from a distance. Had they walked that far?

A flaming pine crashed on the ridge just above them.

CHAPTER 17

Noon, June 20

Smoke and ash polluted visibility worse than morning fog. In the distance, the fire crackled, shooting red-hot flares through the black cloud engulfing the ridge.

Coughing and hacking, Walker controlled his gut fear by rigidly following emergency procedures and hurrying terrified families into cars—until one of the Lucys shouted for Sam and the flaming pine crashed on a pathway near the lodge.

Sam!

Debating protocol, he froze to assess the situation the same way he had when Tess had pulled out a gun.

To hell with protocol. Instinct won—he couldn't let another crazy self-destruct.

Covering his nose with a mask the lodge staff was handing out, Walker crashed into the underbrush. Rivulets of fire crept down the mountain. Hot ash coated the dusty path and his eyes watered from the thick smoke. Tearing pain in his thigh muscle reminded him of his past mistakes. The fire crept closer, beneath the underbrush, through the bed of pine debris. Even the mulch smoldered. Damn, but the whole place could go up like a torch.

Where was Sam?

There was a whole damned hotel full of people he needed to help. . . Why was he chasing the one crazy?

He almost forced himself to turn around—when through the smoke, he saw a slender figure racing toward him. Heart pounding, he increased his pace through the heavy smoke. Without apology, he seized Sam by the waist and flung her over his shoulder.

She beat his legs with her crazy stick, but he refused to drop her.

"I'm fine! Put me down. You left Harvey back there, you know! He thinks he's found water." She wiggled enough that when they reached the parking lot, he had to set her down. She put her hands on her hips and glared at him.

He'd never seen anyone more beautiful and alive.

Walker wanted to strangle her for risking that life for *nothing*. Her face was coated in sweat and soot, looking the way his felt. He resisted the urge to shove loose strands of hair off her moist cheeks. "You followed an idiot into a burning forest to find water? What the hell do you think they're carrying in those trucks?" He jabbed his finger toward the tankers on the dirt path to Menendez land.

"If they could pump water from the ground, they wouldn't have to keep going back for refills! Talk to Harvey." She swung around to indicate the man sauntering from the woods, eyeing them askance. "Tell Walker there's water up there and how to find it."

Harvey shrugged his broad shoulders. "I needed Sam to find it. As I've said before, I'm just a facilitator. You want the aquifer, we climb the mountain."

"You're crazy if you think either of you is climbing that mountain now," Walker shouted his frustration.

"But if they had digging equipment, they could probably reach the aquifer," Sam argued. "The snow cover is still heavy higher up. The aquifer will be full."

"Use your damned brain, Sam! Basic fire equipment works if we don't have to waste time saving people who have no business up here." Walker jabbed his finger at the nearly empty parking lot. "Get a ride out of here, now, or I swear, Sam, I'll lock you up. Only trained professionals belong here."

Before Walker could turn on him, Harvey loped off, shouting "Hoses! This way!" at the staff unreeling the lodge's equipment. He was pointing at the trickle of fire that had followed them out. At least that task was in hand. Now all he had to do was remove this newly irrational woman.

"Harvey and the staff aren't professionals," she argued.

"They're trained volunteers. They know to stay the hell out of the way." He glanced over her shoulder and shouted at the woman preparing to leave, "Mrs. Kennedy, take Sam down with you, will you?"

EVEN KNOWING WALKER WAS RIGHT, SAM FOUGHT IRRATIONAL FURY AS she swung around to see Carmel climbing into the backseat of her Escalade. A ride with Mrs. Arrogant ought to be a real barrel of laughs. She debated swatting Walker with her stick just because, but he was already striding off, duty done. Wretched, miserable. . .

But with Carmen in her gun sight, Sam strode across the lot and opened the door behind the driver. "Official orders," she declared, sliding in, appalled by her own abrasiveness.

Dainty, diminutive *Jade* had taught her to stand up for herself. "Behave as you mean to go on," she'd said, shoving a young Sam onto the stage to explain her science experiment. Her mother had shown her how to face up to school bullies, and later, how to deal with driving instructors who wanted more than her money. In their rural community, with hostility toward her *different* parents rampant, it had been necessary to stand up to the bullies and name callers just to survive.

It had been Wolf who had caught her before she could take a swing at a shrew who'd called him a name. Wolf had taught Sam that some fights weren't worth picking.

So she was both her parents' daughter now—the fighter her mother wanted her to be, and the patient scientist her father had encouraged.

She missed them desperately, but she was a whole woman today because of them. In Wolf's memory, she waited politely for Carmen to fire the next round.

"You called me *step-grandmother*," the lady said under her breath, apparently not wanting the driver to hear. "What do you mean by that?"

"You're the one who has lived here for. . . how long? Thirty years? Have you never talked to Cass?" Sam realized she'd left her purse and backpack in Walker's car. *Damn.*

"Cass and I do not see eye-to-eye," the older woman said stiffly, staring straight ahead. "And I do not exactly live here. My home is in the city."

"And the townspeople are beneath your notice? Not smart, if so. Then we probably have nothing else to say to each other. You may continue living in ignorance. I don't mean to disturb your narrow world." Well, she did, apparently, or she would never have said anything. Unreasonably, it rankled that the Kennedys had never acknowledged Cass and her birth father, even if she'd just learned about it.

Carmen shot her a glare that should have killed. "You're a stranger who knows nothing about us. You cannot come in here and pretend to be family. I will not give up what I've fought so hard to keep."

"Isn't it just a little dangerous not to tell your sons they have relations they don't know about?" Sam said, with only the slightest malice.

Malice! She might occasionally be defiant but she'd never been mean. But even knowing she was behaving abnormally, she couldn't stop. "Someday they might need an organ match or know about an inherited disease or that they're dating *nieces*. That's all I'm saying."

Carmen looked as if she'd swallowed a mouse, but she gathered her considerable resources to produce a withering tone. "They know Cass is a distant relation," she replied as if it hurt to say the words. "Their father's family was small, and the rest have passed on. My sons have better taste than to date women not of their social circle. Are we letting you out here?" she asked with false politeness as the car slowed down in town.

Sam offered a tight smile. "Yes, please, it's been lovely talking with you. And rest assured, I want no part of what is yours. Apparently your husband left my father well off, and the executors have taken better care of the money than anyone did his family."

She got out in the parking lot without watching for Carmel's reaction. She felt oddly drained and wondered what she had thought she was accomplishing. Carmen had been here eighteen years ago when Walker's father had died. She had just told a potential murderer that she was a danger to her precious family. What on earth had possessed her?

Possessed—an ugly word with more than one meaning. Remembering the evil the Lucys kept preaching about, Sam went around back to Dinah's shed where she'd stored the few garden tools she'd gathered. Walker had made it clear that she knew nothing about fire-fighting, so she'd stay out of the way. In the meantime, she needed grounding.

While men bulldozed a dirt boundary around town, she filled her meager watering can. A breeze off the ocean pushed the oily smoke east, back toward the ridge where the fire had started. The flames were no longer visible, so the worst was under control. She could do nothing but watch helplessly, so she returned to the new flowers flourishing in Dinah's planter. She supposed she could prepare sandwiches and drinks for the firefighters, but right now, she needed her fingers in earth, or she might ignite new fires.

She looked up a little later when Xavier's shadow fell over her as she dug in leaf compost. The rental agent and his green blazer looked even grayer than usual.

"Mr. Gump said you'd leave. Why are you still here?" he asked with what sounded like curiosity.

Sam sat back on her heels and studied the man. Really, with his balding head and sagging jaws, he almost looked like a basset hound. She was still keyed up and not feeling cooperative. What the hell did Gump, the city man, have to do with anything? "Why do you ask?"

His stooped shoulders lifted in what might have been a shrug. "It's not safe here. I thought maybe you'd need a better place to stay now that Cass is back."

That was an odd way of looking at things. Originally, she'd been planning on returning to the university, where her knowledge was at least respected. But now that she knew she wasn't in danger of starving, she felt as if she had unfinished business in Hillvale. She couldn't tell if he wanted her to leave or stay.

"I'll let you know if I need a place," she said, reluctant to hurt the odd man's feelings. He seemed like a strangely inarticulate person to hang around self-confident types like Kurt Kennedy and Alan Gump.

Looking worried and confused, he nodded and ambled off across the street. The odd encounter drained some of the tension from her.

Mariah stuck her head out the café door. "If you're done communing with nature, we need more hands on deck in here."

She couldn't rely on her small trust fund to provide a living forever. Brushing off her hands, Sam saluted Mariah and carried her tools back to their storage place.

WIPED, WALKER STRODE INTO THE CAFÉ CARRYING SAM'S BACKPACK AND hoping to find a gallon of iced water to drown himself in. Half the town was there. Before he could even open his mouth, they bustled out of the kitchen with boxes of plastic-wrapped sandwiches and ice coolers he hoped were filled with drinks.

"The landline at the lodge is dead, and we couldn't phone to ask if it was safe to bring these to you," Dinah called as she sliced tomatoes and fed them out on lettuce leaves in an assembly line on the counter. "Want us to send Aaron up while you cool off a bit?"

Walker sought Sam in the crowd but didn't see her. If he were really fortunate, someone had driven her out of town. But with his luck, Carmel had probably murdered her. The backpack hung like a heavy weight off his shoulder. He needed to return it.

"Much appreciated," he said with a nod, taking a glass handed to him. "They're just looking for hot spots now. Send Aaron up. I need to report to the sheriff."

"Any word on who burned the cross?" Mariah asked from behind the counter. She was wrapping the sandwiches Dinah prepared, while the antique dealer carried the boxes out to his truck.

"They have to wait until it cools, but out there on those rocks, they won't find much. If anyone saw anything suspicious, you need to let us know." He glared meaningfully at Mariah, who'd been the last person he'd seen flinging flame around.

"Not us, I swear," Mariah said, holding out her hand palm up. "Crosses are the last thing we'd burn."

"Come sit down over here, dear," Cass called from one of the few booths. "The sheriff allows time to eat."

Dinah handed him a sandwich and Tullah refilled his water glass. Figuring he'd find out more if he talked to the locals, Walker worked his way through the crowd to the back booth. Only when he got there did he see Sam.

"You've got Tullah doing your job?" he asked, then almost bit his tongue. Why the sarcasm? Especially after he'd dragged her off the mountain over his shoulder and then practically thrown her at Carmel. He'd be lucky she didn't cut him off at the groin.

She took the backpack he handed her and studied him warily. "It got you, too, didn't it?"

He stood there awkwardly, balancing his sandwich and drink, until Sam relented and scooted over to let him sit. "Got me how?"

"The evil force," Cass said with cheer. "Sam is finally convinced that evil exists."

"Negativity," Sam corrected. "Negativity is not necessarily evil. Saying spiteful things isn't *evil*."

"Will I regret sitting here?" Walker asked, nearly draining his glass before biting into his sandwich. Dinah could even make cheese and tomato taste like heaven.

"You need to stop talking like a Null if you want my aunt to tell you why your father may have been up here," Sam warned.

Since she was glaring at Cass instead of him, Walker settled down to listen. "And there's a reason she's telling me now?"

"I had no reason to know your father died here," Cass said with dignity. "You deserve to know that it's my fault."

Pow, right in the gut. Walker lost his appetite and studied the old woman. She still looked like a university professor, and she didn't show an ounce of guilt, just regret. "Okay, I'll bite. What did you do?"

"I reported massive land theft and mortgage fraud. I reported it everywhere, to the FBI, to the banks involved, to the attorney general, to the governor. Occasionally, people listen, especially when one has a little money and influence."

Walker ripped off half his sandwich with his teeth and chewed while he contemplated this declaration. He figured she'd used more than money to grease wheels. She'd had evidence. He washed the bread down with more water that had miraculously been refilled while he chewed. He glanced up to see Daisy walking around with a water pitcher. He could easily see how one could lose one's mind up here. Distraction created illusion which led to more distraction. . .

Focus, Walker. "You don't know which agency sent him?"

Land theft and mortgage fraud—that had to be the Kennedys. Cass had turned on her own family? He'd have one of his men find the files, once he knew where to look.

"No, as I said, I didn't meet your father. If he was asking questions, he was very discreet about it. All I felt was his spirit when we tried to reach Zach. I'm so very sorry we didn't try to communicate more. We weren't quite as attentive back then."

"You mean you were doing drugs and you heard voices," Walker said dryly. He knew how that worked. His late wife hadn't talked to spirits, just the characters in her head—until one of them told her to shoot herself and her family.

He had to let that pain go, keep his mind open. Accusing Cass accomplished nothing.

The old woman let his bitterness slide right off her. "Some of us did drugs, maybe, not all. I'm sorry you don't believe the spirits are real, but someone suspects we talk with them. That's why they burned a *cross*, although they misjudged the solstice in their ignorance. They were warning us."

Here was a more relevant subject. Walker eyed Sam as he took a more polite bite of his sandwich. Sometimes, it was just easier to let women talk and sift through the rubble later.

"As I understand it, the Lucys performed an exorcism for Juan to speed him from this plane to the next," Sam said carefully. "That's what appeared to be the magnesium light you saw the other day. Burning a cross has a different function, one that exorcizes *witches*."

Walker's first response was *That's crazy*, but he didn't say it aloud.

"Or they wanted you to think that was the purpose, but their real intent was to hide their crimes or burn out the town."

"Or all of the above," Sam agreed, waiting expectantly for his reaction.

As he was learning, the world was full of crazies, but sometimes, they were right. "We need a different word for crazy," he concluded. "There's crazy that believes in spirits and there's a worse kind of crazy that tries to set towns on fire."

Cass smiled approvingly. "I think you're starting to understand. We cannot call people crazy just because they think or behave or see things differently. For all I know, burning crosses drives out evil. As Sam says, experimentation is required."

"A little hard to observe and test a hypothesis of evil." Walker finished off his water. He didn't want to leave without further questioning, but it was late, and he needed to get back. "You might have to burn a saint to see if you get a different result."

Sam laughed. "Well, yes, killing someone is probably the dividing line between crazy and lucid."

"Whoever burned that cross could just be sending a message to Menendez, which would put the Kennedys right up there as suspects with the Lucys. So unless someone walks in here reeking of kerosene, I think we're back to scientific evidence." Just in case he could persuade rationality out of the stubborn woman, he faced down Cass. "I don't suppose you'd like to tell me about the *massive land fraud*?"

She delicately sipped her tea. "It's old history, dear, over and done. It's too late to do anything more."

Yeah, that's what he figured she'd say. He could still dig into archives. He stood up and left a stack of cash on the table, enough to cover Dinah's costs for the firemen.

"I'll tell her Carmen made a donation, shall I?" Sam asked mischievously.

She knew he could afford presidential suites. The rest of the town didn't need to. "That could go a long way toward mending the rift," he acknowledged. "Thanks."

He knew no one would believe her lie, but he liked that she'd muddied the waters.

He needed to get back to cell phone reception so he could call his office. He had experts qualified in hunting down nearly twenty-year-old mortgage fraud cases.

The question remained, what did any of this have to do with Juan's death and burning crosses?

CHAPTER 18

EARLY MORNING, JUNE 21

BY MIDNIGHT, ONLY A SMALL CREW OF FIREFIGHTERS KEPT AN EYE OUT FOR hotspots on the mountain. Sam's head ached from the smoke. Her feet ached from standing for hours, feeding those who came through and cleaning up after the café closed. She was too weary to miss Walker's company. She walked up the hill to the studio, showered, and simply fell into bed.

Only to wake at dawn from a nightmare of dragons and soul-sucking demons and snakes that spoke with forked tongues. *Forked tongues*, right. Sam wearily wiped her eyes and glared at the clock. The Mexican blanket blocked most of the sun from her bed, but the main room was bright already. No fog today. She would never go back to sleep now.

Deciding to dig up some of the plants she'd located these last days, she got dressed and gulped cereal. She debated whether to take Harvey's walking stick with her. It was a thing of beauty, but she didn't see the necessity. Leaving it behind, she headed over to Cass's gardening shed. Cass had said to use whatever she needed. Sam prayed it wasn't all covered in rust and spider webs.

The wooden shed doors sagged open as if in welcome when she approached. Sam regarded them warily but decided the doors had probably just blown loose. The wind was strong off the ocean this morning, carrying the stench of wet ash and smoke away from town.

She looked for a latch to see if she would be able to close the shed properly, but there was none. Cass apparently didn't mind sharing her tools with anyone who passed by.

She'd brought a flashlight to search the interior. The space was larger than she'd realized. Spotting a light shaped like a lantern overhead, she looked around for a switch. As in the house, the light came on when she stepped inside. Motion sensors in a shed actually made sense and were more modern than she'd expected, considering the ancient sagging exterior.

The tools all looked brand new. No self-respecting gardener had shiny tools without a single dent or worn place in the handle. But Cass had known she was coming. . . .

Preferring not to think about how her great-aunt had all but kidnapped her to bring her up here, Sam found a sturdy, long-handled digger, some like-new gloves, and a bucket for water. She didn't mean to go far. She needed to be at Dinah's in a few hours.

She liked this side of the valley much better than the resort side. Here, birds sang, and the earth simply felt *happy* beneath her feet. The breeze was chilly but fresh, unlike the stench of hell around the lodge. Carrying her tools through the cemetery portal, she explored the overgrown weeds around the gravestones before making any choices.

She didn't think it was sacrilege to take cuttings or divide perennials that would otherwise smother in their own roots. She would leave the graves tended, and the plants would grow better next year.

Wolf had told her the stories of Mother Earth, and she respected the land as his ancestors had. She wasn't so certain her college-educated father had actually accepted the stories, but to her, the earth had always been a living presence requiring respect.

She was pulling weeds and clearing the ground around lily leaves when she realized she wasn't alone. She reached for her shovel and glanced over her shoulder.

Xavier, in his faded green jacket, hovered uncertainly near the

Kennedy vault. He was watching her, but he looked so nervous, she couldn't feel afraid, just puzzled at these odd encounters.

"Good morning, Mr. Black," she called. "Out for a stroll?"

"You shouldn't be here," he said, wringing his hands. "The fire should have driven out the ghosts, but I don't think it did."

She got up to apply her shovel to the clump of lilies, keeping an eye on him as she did so. "If there are spirits, they must be friendly. I like it here."

He seemed interested in that notion, glancing around as if hoping to see Casper the Friendly Ghost. "It's an unhappy place," he finally decided. "Terrible things happen here. The ghosts are angry."

"Perhaps you're a sensitive. I've heard that people feel the sorrow and pain of soldiers who died when they stand on a battlefield like Gettysburg. Have you ever been there?"

"Wouldn't like it," he said.

Remembering she was supposed to be helping Walker, since he'd helped her, she asked, "How long have you lived here?"

He frowned and shifted from foot to foot. "Don't know. Long time. Why?"

"My parents used to live here. I was wondering if you knew them. That would have been almost twenty-five years ago."

He appeared a little curious and his brow wrinkled in thought. "No, don't think so. Geoff died a few months after I moved here. Does that help?"

He'd known the town when Walker's father died! But getting anything out of him wouldn't be easy. Before she could prepare another careful question, he ambled away without a farewell.

Possibly Asperger's? Being a salesman would be tough, if so.

Happy that she'd added one more piece to her store of knowledge, Sam dug in the dirt and decided on her priorities. She needed to talk to Cass more about her parents. What had driven her mother to give her up and send her far away? Her father hadn't overdosed until after she was born, according to the genealogy. Her adoption date was immediately after that. It may have been a grieving widow's decision.

And they still needed a better list of who had been here when Walker's father died—witnesses, potential killers, anything would help. Cass would know more, as would Carmel, she supposed, but neither woman was inclined to talk. Neither was Xavier Black. Would even the lodge staff be reluctant to recall the past?

She cleared the plot she worked on, then carried the starving lilies back to the house. She'd need some good compost to plant them in.

She cleaned off Cass's tools and returned them to the shed—again, the doors opened before she could reach for them. Had someone wired *doors* with a motion detector? Needing to get to Dinah's, she didn't have time to inspect them. She rushed back to the studio to shower and dress.

Reluctant to enter the oppressive pall of wet ash in town, Sam decided to explore the lane of cottages where Mariah lived. Half-way down, at a cottage nearly concealed by rambling roses, an older woman with a thick straight salt-and-pepper mane caught in a black ribbon looked up from her overgrown cottage garden. "I see you found the lilies. I used to tend them, but I can't get up there much these days."

Knowing she would be late, Sam stopped anyway. "I hope you don't mind that I divided them. I want to find some manure or compost to feed them. I don't suppose you know anyone with a stable?"

"I know someone with a compost bin. I'll have him leave a load next time he's by. I'm Gladys. You must be Zach and Susanna's daughter. You look like both your parents."

Someone besides Cass knew her parents! Here was another name for Walker's list, and she seemed more talkative than the others. Sam was dying to ask about her parents, but now probably wasn't the best time.

"I'm Samantha. I can haul the compost if you tell me where to find it. I have to go to work now or Dinah will be swamped. May I bring you up a piece of pie later and we can talk? I'm not familiar with the soil here, but you seem to have a knack." She gestured at the lush garden growing despite the shade.

"That would be delightful but not necessary, luv. Tell Dinah her mother has passed and is sorry for not understanding." Gladys picked up her basket and vanished beneath a rose-covered arch at the rear of the yard.

"Way too much weird for one day," Sam muttered. Almost afraid to pass on the message, she found a shady place in town to store the lilies before entering the busy diner. The rich aroma of coffee replaced the nasty stench lingering outside.

Mariah shoved the carafe at her and indicated the tables by the window. Sam now knew that she had waited tables in high school. Apparently her subconscious had known she could handle the job, even when she couldn't remember it. She washed and began pouring coffee.

Most of the customers today were locals. The tourists who often stopped in after their weekend visit had already left the mountain, which still smoldered in the distance.

Once breakfast was served, they stopped for a break. Dinah cut cinnamon rolls for tasting. Sam sipped her tea and offered the odd information she'd received. "I had a strange encounter with Gladys this morning. She told me to tell you that your mother has passed and regrets not understanding. Is Gladys a friend of yours?"

Dinah's eyes got wide, and she sat abruptly on a stool she kept behind the counter. "I better call my brother," she muttered, looking teary-eyed.

Mariah put down the coffee carafe and joined them. "You have a brother? Is he ill?"

"*Gladys* spoke to Sam. What time is it back there? Noon? I'd better try to catch him when he's at lunch." Dinah got up and hurried to her office, where she kept a landline.

"Gladys spoke?" Maria poured herself a cup of coffee and regarded Sam with interest. "Do tell."

"She had bad news about Dinah's mother, apparently. I don't know why she didn't tell Dinah herself." Feeling uneasy under Mariah's stare, Sam nibbled the mouth-watering cinnamon bun.

"Because Dinah isn't a sensitive," Mariah explained, gesturing with her cup. "She talks about auras and maybe she even sees them, but she's been faking for so long, even she doesn't know what's real."

Sam wrinkled her nose at this non-explanation. "What does being sensitive have to do with Gladys? She seemed quite sensible to me."

"Gladys died of breast cancer last year," Mariah said, watching Sam. "They buried her casket beside her husband in the cemetery, but I have a feeling they buried part of her in her garden."

"What part, her heart?" Sam said with mockery. "And that allows her to keep living?"

"Don't be such a Null," Mariah retorted. "Gladys is dead. But her garden lives. Until now, I'm the only one who has seen her. I suppose the solstice could make the veil thinner, as it does at Halloween, so even a near-Null could see her."

"That's absurd," Sam protested, like a Null.

"Sturdy lady, gorgeous long graying dark hair?" Mariah asked.

"Yes. Maybe it's her daughter?"

Mariah shook her head. "That's Gladys. She had no kids. We're waiting for the Kennedys to realize the lot is being held by the state and to snatch it up for their inventory. But right now, no one lives there."

"Someone does. The garden is gorgeous," Sam argued, not mentioning the compost conversation. She'd thought she'd finally found a source, and it would be too disappointing—and frightening— if she'd imagined a conversation with a *ghost*.

"Some of us try to keep it up to hide the fact that the house is empty, but mostly, the garden tends itself—as if a ghost gardener maintains it." Mariah finished eating her bun without concern.

"Then you'd better hope your ghostcatchers don't catch her," Sam said in disgust, before turning to take orders from a new customer.

But when she walked back up to her apartment after the lunch rush, a dump load of beautifully composted dirt awaited her outside Gladys's cottage.

CHAPTER 19

"The attorney general's office has a closed file on the mortgage fraud dating back over twenty years," Walker's operative reported.

Walker switched the phone to his other ear and started making notes. "When did they close the file?"

"Not long after your father's death. Their main suspect was Geoffrey Kennedy, and he died. His mortgage company was sold and the loans scattered. They were following leads on the Menendez family, and the developer who snatched up the land under a hippy commune, but Kennedy was the money man. How deep do you want me to dig?"

"Give me names, their relationship to the case, and let's see if we can establish a map of land ownership. I'm not entirely certain the fraud has ended." Walker didn't know why he said that. No one had indicated any problems related to mortgages and foreclosures. The laws had changed since Kennedy had gone on his land grab. He just knew the Kennedys and Menendez were still sparring over casinos and condos and the townspeople were worried.

Anywhere else, the town inhabitants would be helpless, caught between two huge landowners. Walker had a gut feeling that the people of Hillvale were a different breed. He hadn't liked taciturn Juan all that much, but he didn't want the security manager to be the first fatality in a new battle.

Since he'd worked overtime during the fire, he had drawn the second shift today. He'd spent the day on his own investigation, but it was time to holster up. He buckled on his gun, picked up his cell and tablet, and was headed for the door when the cell ring indicated his research assistant calling.

Trying to run a business while working a demanding job meant he wasn't doing either task well. "Yeah?" he said into his Bluetooth as he headed for his official vehicle.

"I've been looking into your Ingerssons," Sofia said proudly.

According to the senior management who had taken over the firm after his father, she'd been trying to become a detective since his father had first hired her. She was actually pretty good at the research end. "And why are you doing that?" Although Walker had been equally curious. He simply didn't have the time to look into Sam's maternal family. He no longer had any official reason to become involved in her personal problems.

"I'm not charging anyone for it," Sofia said in indignation. "That poor girl deserves to know what she's getting into. The Ingerssons used to own the land bordering the Kennedy resort and the Menendez property above it. That's where the hippy commune was established. Is there still a farmhouse there? I've always wondered what it was like to live off the land."

Walker tried to picture the area in his head as he started the car and headed out. "May have been once, but there's no house. The fire took out part of that side of the mountain yesterday, so any other evidence of a farm is probably gone. The commune was half a century ago. What does it have to do with Sam?"

He knew Sam's mother was an Ingersson. *Valdis* was Sam's aunt, her mother's sister. Walker's interest was captured despite his disparagement of Sofia's research. Valdis had climbed those hills without fear because they were her home.

"The Ingerssons lost the land to a bank, one in which Geoffrey Kennedy owned a substantial share. There were suits and countersuits, up until your Samantha's maternal grandparents, the Ingerssons, died.

You might add their deaths to your to-do list. They were only in their forties or fifties, I have their ages here somewhere. . ."

"Don't worry, I can figure it out later. How did they die?" Walker demanded. His gut was getting a real workout this morning.

"Apparent heart attack for her grandfather. Overdose for her grandmother. They were part of the original commune, of course, so drugs were common."

"And how long ago was this?" Although Walker thought he already knew.

"About twenty-five years ago," Sofia said. "That's why I thought it might be important."

Shit in a bottle. . . "Just before Sam's mother gave away her baby and fled," he said with finality.

"Exactly—around the time that Samantha's father also died of an overdose."

Had the land fraud his father was investigating begun then? How the hell would he tell Sam? "See who owns that land now," he demanded, then hit the gas pedal and aimed for Hillvale.

"Why are we having a town meeting on a hillside?" Sam asked, wrapping a blanket around her shoulders as she walked. "Couldn't we hold it at Cass's place if there's no meeting hall?" Cass had been avoiding her, which added to her irritability.

Undeterred by the chilly air, Mariah climbed the rocky path as if she were a mountain goat. "The vortex is safer and more effective, especially at the solstice. We tried meeting at Cass's once, but Cass draws spirits, and we have too many sensitives. Valdis went bananas and whatever took over Tullah went after Valdis and it got ugly. Harvey and Aaron carried them out here, and they calmed down, so that's how we've done it ever since."

Sam could actually imagine that, she realized with amazement. She feared this might be carrying an open mind a step too far. But then, she was apparently seeing ghosts, so why not?

"Where's your staff?" Mariah demanded, using hers to propel herself up the rugged path.

"I couldn't carry it and a blanket too." Accepting the staff bothered her somehow, even though she'd paid Harvey now that she had money again.

"It's a weapon. You should keep it at hand, if only to beat back bushes." She whacked at an overhanging branch to prove her point.

Sam changed the subject back to one of more interest. "And how long have these vortex meetings been going on?" Trying to piece together her own past inevitably involved Hillvale history, so she was prepared to listen.

Mariah shrugged. "Hard to say. I've only been here a few years. The older ones managed at Cass's, so maybe it's new blood that has stirred up the spirits. Valdis has only been here a few years more than me, Tullah and Dinah a little longer."

Sam wasn't ready to believe in ghosts yet. Finding water could have been an accident or Harvey playing tricks. The inexplicable compost pile had shaken her, though. She'd not told anyone about that. She'd almost have to either believe in mind reading or ghosts, and right about now, she was spooked enough to believe if they could happen anywhere, it would be in Hillvale. Could her scientific expertise belong in a community like this? She had a sudden longing for the safety of the classroom she'd been teaching in.

"Do we have an agenda for this meeting?" she asked, just to ground herself.

"That's a very Null thing to expect," Mariah said cheerfully. "Just watch and listen and you'll see. It's very free form and driven by what rocks each individual."

Being treated as an outsider was nothing new, but loneliness haunted her with Mariah's words. She was pretty certain Nulls were interlopers, and she shouldn't be here. Once more, she was the odd one out in a group she wanted to accept her.

Discouraged, Sam found a flat-topped boulder that had absorbed the sun's warmth. Now that the sun was setting, the temperatures were dropping, and she almost wished for a fire. She squashed that thought. The stench of smoke and ash still lay across the valley like a heavy pall.

Shadows drifted up the path and from down the mountain and through the trees, filling the natural amphitheater around the vortex.

She hadn't realized there were so many ways of accessing this area—or that there were so many people who believed in Mariah's insane revolution.

Mariah had apparently had an ugly confrontation with the mayor earlier in the day involving developing the burned out land with condos. Apparently the Kennedys expected the scorched landscape to adversely affect the tourist business and had moved to Plan B. Mariah and probably all the Lucys were opposed.

Sam didn't see how the vortex would resolve anything. The energy didn't feel any different from the earth energy she felt everywhere. Perhaps the negative and positive swirled a bit—she couldn't quite tell. Resentfully, she crossed her arms under the blanket and refused to indulge in unscientific theories.

Wrapped in her shedding feather coat, Daisy sat in her own world. Sam almost envied her the coat. Talking animatedly with Tullah and Amber, Dinah evidently sided with the Lucys, whether or not she was *sensitive*. Sam recognized Harvey and Aaron standing with several gray-haired men she'd seen in the diner but couldn't place otherwise. Mariah had a pretty good audience. As the time for the meeting drew closer, all the stone seats had filled and people were standing on the outside, in the woods.

Luminous globes floated from the empty center rocks, the purported vortex. The chatter died down. That was a neat Las Vegas trick, right up there with Cass's automagical lights.

Mariah took a stand on one of the flatter outcroppings and announced, "The Kennedys have chosen to proceed with the condo development and ski resort."

A groan went up from the audience. Voices of protest rose out of the darkness, but Mariah held up her hand, and they silenced. "They own the land. They have the law on their side. There will be evictions. They could raze the entire town if so inclined. But first, they have to level and terrace the hillside on the north end of the valley."

The valley around the lodge, below the Menendez land, Sam now knew, the area partially consumed by the fire. She could almost feel the despair swirling around the circle. Did that many people live up there? She hadn't thought so.

"They need Menendez to agree to access," Harvey said from outside the circle. "Do they have it?"

"They seem to think they do," Mariah said.

"Bulldozers on sacred ground," Daisy said sadly from her seat on the rocks. "The Evil One uncovered. It will seek and destroy us, as it has before, and take away the Earth Mother. We must send her away again."

"It is because she has returned that this is happening," an older woman shouted from further down the hill. "We sent her away for a reason!"

"I brought her back for a reason," Cass said, striding into the clearing. "The heart of the town is being sucked dry, and we are growing weak. If we don't turn the tide now, we may as well pack up and leave and let the Nulls win."

Sam felt an icy chill down her back. Were they talking about *her*? Amber had called her an *earth goddess*. Earth *mother* was only slightly less whacky. She would get up and leave, but she'd have to climb over rows of people to do so.

"She can't fight city hall," Harvey said in a scoffing tone. "Better to keep her safe. It's not as if any of us are making enough of a living here to make it worth a sacrificial lamb."

"You're young," one of the older men said. "You don't know what we've done to keep this place safe. We have nowhere else to go."

Voices clamored from every side. An eerie wail keened above the clearing. Shadows shifted, and the weird luminous balls multiplied, flitting back and forth overhead. Chilled, body and soul, Sam started to rise, but a hand pressed her back again.

"It's all right," Amber whispered behind her. "Theatrics is always a given in this crowd. Now that you have fire out of the way, you have the Magician and the scarecrow on your side. I'll read your cards again in the morning, if you have time to stop by."

Amber's sensible voice settled Sam's nerves. *Theatrics*, of course. Magicians had used them for ages to distract from their illusions. She settled in to enjoy the show.

Cass waved her hand in the air, and the light balls swirled around Dinah. Apparently taking that as permission, Dinah stood to speak. "I have nowhere else to go. My café is profitable here. Where else would I find better customers? But I rent from the same place everyone else does. If they don't renew my lease, I have no choice but to pack up."

One by one, the story was repeated—the Kennedy leasing company owned the land the town was built on. If they protested development —who knew what would happen?

A gray-bearded man in flannel shirt and overalls rose slowly when his turn came. "Listen to us! The vampire has sucked our souls, our ability to fight, and made us what we are today. We fought the Evil One once and won—at a cost. Where will we find the strength to do it again?"

"This sounds like something out of a fantasy novel," Sam murmured in exasperation.

One of the older women she'd met at the séance patted her knee. "Exciting, isn't it? The spirits have been demanding action for years now, and we've been too comfortable to listen. Finally, we can act."

Sam wanted to suggest that a lawyer would make more sense than theatrics, but she had no cat in this fight. She'd be gone long before they settled anything. An argument broke out that had the lights circling madly, and she got antsy again. She glanced around and thought she saw Walker in his cowboy hat coming up the path they'd taken earlier in the week, when she'd told him about her memory problem. She longed to go to him, but it would be foolish to do so.

The weirdly liquid banshee wail was coalescing into words, and Sam grimaced, recognizing Valdis. Was this really her aunt—a melo-dramatic, mentally unhinged aunt?

"The Evil must be expunged from this plane," Valdis cried in a voice that carried like an owl's hoots in the night air. Standing on a rocky ledge above the others, she waved a long black cloak like bat wings. "The Earth belongs to the Mother. She must take up the battle and lead the way."

Oh yeah, right, auntie, so not happening, Sam thought grimly.

"She's a Kennedy," someone else shouted from the woods. "She's probably spying on us right now. I say send her back where she came from. We were fine until she arrived."

Oh well, thank you so much. "I don't like this," Sam whispered. She felt as if she were back in seventh grade with the mean girls writing

Her parents are weird and she smells like goats. She couldn't punch an entire town. "I don't belong here."

Amber hugged her. "Of course you do, poppet. Cass brought you here for just this reason. He's right, the energy vampire has weakened us, but you will bring us life again, just the way you have nourished our planters."

"Because plants and people are no different?" Sam asked with an edge of sarcasm. "I should dump manure on you?" But no one responded to her nervous anger. She didn't *have* to stay.

She simply longed for the peaceful land she'd had before her parents died—one where she was normal and felt at home. . .

Heated mutters rose on the wind, disturbing the fantasy drama. The light balls flickered and started fading. Mariah and Cass shouted over the buzz of voices, but it was obvious old animosities had been stirred. Sam decided it was time to go. She stood up, and this time, Amber didn't stop her.

"Go and keep on going," a male voice shouted when she tried to find a path up the rocks. "We don't need no Nulls here," a second, female, voice cried. "She's the reason Juan died!" another cried. "The Evil One spewed the skeleton because of her!"

Rattled, defiantly refusing to cry, Sam fought her way through the bodies blocking her in. They shifted, parted, let her pass—until a large masculine frame blocked her way. She almost flung herself into Walker's arms. "Get me out of here," she whispered.

"Not like this. You have to play to the crowd." He swung her around, forcing her to face the mob. He shouted to be heard. "*Cass* is a Kennedy. Do you call *her* a Null?"

Mariah echoed his cry. "Have you taken time to see what Samantha has done with our planters in town? Those weeds she planted in the alley—have you seen how they're blooming already? And you call her a *Null*?"

Resentfully, Sam wanted to shake off the strong hands holding her pinned to the spot. But. . . People had noticed her planters? And thought them special? Why?

Below, Cass and Mariah were casting their magic again. The lights were back, and Valdis's wail had ceased. That alone was sufficient to let the hair on the back of her neck rest.

"She knows how to use a staff," Harvey called from the woods.

"I've been inside her head, dears," Cass said, drawing the remaining balls around her. "Don't be foolish. Sam is one of us."

Cass's admission that she'd been inside Sam's head silenced even Sam. She'd hated being treated like an outsider. Now she wasn't entirely certain she wanted to be an insider. One would have to be crazy to live like this.

"United we stand," Mariah called. "Are we united in fighting development?"

Walker muttered an expletive as a shout rang around the clearing. "I think we're done here. Coming with me?"

Wordlessly, Sam followed him out of the shouting crowd. She heard warm murmurs of farewell from the women surrounding her, but she still felt the hostility of strangers packing the arena. She'd thought she'd found a place of welcome. Maybe no such place existed.

"You knew they were talking about me?" she asked as the silence between them became unbearable. "You knew they were blaming *me* for Juan's death?"

"Small minds in narrow worlds look for simple cause and effect. They don't have the experience or education to envision broader possibilities or even shades of gray. The Lucys are about as small a world as you can get, and they're superstitious as they come. I've been talking to the old-timers, sounding them out about my dad, and I've heard the rumors about you. They know your history. The older ones know your families. But the past frightens them, and they're just not talking about it. Cass and Mariah will give them another sacrificial goat before the night is over."

He limped a bit, as he did when he was tired. But as they found their way in the dark down the crumbling pathway, he placed a steadying hand on the small of her back, and she enjoyed the gesture. She liked a whole lot about this sensible, self-assured man—except for his protective need to control. She knew getting in deeper with a Null who sought security was a straight road to heartbreak if she continued pursuing her weird Lucy leanings. But the stiff deputy had *stood up* for her place as a Lucy.

"Are you on duty?" she asked, grimacing as his uniform became more visible once they reached the paved highway.

"Until midnight," he said in regret. "Want a ride back to your place? I can take a look around, make certain no one is lingering in the bushes, pretend I'm working."

She entertained that idea for all of a minute before deciding she was too wound up to go to bed, alone.

"Is there anyone at the lodge? Do you think the utilities are operating again? Cass has no internet service, and I'd like to use the computer." And she didn't want to be alone when the meeting broke up or be around if Mariah or Cass came by. She needed *normal*.

"The lodge is open for business," he said. "Although there aren't many guests. Would you like to hang around until midnight?"

She heard the suggestion in his voice. It matched her need. "I can do that," she said with what she hoped sounded like adult decision and not a teenager's hormonal heart-pounding.

Walker circled her waist and squeezed her close before he helped her into his cruiser. She almost leaned her head against his shoulder, but that would have been needy.

"Kurt will want to know about the meeting," Walker warned as he climbed in, smelling of warm man and musky aftershave. "If you tell him, you will be colluding with the Nulls just as they said."

"I am not going to be drawn into this," she said fiercely. "It is not my fight."

He started the car and drove silently for a minute before replying, "The Lucys may be right. You might very well be the reason for the fire. My secretary called a little while ago."

Sam hugged her elbows and waited, not liking the tone of his voice.

"A lawsuit against the Kennedys' mortgage company and the bank resulted in the Ingersson farm being returned from default and put in a trust with the proceeds from the suit when you were an infant. Since your grandparents were both dead by then, an executor was named. Once you reached twenty-one, you and Valdis became jointly responsible for any sale of the land."

"And the Ingersson farm is what?" Sam asked, almost angrily. *Valdis*? She was essentially responsible for her insane aunt's land?

"The farm is the linchpin allowing access from the town to both the Kennedy and the Menendez properties on the mountain. The Nulls and Lucys are essentially fighting over your land."

"Cass," Sam hissed. "This is why she dragged me up here. This is all Cass's doing."

CHAPTER 20

Late evening, June 21

SAM MARCHED DEFIANTLY INTO THE LODGE LOBBY TO INQUIRE ABOUT THE computers. Walker followed her, like any good escort. Apparently, the desk clerk had no orders to keep her out, so she pressed a kiss to Walker's stubbly cheek, inhaled his confidence, and headed for the guest business office off the main lobby as if she'd spent her life using hotel computers.

She now knew she'd been in hotels a few times, traveling with her parents to San Francisco, but Wolf and Jade hadn't taken vacations the way other families did. Wolf had been a pilot, and he'd flown them back to visit with his family in Arizona, where they'd stayed on the reservation. Jade had a small family in the San Francisco area. They'd stayed in their homes occasionally. Or they'd gone camping. Business hotels weren't part of the experience.

She was aware now that she had adopted family, cousins and aunts who could take her in, if she needed familiar faces and *normal*. She didn't have to stay in Hillvale. Until tonight though, she'd felt more at home in Hillvale than she had with her adopted relations. The realization unnerved her.

Biting her lip in frustration, she opened a computer and checked her email box to prove she was still who she used to be. She responded to friends who were too busy with their own lives to worry about her. She had a message from one of her professors about a job he thought she might be interested in—in Alaska. Academia was boring but safe. She'd assumed that would be her career path, maybe in a more multi-cultural area.

And now. . . ? She was jumpy and on edge, but her parents' admonitions of *don't back down* and *persevere* forced her to clench her jaw, straighten her spine, and keep digging into who she really was—which wasn't necessarily who she thought she was before she came here.

She'd given Walker her email address earlier. As promised, he'd sent her links to all the files he possessed on her birth family, including the genealogy chart. She studied the visual, trying to assimilate all the information he'd collected. How had the Ingersson farm ended up in a trust? Shouldn't it have gone to her mother instead of to an infant and a woman deteriorating into madness? Although Val had been young and presumably sane back then. The legal document didn't reveal the court's thoughts.

As Walker had predicted, Kurt Kennedy knocked on the door before she'd dug too far into the files. Sam closed the browser and cleared history as Kurt entered.

"Hope I'm not disturbing important research," the lodge manager said. Despite his bespoke suit and expensive haircut, he looked older than the early thirties she knew him to be. He was a well-built, striking man, but he possessed the charisma of a dried oak leaf—as if the life had been sucked out of him.

Now she sounded like one of the Lucys!

"Just checking email. I have an offer of a possible position as a federal environmental program manager in Anchorage," she said brightly, just to prove she had a life outside of waitressing in a small-town café.

"And I don't suppose you're going to take it?" He sat on one corner of the printer desk and played with a rubber stress ball someone had left there.

"I might send a resume, but no, I don't imagine I'll pursue it." She didn't give him more than that but let him take the lead.

"You were at the town meeting tonight?" he asked. "Has Cass talked them into burning us at the stake?"

Sam leaned back in her chair and tried to work out what was expected of her, but she couldn't. Honesty and openness were all she'd been taught. "I'm wondering if my mother gave me to my adopted parents because they were the most down-to-earth, honest, upright people she knew," she said, not giving him an answer yet.

"And your adopted parents lived someplace so barren of magic and imagination that she thought you'd be safe from this town's craziness?" he asked with both amusement and sympathy.

She almost liked her uncle at that point.

And then he had to add, "Cass hates us. She won't be happy until she brings us down. It really isn't about smoke and magic, just plain old family feuds."

Sam shook her head and said gently, "I don't think so. I know I haven't been here long, and I'm far from understanding all the nuances, but Cass isn't a woman who hates. She's afraid, maybe, and possibly bitter, but hate. . . ? No, that's much too strong. She and Mariah and the other Lucys oppose what you want, maybe even what you stand for, but that's not the same as hate. Yet. There is still a chance of reconciliation."

He grimaced as if in thought, then rejected the notion. "No, I don't think so. They live in a utopian world that doesn't exist. We live in a world that requires we pay the mortgage and payroll. I hope you don't fall for their idealistic bullshit."

Sam was debating how much she ought to tell him, when a large shadow passed the plate glass window and shoved open the door. *Walker.*

"It's midnight; the witch's spell has broken," Walker said in a cool tone that covered many layers of meaning.

Sam warmed at the look he gave her, but the way he took a confrontational stance in front of Kurt gave her cold chills. Walker had a defensive streak a mile wide. She needed to establish boundaries.

Kurt returned to his feet, one bull facing another.

"You'd do better to talk to Cass or your mother than to Sam," Walker said in a deliberately casual tone. "You're placing her in a tough position by putting her in the middle."

"I don't know what the hell you're talking about, Walker," Kurt said. "We were just discussing generalities. It's been a long day, and I thought talking to someone who wasn't from Hillvale might wind me down."

"A pretty someone," Walker supplied for him. "Sam, you really need to explain who you are so Kurt here doesn't get any odd ideas."

Sam didn't know whether to laugh or roll her eyes. "Don't go all macho on me, Walker. I'm trying to be polite by telling Mr. Kennedy he needs to talk with Cass. If Carmel hasn't said anything by now, I don't think she intends to open communication. The Nulls and Lucys need to find channels for talking besides me."

Kennedy made a face. "Don't make me feel older than I already do. Call me Kurt, please. And I may be busy, but I'm not ignorant. I know Cass was my grandfather's daughter by his first wife, that she inherited a large portion of his assets and has blocked any expansion in the direction of her property. My mother despises her and anyone who has anything to do with her, which means Sam. Sam, you tell me Cass doesn't hate, but my mother does, so don't be too certain about Cass. What two old women do means nothing to me. I make my own decisions. And I have no reason to talk to the Lucys."

"You should," Sam said, standing. "Because apparently I'm one of them, *Uncle* Kurt. Talk to your mother. Talk to Cass. I won't be here long enough to resolve the problems you're not seeing."

She walked past both men and into the dim corridor, in an emotional turmoil she had no experience in handling.

"*Uncle* Kurt?" Kennedy asked Walker in shock, watching Sam walk away.

Walker shrugged. "I was raised to respect my elders. You probably ought to learn to talk to yours, as Sam said. She apparently thinks it isn't her place to explain what the whole damned town keeps hidden, but she's leaving you holes wide enough to drive a Cadillac through. And chances are very good, when you start digging deep enough, we'll get closer to what happened to Juan." Walker opened the door but gave Kurt a moment to gather his thoughts and follow up that statement.

"What happened to Juan? It wasn't cougars?" Kurt shoved the door closed again.

"He was shot in the back at close range and dragged up the hill for the cougar to maul," Walker told him. "The fire conveniently wiped out any evidence we didn't collect earlier."

"As well as the cats," Kurt said, running his hand through his hair. "They'll be on the other side of the mountain by now. Damn, Juan's death was a tragedy, but this. . ." He shook his head as all the implications arose. "You'll have this place covered in cops again. My mother just left for Hawaii."

"Expect the sheriff's team in the morning. They were waiting for the autopsy before coming out with a warrant, not that there's much left to search now, unless he was shot inside. Maybe it's a good thing your guests bailed." Walker hauled the door open again and this time, he limped out after Sam.

He shouldn't feel sympathy for the poor rich guy, but Kurt had lived too long in his protected bubble. Hillvale was about to rip it wide open. He didn't want Sam caught up in the fight any more than she did.

She was waiting for him on the lodge porch, hugging herself as he'd seen her do earlier this evening. Walker wrapped his arm around her waist and led her toward his car. "Your place or mine?"

She threw him a haunted look. "If your place is a thousand miles from here, let's go. Otherwise, mine will have to do."

"Other than a room at the lodge and the apartment in Baskerville, I have a place in LA, but it will be tough to make it back to work tomorrow." He helped her into his official vehicle and started the engine.

She snorted in what he hoped was humor. "There is that. So, do I stay here or move on?"

"Why don't you hit me with that in the morning? Right now, I have better things on my mind." Like the smoking hot woman he should be keeping his hands off of until she knew where she was going and how. He refused to believe Sam was as unbalanced as his late wife had been.

"On your *mind*, or elsewhere?" she asked with a laugh. "I'm all for mindless right now. Any more Hillvale and I'd have to pack the car and drive far, far away."

"It's intense at the moment, but the town is usually pretty laidback and friendly. There's something to be said about you stirring the hornets, but it's in the hornets' nature to be stirred. You either let the bugs drive you out or you find cold water and douse them." He steered through the quiet town, keeping his eyes open.

"Water," she murmured, not offering an explanation. "There could be something in that."

"Water rights are complex out here," he warned. "Whatever you're thinking, don't count on it."

As they drove up Cemetery Road, Walker could see all the lights on in Cass's place. Beside him, Sam tensed. "You need to see what's happening?" he asked.

"I do—and I don't." She crossed her arms and rubbed her elbows. "How comfortable are you with one of them heading over as soon as we pull into the drive and go upstairs?"

"If you're asking if I want to keep our sleeping together on the down low, it doesn't matter to me. You're not my case anymore, and Cass isn't stupid. This comes down to how much you want the town to know about you."

She slanted him a look that probably would have curled his toes if he wasn't concentrating on the road.

"Let's go to my place and see if the Lucys are crazy enough to disturb us." She unbuckled the instant he pulled up her drive.

She was as eager as he. Walker laughed softly. "We could hang a tie on the door."

"Did that ever work for you?" She opened the door and climbed out before he could come around and get her. Her urgency excited his.

"The tie worked for me, when I bothered to use it." He loped after her, ready to carry her up the stairs if that got them to bed any faster. "Mostly, I stuck a chair under the knob because the chicks got off on manly-man crap."

"I have a feeling neither chair nor tie will work with Lucys." She laughed in a low throaty voice that raised his pulse a few more notches.

The marmalade cat strolled out of the bushes to check them out.

"Even Emma doesn't want to be near Cass tonight. Smart cat." Walker enjoyed the sway of Sam's hips under his hand as they followed the cat toward the stairs. It meowed and waited for them.

Sam's haste abruptly halted at the foot of the stairs. "What's this?" Giving evidence of the wariness she'd learned these last few days, she didn't touch the object that had raised her curiosity.

Walker leaned around her, removed his flashlight, and turned on the beam. He relaxed and chuckled. "That's one of Daisy's sculptures. She calls them *lamassu* and I think they're supposed to be protective spirits."

He picked up the palm-sized collection of wired rocks and crystals to show her. "Yours almost looks like a butterfly."

She smiled in delight and took it from him. "How does she do this? I'd never be able to get all those stones to hang together long enough to wrap them with the wire. Look, it even has some tiny blue stones glued to the head. For eyes?"

"*Sapphire* for your eyes," he suggested.

"That's sweet that you noticed my eyes. I can't imagine Daisy has." She kissed his cheek, and then they hurried up the stairs to the apartment. Sam handed him the statuette so she could dig her keys from her purse. Stopping at the top of the stairs to scratch Emma's head, she jerked back, as if startled. "Mr. Black? What are you doing here?"

"Xavier?" Walker pushed past to see the rental agent slumped in the wicker porch chair, unresponsive. He flashed his light at the visitor and his gut froze. "Go get Cass," he ordered curtly. "I'll call for an ambulance."

Although Xavier Black looked past the need for a hospital.

CHAPTER 21

"I know CPR." Sam tried to push past the obstacle of Walker's arm while the cat dashed back down the stairs. "We should at least check his pulse."

"It's a potential crime scene," Walker warned. "Stay there," he said curtly, pointing at the stairs. "I'll check. That's a kerosene can beside him."

Astounded, Sam stayed put. *Kerosene*? That dazed old man had burned the cross? Had he intended to burn her home?

She took Daisy's artwork from Walker and set it aside on a mosaic table. So much for protective spirits.

Or had the spirits stopped him? Maybe she was the one who needed to broaden her thinking.

Walker pulled out his radio and ordered an ambulance, then reached over to check the old man's wrist. "It's weak, but I think I feel something."

"How long will it take for an ambulance?" she asked anxiously, helping him lay Xavier flat on the balcony. His green blazer hung loose on an almost skeletal frame.

"Too long. Run over to Cass's." Walker began compressions, counting out the pace. "There's a nurse who lives up here somewhere. She'll know. It might be diabetic shock for all we know."

"Why on earth would he be on my porch with kerosene?"

"Keep him alive, and we'll ask," Walker said grimly, pumping. "After you fetch Cass, find the evidence bags in my car. We need to bag up that can."

Sam took his keys and ran down the stairs, but before she could cross the lawn, she saw Cass's irregulars on the move. She opened Walker's car and found what she hoped was an evidence bag as the women approached, then dashed back to the balcony to warn Walker. "Here comes the light brigade, right on schedule."

While she bagged the can and Walker kept up the compressions, Sam called to the approaching crowd. "We need medical help. Walker says there's a nurse nearby?"

"I'll fetch her," Mariah cried, peeling off from the pack and jogging down the path to the cottages below.

"Who is it?" Cass demanded. She carried a large flashlight and led the way for the others.

"Xavier Black. Does anyone know if he's diabetic or has a heart condition? It will be a while before the ambulance arrives." Sam eased to one side, allowing only Cass up the stairs before blocking the others. The balcony wasn't large.

Cass checked under Xavier's eyelids, then called to the women milling about below, "Who has the naloxone?"

"Crap," Walker said, sitting back on his heels and turning Black on his side. "He's an addict?"

"Painkillers mostly," Cass said crisply. "He self-medicates but usually not to this extent."

"I won't ask how you come to have the antidote," Walker said grimly.

One of the older women ran up the stairs and handed over a box that Sam passed on to Walker, who seemed to know how to handle the nasal spray. Xavier coughed briefly but didn't regain consciousness.

Walker took his pulse. "Stronger. Give it five minutes to kick in. Anyone know why he was on Sam's porch?"

"He's kind of been hanging around me a bit," Sam said, fretting at her bottom lip. "I had the feeling he wanted to say something but couldn't find the words. I really didn't sense any harm in him." Of course, he hadn't been carrying kerosene at the time.

Cass muttered an unladylike expletive and gestured at her audience. "You'd best all go home before the police arrive."

Amazingly, they did as told. Wide-eyed, Sam watched everyone depart, chattering. "Police?" she asked. "Walker is the law up here. Why would they need anyone else?"

"I'm off duty," Walker reminded Cass. "I didn't ask for back up, and no one is likely to be here until morning, when the sheriff heads for the lodge. A drug overdose won't rate suspicion, yet."

He checked his watch and Xavier's pulse again. The old man seemed to be stirring.

Ignoring them, Cass lowered herself to the top step. Emma arrived to bat her furry head against Cass's leg until she was petted. Worried, Sam glanced from Walker and the unconscious man on her doorstep, to her great-aunt, who looked worn thin.

"You know something," Sam concluded. She sat cross-legged on the only space remaining between Walker and Cass. She'd hoped to have Walker naked and in her bed about now. He sent her a glance that probably meant he was thinking the same thing. That revived her a little.

"I really haven't given any of this enough thought," Cass said. "Mariah dumped the announcement on us that the Kennedys are going through with the construction we thought we'd stopped all those years ago. I never wanted to look for the names of people who were here when your father died. It would have stirred up all those old ghosts. Most of the people involved are gone, foreclosed on, dead, retired—there just aren't that many of us left. It didn't seem relevant."

"But Xavier Black was one of them," Sam said. "I learned that much. He said he moved here about the time Geoffrey Kennedy died, but he didn't seem particularly coherent. I thought perhaps he had some form of Asperger's and didn't know how to socialize."

"He was a friend of Geoffrey's back then," Cass said. "He socialized just fine. He had a law degree but chose to become a mortgage broker. He talked people into taking out loans for *improvements* that they couldn't afford. He sold them on easy loans that go up with the interest rates or had balloon payments."

"Free market," Walker said cynically, administering another dose of the spray. Xavier began to cough again, spitting up the meager contents of his stomach. Walker moved out of the way but kept a moaning Xavier tilted on his side so he wouldn't choke on his own vomit.

Sam sent a little prayer of thanksgiving that he wasn't a corpse.

"Yes, dear, the fine line between legal and moral. Geoff's bank *knew* those people wouldn't be able to afford higher rates, but they gave the loans anyway. That was one of my allegations when I hired lawyers to sue. That brought in the federal regulators, but much too late for most of them, the store owners in particular. Carmel always hated that I'd deprived Geoffrey of half the Kennedy fortune. She's been determined to make up for it ever since. That's how the Kennedys' leasing company came to own most of the town."

"What happened to Xavier?" Sam demanded, recognizing her aunt's procrastination.

"He spent the night in the cemetery." She sounded almost proud. "The law couldn't provide justice, so we did."

Sam exchanged a puzzled glance with Walker, who shrugged and steadied his waking patient. "You knocked him out and left him in the cemetery?" she asked when Cass didn't continue.

"Really, I shouldn't say anything with the law as a witness. It implicates others. Let us speak in theories. If one believes in ghosts and spends the night in a haunted house, what happens?"

"One imagines ghost and goblins and runs screaming from the building," Walker said dryly.

"Yes, well, if the door is locked, then there's no leaving, is there?" Cass leaned her back against the concrete stair wall. "The spirits cleansed him. Xavier was a changed man. Geoffrey fired him. We didn't have a mayor or an official town back then, but we had already signed a petition to start one. So we appointed a temporary mayor who set Xavier up in one of the empty storefronts and gave him a list of properties to rent out. He's been there ever since. Of course, since the Kennedys have bought the bulk of the rental properties, he's essentially working for them again."

Mariah arrived at the bottom of the stairs with a stranger. Cass and Sam moved out of the way.

"Brenda is a nurse practitioner," Mariah said, remaining at the bottom.

"I'm retired," Brenda protested. Small and wiry, Brenda didn't appear old enough to be retired.

Walker explained what they'd done so far, then held up his flashlight so the nurse could check under the patient's eyelids and take his pulse. She had Walker hold the light over Xavier's shaking hands and on his face again.

"I'm not sure this is Vicodin. That's his usual escape, but there's blue around his mouth. There's some alcohol on his breath, but he knows better than to have more than one drink. His temperature is elevated and so is his pulse. Bring me some cold water and towels."

Sam jumped up to unlock the door, fetch her meager stash of towels, and rummage for a bowl for the water. She could hear the others talking as she filled the bowl.

"Coke?" Walker asked. "There's a dealer up here?"

"Not anymore," Cass insisted. "We're all into yoga and health foods. We learned our lesson long ago."

"I'm no expert," Brenda said. "I'm only operating on what little I know. But drug use isn't all illegal. Hillvale has a large older population. We all have medicine cabinets full of prescriptions. It could be a prescription or a cocktail of drugs I don't know about."

Sam supplied the water and helped apply the compresses. "Can you check on the ambulance?" she asked Walker as Xavier began to shake.

Walker took his radio inside the house, out of the way. She was pretty certain she heard him mention *suspicious circumstances*. Her heart sank to her feet.

She glanced at Daisy's little statuette and her anxiety rose even more.

Crazy Daisy may have been here when Xavier arrived. What did that signify?

~

THE AMBULANCE TOOK XAVIER AWAY. BRENDA WALKED CASS BACK TO HER house. Walker stayed with Sam, hugging her close while she wept from the aftershock of the night's events.

"Given what we know about Juan's death," he told her, "the sheriff will try to expedite the blood tests on Xavier and turn this into a crime scene. Better get some sleep before they start tramping up the stairs."

Holding Daisy's artwork, she nodded against his shoulder. If this was a crime scene, it had already been seriously disturbed. Still, he'd have to tell the sheriff about the kerosene and the butterfly in the morning.

Taking Sam's nod as permission to lock the door, Walker guided her behind the colorful blanket to her bed. "Anything look out of place in here?" he asked, switching on the lights.

She jerked back, surprised. "You think someone was in here?"

"The door was locked, so no, I don't think so, but I thought it best to check before we mess up anything else." He really wanted her in that bed. He needed sex, not tears. No more tears, no more crazy, no more responsibility for anyone but himself.

Setting her stone butterfly on a wall shelf in the front room, Sam pushed back the curtain. She checked the suitcases she seemed to be living out of, went into the bathroom and looked through her personal belongings, and came out to examine the open studio. "That first time, I could tell someone had been in here. This time, nothing."

Her space was limited, neat, and easy to tell if anything was out of place. Walker nodded agreement. "Since Xavier probably has keys to every rental in town, he may have been the one who searched your place earlier. If he meant to do it again, he could have. So he must have come for another reason, then passed out waiting for you."

"A purpose besides burning me out? What would have happened if I'd been here?" she whispered in a mix of panic and horror.

"If you'd been here, you might have seen whoever gave him the drugs. Or you might have been accused of giving them to him. It's a damned good thing you went with me to the lodge." He shouldn't have said that.

Her eyes grew wide and looked almost purple in this light. "You think they may have been framing me?"

"You seem to hold the key to the Lucys, but let's not speculate.

Come on, let's go to bed. We can just sleep, if that's what you want. It will be a short night."

Fortunately for him, Sam wasn't ready for sleep. They worked off their adrenaline overloads together, without any need to discuss where their non-relationship was going. Walker thought he might be able to handle this friends-with-benefits business they had going, especially with an intelligent woman like Sam. Even when she was being Lucy crazy, she had her head on straight.

In the morning, they explored the tiny shower together. For the first time, Sam studied his damaged thigh, running her fingers over the puckered skin and injured muscle. Walker stood still for it. He supposed he had to explain sometime.

"I only read the small piece in the newspaper," she said hesitantly.

"My late wife heard voices." She needed to understand the true extent of his damage, that he wasn't whole on the inside or outside. "She was a writer, said medication messed with her work."

"You don't have to tell me if it still hurts," she whispered, caressing his chest.

Keeping sex upfront somehow distanced the pain. He knew talking would help, but he had to grit his teeth to continue. "The voices told her our son was a distraction she didn't need. She took my gun out of its case and opened fire."

Here was the hard part, and he hugged Sam close while he talked over her head. "I should have jumped on her and taken the weapon. But I followed protocol and took the safe route. I grabbed Davey and rolled beneath the car. Tess kept firing until she only had one shot left, then turned the gun on herself."

Emergency services had arrived too late to save Davey from that first direct shot or his wife from the last one. Intellectually, he knew he couldn't have done better, but the *if-only* leech sucked at his soul.

He felt her hot tears against his skin even through the stream from the shower. She didn't question his actions as he'd been doing for months. Instead, she kissed his chest and said, "You must have been in rehab for months."

Tension seeped away. He despised sympathy, but she was simply acknowledging a truth. He lifted her chin and kissed her thoroughly, before turning off the water and reaching for a towel.

"Months in which I decided life was short, and I wanted more than a desk job," he said, watching as she rubbed her hair dry, leaving the rest of her gorgeous body visible for his perusal.

"And being a small-town deputy fit the bill?" she asked, rightfully dubious.

"Looking for the reason for my father's disappearance fit the bill." And it still did. He wasn't ready to give up on finding the killers, now that he knew for certain that his father had been murdered here—and that the murderer might still be on the loose.

She wrapped the towel around her and ran product through the tangle of her hair. "That's how I feel. I want to know what happened to make my parents abandon me. Cass knows a lot more than she's telling."

"I think it's all starting to unravel, but it's hard to imagine even a Lucy with a grievance killing anyone. My bet would be on one of the store owners whose livelihood got stolen." Walker missed the fresh uniform he had waiting at the lodge, but he hadn't been thinking of clothes when he'd led Sam out last night. He strode into her bedroom to gather his discarded uniform.

"You don't limp as much in the mornings," she called after him.

"Muscle tires out. I'm supposed to be doing exercises to build it up again. I figured hill climbing works." He yanked on briefs and trousers and reached for his shirt.

She appeared in the doorway, combing out her shoulder-length hair. "Do you believe in evil yet?"

"Haven't defined it yet," he countered. "Dinah's for breakfast?"

"What if evil is all the venal things inside us—the jealousies and greed and hatred? And yes, Dinah's. I work and she feeds me for free."

She bent over to rummage in her suitcase, giving Walker a heart-stopping view of her rounded buttocks. He was a goal-oriented man who didn't waste a lot of time thinking about sex, but Sam could easily change that.

As long as he kept it to just sex. No more commitment and family and the painful strings that tied him in knots. He'd not been able to protect the child he'd been given. If he meant to get back into action, he wouldn't be leading the kind of safe life a family needed—as his father had proved.

"So where does strung-out on drugs and stupidity fall on the scale of evil?" he countered, to keep from thinking of what couldn't be changed.

"Admittedly, nebulous." She wiggled into a tight camisole. "So we're back to negativity instead of Biblical evil. If we're infused with negativity, we get depressed, take drugs, blame others for our woes..."

"And end up like Xavier, passed out on a stranger's front porch. Give it up, Sam. Hillvale is not inhabited by evil or negativity. It's a bunch of old hippies who hug trees and believe in earth spirits instead of a Great Creator or whatever. People need to believe in a larger power than their own." He tucked in his wrinkled shirt and wondered if he'd have time to change before the sheriff and his crew arrived.

"That's what I would have thought until I was out on that mountain during the fire. I know I have a smart mouth, but I'm usually cautious and never mean. I said things to Carmen—a complete stranger—that I would never have said under any other conditions. And you were behaving like a Neanderthal and even Harvey had a greedy gleam in his eye."

"Tension, stress, human nature. Don't make too much of it." Walker waited for her to finish dressing.

"So you think my planter boxes are normal, and Xavier imagined ghosts in the cemetery, and Val found your father's skeleton by accident?" She shimmied into a pair of jeans.

"Or she knew he was there all along and just decided it was time for the world to know. Don't let the Lucys get to you. They know things others don't because they're a close-mouthed bunch and don't tell all they know until they decide it's time to be said. Xavier's story is a good example." He checked out the window to be certain no more bodies were on the doorstep and no crazies were burning crosses.

"You skipped over the planter boxes," she reminded him. She watched him from beneath long lashes as she braided her hair.

"I don't know anything about flowers," he admitted. "They look pretty and much better than before."

"Fine then," she said with a shrug. "We'll collect some of my ghost compost on the way down the hill. Cass said I could use her wheelbarrow."

"Ghost compost?" he asked warily as she marched for the front door. He'd stupidly been hoping for a kiss or a hug or some token of affection after the night they'd shared. But they were doing sex, not affection, he reminded himself.

The arguing was just the same.

"The dead lady promised me compost and she provided," Sam said airily as she grabbed a walking stick and headed down the outside stairs. "Or perhaps you need to take your car back to town. I want that compost before someone else collects it, so I'm walking."

Abandoning his car, Walker followed her along the overgrown path to Cass's place. He watched in puzzlement as she waved her hand at a half-rotted wooden shed and the doors fell open as if on well-oiled springs. She disappeared inside, and he peered in after her.

The immaculate interior was easily twice the size of the exterior.

CHAPTER 22

MORNING, JUNE 22

SAM TOOK WALKER'S SILENCE AS INCREDULITY AT THE SHED, NOT HER comment about ghosts. Men were so very *visual*.

After his painful revelation of how he'd lost his wife and son, she understood he was entitled to cynicism. She admired his fortitude in finding a means to move forward despite the emotional and physical obstacles. Her loss of her parents had been traumatic, but nowhere on the level he'd suffered. She was in serious danger of opening her heart to him, but she feared, after his experience, he'd never believe she wasn't crazy if she talked to ghosts.

Without speaking, they borrowed Cass's wheelbarrow and shovel. They crunched down the lane to the ghost house, where they collected very real, very smelly compost. Sam's scientific mind acknowledged that someone may have overheard her talking and decided to spook her, as they had poor Xavier. But the part of her head that Cass had inhabited wanted to believe she'd talked to the ghost of the woman who had created this wonderful garden.

While they shoveled, Walker studied Grace's house and yard, probably looking for evidence of how the mound had been delivered. Sam didn't care. She had what she needed, and he didn't object to pushing the heavy wheelbarrow the rest of the way down the lane.

She handed him the apartment key before he loped back up the path to collect his car. "In case the sheriff needs to examine the crime scene. Just drop it off when you're done." She stood on her toes and kissed his bristly cheek—he hadn't had a razor with him. "Let me know if you need more Lucy translations."

He kissed her back, a little more fervently than expected after his silence.

Feeling a little foolish carrying a beautifully carved walking stick into a restaurant, Sam tucked it behind the counter, then washed, and put on a clean apron. After last night's craziness, she was heeding Mariah's warning to carry a weapon.

"Anyone heard how Mr. Black is doing?" she asked as she carried the coffee carafe up and down the counter, filling cups.

"Brenda took Cass down to the hospital this morning," Mariah said, setting out a plate of poached eggs for Harvey. "They can call Dinah's landline and let us know if they hear anything."

"Is Dinah okay?" Sam asked in a low voice, nodding at the kitchen.

"Yeah, her mother's funeral was yesterday, so there's no purpose in her going home now. It was cruel of her brother not to let her know."

"No need to go talking behind my back," Dinah said with dignity, appearing in the doorway carrying a plateful of powdered beignets. "Tullah will help me speak with *Maman* when she's ready. I forgive those who hurt me. Their ignorance only hurts them."

"Nice attitude," Sam said in admiration.

"We need a national Forgive the Ignorant Day," Harvey said cynically, eyeing the beignets with a gleam of hope in his eye.

Dinah slapped the plate down in front of him. "Here, this is partial payment for Sam's staff. You behave, and you'll get more. She's going to be a valuable asset to this community."

"I paid for the walking stick," Sam admonished. "Unless, of course, you wish to kill Harvey with kindness. In that case, I'm all on board with that."

He slanted her an evil look from under his sinfully long black lashes, but with a mouth full of hot grease and sugar, didn't respond.

She started to inquire about Daisy's *lamassu* but decided the fewer people who knew Daisy had been there last night, the better off she was. Daisy would not do well under interrogation.

"Has Mr. Gump abandoned us?" she asked, for no good reason other than to hear about the Kennedys' decision to develop their land.

"He was at the lodge last night but must have driven back to the city," one of the lodge employees said. "He's talking about opening an office up here once the construction starts."

That was not a statement to unite community spirit. The café went silent.

"Was that mural painted when the café opened?" a young hiker asked, oblivious to the animosity. He nodded at the faded painting behind the appliance counter. If his scruff was any indication, he'd been camping in the woods. He hungrily eyed Harvey's beignets.

Sam turned around to study the faded paint lost among the appliances and dishes. Now that she knew her adopted parents were artists, she understood why the mural and the paintings elsewhere called to her.

Harvey pushed the plate toward the hiker, grabbing a couple more for himself as he studied the mural. "No idea. Anyone else?"

Dinah glanced at it. "It was here when I opened the place. I keep meaning to either clean it up or paint it over, but it grows on me."

Sam had been meaning to take a look since she first noticed it. Taking this opportunity, she pushed aside the huge coffee machine to see the bottom right corner. "It's not just dirty, I think it's tempera!" she said in surprise. "It's been varnished over."

Spitting on one of the clean rags Dinah kept under the counter, Sam dabbed at a corner of the paint, hoping to find a date or signature under the grease and grime. "Why would anyone use anything as difficult and delicate as tempera in a *restaurant*?"

"What's tempera?" Mariah leaned over to watch.

"It's an ancient form of paint, made from egg yolk, used well before oils were invented. Many old European murals still survive because the stuff lasts forever, but it's thin and cracks easily. Cleaning it isn't a good idea."

"And you know this how?" Harvey asked, licking powdered sugar from his fingers.

"My parents were artists. They had long involved discussions with other artists and insisted on showing me every ancient painting that ever existed in our corner of the world." Which was a curiosity in itself since she'd never shown any interest in art. Sam shoved that thought aside for later reflection.

She removed pots hanging over the mural and pushed the juice machine to the side. "Mostly, tempera is a medieval medium, but Andrew Wyeth and a few other twentieth-century artists dabbled in the stuff, probably as a back-to-nature statement."

"The hippies," Harvey said, finishing his last beignet and dusting off his fingers. "They were into living off the land. Doesn't get more natural than eggs. Yuck."

"They make a modern tempera now, and I'm not expert enough to know if this is from a jar or the real egg yolk kind. The natural kind can be dangerous, since natural color additives can be poisonous."

The minute she said *poisonous*, the café grew quiet. Dinah joined Mariah in studying what little they could see of the muted colors of the painting.

"It's kinda pretty," Dinah said, stepping back to admire the representation of the café and its customers in a different era. "Not real bright but quiet and peaceful like. Like in the churches," she added in surprise.

Sam didn't dare touch the mural again but nodded. "The old church artists knew tempera works best with solid objects like stone, so they used it on church walls or painted on boards for religious icons. It lasts forever." Sam rapped her knuckles against the wall. It felt like concrete.

"Is the painting valuable?" Mariah asked.

"I have no idea." Sam stepped back to admire what she'd uncovered. "I could call around and see if anyone would be interested in looking at it. Do you have any famous artists from this area? That would lure someone up here faster."

She turned around to greet a customer just entering—one of the sheriff's men, she guessed, even though he was in plain clothes.

He simply asked for eggs and coffee, but the mural conversation ended. The Lucys didn't talk in front of authority—except for Walker, who had apparently gained their trust.

The hiker, however, didn't know to keep his mouth shut. "Didn't

Lucinda Malcolm live up here in the sixties? We had an art teacher who knew her and never shut up about her."

"Seventies," Sam said automatically, because Jade claimed she was a relation to the famous artist. "I'd think she must have been pretty old by then. Her work dates back to the early twentieth century, but she didn't become well known until late."

"Yeah, that's her," the hiker said, satisfied. "Do you think she could have painted that mural?"

Sam was about to say the painting looked as if it had been done in the seventies, judging by hairstyles. But Mariah untied Sam's apron and shoved her toward the door. "Time to go play in your planters. We can take it from here."

More secrets. Sam scowled and tossed her apron under the counter where she kept the walking stick. Harvey got up to accompany her out.

"I'll tell Cass," he said quietly as they walked out together. "No one tells me anything either, but there are rumors about the artists who lived up here over the years. Not just artists, but writers and musicians and other creatives. It's one of the reasons I'm here."

"If they all turn out like Daisy, you'd be better off going back where you came from," Sam said irritably. "I don't like secrets and gossip. I'd go with you to talk to Cass but she isn't home."

"It's okay. We'll know when she is. Keep the staff with you, though. There's something funky happening here, and you do seem to be the eye of the storm."

"Oh, thanks for that." She glared and then peeled off to go down the alley to the compost pile Walker had hauled down for her. She'd rather plunge her hands into manure than keep secrets.

Maybe she'd confront Cass when she got back, and then leave Hill-vale forever.

Or maybe she'd go back to the studio and call the art gallery that showed Jade's art. The owner was the one who had talked so fervently of Lucinda Malcolm's work—and the mystery of who Lucinda really was, since the name was a pseudonym.

At least she'd left the diner before disclosing *that* secret to the hiker.

~

AT THE END OF HIS SHIFT, WALKER DROVE INTO HILLVALE AND PARKED HIS car. He paid particular attention to Sam's planters. As he got out, he could smell the malodorous gunk she'd put into them. The damned flowers seemed to have doubled in size since yesterday. He couldn't believe Mariah had told the whole damned town that Sam was a Lucy because of them.

He'd just thought the blooming pots were artistic and the Lucys should appreciate her. But now that he really looked at them. . . The tiled and painted planters were filled with an amazing collection of exuberantly colored plants that spilled over the sides as if they'd been growing for months.

Flowers were flowers, and he didn't have a scale to judge their growth by. But that shed of Cass's. . . that he knew was *all* wrong. If he hung around Hillvale much longer, he'd be as crazy as the Lucys. He'd have to check the back of the shed sometime and see if it was an optical illusion built into a hill.

As he'd hoped, he found Sam helping with the dinner rush. She acknowledged him by lifting one plate-filled hand but went on to deliver her orders. He settled on a counter stool to wait.

Tarot-reading Amber had set up her cards in a booth and was doing a reading for Dinah, who ran out of her kitchen to flip a card, then ran back to finish whatever was cooking.

Ever-nosy Mariah came over to bring him water and take his order. "So, did the sheriff find anything interesting up at the resort?"

Walker shrugged and hid a grin behind his water glass. "No ghosts," he reported.

She took the plastic menu from him and swatted his hand. "Dinah is fixing muffulettas tonight. You'll have that."

"I don't like olives, so give me a burger." Walker didn't bother snatching back the menu. Dinah would give him whatever she wanted anyway.

Keeping her voice low, Mariah wrote down his order. "You're so boring, I don't know what Sam sees in you. You can't even give us information that might be vital to our survival. We should know if we're living with a killer in our midst."

"I can tell you that the sheriff can't find Daisy to see when she left her lamassu at Sam's door." Walker grinned at Mariah's disgruntled expression.

She huffed and stuck his order on Dinah's spindle.

Sam came over, but not to rescue him. "The detective who checked my place went over to the Kennedy vault. Did he find the gun there?"

Exasperated, Walker narrowed his eyes at her. "You know I can't tell you that. Do I need to eat up at the lodge?"

She leaned over to kiss his cheek. "No, honey pie, because we're just looking for confirmation of what we already know. They took fingerprints of the entire resort staff, including Uncle Lance and all available Kennedys, so they're matching against something. And the sheriff personally returned my key, so I'm hoping I'm not a suspect, yet."

Dinah emerged from the kitchen and slapped a sandwich in front of him, with fries big enough to feed a family of four. "No olives. What's the word on Xavier?"

"Cass didn't call you?" Surprised, Walker bit into his sandwich. He was starving. Filled with thinly sliced hams of various types, topped by an Italian style dressing and fresh tomatoes, whatever in hell he was eating made his mouth water.

"She did, said he was rambling," Amber said as Dinah stopped by her table to turn another tarot card. "We thought you'd know what happened to him."

"That's private information," Walker said between bites. He wished for a beer, but Dinah didn't have an alcohol license. Felons couldn't get them.

"We need a mind-reading psychic." Sam refilled water glasses up and down the counter. "Xavier knows something."

"Daisy might help. Anyone seen her around?" Aaron the antique dealer spoke up from the end of the counter, where he'd been checking his phone.

"You got reception on that thing?" Walker asked, curious.

"Nah, I can pick up the mayor's wi-fi. Someone ought to check on Daisy, though. I saw her taking that golf cart of hers toward the burn area after Mariah's meeting last night."

Walker wanted to question how Aaron had the password to

Monty's private communications, but the question about Daisy had silenced the room.

"She left a stone butterfly on my stairs," Sam offered to the room in general. "But she may have left that before the meeting."

"Isn't she with Valdis?" Dinah called from the kitchen.

"Haven't seen Valdis since the meeting either," Amber said, inching out of her booth. "She didn't come to Cass's."

All around him, the locals were paying their bills and gathering up their dinners. Mariah rushed out of the kitchen to distribute recycled paper bags—no Styrofoam containers for the tree huggers. Walker finished off half his sandwich and stuck the other half in a bag Sam handed him.

"They can't wander off for a day without everyone getting worried?" he asked in a low voice.

"Apparently not. I'm guessing I better go with them." Sam removed her apron.

"They're adults. I can't radio the sheriff unless we know for certain they've been missing at least twenty-four hours. And there isn't much we can do now. It will be dark in a few hours." Walker stood up and followed Sam and the rest of the crowd out.

"Where did we see them last?" Aaron asked of the gathering circle in the parking lot.

"Daisy drove me into town on her golf cart after we left the vortex," one of the more frail, elderly ladies said. "I thought she was heading home."

"Anyone else see Daisy or Valdis after that?" Mariah asked.

Aaron gestured toward the burned-out hill looming over the town. "I saw Daisy driving that way. Anyone else?"

Silence. Out of curiosity, Walker waited to see what they would do next. He checked his watch. The public meeting at the vortex had started breaking up after ten last night. In a few hours, he could call the office, but no one would instigate a night search unless he reported the women had fallen off a cliff.

It would be a simple matter to look for the cart. He could lead a team, if that's what they decided to do. But this was a Lucy gathering. Stepping in with the voice of authority would only send them to the hills without him.

"Aaron, do you know where they were sitting in the amphitheater?" Mariah asked. "Can you run up there and get a feel for them?"

Okay, that wasn't the direction he'd seen this going. Walker watched with curiosity as the antique dealer jogged off up the hill.

"We need our staffs," Tullah called, locking up her shop, apparently apprised of the situation by one of the older women who accompanied her.

"Flashlights, water," Walker told them in resignation, gathering that practical wasn't on their minds. "If we're going up to the burn site, you'll need stout shoes. Boots preferably, for snake protection." He glanced down at Sam's sneaker-clad feet. "You should stay here. We'll need a communication center."

Ignoring his admonition, Sam called, "Tullah, do you have any boots that might fit me?"

The tall woman raised her walking stick, unlocked her door again, and gestured inside. "Got a few pair. Come try them on."

From across the street, Pasquale, the grocery store owner, came out carrying a case of bottled water. As if tuned in to a radio wave frequency beyond Walker's hearing, more locals hurried down from the cottage lane. A few cars pulled into the lot. Harvey returned, holding a selection of carved staffs for anyone who didn't have theirs.

Water bottles were distributed. The crowd grew larger as the sun lowered in the sky. Walker chewed the rest of his sandwich while waiting for Aaron's return.

The crowd grew quiet the moment they saw him jogging back down the hill.

"Valdis wanted to commune with her parents," Aaron called when he came close enough for them to hear.

How the hell did he know that, Walker wondered, but he kept his mouth shut.

"I checked and she's not at the cemetery," Aaron continued. "The police have trampled the place, so there's no sign of her."

They waited until he caught his breath and gulped from the water Mariah handed him.

"Daisy went to look after the artwork," Aaron finally said, wiping his mouth.

"What artwork?" Mariah demanded.

Everyone else looked equally mystified.

CHAPTER 23

EARLY EVENING, JUNE 22

SAM STOMPED HER NEW-OLD BOOTS TO TEST THE AMOUNT OF GIVE AND listened to the Lucys argue over what Aaron *felt* about what Daisy *thought*. She had as little understanding of the conversation as Walker. He was frowning, looking at his watch, and glancing up at the sun. At least she understood his concern.

She took his hand and nodded at the burned swathe of mountain above the town. "If they saw Daisy driving toward the burn site, then let's follow the road," she murmured. "I'm hoping Valdis is just sleeping on a gravestone, but the burn site is dangerous."

"Leadership required," he said with an understanding laugh. He squeezed her hand and loaded bottles of water into his pockets. "I don't suppose Tullah has backpacks in that magical shop of hers?"

"I didn't ask and didn't receive," Sam said with a frown. "I guess I'm just assuming Daisy can't get far from her cart. She has hip problems, and the road runs out, doesn't it?"

Walker nodded. "About a mile up. Okay, let's go. Let your magic stick lead the way."

She shoved bottles of water in her camp short pockets. Even

knowing Walker was poking fun at her walking stick, she followed its vibrations toward the nearest hiking path up the mountain.

A few moments later, Harvey and Tullah joined them.

Since they gave no explanation, Sam figured it was up to her to draw them out. She needed to find out more about this odd town from which she apparently came. "How did Aaron know Daisy was thinking about artwork?"

"Psychometry," Harvey offered. "He believes he can capture or read the thoughts and emotions of objects people have touched. Psychologists call it wishful thinking and delusional."

Sam's eyebrows shot up at this amount of information from the usually taciturn musician and wood carver.

Before she could question, Walker added, "Whatever Aaron does, he's good at it. His antique store is just a front for hanging out up here. He's an international art and antique dealer and owns a fortune in old crap he keeps in warehouses around the country."

Tullah gave an unladylike whistle. "I didn't know that. He's a bit of a grouch, but he's identified some of my finds as belonging to old-time movie stars, even found stills from the films in some cases. I make enough selling them on the internet to keep operating. Wish I could take him with me when I go shopping."

"If you're making a profit, why don't you and Aaron own your own shops?" Sam asked, still torn by the knowledge that her father's family might heave all these people out of their businesses.

"A few years back, when I started, I was leery of my reception, so leasing made sense. Aaron was probably the same. We're newcomers, but the old-timers welcomed us with open arms. But now when we want to buy our own shops, there's nothing available." Tullah sounded sad.

"It would be a shame to lose the community," Sam said, when no one else did.

"Amber says *you* can stop that from happening." Harvey pounded his stick in the ground, then cut away from the road toward the blackened edge of the fire's path.

Sam could actually feel the vibration he was following. She didn't know what it was, just that the *energy* was different in that direction. Maybe she should have taken physics. She knew about tectonic faults and how the earth moved, but no one had told her she might *feel* an earthquake coming—although animals were said to sense it. Daisy was hardly an earthquake though. And feeling energy wouldn't save a town.

"Wishful thinking," Walker said, repeating Harvey's own words. "Sam was a student a few weeks ago. You can't lay all your problems on her."

Sam squeezed his arm and nodded downhill. "We have company. Tell us how to start a proper search."

The Lucys had finally divided up and were ready to follow direction. To Sam's surprise, the man Mariah had once pointed out as the town mayor, Sam's Uncle Montgomery, had joined them. He and Walker were the only ones without one of Harvey's staffs.

Walker waited until they were all within range of hearing to ask, "Does anyone have any notion of where Daisy might go up here?"

"Only thing up here is the old Ingersson farm," Monty responded.

Sam studied him in the growing dusk. She knew he was only about five years older than she. He had a healthy California bronze look, including sun-touched gold tips in his light brown hair. He wore an easy smile, making him seem remotely more approachable than his older brother.

"Would the farm be in that direction?" Sam pointed to the south, away from the lodge and Mendoza land, in the direction Harvey was taking.

Monty narrowed his eyes at her. "Yes, on the other side of that ridge was the farmhouse. Most of the land we're standing on right now was part of the farm."

"Still is," she asserted, without really knowing the facts. She just *felt* it. It was an extremely odd feeling. She didn't want to get too excited about having her own land again.

He didn't respond. She had a feeling he was a man who didn't waste time arguing.

"Our staffs are tugging us that way," she said as boldly as she dared, even though it was an insane declaration. "Walker, can you put me in the same part of the grid as Harvey?"

Harvey was already halfway down the hill.

"Your staff is tugging you?" Walker asked skeptically, but he was wearing his shades again, so she couldn't read his expression. When she merely waited for agreement, he nodded. "Fine, then, you, Harvey, and Monty head that way. I'll divide up the rest of us. Keep each other in sight and hearing at all times. It will be dark before long, so if you don't have a flashlight, make sure you're partnering with someone who does."

Monty waved his flashlight. Taking a deep breath of resolve, Sam followed her weirdly twitching staff and set off in the direction it led, which seemed to be a rutted lane of sorts.

Harvey was veering off of it, scrambling down a hillside.

"You don't really believe that stick business, do you?" the mayor asked when they were out of hearing range. "You just wanted to see the farm."

"You think my subconscious guides it?" Sam asked with interest. "Ideomotion? It's one theory."

"You've already researched Lucy weirdness?" he asked in surprise.

"I'm a scientist. I do not accept anything on faith and looked up divining rods. Google doesn't explain what I feel. You'll have to take my word that I had no idea where the farm was. It's not as if there are directional signs, and I've only been here a few days. So the jury is still out on what this stick can do as far as I'm concerned." She walked along, unconcerned, studying how the fire had skipped patches of scrub and trees, depending on how the wind blew. The firemen had almost had the flames under control by the time it reached this area. The stench of wet ash and smoke was overpowering.

"I understand from Kurt that I'm supposed to welcome you to the family," her half-uncle said. "I should have done so sooner."

"But you had me investigated first," Sam said in amusement. "I can understand that. I'm still investigating me too."

Harvey had disappeared. Walker had said they were supposed to keep each other in view, but he'd also said that Harvey was a vampire who walked these hills at night. She had to assume Harvey knew what he was doing.

"Walker says you're the real deal, but he's not telling me everything." That sounded almost like a mayoral grumble.

"Walker considers everything is on a need-to-know basis," Sam acknowledged. "I didn't know all that about Aaron, either. And he probably knows a lot about you that he's not telling. Walker is a font of undisclosed information, but I trust him." And she did, even though her circumstances were so weird, she shouldn't trust anyone. Jade had taught her to be suspicious of other people's motives, so she wasn't naïve. There was just something about Hillvale. . .

She crouched down to examine a pine seedling that had survived behind a boulder. The mountain would recover in a few seasons. She wasn't certain about the resort or tourism.

"Walker is a professional," Monty admitted grudgingly. "I don't want to believe we have a killer in town, but Juan didn't shoot himself in the back."

"The police haven't told you if they found anything?" Sam asked. "I thought for certain all that fingerprinting would help."

Monty shrugged. "They searched the family vault and found a gun, but there are multiple sets of prints on it. They're still testing ballistics to see if it's the gun that shot Juan. The sheriff seems to think Juan was shot in the security office, but the entire staff has access to it. Even Uncle Lance has been in there to get keys to his studio when he lost his. My mother keeps spare sets of keys there. There are fingerprints all over. With no motive, they have nothing."

"What about opportunity?"

Monty shrugged. "Shots were reported before midnight. I won't go into the condition of the body, but the cops figure the time line is about right, a few hours before or after if there were any unreported shots. A lot of people were still up and around, but who goes back to the security area at that hour?"

"That's about the time we heard the howling ghost. Surely they can make a list of people up and around then. I saw Harvey walking toward the cemetery right about that time."

"Howling ghost?" Monty shook his head in disbelief. "Harvey would have to hike several miles to reach the cemetery from the lodge. There were a lot of people closer. Walker said several of the Lucys, including Valdis, were out and about within half an hour of the shots-fired report. He said my uncle was in his studio then. That's close to the security office, but Lance claims to have seen nothing, which isn't unusual for him. Alonzo and Bernard were working the night shift and saw my mother's Escalade go out, although no one saw who was driving. My mother said she was asleep and Francois claimed no knowledge of it. Kurt and I had just had a meeting with Xavier and Gump. And then there's half the resort staff and the guests who could have come and gone without anyone really noticing. *Everyone* had an opportunity."

"I hope they don't suspect poor Xavier now. I'm afraid if he held a gun in his hand, he'd put it to his head. He seems to be an unhappy person."

But Xavier had carried a kerosene can. Would the same person who burned the mountain be the one who shot a man in the back?

"I remember Xavier from when my father was alive," Monty said thoughtfully. "When he first started coming here, he didn't pay Kurt or me any attention. But he seemed to change overnight, into a ghost of a man who jumped if we said *boo*. I assumed he fried his brain on drugs, but he manages the rental office fine. He must have been sharp once. I can't imagine him shooting Juan for any reason."

Sam hid her excitement at finding someone actually willing to *talk* to her. Walker was too professional to reveal police findings, and he hadn't lived here all those years ago. "Do you think Juan's death is related to the finding of the skeleton?"

"Yeah, I'm afraid it may be," he said grimly. "Which will tie it to my family now that Walker's father has been identified. My mother has suffered enough over all these years. I don't want her put through that kind of grinder. I hope she stays in Hawaii until this settles. It always relaxes her to get away."

"She's sensitive to the negative energy, I suspect," Sam said aloud, forgetting she was talking to a Null.

Her half-uncle went silent again. *Oops.* She cast him a look, but he was studying the terrain ahead.

"The farmhouse used to be over by that patch of green on the left. Looks like the bluff protected the shrubs from the fire. There's a stone foundation in there. Usually, morning glories cover it, but they won't be blooming at this hour, if they survived. There aren't too many hiding places."

"Where would she hide a golf cart?" Sam studied what must have been her grandparents' home, but in the twilight, it didn't look any different than the rest of the mountain. She felt a connection to the land but nothing else.

"Daisy gets her stones from somewhere. I guess this is as good a place as any. She probably has a favorite spot for that ugly lump of metal. Daisy!" Monty shouted as they headed down the hill into the secluded basin.

A few of the bushes appeared to move. Sam hurried in that direction. "Daisy!"

A stick raised up above a sprawling manzanita hedge singed by the fire. The staff swung lazily, so the bearer didn't seem to have any urgent message.

"Not having cell phones is a real pain," Sam muttered, hurrying down the rocky, burned-out path.

"If she's hurt, I'll jog back and find Walker. She's not large. We can haul her out easily enough, especially if the cart isn't out of gas." Monty strode along with confidence, apparently knowing the land.

Sam wondered if he knew she and Valdis were purportedly heirs to the property. Surely, if he'd been researching property rights, he had a full-scale map of every lot. But he wasn't saying anything. Interesting.

Before they reached the hedge, Sam nearly stumbled over what at first appeared to be a stack of stones. On this side of the bluff, the shadows were long. She took Monty's flashlight and flashed it over the ground.

Lined up around what appeared to be the farm foundation was a military row of small stone statues similar to the one Daisy had left for Sam last night. These weren't quite as artistic, consisting mostly of three stones maybe a foot high, wired together with whatever bits of flotsam Daisy could summon from her surroundings. Manzanita arms were the primary decoration. One or two had shiny pebbles as ornaments—decorated generals maybe, Sam thought with amusement.

"What the. . ." Monty bit off the rest of the curse as he examined the line.

Sam's staff quit pulsating. "Daisy, is it okay for us to cross the line?"

The bushes parted and Daisy's graying head peered out. Sam breathed in relief.

"Yes, yes, come along." She disappeared behind the bushes again.

"Are you hurt? Do you need help?" Sam asked anxiously, stepping across the statues.

"I'm fine. Montgomery, go home. You're useless," Daisy called, actually sounding coherent for a change.

"You can tell the other searchers to go home," Sam said, holding back a sigh of exasperation. "I'm sorry you got dragged away from your busy schedule."

Monty almost chuckled. "Par for the course up here. Valdis is probably engraving stones in the cemetery. But I needed the exercise. It's good to remember what the mountain is about, and I wanted to see how much damage the fire did."

"I think this part of the land will be fine with a little care," Sam said cautiously. "I studied controlled burns. There are recommended actions that can be taken."

He nodded without expression. "I'll send a few of the women down with flashlights. You'll all have broken ankles stumbling around in the dark."

"I'm not hanging around to be found by snakes and cougars," she said tartly. "But I'll stay with Daisy until the others decide what they want to do."

"Glad you understand she won't be persuaded away until she's ready." He handed her the flashlight and stalked back up the way they came.

"Good, he's gone," Daisy said from behind the hedge. "We need more lamassu. I should have thought of this sooner. We can't have bulldozers here."

"Why do we need spirit protection?" Sam asked, pushing through the thick prickly hedges to find Daisy sitting on a part of a stone foundation not covered in branches. She had rolls of rusty wire and piles of stone and several sets of wire cutters scattered across the rocky clearing. Sam thought she caught a glimmer of metal buried in the manzanita that might be the golf cart.

She examined what must have once been the farmhouse where her grandparents had lived. It wasn't large. Several old square timbers still remained, perhaps from the original cabin. If there had been plaster walls, they'd deteriorated into the general debris. There might have been a concrete floor but there was so much dirt, it was hard to tell. A mudslide may have covered it. The bluff didn't look particularly stable.

The remains of an old stone chimney were the only real proof that a house had existed.

"Evil drives the bulldozers," Daisy said. "Here, add this to the line." From beneath her feather coat, her hand stuck out, holding a new statue. "Not having to get up will save me time."

"You need to sleep and eat," Sam remonstrated. "We have lots of time before bulldozers come up here."

"No, no." She shook her long hair. "They'll come in the dark and raze the trees while we're sleeping. We can't let them find the art!"

Gazing at the *treeless* basin, Sam winced. Mariah called Daisy's irrationality time-walking. It sounded more like hallucinations to her.

She carried the stone figurine out to the line apparently meant to circle the foundation. She set it about the same distance as Daisy had the others. Taking the flashlight, she studied the small army. Even hastily constructed, the stone and stick figures were all tiny works of art, expressing excitement, anger, tension—all the emotions generated by the outdoor meeting. Sam marveled at Daisy's talent and wondered if the figures could be sold in places like state park gift stores. She needed to call Jade's gallery owner. She had contacts.

Tullah and Walker appeared at the top of the ridgeline. They'd apparently met up with Harvey, who started down the hill, carrying an armload of dry branches. Sam waved. It was still new and exciting to have found a few people who might possibly accept her, even when she talked about shivering sticks. Back at the university, they would have been horrified that she wasn't sending out her resume. Her friends from high school would have giggled over these diverse and eccentric people. But Sam sensed only concern and interest as the others strode toward her.

Walker hugged her as he followed her through the manzanita hedge. Tullah and Harvey stopped to check the lamassu army as she had just been doing.

Daisy held out another figurine. In the beam of the flashlight, the crystals in the rock glittered. "Tullah can gather the stones. Tell Harvey I need more pine and sage and there's still a laurel up there on the ridge. He'll know."

How did she know who was out there? Sam tried to peer through the hedge from Daisy's perspective but it was too thick to see anything.

Walker took the figure but studied Daisy. "You okay? Can you get up and walk around so we don't worry?"

She shoved her hair out of her eyes. "You could have brought food." She picked up her staff and used it to pull herself to her feet, then shouted her commands at the two on the other side of the hedge.

At Walker's expression, Sam hid a giggle. He'd removed his sunglasses in these shadows. She was amazed he wasn't rolling his eyes.

"I think you better come down for a rest," she told the older woman with concern. "We'll bring an army of people up in the morning to help you."

Daisy frowned but wavered uncertainly. "Where's Valdis? She promised to help."

"We don't know. We're looking for her too." Sam's unease turned to her aunt. Younger than Daisy, Valdis had the limber strength of a mountain goat. Sam hadn't been worried about her, until now.

Daisy looked reluctantly at her treasure of junk. "I really shouldn't. But Valdis heard the spirits call. We'd better see what she's found." She nodded appreciatively, if absent-mindedly, as Harvey pushed through the hedge to deposit his load of twigs in her workplace. Sam thought maybe he'd been here before.

Leaving her tools, Daisy hobbled over the low stone foundation with Walker's help. Harvey was already cutting branches from nearby trees, and Tullah had a skirt full of stones of different sizes. Sam shook her head in astonishment that seemingly intelligent, educated people would follow Daisy's crazy orders.

But this was what community did—accepted each other as they were, Sam was beginning to understand.

"We'll leave these for you to start with in the morning," Tullah called. "We'll come right down after you."

"Cougars," Walker said. "Move it quickly."

Sam took Daisy's left side and Walker her right and together, they climbed out of the hideaway.

"Is the cart operating?" Walker asked.

"Should be, but I banged the bumper. Valdis won't be happy." Daisy gestured at the back end of the camouflage-painted golf cart.

"I'll back it out, see if it still runs." Walker shoved aside broken branches to expose the now well-scratched sides of the cart.

"Thank you for my lamassu," Sam said while they waited.

Daisy nodded absently. "Bad spirits can go in good places. Let him guard your door."

"Did you see Xavier there when you stopped by?" she asked as nonchalantly as she could.

Walker shot her an approving glance as he backed out but stayed silent. He did that a lot, Sam noticed. He listened and waited and when it was time, he acted. She liked the way he'd taken charge of the search, while letting others do their own thing.

"He's haunted," Daisy said. "Evil has drained his soul. I told him to rebuild by doing good deeds."

She sounded perfectly rational, as if discussing last night's dinner. It was the content of her speech that had Sam shaking her head. It was rather like having a sideways conversation.

"He overdosed. He's in the hospital now. Do you know why he might have stopped by my place?"

Daisy stopped and frowned at the darkening sky. "He knows who wants to kill you. He consorts with the Evil One."

CHAPTER 24

EVENING, JUNE 22

BY THE TIME THEY REACHED HILLVALE, IT WAS FULL DARK, AND BOTH search parties had either gone home or gathered in the café. Walker noted the Kennedy Escalade parked in the lot, with Francois sitting inside, drawing on his cigarette. Did that mean Carmel had returned?

Inside the café, Monty and Mariah were glaring at each other, but at least the mayor had waited around instead of driving back to the lodge. No other Kennedy was present though, so why was Francois here? Monty's Tesla was usually parked behind his office.

Seeing a graying blond head at the far end of the counter, Walker answered his own question. Carmel's artist brother didn't drive or even come to town often. The chauffeur must have brought him. Lance was contemplating a selection of pastries as if they were a still life to be painted. Walker almost laughed when Lance moved a beignet into a more artistic composition with the fruit tarts on his plate.

Oddly, Alan Gump, the real estate magnate from the city, was also at the counter, drinking coffee and telling loud stories to a group of business owners. Why was he here at this hour? Had he already set up his development office?

The Lucys gathered at the far end of the counter from the Nulls, near the entrance. They hugged Daisy in excitement at her return, chattering and keeping their voices low, so the Nulls couldn't overhear.

Walker was glad these people weren't normally violent because the divisiveness was becoming more apparent every day.

Sam settled Daisy on a stool so Dinah could pamper her.

Confused by the way Sam, the scientist, fit in so easily with the crazies, Walker sat beside Monty for a normal summary of events. "Valdis?"

"Mariah said they searched the cemetery and didn't find her. For whatever reason, they're waiting for you and Sam to come up with a better solution. Got any?" Monty slugged his coffee as if it were whiskey.

"Bloodhounds? Wiggling sticks?" Walker gratefully accepted the burger Dinah slapped in front of him. He didn't quibble over the avocado and sprouts because the bite of sriracha sauce made nutrition worthwhile.

Monty went back to glaring, this time at the mural. Lance appeared to be studying it almost surreptitiously, in between rearranging his food. And *there* was the reason Carmel's artistic brother had deigned to descend from the mountain—he'd heard about Lucinda Malcolm and the mural that had been staring them in the face all these years.

Finding Cass looking gloomy in one of the booths, Walker decided if he had to look at misery, it ought to at least be female, he picked up his plate and sat across from her. "How is Xavier?"

"If you've tested the kerosene can for prints, you already know he burned the cross," she said without hesitation.

Walker raised his eyebrows in surprise at this admission. He knew the story he was about to hear would have nothing to do with rationality, but he asked anyway. "He burned the mountain so the Kennedys had to go forward with the condos?"

Cass glared at him. "He says the spirits made him do it, but he thought they were the *good* spirits telling him to cleanse the evil. He says he only planted the cross and didn't start a fire. So now he's not so sure if the spirits were good or evil, and he wanted to ask Sam. Why would he want to ask Sam?"

"Because he's crazy like everyone else up here?" Walker suggested. "Did he say where he got the drugs?"

Cass cast him an evil eye, but at least she was looking less depressed. "Are you going to arrest him? He needs medical help, not prison."

"Is anyone pressing charges? If he lit that fire, he pretty much destroyed the resort's business, so it's Kurt and Monty you need to talk to." Which is why Xavier had gone to Sam, Walker realized. Cass wouldn't talk to the Kennedys, but Sam might go with him to explain. The man was only half-crazy.

"The sheriff's office will press charges if you tell them to," Cass said.

"The sheriff's office will do whatever the D.A. says," he corrected. "I'll take a wild guess and assume the D.A. will have difficulty convicting with only a drug-addicted mental case's half-confession, unless there is other evidence. The kerosene can was a plant to make sure he was implicated and probably to explain his overdose. It was wiped clean of prints."

Cass's eyebrows shot up in surprise. Then she narrowed her eyes and glared when she realized she'd given away Xavier's confession for nothing.

Walker continued without waiting for her protests. "I can't imagine Xavier was lucid enough to wipe fingerprints if he meant to confess. They can't even get him for possession, since he had nothing on him. And last I checked, they still didn't have the blood analysis. From what was said the other night, chances are good that this wasn't a normal overdose and someone tried to *kill* Xavier. That's the person I want."

Cass looked thoughtful. "We don't do drugs up here anymore. Maybe I can pry his source out of him. I was reluctant to ask for fear he'd incriminate himself more."

"We want killers, not demented old men, although if Xavier is in the habit of burning out the spirits, he may need help." Walker waited, but Cass didn't respond. Dementia had many disguises in Hillvale. "Where do you think Valdis might be? Is this unusual for her?"

"I don't think she's conscious," Cass said worriedly. "She has a very strong presence. If she was awake, I'd eventually hear her or she would hear me. She said she wanted to visit with the spirits of her parents before she followed Daisy. As far as I'm aware, that's the last anyone saw of her. I'd hoped she was with Daisy."

Walker didn't know how to react to Cass *hearing* Valdis. But the possibility that Xavier may have been given a lethal overdose on purpose escalated the possibility that a killer was targeting the Lucys for a reason. Not that Xavier was officially a Lucy, but he lingered there on the edge, betwixt and between—as did Sam, Walker realized worriedly. And both had connections to the Kennedys—if that had any relevance.

Since land fraud had been the reason his father was killed. . . Still no obvious connection to recent occurrences. If the Kennedys and the development company were working with Mendoza, they had all the land they needed. The Lucys were barely a speed bump on their highway to riches.

Xavier had been in Hillvale when Walker's father was killed. Valdis hadn't. But Valdis was Sam's aunt—and part owner of a rather valuable piece of land. *As was Sam.* Instinct roiled.

How many people knew the farm still belonged to Ingerssons? Did it matter?

Walker finished his burger and slipped out of the booth. "I want to take another look at the cemetery. If I don't find anything, I'll put in a report to the sheriff's office, persuade him Valdis might be in danger so he'll organize a search party."

"You're a good man, Walker. I'm sorry about your father, but if it brought you up here when we need you, Fate has served its purpose."

Walker wasn't any too certain of that, but Sam met his eyes as he returned to the counter, and he almost started believing in the stars and planets and Fate as well. They were in synch in ways he couldn't explain. He saw her concern, and it was the same as his.

"I want to give the cemetery another search," he told her, keeping his voice low.

"I'm going that way," she said, agreeing without saying the words. "Do you want anyone else?"

Walker cast a glance over the crowd. He'd like to have Harvey and the mayor, since they hadn't searched the cemetery earlier, but he didn't see a good way to extricate them without everyone zooming in.

"One of them could very well be a killer. If they sabotaged the search earlier, I'd rather not have them do it again."

That raised her eyebrows. She obviously didn't have his experience with the criminal mind. And at this point, he feared he was dealing with a killer who planned ahead, not a flake who OD'd. Homicide was not his division, in his real job or this one, but his background and education had developed his instincts for danger.

Following his example, Sam casually waved at Dinah. "I'm too tired to think. I'll be down early to clean up, Dinah, so leave everything in the sink."

Hoots and catcalls followed them out, but Walker didn't give a damn. He steered Sam to his official vehicle and kept an eye out to see if anyone followed.

Monty and a blustering Alan Gump emerged, arguing vociferously. Both men were large, but Gump was older and carried more fat than muscle. Unless Gump was carrying a gun, the mayor could hold his own. Walker fastened his seatbelt and kept an eye on his rearview mirror. Lance trailed out to the Escalade, looking morose. By the time Walker had his vehicle in gear, half the diner had emptied and some were striding toward the cemetery.

"I don't think you can keep what we do quiet in Hillvale," Sam said in amusement, watching the side mirror and following his thoughts.

"I shouldn't have told Cass I was taking another look around. Damn, when will I learn?" Just in case he might fool anyone, he drove the SUV down Cass's drive and parked in front of the garage/studio.

Anyone following would most likely be on foot and take a while longer to catch up.

"Let me run up and get another flashlight." She dashed up the stairs and came down in an instant, shoving flashlights in her pockets and dangling a small backpack off her shoulder. "I brought a snakebite kit, just in case."

Walker was out of the car with his own flashlight in hand. "What's your hang-up about snakes? They're more afraid of you than we are of them."

Swinging her walking stick, she easily fell into stride with him, cutting across Cass's yard and keeping to the concealment of the shrubbery. "Got bit when I was a kid. The pain was beyond excruciating. Only time I ever saw my parents go into full-scale panic. They were screaming at each other. I was terrified, and I'm sure they must have been out of their minds with fear, but it was their screaming that told me I was in trouble. They *never* argued."

"So you associate snakes with dying and panic?" he asked, trying to grasp her fear.

"Mostly, I think I associate it with losing the ones I love. I was afraid they were going to divorce and go away like the parents of some of my friends, and that made me panic even more. I know it's an unreasonable phobia, that snakes are good for the environment, but I can't even look at one long enough to identify it. I just freak and run."

"At least you have a good reason. Most people freak without thinking." *Like Tess.* Walker tried not to compare, but his mind kept wanting to believe Sam was different, that she might be the partner he needed. But that was loneliness speaking. And good sex. OK, and she fascinated him—always a dangerous sign when a woman engaged his brain.

She swung her stick and stayed silent. He liked that she didn't talk for the sake of talking. When they reached the cemetery, he concentrated on looking for footprints in the dry ground, but too many people had traipsed this path and dust wasn't permanent.

"She's not here," Sam said abruptly. "I want to check the amphitheater. I'll meet you back here in half an hour."

Walker fought the protective urge to follow. Sam was an adult. She didn't need a babysitter. And she'd just told him Valdis wasn't in the cemetery as if she *knew* something he didn't. As if she heard voices in her head?

Clenching his molars, Walker stomped up to the cemetery, alone.

AN OWL HOOTED AND FLAPPED ITS WINGS OVER HER HEAD. SAM JERKED nervously. Walking up to the vortex had been different in daylight, or when she'd been surrounded by people she knew. Out here on the rocks, all alone, the hike was a little intimidating. If she tripped, she'd have to scream loudly for help, and she wasn't certain anyone would hear.

She tried not to think about snakes and cougars or nasty spider webs.

The trees had been logged long ago. It was just scattered underbrush and rocks—and forces that drew her staff as if iron to lodestone. She wondered if that was part of the magnetism of the vortex—a layer of magnetite beneath the layers of sandstone and granite. But magnetite wouldn't draw wood. She could swear the staff twitched from *vibrations*, and the crystal eyes in the handle possessed an ethereal gleam. Refusing to believe in the supernatural, she wasn't afraid, just curious. She followed its direction around the top of the amphitheater, not into it.

She had to assume twitching staffs were ideomotion. She wanted to find her aunt, therefore her brain provided sympathetic pulses so she imagined she was helping. She should be searching with the others. If Valdis was dead or injured, Sam couldn't send psychic help messages to the universe. She needed real live cell reception.

If the Kennedys wanted to build condos out here, they'd have to build cell towers first. How did one go about doing that?

What if cell towers interfered with the vortex? Not that she believed the vortex had special energy. . . But someone ought to study any possible energy effects before the vortex was lost. A seismograph might give some indication of underground vibrations, but she wished she could use satellites to help find imbalances and measure heat the way climate change was tracked. Differences in heat energy would explain a lot.

The stick twitched to a path leading up another hill, away from the amphitheater and the cemetery, in the direction Walker had called the Ingersson land. Which was when Sam had a horrible thought—*what if her grandparents weren't buried in the cemetery*? She hadn't seen a gravestone for them.

She froze to consider what she was doing. It was dark and getting cold. If she were a snake, she'd be slithering into a warm nest about now, except she had a vague recollection that rattlers hunted at night. She wore sturdy boots, but she had no idea how old the batteries were in her flashlight. A sensible person would go back and *ask* about the graves—but if anyone knew, wouldn't they have mentioned it already? They'd died nearly a quarter of a century ago.

A sensible person wouldn't be out here paying attention to the frantic tugs of a dead tree branch. She knew she was following this insanity out of fear. Valdis had been out in the heat and cold without water or food for twenty-four hours. How much longer could she last? What if she had a heart condition? What if she'd been bitten by snakes?

What if someone had tried to murder Valdis as they had killed Juan?

Instinct and emotion. . . or science and fact?

She'd spent her life with science, enough to know that book learning wouldn't help her now. The time had come to extend her experience beyond the ivory tower.

She followed the damned twitching stick. Walker would never speak to her again. She regretted that, but he'd never promised more than good sex. He would be going back to LA and his executive position, and she was pretty certain by now that she wouldn't follow. Her hands belonged in dirt, not on computers.

It tore at her lonely heart to give him up, but maybe she'd find a home in Hillvale. She missed having a family. She needed to figure out what kind of life she wanted to make for herself, and what people she wanted populating it. Even if she eventually had to leave to make a living, she would like to think she had a place to come back to, where people knew her.

The staff led her up a crude path through shrub untouched by the fire. She sensed she was heading in the same direction in which they'd found Daisy, but this was higher ground. Surely Valdis wouldn't have buried her parents way up here? Why?

If she could see below, she was pretty certain she'd see the farm in the distance. This had to be the ridge high above the bluff that had protected Daisy's little hideaway. She sensed the oddly *bad* energy on this side of the vortex. If she was into woo-woo and spiritualism the way the other Lucys were, she'd be concerned too. Instead, she wondered about polluted aquifers or an earthquake fault hidden beneath the pines and manzanita.

Of course, if she could find those, she might be able to stop the development with science. Her other family would hate her.

An anguished banshee howl lifted the hairs on the back of her neck.

CHAPTER 25

Sam fought rising panic. Had she come all this way only to find her aunt totally mad and howling at the moon? She glanced nervously over her shoulder but didn't see any moon, full or otherwise. The fog was drifting inland.

"Valdis?" she called.

"Go back," Valdis wailed. "The serpents nest under me."

Serpents. *Deep breath, Samantha, there be no dragons here.* "Can you come down here where I am?"

She tried to see her aunt, but the flashlight revealed only large boulders tumbled from a long-ago mudslide.

"Twisted the damned ankle," her aunt said in a perfectly prosaic voice.

Sam was so relieved by the normality that she almost shook with laughter, until she realized Valdis had been up here for twenty-four hours without food and drink. Or drugs. "I have water and a first-aid kit in my backpack. How do I avoid the serpents?"

"They're in the rocks, hunting. You can't. Don't waste your life for mine. You are the only hope of eradicating the evil. It's spreading.

Even Lance is infected now. This is all Susannah's fault. You were supposed to learn art, not science." This time, despair and a hint of doom crept back in her voice.

Art! She couldn't draw a straight line. She *could* go back and get help. But she hated abandoning her aunt—and leaving her in danger of snakes.

Sam shuddered, realizing Valdis probably meant she was sitting above a snake nest.

Faced with family or phobia, Sam girded her figurative loins, held her breath, and cautiously poked her staff among the rocks. If she believed in magic, she'd hope the stick would guard her safely past snakes and up the boulder path.

A bite would cause excruciating damage before they could reach anti-venom supplies. Snake-bite kits were mostly for pretending something was being done so the victim stayed calm.

"Why can't Cass hear you?" she asked, hoping to distract herself if not Valdis as she climbed.

"Unconscious," Valdis said in disgust. "Not good with pain."

"Well, start sending magic signals to Cass now. I'm coming up."

Swallowing hard, fighting panic, Sam stepped up on the first rock in the slide area, beating her staff against the stone and underbrush. She almost wished her memory hadn't returned.

Valdis started to moan, not in pain, but as if possessed. Now, it wasn't only the hair on the back of Sam's neck standing up. She had goosebumps up and down her arms.

"He's here," Valdis wailed. "He's here. He's come back! Be careful. I don't know him anymore. The evil. . . He doesn't know what he's doing. Promise me, you'll take care of them. Don't let them give in to temptation. . ."

Sam beat her stick against the next rock, whacked at the bushes, and prayed to whatever gods or spirits looked after mad women. "Who's back?" she called, just because. She was fairly certain this was her aunt on spirits, not drugs.

"Go away!" Valdis shouted in a voice not her own, confirming Sam's suspicion. "Go back! Leave this place. Let the evil die here as I did!"

"Okay, that's not a positive attitude," Sam muttered. "Valdis, block that jerk. You're not dying. Find someone useful."

Maybe she had started channeling Cass and her acerbic take on life. No wonder her great-aunt was a little weird if she'd lived with people in her head all her life. That sounded like a description of schizophrenia if she'd ever heard one.

Valdis fell silent. Biting her bottom lip, Sam climbed a little faster, questioning her sanity as she went.

In the silence, she heard the unmistakable rattle of a diamondback. Sam froze.

Valdis chose that moment to start howling. "It's in the paint! I see the demons, and they see me! Stop them, stop them now, bury the demons before they reach us!"

Snakes, paint, demons. . . *Snakes*—snakes were real. The rattle was loud and threatening. She was in its territory. *Stay calm, don't panic.* What did the books say she was supposed to do? *Freeze. Respect the snake.* Okay, she was completely frozen. If respect meant frozen with fear, yup, she was all over it.

"Don't worry, he's gone." Valdis spoke in a sing-song voice with a slight accent—Scandinavian? "You'll do fine if you don't give in to greed as the others did. Don't play with the crystals and be strong, dears. It's up to you to rebuild our beautiful farm."

Don't play with crystals?

The new voice almost sounded coherent. Either that or Sam figured she was as nuts as her aunt. She'd feel better if the voice had said don't play with *snakes.*

Heart pounding frantically, she listened for the rattle as Valdis grew quiet again. Sam ran the beam of her flashlight over the rocks until she caught movement. She inadvertently stepped backward to avoid the slithering shadow and lost her footing on the boulder. She screamed.

Stalking out of the cemetery, surrounded by chattering Lucys, Walker irritably decided he wanted one of Harvey's big sticks too. They'd be useful in batting off the crazies.

The scream shivered every nerve in his body.

Without hesitation, he ran toward the amphitheater. The scream had been much more distant than the vortex, but it was Sam's, he knew it. Fear escalated his pulse.

He pulled out his radio and was calling for an ambulance before he gave it a second thought. His training had taught him better, but he wasn't following his head. He was following his damned. . . what? Instincts? Heart? He'd been around the Lucys too long.

He swept his big flashlight around the arena, finding no way of tracking Sam on rocks. How the hell would he find her?

Harvey stepped out of the shadows ahead. Harvey, the night-walker, the maker of crazy sticks—but Walker knew nothing against him. As far as he'd been able to tell, the musician was just exactly what he seemed, an underpaid creative who carved sticks for a living.

"Valdis goes up on Bald Rock when she wants to commune with the spirits," the long-haired man in black said, pointing one of his sticks at the mountain.

"Why didn't anyone say that earlier?" Walker asked, stomping out his anger and fear by following the direction indicated. "And that was Sam's scream, not Valerie's."

"No one will go up there but Valdis. Sam wouldn't know better. She would have followed the vibrations." Harvey fell in step with him. "If you've called for help, I'll direct them up there, but I'll only go to the bottom of the path. The rock is haunted, and not by friendly ectoplasm."

"Charming," Walker grumbled. Did he hear moaning? "You've personally seen ghosts?"

Harvey hesitated. "I've personally seen evil. That's enough to keep my distance. There's something bad happening out there. That's all I can tell you."

"And Sam and Valdis may be up there doing battle with demons?" Walker said cynically. "And everyone is abandoning them?"

"Put that way. . . yes," Harvey muttered. "So, we're cowards. We're artists, not heroes."

"You're superstitious idiots." Walker halted to listen. Did he hear voices? "Sam?" he called, hoping for a response. . . hoping Sam's vibrant life and laughter still lived.

Maybe he was fooling himself, but he thought he heard "Okay," float down. He picked up speed, tramping on Harvey's heels close enough to make the other man hop faster.

"No, we're neither superstitious or idiots," Harvey said emphatically. "If you stay here long enough, you'll see what we mean. I heard about the *fouled brilliance* of the commune, as my father called it, and came up to find out for myself. There's not much talent left up here to be brilliant, but the *foul* part is subtle and doesn't need talent to cause harm. Sam called it negativity, and she might be closer to the truth, but how does one put negativity into dirt?"

"Explain negativity." Walker needed a distraction from the horrifying images filling his head. Snakes and landslides and broken necks provided more than enough evil without throwing in demons. But *negativity*, that almost made sense. The world was full of it.

"Talk to Lance sometime," Harvey suggested, almost angrily. "Look at his artwork. There's a reason Daisy hands out guardian angels, although I don't know why the devil she's using stones from the Ingersson farm, since that's where the evil erupted."

Now they were getting somewhere—the hippy farm, where drugs and art ruled. Hallucinogens were probably part of the routine. Cass had learned how to wipe Sam's memory with that nasty hypnosis trick somewhere. "And you know this how?"

"Listening to the old folks and my father. He was a kid when he lived up here. My grandparents wrote music, played a dozen instruments, got pretty famous there for a while. A lot of the people who lived here were talented. Only the ones who got out survived the evil. My grandmother hauled my father out when he was still young, but my grandfather stayed behind. He was laid to rest on the farm, along with Valdis's parents."

Valdis's parents were buried *on the farm*, not in the graveyard? Why the hell had no one told him? Because they were superstitious idiots and didn't want to come out here. Walker thought banging his head against boulders would be more useful than talking to the people in Hillvale.

"Sam!" he shouted again as they climbed high enough to see Bald Rock.

"Valdis is injured." Sam's voice called down, sounding sane and safe.

Walker stopped to take a breath and wing a prayer to the universe. "And you?"

"Bruised, embarrassed, but in one piece. There are snakes," she yelled back. "Be careful."

All right, keep breathing, he could deal with snakes. No guns. No mad women. No children. Just snakes and rocks and. . . *evil*. He could almost hear his mother's voice warning of the evils of vice whenever she caught him with alcohol or pot or flashing cash to impress. She'd chattered at him in Mandarin, smoked sage in his room, cut off his allowance, and invoked the memory of his father. And when he'd really been difficult, she'd planted bamboo outside his window and installed water fountains outside his door—to encourage *positive energy* flow. So, yeah, he understood superstition.

He'd still grown pot in his dorm room and played beer pong with everyone else, but he'd outgrown flashing cash to impress. Well, maybe his BMW was the adult method of impressing. So sue him. He wasn't evil, and he still didn't believe bamboo helped.

"You're going to leave it up to Sam and me to help Valdis down?" Walker asked Harvey, trying to keep his tone neutral.

Harvey mumbled a few curse words under his breath. Or maybe he was chanting spells.

Valdis chose that moment to begin a chant in her own voice. "Go now, go back to the hell you created," she shouted. "Take your greed and your pride, leave us this earth we were given."

Walker's hackles rose, and he increased his stride, pushing past Harvey.

"She's praying," Harvey offered. "She hears dead people, if you want to put it like that. It sounds as if she's talking to one she knows, but she never explains, so we can only guess."

"He shot me," Valdis shouted in a deeper, different voice.

Harvey cursed louder and followed after Walker, beating at the bushes to warn the snakes.

"I'm guessing she's not praying now?" Walker said wryly, leaping from rock to rock. For one insane moment, he wondered if Valdis might be channeling his father.

"She may have a broken ankle," Sam called back in the voice of sanity. Walker wafted another. . . normal. . . prayer to the powers that be.

"They have all the *dinero,* the easy job, and I live in a hovel!" It was Valdis speaking, but in a gruff voice with a slight accent.

"Juan," Harvey said in horror. "She's channeling Juan."

"Sam, ask who shot Juan," Walker called. Not that he believed Val was channeling ghosts so much as voices in her head, but he needed the distraction to keep his mind focused as he looked for safe places to put his boots.

He could hear her more clearly, so they were getting closer.

"Who shot you?" Sam asked, as if she were sitting in an interrogation room talking to a damned ghost.

"That freak Francois told his boyfriend," the sepulchral voice shouted furiously. "How could I know he was listening? It was a private conversation!"

"Did Francois shoot you?" Sam asked in a carefully neutral voice.

"He got the gun! No way that sleaze would have one. The Kennedys ought to pay!" the weird voice cried.

Walker's hackles rose even more. He was almost as reluctant as Harvey to climb higher. This was worse than watching some weird horror film. He expected a freakish puppet to twirl out of the darkness at any moment. But Sam was up there—he had to reach Sam.

"They get away with murder, they should pay," the voice continued angrily.

"Who did the Kennedys murder?" Sam asked in genuine puzzlement.

Walker climbed faster. Was Valdis a danger when she was hallucinating like this?

Hell, yes. He just had to pray she didn't have a gun. But she was strong, stronger than Sam.

Heart in throat, he lengthened his stride, while Harvey beat the shrubs with his stick.

CHAPTER 26

"Who killed you?" Sam asked again, not daring to touch Valdis. Her aunt sat on a precarious ledge that couldn't hold more than one. She swayed when she spoke.

Sam had fought past her terror of snakes to reach her aunt. Only now she was almost as afraid of Val's insanity as the snakes.

"The old fraud," Valdis muttered in the guttural tone Sam had to assume was Juan. What had Cass said? Juan's spirit was angry and would linger to speak when he was ready. Did she believe that out here on this eerie hillside, Valdis was channeling the security guard's spirit? Or was this more theater?

"What old fraud?" Sam asked, unable to do more than listen for ominous rattles and to Walker climbing closer. She didn't think she could even hand her aunt a bottle of water while she was in this state.

"I thought the boss did it," the spirit voice grumbled. "But *he* was there then. Maybe it was him all the time. *Killer*!"

Apparently spirits didn't remember names.

Valdis spoke more quietly and was starting to shudder. That

couldn't be good. What should she do now? Sam wished Cass was here.

Take her hands. Talk her down, a voice whispered in her head.

Sam freaked for half a second. Voices in her head were even worse than Val's spirit voices. But then, insanely, she recognized Cass, who had apparently occupied her head for nearly a week. And the advice made sense, so she wouldn't freak just yet.

Taking a deep breath to settle her rattled nerves, Sam stood and approached her aunt's higher position. "Aunt Valdis, I think it's time to come back. Cass says so." She reached up and caught a bony hand.

Valdis clasped her hand and began moaning again.

Tell her to let go, to let the spirit free. Wish him into the light.

Sam wasn't entirely certain the spirit belonged in the light, but lacking any better knowledge, she repeated Cass's refrain aloud and stood on her toes to take Valdis's other hand. Valdis continued swaying and shaking but fell silent, which was almost a welcome relief.

With relief, she felt Walker reach the rocky plateau. She wanted to fling herself into his arms and have hysterics, but she was no longer a helpless child. Clinging to rational, she repeated Cass's words aloud and tried to bring Valdis back, grateful when Walker added his strength by clasping her shoulder with his broad hand.

As if the contact provided a grounding wire, a shock wave jolted between her hands and her aunt's. Valdis slumped.

Before Valdis could slide off her perch, Walker was there, catching her, lowering her to the plateau they stood on. Her aunt wasn't a small woman, but Walker cradled her like a child.

To Sam's surprise, Harvey reluctantly climbed up to join them.

"She's been without food and water for twenty-four hours. She says her ankle is sprained." Sam dropped to her knees to push her aunt's ragged black skirt away from her ugly black boots. Valdis had apparently opened the laces on her right boot. Sam tried to pull it off, but the leg was swollen. "I need a knife to cut this off. She can't walk like this."

"We'll let the medics cut the boot off. They should be waiting by the time we get her down. I didn't call search and rescue, so we'll have to carry her ourselves." Walker shoved aside Valdis's lacy veil to reach her cloak ties.

Sam gasped at the sight of the red scar marring her aunt's elegantly-boned face. Apparently already aware of the disfigurement, Walker unfastened her heavy black cloak.

Harvey apparently grasped what he intended. He took the other end of the cloak, and the two men tugged on it, testing it for strength.

"It should work," Harvey said, handing his staff to Sam. The wood vibrated with an intensity deeper than hers, and she almost dropped it. "You'll have to lead the way down. Walking backward is not one of my skills, but I should be able to follow the stick."

They wanted *her* to lead the way? As she stood there, stunned and shivering, Walker hugged her and planted a kiss on the top of her head. "We've made enough noise to scare snakes into the next state. Just go slow."

"What if she wakes up?" Sam asked, worriedly studying her unconscious aunt.

"We could make a straitjacket of this thing," Walker suggested. "Bundle her up like a butterfly."

"Caterpillar cocoon," Harvey corrected grimly. "Or bat wings. With Valdis, that's our best bet."

Sam helped them lift her aunt and lay the cloak under her, then roll her back on it and wrap it around, with room to spare. Without the drama, Valdis seemed much smaller.

"Do you think she was really talking to Juan?" Sam asked, flashing her light down the jumble of rocks.

She might never overcome her dislike of snakes, but she'd learned people were more important than her fear. That had to be a step in the right direction.

"If it was Juan, he didn't tell us much," Harvey said disparagingly, lifting his end of the bundle. "Except that Francois has a boyfriend. Should have guessed that."

Walker snorted as he lifted his end. "The epaulets didn't give it away?"

"Bigot," Sam called back as she scrambled down the path. "Wearing costumes doesn't mean a person is gay."

"He's seeking attention," Harvey suggested. "That doesn't make him a killer."

"Francois was there when Carmel visited the vault," Walker argued. "If that's where she kept the gun, he knows about it and had access to it. And he would have had the keys to drive back up to the vault after Juan was shot."

Sam considered that but shook her head in disagreement. "If we are going to believe that was Juan talking through Valdis—and not just Valdis being dramatic—then it sounded as if the *boyfriend* was the killer, not Francois."

"The old fraud," Walker repeated. "And the reference to the boss *back then* makes me wonder if Valdis doesn't know something about my father's death as well."

"Valdis wasn't here *back then*," Sam reminded him. "So she would have had to have heard it from someone else."

"Like Juan," Harvey suggested dryly. "I'm not liking this backward thing. Give me a second so I can try holding her behind my back."

"Earlier, before you arrived, Valdis was channeling other voices." Sam waited as Harvey lowered his burden and turned around. "One voice said we should leave and let the evil die up there as he did. That voice also muttered about paint and demons burying us. The other sounded like a woman with maybe a Scandinavian accent. She said we would be fine and we should save the farm. It all got mixed up with art and crystals and Valdis telling me it was Susannah's fault that I'm not an artist."

"Hallucinating," Walker said. "She was up there too long. She's dehydrated."

"I wish I could have got some water in her, but I'm afraid she'll choke if I try now," Sam said worriedly.

"Believe me, it's much better to leave Valdis unconscious." Harvey strode with more assurance now that he was facing forward. "She has the strength of a pit bull and her bite doesn't let go."

Sam flashed her light up the hill to check on Walker. The muscles had tightened over his cheekbones, but she didn't think it was from the strain of carrying his burden. He had his grim cop look on. "You're about to tear Francois into shreds—just in case Valdis knows something, aren't you?"

"I dismissed him. I shouldn't have. He's lived up here as long as the Kennedys."

"Keep it moving, Sam," Harvey said. "You can admire your boyfriend once we get off this damned mountain."

Sam marched on, feeling somehow safer and a little triumphant that she had conquered her fear and maybe, sort of, accepted that her aunt spoke to people on another plane. This was not university material by any means. And maybe it was only the theatrics that made her believe. But if Valdis had given Walker a clue that could lead him to his father's killer. . . She didn't care how it came about.

The ambulance was waiting on the cemetery road, as was half the town, it seemed. Men met them at the bottom of the path to take Valdis and carry her out to the road. It took four, because she started to struggle.

Harvey reclaimed his staff and disappeared into the woods without speaking to anyone. Walker draped his arm over Sam's shoulders and nuzzled her ear. "I'm thinking LA about now."

"Nope," she said. "It's too far and we're too tired and I want to know what happens."

"Like a damned soap opera," he concluded. "That's what really bites about the investigation business. You can't just put it down and walk away."

"My mind is racing, but the rest of me is ready to crash. And now I'm wondering if I should have said anything in front of Harvey. We really don't know much about him—except apparently his grandparents were part of the commune." Sam let Walker lead her through the crowd of concerned citizens. Cass wasn't here. Had she put herself into another trance?

She stopped and cornered Amber. "I heard Cass in my head. Can someone check on her?"

Concerned, the tarot reader nodded, grabbed Tullah, and the two hurried down the path to Cass's. That and the ambulance departing broke up the crowd.

"I probably should have gone with Valdis," Sam said anxiously.

"The medics will work better without you crowding them. I'd take you down in the morning, but I have to report to the office." He hugged her again.

"We'll worry about it then," she agreed, too tired to argue.

She probably should have argued when Walker took her home and came inside without asking, but she didn't, and that wasn't because she was too tired. Walker's arms around her were the strength she didn't have, his kiss was the energy boost she needed. And when she wrapped her legs around his hips, he carried her straight to bed, where they both belonged.

~

Morning, June 23

THE NEXT DAY, WALKER WAS RELIEVED THAT SAM DECIDED TO HELP DINAH with the breakfast rush instead of driving into town with him to check on a crazy woman she barely knew.

"You'll hear more if you stay here," he told her, pulling on his wrinkled clothes again. He'd have to think about carrying a suitcase in his trunk at this rate. "Ask around about Francois."

"And maybe I can ask about crystals and art a bit." She was still naked after their shower, running a dryer over her wet hair.

Walker soaked up the sight and wondered how hard it would be to leave her here when his job was over. Pretty damned hard, he feared. He wanted to know everything about this witchy woman. He was thinking it might take a lifetime though, and neither of them had an inclination for that.

"You could ask Daisy where she gets the shiny bits she uses on her statues," Walker agreed, catching a glimpse of the stone butterfly reflecting sunlight from the windows. "I can't see how they have anything to do with anything, but if Valdis was speaking from some past memory, it must be a strong one."

"That's how I'd like to think about it—she's calling up voices from her past. But that bit about Francois was pretty freaky. How will you go about finding his *boyfriend* and questioning him?"

"Carefully," Walker admitted. "He's been with the Kennedys forever. I don't know how he could have hidden a lover for long in this town, though."

"Well, Valdis could have got the relationship wrong. It's hard telling what she's seeing or hearing. *Old Fraud* doesn't tell us much. A lot of old people here, and I'm guessing half of them are charlatans." After pinning her hair in a stack on top of her head, Sam shimmied into her underwear.

Walker had to turn away to fasten his belt or he'd never get out of there. "The only legal fraud I know would have been Geoff Kennedy, and he's dead. I need to go over the attorney general's old report and run the names of his cohorts through my files to see if anything matches. Nothing leaped out at me in the first read-through."

"They would have all been eighteen or twenty years younger than they are now. Women could have married and changed their names. People who were merely assistants back then could be bigwigs now. Maybe their names weren't even in the report."

He couldn't resist kissing her again. "I'll have intrepid Sofia look up the names of the lower echelons at the bank and mortgage company back then."

She kissed him with enthusiasm, then stepped away so she could finish dressing. "She may have to hack computers. That doesn't sound like anything that would be public."

"Payroll reports, human resources, employment agencies, there are always back doors if you know the right people. If we can find evidence that someone from back then was up here the night Juan died, I can have a judge subpoena the company files— although convincing them Juan's case involves *old fraud* should be entertaining. I need to drive down and check in at the office. Should I drop you off in town?"

She hesitated, then shook her head. A few recalcitrant strands of platinum hair fell and caressed her elegant cheekbones. "I want to walk down the lane. I haven't met everyone here, and the ghost house fascinates me."

Walker felt his insides grind, but he nodded knowingly. "You're planning on staying here, aren't you?"

"Maybe. The ghost house has this beautiful garden. . . But I don't know what I want yet." Her sapphire eyes begged him to understand.

And he did, sort of. He understood they were two very different people, with different life experiences, different needs. He brushed aside the dangling curl and kissed her cheek. "See you when I see you then."

He skipped Dinah's and drove down the mountain to change clothes and check in for roll call. The routine was starting to irritate, but he needed legal power to question people like the Kennedys. His usual work didn't include active criminal investigations, until he uncovered a crime. Then he handed the case over to the authorities. He was enjoying having the ability to follow through on the cases, but he disliked the bureaucracy. Or maybe he just disliked not being his own boss.

In a fresh uniform, Walker reported in at the office and went over the files. The blood analysis on Xavier was still incomplete, although the hospital's staff had concluded an overdose of cocaine. Not knowing Xavier's drug of choice, he couldn't reach a conclusion.

The ballistics report on the gun from the Kennedy vault had proven it was the weapon used on Juan. Muttering a curse under his breath, Walker looked over the fingerprint report again—too many smudges and attempts to wipe it clean. Traces that matched those in Carmel's bedroom, partials from Francois, but also some identified from Geoffrey Kennedy's old files, and even one from a maid who had probably picked it up to dust under it. It was practically a public gun.

He read through the homicide team's notes. Francois claimed he'd never touched the gun. He'd lied, since they'd found a partial of his prints on it.

Walker needed more information on the Kennedys' driver, as well as names of people who'd worked with Geoff Kennedy, the bank, and the mortgage company from twenty years ago—although that wasn't part of the sheriff's investigation.

He gave the detective a head's up about Francois, then called Sofia to start digging into mortgage and bank employees from twenty years ago. He was getting a jumpy feeling that he was leaving Sam alone too long.

No one had attempted to harm Sam or Valdis yet, but Walker had a nasty fear that their land had a part in whatever was happening up there. Maybe that's what Valdis was ranting about—she believed that land ownership was somehow dangerous.

Nah, that was too rational for the old witch.

He stopped at the Baskerville hospital where both Xavier and Valdis were patients.

As he drove his official vehicle into the lot and hunted a parking space, he noted Alan Gump of the garish blond hair and bespoke suits climbing into a Lamborghini. Real estate moguls had to stand out in a crowd, Walker supposed, but flashing that much wealth in a district predominantly occupied by people barely scraping a living seemed. . . offensive.

He rolled his eyes. That was his mother's voice in his head, nattering about the evils of flashing wealth to impress. He was spending too much time with the tree-hugging Lucys.

Walker checked on Xavier first, but he'd been moved to a drug rehab facility in Monterey. Damn.

He would compile a list of questions and see if one of his men could get in to see the old goat.

Then he stopped in to visit Valdis. She was hooked up to an IV and despite the scar, looking almost healthy without the grim black clothing. Tullah, the tall, elegant, thrift shop owner, and Amber, the tarot reader, were already there, shaking out clean dresses—all black—apparently for Valdis to choose from. Walker grimaced and almost turned around rather than face a room full of Lucys.

But he gritted his teeth and entered. All three women looked at him as if they were ready for him to be gone before he even spoke a word.

After exchanging pleasantries and learning that Valdis would be released soon and had a ride home, Walker attempted to at least get in one formal question. "How much do any of you know about Francois?"

"He's a slimy creep who would sell his soul for cash or drugs," Tullah said without hesitation. "But only if it meant he didn't have to lift a hand or do more than exist."

Walker quirked an eyebrow. "Not many people turn over cash or drugs for nothing."

Looking like a warm cuddly teddy bear, Amber snapped a dress with unusual ferocity to shake out wrinkles. She began folding it away, leaving a trailing long skirt of black gauze across the bed. "She means he's a snitch," she said in disdain. "Give him a toke, and he'll tell you anything."

Valdis picked anxiously at the black gauze and didn't look him in the eyes. "He spies for Carmel," she whispered. "He worships her."

"But he wouldn't kill for her?" Walker asked, ugly suspicion rising.

All three women looked uncertain.

Oh, crap. Would Carmel order a security guard killed? Why?

CHAPTER 27

MORNING, JUNE 23

DESPITE THE LINGERING SMELL OF ASHES, SAM HAPPILY TRANSPLANTED salvia and sage from the ghost garden to a sunny spot beside the town hall. The two-story wooden building was at the end of the row of shops. The town could easily expand the land around it into a park, if her Uncle Montgomery gave up the driveway to his private parking spot in the back. She envisioned benches and a fountain—tile or stone? —and pebble paths surrounding beds of flowers that bloomed all year around.

She thought best with her hands in dirt. If she stayed here, could she obtain a grant to study the earthquake fault and how it might affect the aquifer? Having grown up on a farm in a small rural area, she didn't miss the city lights. Although *fitting in* had always been a problem for her. She knew where she belonged at the university. Here. . . She had no idea where she stood.

She might miss a social life once Walker returned to LA. She didn't want to think like that. She had no claim on Walker. That had been understood from the first.

She would miss Walker reassuring her with a shoulder squeeze when she needed an extra zap of strength. Admittedly, his protective streak could use a good trim, but he wasn't the type of macho man who shoved her aside and told her he'd do whatever needed doing. He just offered to be there if she needed him. She felt as if he'd cut open the cocoon binding her so she could spread her wings and fly anywhere she liked.

Like the tarot card Amber had shown her—the strings tying her up had been snipped. Freedom to choose her own road was scary.

She knew Walker was among the walking wounded, that he had issues over his son's death and needed to resolve his father's murder before he could move forward. And even knowing it meant he would be leaving her, she wanted to help him solve the case—as he'd helped her when she thought she'd lost her mind.

Voices rose inside the town hall. She tried not to eavesdrop. It was so peaceful here, marking out a garden, planning the colors and sizes of the flowers she needed.

"Keep your mother away," Mariah shouted inside.

Mariah didn't normally shout. Sam frowned.

"That's impossible," a low male voice rumbled. The mayor? "She's responsible for the well-being of everyone in this damned town."

"She's responsible for *destroying* all this! She's been here too long, Monty. The demons are sucking her dry. She retaliates by feeding on your energy and Kurt's and everyone else's that she encounters. Keep her healthy, happy, and anywhere but here."

"And you know all this because your little nets are clean?" the mayor asked scornfully. "Don't be ridiculous. You'd be out of work in that case."

"No," Mariah said wearily. "The place is possessed by centuries of souls that can't pass on. You want a Valley of Death, call it Hillvale. Go look at your uncle's art sometime, really look at it. I know you won't believe that she's draining you and Kurt, but study your uncle. Does he look healthy?"

Sam quietly set her tools in her garden basket and stood up.

Daisy had been *protecting the art.* Dinah's mural could possibly be painted by one of the most brilliant artists of her era, and it resembled another in the lodge's dining room. Valdis had talked about demons and *paint*. Mariah was fairly rational and even she was talking about looking at the art. Maybe it was time to do so.

Sam returned the garden tools to Cass's shed and went to her studio to look up the phone number for the San Francisco art gallery where Jade had sold her work. Sam had always assumed the gallery was called Malcolm Magic after Lucinda Malcolm, the pseudonymous artist. It specialized in surreal fantasy but often included more realistic styles with hidden fantasy elements that Jade had found fascinating. Sam couldn't see enough of the mural on Dinah's wall to find hidden elements, but the style had resembled the art Jade had admired.

She dialed the old landline phone with trepidation, but it rang appropriately. Good to know it still worked. The gallery receptionist put her on hold, and a moment later, Elaine Lee answered.

"Samantha! How delightful to hear from you. When are you coming to visit?" Elaine spoke with a slight Cantonese accent, although Sam was fairly certain she'd lived in San Francisco most of her life.

"Actually, I'm in California now," Sam told her. "I'm not sure I'm ready to drive in the city, but I've found a painting out here in the middle of nowhere that made me think of you."

"Anything that makes you think of me is good," Elaine chirruped. "I do *hope* it's good. Where are you?"

"Hillvale." Sam waited. As she feared, the normally chatty Elaine went silent.

"Hillvale?" she asked after a moment, with a degree of hesitation. "Why are you there?"

So even Elaine had known some part of her story—layers within layers to uncover.

"It's a long story. I'd love to tell you sometime," Sam said, not explaining. "I'm kind of caught up in something and can't get away. But I've found a mural that someone tells me could have been painted by Lucinda Malcolm, and I thought you might be interested."

It wasn't as if Elaine could sell a mural. She would have no real reason to come up here. But Sam had hoped curiosity would drive her —and she might learn a little more about her birth parents.

"Lucinda lived in Hillvale for a time," Elaine acknowledged. "Have you found any more of her work?"

"I'm no expert," Sam warned. "I saw a piece resembling the mural hanging at the lodge. And one of the locals mentioned a cache of art hidden up the mountain." That was almost pure fabrication. Daisy could have been *time-walking* when she saw art. But instinct demanded that she bring someone up here who understood more about painting than she did.

Elaine stayed silent long enough to indicate a lack of enthusiasm. "Hillvale isn't healthy for artists," she finally said.

"Did my birth mother tell you that?" Sam asked, baiting the hook. She wished she could see Elaine's expression through the phone, but the resignation in her voice sufficed.

"Jade feared this day would come," Elaine said with a sigh, not admitting anything. "Fine. I'll take a look at my calendar and get back to you. Tell me how to reach you."

Sam gave her the studio's phone number and the one at the café. "I'll give you my cell too, but it won't reach me unless I'm off the mountain."

"I do wish you'd come down here, Sam," Elaine said anxiously. "I could meet you in Santa Cruz or somewhere if you don't want to try city driving."

"It's all right, Elaine. I'm hearing the stories I need to hear. Keep in mind, I'm a scientist, not an artist. Wolf would be proud of me."

Elaine's voice brightened. "That's true. I have a gallery opening this weekend, but I'll get back to you as soon as I clear a place in my schedule. Just be careful!"

After reassuring her mother's friend, Sam changed clothes, got in her Subaru, and headed for the lodge. The car shouldn't sit idle for too long, she reasoned. Now that she had her license back, she didn't need to walk everywhere—although the exercise certainly allowed her to eat as much of Dinah's wonderful food as she liked.

Once she parked at the lodge, she wasn't entirely certain what approach she should take. Lance wasn't likely to be hanging around the computer room, and he was the one she really wanted to see.

The sheriff's car was there, pursuing the ongoing investigations, so she assumed she couldn't be in too much danger. She really didn't want to talk to any officialdom except Walker though. She parked behind the lodge, near the small building she'd been told Lance used for his studio.

Deciding she'd use Elaine as her excuse for stopping by, she walked up to the studio's open door as if the Kennedys really were her family and she belonged here.

Lance looked up from his work when Sam knocked on the door frame. Remembering Mariah's warning, she studied him. He'd pulled his graying blond hair back in a piece of string at his nape. He had the same Viking bone structure as his sister. His jutting cheekbones and square jaw were just more masculine. If she did not mistake, his color was healthier today. He was tall and lanky and not muscular by any means, but he didn't look like a weak man.

"Samantha," he acknowledged with a nod, cleaning off his brush. "You have been very much a topic of conversation lately."

Huh, she didn't even need an excuse to stop in.

"Have I? Should I apologize?" She entered even though he hadn't invited her. She was used to the absent-mindedness of her adopted parents. She stopped to examine a collection of small portraits grouped on one wall.

"No, not at all. I gather my nephews are somewhat bemused at learning their father wasn't a model of good behavior, but he died when they were young. There was no reason to enlighten them." He pointed at the photo-sized portraits she was admiring. "What do you think? I understand you were raised by professional artists."

"That doesn't mean I understand art," she protested. "I'm just like everyone else, admiring for personal reasons and not necessarily for the right ones. You've captured likenesses extremely well as far as I can see. In this one, Mariah shines almost as brightly as the crystals she hangs in her nets. But in this one, Kurt is looking a little tired."

She studied another of a gorgeous blond woman wearing what appeared to be a *Hello, Dolly* type of costume. The face looked familiar but she couldn't quite place it. "Who is this?"

Cleaning his brush, he leaned over her shoulder. "Valerie. Isn't she gorgeous? I had to do that from memory. While she's on stage, I'm too enthralled to even sketch. Her voice is magnificent."

"Valerie? *Valdis*? She was on stage?" That explained the carrying voice!

"That was a long time ago. She's extremely talented, but she retreated from the public eye after her. . . accident." He put his brush back in a mason jar holder.

Guessing he wouldn't tell the story, Sam moved on to the next portrait. "Who is this person with the red eyes?"

"Juan," he said curtly, reaching over her shoulder to take down the image. "Something in the paint erodes the color after a while. I've been experimenting with the formulas used in the seventies, but I cannot achieve their clarity. Although I do recollect others developing the unfortunate redness, so perhaps the crystals they used were impure."

"Crystals?" Sam studied the rest of the miniature portraits. He did have a gift for capturing a likeness, although she couldn't see much personality in the people represented. Monty and Kurt could have been stone statues for all the life they exhibited. She was surprised to find Dinah in the collection. She didn't think Lance went to the café often. And was that Valdis again—without the scar and looking much, much younger?

"The formula included grinding crystals into whatever media they used for coloration. I've experimented with both their formulas and my own, but every so often, they still deteriorate." He studied Juan's image, shrugged, and added it to a stack turned to the wall.

"Perhaps Juan's family would like the painting?" Sam suggested. "Can you blot out the red?"

He hovered uncertainly over the stack of canvas turned to the wall. "Juan was an unhappy man. When they were younger, my nephews had to buy his silence with their allowances when he caught them out past their curfew, until they started telling their mother rather than hand over the money. Thought that rather smart of them. So I did the same when he tried to blackmail me over a trifling incident. Not a very bright fellow. Do you really think his family would like the portrait?"

Sam remembered her one encounter with the surly security guard. He hadn't seemed to be a bad man, but unhappy might describe him. Was that what Valdis had channeled—Juan's unhappiness that he was poor and the Kennedys were rich? Her aunt could have picked up on that while Juan was still alive.

"I think they'd like it," she said, keeping her voice light so as not to encourage him if he didn't want to do it. "Families always think the best of their relations."

"I'll cover the red with a dab of tempera. That seems to limit the corrosion. Maybe Monty will take it to the family for me."

He finally took the time to study her. "You are more interesting than the Kennedy side of the family. You resemble the Ingerssons. Valerie has those same delicate cheekbones."

Ridiculously pleased that he'd noticed a family resemblance, Sam brushed at her cheek. She hadn't realized anyone knew of her relation to Valdis. "My parents tended to paint me as square blocks or eagles or other weirdnesses, so I don't see myself as others do."

He nodded understanding and began rummaging through a stack of paintings. "The Ingerssons and their tribe eventually gave up portraits, probably due to the paint corrosion. But the artwork that survived is quite distinctive."

He pulled out a faded canvas and held it in the sunlight. The subject appeared to be artists painting other artists, a vain conceit, but Sam recognized her own face in that of the woman being painted. She touched the woman's wild mane of hair. "My grandmother?"

He nodded and pointed at one of the artists in front of an easel. The man's face was turned away. Only his blond haystack of curls was visible. "Your grandfather."

"Well, I see how I came by the unruly hair," she said, forcing a lightness she didn't feel. How did he know about her family? "You didn't paint this, did you?"

"No, this was done before Valerie was born. She's a little younger than I am, so I'd say this work is over fifty years old, just before your grandfather's art became famous and brought notoriety to the commune. It's not signed, but Valerie says it looks like her mother's style. They were probably standing in front of mirrors so she could capture both of them at work. It used to hang in the lobby but Carmel had it taken down."

"This paint didn't corrode," Sam noted with interest.

"But it faded, so they were experimenting with different media even then. We can learn so much from examining the work of the masters." He set the oil back in the stack.

Sam wouldn't call her grandparents masters if that was an example, but she nodded agreement anyway. "I noticed a painting in the dining room that resembles the mural in the diner. Was that done back then?"

He frowned. "Given its condition, most likely, although it appears a good deal of paint was applied in some attempt to repair it. I never met most of the people the mural represents, so I can't say if they're a good likeness."

"Perhaps the lodge's canvas just needs a good cleaning, like the one at Dinah's. Do you think anyone would mind if I took a look at it?" Sam wasn't certain if she was learning anything valuable, but talking to Lance had been interesting. She'd have to ask Elaine about using crystals in paint.

"Not at all." He waved vaguely in the direction of the lodge. "Go before the lunch hordes descend, and no one will know you're there."

Feeling as if she'd been dismissed, Sam thanked him for his time and headed for the lodge. She hadn't done a study of the Santa Cruz mountains, but along an oceanic fault, she assumed she would find sandstone and granite. If Daisy was finding *crystals* for her sculptures, and artists were grinding them into paint, she would guess there was some form of quartz diorite along this fault. She wasn't a geologist, but she liked rocks. Diorite polished up nicely and made pretty kitchen counters. It was too hard for detailed carving, but she supposed it could be ground to add sparkle.

The dining room was empty. The resort's business hadn't picked up since the fire. She'd hate to see the town dry up and blow away if the tourists didn't come back. But she had ideas bubbling of how they could work with the burn site—if her step-grandmother would listen. Except Mariah wanted to keep Carmel away—odd.

Sam found the painting she'd noticed the one night she'd eaten at the lodge restaurant. It was too dark to really see it. Looking around, deciding there was no one to notice, she lifted the frame from the hook and carried it to a window. The porch overhang prevented too much sun from entering, but the light by the window was brighter.

She had seen Lucinda Malcolm's work. This wasn't it. She'd hoped it might be a valuable piece the Kennedys could sell to help cover expenses until the burn site was restored. But this was just what Lance had said—a repaired oil, probably from half a century ago. It was another trite conceit—the artist portraying himself and his friends as the disciples at the Last Supper. The Jesus figure in the center was sitting behind a counter that looked like Dinah's and resembled the curly-haired man Lance had identified as her grandfather, although his hair was considerably longer in this work.

Anyone who portrayed himself as the Savior had to be an arrogant prick. She assumed his *disciples* were other members of the commune. They were all very young. Disappointed, she returned it to the wall.

Turning around, she almost pressed her nose into Alan Gump's expensive vest. Off-balance, she stepped back and her spine hit the wall. "Hasn't anyone taught you about personal space?" she asked irritably.

There was something about the resort that made her say things she shouldn't.

The bulky man shrugged and stepped aside enough that she could sidle past him. "I was just trying to see what you saw in that old piece of junk."

"Bullies intimidate by occupying personal space," she continued, easing toward the door. "It's not a good policy around people who carry weapons."

Who in hell was this talking? She didn't carry weapons. Sam wanted to bat her ear to see if Cass was inside her head again. But she didn't sense Cass. Alan Gump just turned her into a porcupine for some reason. Maybe this was why the Lucys didn't talk to him.

Ignoring her comment, he continued studying the painting. "Did you recognize anyone in this?"

Sam put a few tables and chairs between them. "Considering the painting is over half a century old, hardly."

"I was told they were a cult. This seems to prove it." He turned his back on the artwork to regard her. "The Kennedys are too polite to say so, but they don't want you up here. I can set you up with a fine place in Frisco. Pretty girl like you shouldn't be wasting her time with these nuts."

Appalled at the implication, Sam retorted, "Rich sexists like you don't belong anywhere." She swung on her heel and marched out.

She felt as if she'd just left a load of filth behind, but she was more

worried about the words spouting from her mouth—as if they weren't
her own.

CHAPTER 28

LATE MORNING, JUNE 23

IN SEARCH OF FRANCOIS, WALKER ENCOUNTERED SAM EMERGING FROM the lodge looking pale and angry. His insides lurched dangerously in a way he should ignore but couldn't. Since she wasn't looking his way, he stepped into her path.

Her fingers were clenched in balls, and she stared at him blankly for half a second before visibly relaxing.

"Mariah is right. I should carry my staff everywhere." She practically spat the words.

"Want to talk about it or go find the stick and whop someone first?" he asked. Until she explained, he didn't know whether he ought to be amused or angry. He knew better than to say she looked beautiful when she was mad.

"Neither," she decided. She shoved her recalcitrant hair back from her face and finally smiled up at him, nearly melting him on the spot. "I'll carry the stick from now on. How's your day going?"

"Valdis is looking good. Her Lucys practically threw me out of her room, but not without implicating Francois and maybe Carmel in any and all dastardly deeds. Since they're Lucys, I take their warnings with blocks of salt. Xavier has been transferred to rehab, where he's not currently accessible. And your day?" He leaned against her Subaru, crossed his arms, and waited. Communication was supposed to be a two-way street.

She didn't answer immediately, as if deciding what to share. "I've been busy. You might want to talk to Lance, though. He claims Juan was in the habit of blackmailing people. So maybe Valdis was on to something when she channeled him—although again, she gave it a Lucy twist to implicate the Kennedys. I need to help Dinah with the lunch rush, but if you have time, stop by later, and I'll try to catch you up." She kissed his cheek and reached around him for her door handle.

The casual familiarity gave him a thrill, making him feel as if it might be possible to more than exist someday. Walker caught Sam's long hair, tilted her head back, and planted a more satisfactory kiss on her mouth. She responded with enough electricity to momentarily gratify him.

"See you after dinner, then. I can't ignore Lucy warnings entirely, so I'm off to interrogate Francois. Wish me luck."

"Carry a big stick," she warned. "This place is infested with termites."

Wondering what that meant, Walker let her go. He wanted to believe that Sam was sane and could take care of herself, that he didn't have to fight any battles for her or with her. He'd never realized how his love for mentally crippled Tess and his need to help her had been an anchor tying him down, despite doctors telling him there was nothing he could do.

Before he could figure out the rest of his life, he had to find out who had killed his father. He had the sneaking suspicion that Juan's death was in some way related to the discovery of his father's corpse, although that made sense more in his mind than on paper.

Juan had been blackmailing people? *Damn.* That opened whole new avenues.

He'd already checked and knew the Kennedy Escalade was parked in the reserved spot. He'd never bothered to learn where Francois hung out when he wasn't driving. Since the homicide team was here, he tracked them to a meeting room.

"Have you interviewed the chauffeur yet today?" he asked after providing a report on what he'd learned from the Lucys about Francois being a snitch and possibly a stoner.

"He's on the list," the detective in charge said. "But we have no motive. We were hoping something would turn up before we questioned him."

"Loyalty to an employer is weak. But if he likes easy money and drugs, there's potential," Walker said. "And if Juan was in the habit of blackmailing people, what are the chances he might have had something on Francois?"

"Shooting someone in the back might be the MO of a slacker like Francois," the detective admitted.

But would Francois hit a man over the head with a shovel? Or could they have two murderers on the loose? Walker shifted his shoulders uneasily inside his shirt as he waited.

Kurt returned with the officer sent to find Francois. Kurt nodded at Walker but spoke to the detective in charge. "Francois had some kind of breakdown last night. We had him taken to the city for evaluation. My secretary can give you the name and the number for the facility. I'm sorry. I didn't know you'd need him for further questioning. He's an old family retainer, and we treat him like one of us."

"What kind of breakdown?" the detective asked impatiently.

Kurt looked uncomfortable. "The lodge has a reputation for being haunted. I'd rather you didn't carry this further than this room." He waited expectantly. When no one responded, he continued, "Francois began screaming Juan's ghost was haunting him. He grabbed the keys to the car, but I didn't think he was in any condition to be driving. When I took the keys away, he had a. . . meltdown. He began babbling about ghosts and fires and then rambled about how he'd only wanted to help us. He wasn't coherent."

"Does he do drugs?" the detective asked curtly, making notes.

Again, Kurt hesitated, before giving a brief nod. "I think so, although probably just pot and only when he isn't driving."

Walker hid a grimace and accompanied Kurt out when he was done.

"That didn't go well, did it?" Kurt muttered as he stalked back toward his office. "But that old man wouldn't hurt a soul."

"Even out of loyalty to your family?" Walker asked.

"Shit." Kurt halted and stared at one of the more modern artworks on the corridor wall. "But my mother isn't here. He's loyal to her, not any of us."

"But the resort represents her. If he suspected someone was a danger to the resort?"

"Like Juan? Juan was our head security guy. No, that doesn't make sense either. The only thing that makes sense is that everyone up here goes crazy," Kurt muttered bitterly.

"I think that's what the Lucys are saying," Walker said in amusement. "But the cover-up could go further back than Juan. Was Francois here when your father died?"

Kurt glared at him. "You mean when *your* father was killed? Francois would have been here, yes. He's the son of a cook my family employed in the city. He was unambitious then, and he hasn't improved with age. But he can drive a car, and he'll do anything for my mother. I doubt that even she could persuade him to dirty his hands and lift a weapon heavy enough to crack a skull."

Walker nodded agreement. "Yeah, he sounds like a victim more than someone who takes action. You might want to send a lawyer to be with him when they question him."

Running his hand through his hair, Kurt nodded. "Thanks. That's something I can do."

Walker shook hands and walked off. Kurt Kennedy was a man who liked tight control over all aspects of his life. A murder investigation on his doorstep had to be driving him around the bend. . . right along with the Lucys, he thought in amusement.

Sam was right. They needed a better definition of crazy.

~

MIDDAY, JUNE 23

"THEY'RE BRINGING VALDIS HOME," MARIAH MURMURED AS SHE TIED ON her apron and passed Sam behind the counter. "She and Daisy will be staying with Cass tonight so they can be sure she's stable. Don't spread the word yet."

Sam thought she ought to ask why not, but sometimes it was safer to see for herself. Around here, everything was subject to interpretation.

Alan Gump came in for lunch with a group of men in business suits. It seemed odd not to see Xavier's green jacket in the crowd, but Sam did as the others had warned her earlier and didn't speak to the asshat.

The burly real estate mogul in his designer suit behaved as if she didn't exist, and that was fine too. Bringing the group their drinks, she heard them talk of access roads and engineers. She really needed to see that trust fund document Walker claimed existed. She should have the lawyer handling her parents' estate look at it.

Maybe she ought to have a will drawn up first.

Where had that stray thought come from?

Feeling restless and uneasy, fearing Hillvale might be starting to get to her, Sam hurriedly cleaned up the counter and tables after the lunch rush. "I want to talk to Cass about her roses," she told Dinah as she tugged off her apron.

"Take some of those sandwiches with you," Dinah called. "You may need to feed that man of yours."

Her man? Sam smiled and took the sandwiches, but the notion of having a man of her own—was a little unsettling. Of course, she was in a nervous mood anyway. She conjured up a memory of Walker's bronze visage, wicked smile, and cowboy hat, and felt a warm rush that steadied her.

By the time she put the food in the studio refrigerator, showered, and grabbed her walking stick, Mariah was already sitting with Cass and Valdis on the Victorian front porch. Valdis had her bandaged foot propped on a cushioned wicker stool with an ice pack on it.

"Where's Daisy?" Sam took the seat on a wicker settee Cass indicated and accepted a glass of whatever they were drinking—spiked punch from the taste of it. She could be generous and call it sangria since orange slices were involved.

"She's back at the farm, making more lamassu." Valdis didn't seem any worse for her ordeal. The black gown she wore looked as if it belonged in a Spanish Doña painting—all black embroidery and heavy rustling damask. She'd thrown her veil off her face so she could sip from her glass. All the black made her fair complexion even paler and the scar on her jaw more livid.

Sam searched for some sign of the beautiful woman from Lance's portrait, but Valdis had done all she could to erase her past, even using dark eye make-up to enhance the paleness of her fair skin. After the prior night's ranting, though, she seemed almost normal.

"How are you feeling?" Sam asked.

"I'm fine, thank you," Valdis said politely. "How did you find me? I thought my time had come."

"Harvey's walking stick." She ought to feel like an idiot admitting that, but oddly, a dowsing rod that found people made insane sense here. "It would have been a lot easier if I'd been told earlier that your parents weren't in the cemetery."

Mariah looked surprised. Cass didn't.

Valdis shrugged. "Their spirits belonged in the land they polluted. Their mortal remains are irrelevant. They were both cremated and their ashes scattered on Bald Rock."

"It's no matter," Cass said, passing a tray of shortbread cookies. "What matters is who else knows that Sam is an Ingersson? The name alone makes you a threat to the Nulls."

"I wish everyone would quit calling them that," Sam said irritably, probably because she shivered at the perceived threat. "Name calling does not lead to rational discussion."

"Sorry, a bad habit, you're correct. But the land destroyed us before and will do so again, unless we exercise caution." Cass rocked in a golden Bentwood rocker piled with red pillows.

"Explain why being an Ingersson is a bad thing?" Mariah asked from her seat on the steps. She worked one of her nets as they talked.

Valdis remained silent. Cass looked to Sam and asked, "You know, don't you? That nosy cop of yours knows everything."

"If Walker knew everything, he'd go back to LA. I keep telling you that secrets can only hurt. If we'd known the Ingersson graves were on the mountain instead of in the cemetery, we could have found Valdis sooner." Sam bit into her shortbread in hopes it would sweeten her disposition.

"So all of you know something I don't?" Mariah complained.

"You're a fine one to talk. How long have you and my mayoral uncle been holding secret meetings?"

The shade of an old pine tree hid Mariah's color, but Sam thought heat darkened her friend's brown skin.

"Monty isn't like Kurt," Mariah protested. "He may not believe in ghosts, but he accepts that I can send them on."

"Like the Grim Reaper?" Sam asked, just because.

Mariah snorted and took a sip of her punch. "A scythe would be wonderful. I could try carrying one if it would help. But no, I just see ectoplasm and have the ability to zap it beyond the veil. And you're diverting the subject."

Ectoplasm? Sam tried to piece that into the world as she knew it and failed.

"If Mariah is consorting with the enemy, it's better you don't tell her everything just yet," Cass warned. "Too many people died last time. I don't think I can bear to lose more."

Last time—as in twenty-five years ago when the nephew Cass had raised as her son had died, along with the Ingerssons. And the Ingersson daughters had fled Hillvale and not returned. But now Valdis and Susannah's daughter were back—and it was all about the land somehow. Evil and ghosts and even water rights and fire all led back to the land.

"I don't think Monty and Kurt are like their father," Sam said tentatively, trying to sound Cass out. "Things have changed."

"They consort with Evil," Valdis chanted in her banshee voice. "It infects the land and the people who dwell on it."

"Short of an earthquake, I don't think you can eliminate the mountain," Sam said gently. "Are you saying the farm contains toxic chemicals?"

Cass gave a curt laugh. "That's one way of looking at it, I suppose. Who knows what the crazies mixed into their paints and hallucinogens? And sanitary conditions weren't the best. They used chemicals on the marijuana they grew. If it makes you feel better to call it pollution, go ahead."

"Greed," Valdis intoned. "Greed infects the land. Greed and ambition and unhealthy desires."

Sam exchanged glances with Mariah and refrained from snickering. Did Valdis even know what unhealthy desire was?

Then she sobered. If Valdis once had a real life in the theater, she had once been young and alive and extremely talented, if Lance was to be believed. What had brought her back here?

CHAPTER 29

AFTERNOON, JUNE 23

WALKER WAS PATROLLING THE ROADS, BORING HIMSELF BY LOOKING FOR DUIs and speeders, when his personal cell rang. He was far enough down the mountain for reception, so he pulled over and answered.

"I may have found something, boss," Sofia said.

"I'll be off duty early. Just shoot me an email," he advised. Being a deputy might be the world's dullest job, but he wouldn't take the county's money and shirk his tasks for his own personal gain.

"It's got to do with now as well as then," Sofia said, sounding excited. "You told me to see if anybody from eighteen or twenty years ago is still in Hillvale now, besides the ones you know about."

Walker picked up his tablet and opened his notes. Getting Sofia off the phone would be faster if he listened. "Go ahead. I'm ready."

"He doesn't live there," she warned. "I'll email you the file, but I thought you ought to know that an Alan Gump worked in the development department of Commercial Contracting before they went belly-up with the dissolution of the Kennedy mortgage company eighteen years ago."

"Gump, the real estate guy working with the Kennedys now?" Walker opened his notes, scanning the file on the condo developer.

"One and the same. He was prettier when he was younger," Sofia said with a chuckle. "I'm comparing the old brochure with his current website. Definitely same guy, although that green coat they're all wearing back then doesn't do him any favors."

Green coat? Why did that ring bells?

"Have Dave run a financial analysis of Gump and his condo company and look for connections to the bankrupt contractor. It could be nothing. He would have been a junior employee back then. That doesn't mean he had any access to Hillvale at the time."

"He was in Hillvale all right," Sofia said. "He was photogenic, so they must have hauled him up for the condo brochure. It shows him in a group of smiling faces with Geoff Kennedy in front of the lodge. And one more thing—"

Walker waited for the bombshell she'd saved for last.

"There's a Menendez listed on Commercial's board in the old brochure. I think Dave already sent you their file. I've scanned the brochure into it."

He'd investigated the Menendez clan inside and out. They were mostly prosperous and scattered around the country. The only one of the family currently interested in Hillvale was Hector, who owned a small share of the family plot. He was too young to have been featured in a twenty-year-old brochure. But back then—one of the family patriarchs might have had a foot in the door.

"Good job, Sofia, thanks. I'll start asking questions."

He hung up, opened his email, took a look at the brochure scan, and agreed the skinny blond kid in the green sales jacket and tie was the same Alan Gump he knew today. There was no photo of the Adolpho Menendez listed as a director.

As far as Walker was aware, the Menendez land hadn't changed hands in a century. They came out of the Kennedy debacle just fine. What reason would they have to want his father dead?

Alan Gump had been too young to be a major player in the commercial company that had collapsed when the Kennedy fraud caught up with them. Could he have had family wealth invested—money he'd lose if the company went belly up?

If Xavier Black was the lawyer working with the Kennedys, as Cass had said, then he might know more about the contracting company. Xavier supposedly had all his wits back then.

Deciding he wasn't shirking his duty if he was working an open case, Walker forwarded the information on Gump to the detective handling his father's file. Then he called the agent he'd assigned to follow up on Xavier. Xavier had to know more than he was sharing. Whether he was coherent or not was a different question.

"He's awake," his field agent reported. "The cops have already been there and the facility is reluctant to let me in, said he was extremely agitated after the last visit. Want me to keep on it or do you need to check with your cop buddies?"

"Hold off unless I call you back. I need to see what they found out." Hanging up, Walker put the car in gear and drove down to the office. He could finish a few reports and check on what they'd learned from Xavier before signing out for the day.

How was this new condo company planning on developing Hillvale? Had the Menendez family finally sold out? Sam and Valdis certainly hadn't. Maybe the land under the town was sufficient for now, and they just planned to squeeze the Ingerssons out later.

But the situation made Walker edgy. Eighteen years ago, his father had died while uncovering the fraud that had driven out half the town. Was this an extension of the same scam that had claimed the Ingersson property before that? The Ingerssons had died long before his father had come to town. They'd died while still fighting the bank, and even after the family had won, the daughters had scattered to the winds— for a reason?

That's what he kept coming back to. Sam had inherited a troubled legacy and been sent far away with no knowledge of it—as if someone hadn't wanted her to know about her family farm. To prevent the land from being sold?

And now she was back. How many people knew she and Valdis owned that mountain?

MARIAH'S QUESTION: *EXPLAIN WHY BEING AN INGERSSON IS A BAD THING?*

still hung in the air. It was obvious not everyone knew about the farm's ownership.

"Walker is still working," Sam told the others who waited expectantly for her answer—the one Cass refused to repeat. "Will Monty be in his office? I want to say this only once."

The sangria tea party had expanded and gone inside with the arrival of Amber and several of the other Lucys. While they talked of how they could stop development with protests and hiring environmentalists, they weren't telling her what she needed to know about her family and heritage. It was time to move matters forward.

"Our mayor is always in his office. You'd think we were a megametropolis requiring a squadron of paperwork." Mariah watched with interest as Sam divided Amber's tarot deck into piles on Cass's dining table. "But he'll know something's wrong if I walk in with you. What you have better be good."

"I have no understanding of what you just said, and what I have is probably not good, so maybe we should call it off. We can go help Daisy make lamassu." Sam sat back in her chair and let Amber do the honors of turning the cards.

Amber flipped the first three and looked alarmed.

Plied with Cass's sangria, Sam wasn't too concerned. "If you don't like what you see in the cards, do we need an astrologer to tell us if the sun is in the wrong house?"

"The *planets*, poppet, and no, the cards are enough. Maybe you shouldn't go anywhere today. I've never drawn the Devil, Death, and the Hanged Man in sequence before." Amber stared at the cards. "The forces are very strong right now. Forget Monty. Go home and stay there."

"You've told me the cards have multiple meanings. Death can mean the end of a project or a way of life or any number of things. Maybe it means the death of secrets." Impatient with their superstition, Sam tapped the Hanged Man card. "We make our own fates."

Amber didn't look any more relieved. Sam couldn't help that.

"Maybe you should listen to Amber, dear," Cass said, her usually smooth face lined with worry. "Her interpretations are in tune with the Universe. Visit Monty another day."

Cass had to know what Sam intended to tell her other family. But her great-aunt had brought her to Hillvale knowing the disturbance she would cause.

Sam retrieved her staff and stood up. Some Lucy superstitions had a practical base. *Speak softly and carry a big stick* suited her, if she'd just learn to keep her big mouth shut. "And tomorrow may never come. Procrastination only drags out the anxiety."

"If we visit Monty in broad daylight," Mariah murmured as they left the older Lucys frantically flipping cards, "everyone in town will know."

"And this is a bad thing why?" Sam started down the hill toward town.

"They'll say we're conspiring with the Nulls. They'll shut us out." Mariah reluctantly followed.

Reject her, as she'd been rejected so often. Sam hated being an outcast in this town to which she had so many ties, but maybe she'd grown up a little. Being herself first mattered, she finally understood. She couldn't be everyone's good little girl.

"No," she argued. "No more secrets. The only way we can move forward is to open all lines of communication." Sam hoped she knew what she was doing. It wasn't as if a master's degree gave her experience in the real world. She prayed announcing to the Nulls who she was and who owned the farm above town wouldn't get her killed, as Cass seemed to fear.

"This better be worth ruining my Lucy reputation," Mariah said grumpily.

The front door of the town hall was open, but no one occupied the reception area. It looked like a Chamber of Commerce tourist center with brochures advertising local entertainment and maps for hiking trails.

Mariah indicated the empty office. "No money for staff."

"And no cash to be guarded, I get it." Sam started for a door marked *Employees Only* calling, "Anyone home?"

Mariah muttered a curse, pushed ahead, and opened the door. "Company, Kennedy!"

Sam entered a short hall adorned with aging paintings and photographs. At the end, Montgomery Kennedy stepped out, frowning and shoving his hair out of his face. "What is this, an invasion?"

"A mayor should be accessible to his populace," Sam said cheerfully. "I'm here to prevent revolution. Are you willing to talk?"

"Revolution? You mean the Lucys holding a sit-down in the parking lot? By all means, let the negotiations begin." He gestured to the door behind him.

"You have no idea what we can do, Kennedy," Mariah said defiantly. "We're organized. We'll sue if you try to take our town away."

"Stand down, Mariah. We've come to talk, not threaten." Sam followed her uncle into his office. She studied the serious lack of décor and amenities and chose a worn-out chair that appeared to have been discarded from the lodge lobby.

Mariah sat cross-legged on the floor, forcing Monty to take the other shabby chair on the visitor's side of the desk if he wanted to see her.

"What do we need to talk about?" the mayor asked wearily. A normally affable jock, he had faded to almost the same shade of gray as his brother today.

"Openness and honesty," Sam said, feeling a tug of concern for her overworked relative. "Before I have my lawyer start looking into the documents Walker claims exist—did you know that I'm an Ingersson and that Val and I own the farm?"

Monty shook his head. "The land, no, of course not. That's foolish. I did hear talk about you being related to Val, though. I'll accept it if you do, although I don't see the resemblance."

Mariah snorted. "That's because you're too blind to see people instead of numbers. Val dyes her hair and hides behind veils. If you ever looked at her, you'd see the resemblance, although admittedly, Sam looks more like Cass and your lot."

Monty waved his hand in concession. "I'm not arguing about family ties. The problem lies in the rest of the statement. Val's land was lost long ago. We hold the deed now."

Sam's stomach tied in knots, but this was why she had to put everything out in the open. Walker had professional reasons to keep quiet. She didn't. "Walker has had men investigating me, and in the process, they have searched the property office. This is public information. You can look for yourself. The farm is owned by a trust. He says the documents he's located show Val and I are the beneficiaries of that trust."

Mariah looked stunned. "How is that possible? No one even knew you existed! What if you hadn't found your way up here? Who would get the land then? Are you sure Walker isn't perpetrating some scam?"

Monty shook his head. "Sorry, not to demean Walker in any way, but that's dreaming. The condo company has the deeds or they wouldn't be spending money to draw up development plans. My father set it all up long ago, but we've tried to stay out of it until now. I don't doubt Walker's done his job, but there is apparently a missing piece."

"And that's me," Sam said quietly, thinking about what Mariah had just asked about who might get the land if she hadn't shown up. "As long as I didn't exist and Val barely clings to reality, there might have been some hope of fighting for ownership."

"That's ridiculous," Monty said. "No respectable company spends money based on wishful thinking!"

Sam shook her head. "Cass knows about us, she's just not talking. I think she's afraid more people will die if she does. She raised my father as her son, and losing him must have hurt very much. I don't know what it cost her when my mother sent me away as an infant. You and Kurt were just kids and wouldn't care. I think everyone simply kept quiet after your father's death and the threat of development faded away."

Monty glared as if he'd like to snap logs. "I'll call my lawyer. This is ridiculous. Too many years of planning went into this development to believe this Lucy nonsense."

"Your lawyer and mine probably ought to look into this together," she agreed, putting her executor's business card on the desk. "But if what Walker has uncovered is the truth, and he has no reason to lie, then someone worked very hard and sacrificed a lot to keep you from ever developing the farm. It may be time to locate my birth mother."

Mariah was still looking stunned. "How is any of this possible? How can land sit there for twenty-five years and no one own it? The taxes alone would ensure the county moved in."

"If the trust works like the one my father inherited, then an executor is handling it. He has no authority to sell while we're alive, but there was apparently money involved in the settlement suit. I don't know how much is left, but if someone intended no one to develop that land, the money must be invested to produce enough income to cover taxes."

"And executor fees," Monty added. "And this is all highly improbable. I was too young to know the details but Alan assured us that the court favored the bank, the foreclosure was allowed, and his company took over. The Ingerssons died shortly after the suit was settled. I vaguely remember them stubbornly refusing to leave and living in a tent after fire wiped out the farmhouse. But I was only five or six at the time. I don't remember their deaths. I'm sorry Val feels as if she was cheated out of her home, but the past is past."

"Could you call your development people and ask to see a copy of the deed?" Sam suggested.

The land meant nothing to her, but the town was important to her friends and the condos were important to her family. She was damned no matter which way she turned.

Monty scowled but picked up his landline and dialed a number he apparently knew by heart. "Is Gump there? Fine, then tell him I need to see a copy of the deed on the old Ingersson property." He listened for a minute and his scowl deepened. "I want to frame photos of the land as it is now and include deeds as part of the montage. Right. Let me know when they're available. Thanks."

He hung up and glared. "There's no one in the office who can produce them right now. They'll get back to me."

Mariah stood up, looking militant. "Hitch up the lawyers, folks, it's time to visit the courthouse. Someone, somewhere is lying, and my bet is on *your* development company."

Monty stood, frowning formidably and looking at his watch. "It's too late now, but I'll call my lawyer in the morning. A deed to a trust is meaningless without looking into ownership of the trust."

He nodded at Sam. "Thank you for bringing this to my attention. I'll see if Kurt has done his homework, but we're not lawyers. We rely on the people we work with to be trustworthy. I have no reason to doubt a company that has spent years and hundreds of thousands of dollars on planning this development, but it's good to double check. You need to do the same."

"I intend to, but I didn't want to do it behind your back. I'd really like to make Hillvale my home, but I can't if my families are at war. I've lived without a home for six years. I can do it again. But I'd hoped there might be a place for me here," Sam said wistfully. She stood and wished she had the right to hug her uncle. His affable smile had disappeared. But she didn't think he'd appreciate the gesture.

Since she may have just destroyed his hopes for the future as well as her own, she understood.

Instead of taking the door they entered, Mariah opened a panel in the office wall, exposing what appeared to be the bluff. "This way. I'll show you a shortcut. Amber said you need to lie low, and this might be a good time to listen. Dinah needs to do without you until all lawyers have checked in. Half the town could be out there waiting anxiously for good news."

"They saw you come in," Monty grumbled. "You ought to go out and face them."

"I'll tell them we held a sit-in protest all night but you crawled out a rat hole," Mariah retorted.

"Then I'll go out the front and let them believe I killed you, give them something to meddle in," he snapped. "You can't keep hiding who you are."

Sam waited for that enigmatic argument to be explained, but Monty merely waited as Mariah led Sam out to a narrow protected area where a Tesla concealed a set of steps carved into the bluff face. Skirting the car's hood, Mariah started up the stairs, saying, "You might as well know how to get to your farm from every direction."

Her farm. Sam actually thrilled a little, for the first time, at the possibility that she might own land here, but she forced herself to stay practical. "Walker will be coming up after he gets off duty. How much time will this *shortcut* take?"

"Not much," Mariah assured her. "Fifty years ago, the Ingerssons— and their tenants in the commune days—didn't have a lot of vehicles. They walked to town for their groceries and supplies. This is pretty direct, just really steep. Daisy can't walk it, but Val can. She grew up here. She knows all the nooks and crannies. It's how she gets around with no one seeing her."

The western sun lit the way up the first set of steps, but then the path turned behind a wall of rock, and they walked in the shadows of the bluff. It was easy to see why people talked of ghosts. The wind whistled through this narrow canyon, and the light shifted uncertainly. Above, Sam could see the tall pines she guessed were the ones she'd seen from the farmhouse foundation. They probably provided a windbreak.

"If Daisy is up here, we should have brought her food." Sam started to turn around.

"Oh, shoot, yeah. I'll run down and procure provisions and explain to Dinah why she's on her own for a while. You assure Daisy food is coming. She'll point you to the path that leads to Cass's so you don't have to come back this way. The farm really is the key to this town. I can't believe you own it!" Mariah pressed past Sam to go back down but squeezed her arm with excitement as she did so. "Bless you for finding us! I haven't felt this positive in ages."

"You have a way of getting into town without walking through the town hall again?" Sam asked in amusement.

"I drop over the wall and onto Monty's car most times. Haven't heard him leave. But if he has, the drive will be clear. I can go around the building."

That sounded like a precarious path. She'd have to study it better later. But now, curious to see where the stairs came out, Sam kept climbing. Maybe she could persuade Daisy to show her the art she protected with her stone statues.

The stairs at the top were more crumbling sandstone than solid granite. She had to watch where she put her feet. She was grateful she'd taken Harvey's staff with her. She pounded the rocks at any crevasses where snakes might slither.

At the top, she reached the wooded area that served as a windbreak. She could see now that someone had planted redwoods among the pines, and she ran her fingers over the peeling bark, trying to guess the age. The area had obviously been logged of old growth, but the new trees were doing well in the shadow of the Douglas firs. One day, they would tower over the mountain again.

She even found a few California rhododendrons surviving in the damp fog that rolled in off the ocean. What a wondrous place this must have been! And it might be hers? Did she dare let excitement build? Probably not, given the land's history.

Once out of the wooded area, she was back on unhospitable rock and the burned remains from the recent fire. She knew the dirt between the rocks would grow habitation, but it needed water. Without the pines and redwoods to catch the moisture in the air and provide shade, the rocks dried out.

She studied the open landscape in the light of the setting sun. The light was probably fabulous for artists. And if she climbed up high enough, she might even see the ocean. She hadn't gone up on Bald Rock with Val, but that was probably a good perch. She could see it looming over the plateau, well above the hedges surrounding the farmhouse.

She called Daisy's name to let her know she was coming. A staff raised above the manzanita, indicating she'd heard.

The line of protective statues had nearly doubled to surround the old stone foundation. Daisy had been busy.

"I've brought water but Mariah had to go back for food. I didn't know we were coming up here." Sam pulled an unopened bottle of water from her cargo shorts and stepped over the guardian border.

Daisy looked up with a frown as Sam pushed through the hedge. "You shouldn't be here. The mountain will tumble in your presence."

"Uh, well, sorry." At that warning, Sam glanced nervously at the tall bluff and evidence of previous rock falls, but there wasn't any good reason for them to fall after the winter rains had stopped. Sam handed her the water. "I'll leave when Mariah returns. Can I help?"

Daisy gestured at her dwindling collection of sticks and stones. "The hills are not safe. The village is hungry. They have sent their bravest warriors to hunt the Great Bear, but the warriors do not return. The women dance in mourning around the fires, and the children cry."

Listening to Daisy's chanting voice, Sam could almost travel with her through time, smell the campfires and see the shadows of long-lost huntsmen tracking grizzlies with bows and arrows. In a place this isolated, the spirits just might linger. "And then the Spanish came, I guess."

If she couldn't get sense out of Daisy, she might at least hear some history. In comfortable silence, she gathered stones and lined them up by size.

"The men with spears took the people as slaves," Daisy said sadly some while later. "The women weep for their homes and the sons who lived and died here."

"The grizzlies are gone, aren't they?" Sam thought Daisy was getting too heavily into doom and tried to bring her companion back to better times.

"The Great Bear hunts us all. White men bring evil and the wrath of the gods. You should leave."

Sam quit asking questions and wandered further afield, searching sticks and stones. When she heard the sputter of an engine, she breathed a sigh of relief. She didn't want to leave Daisy alone, but she didn't know how to talk to her either.

Daisy heard the sound and gestured dismissal. "Take Valdis back with you. Don't make the Evil One's job easy. Go far far away."

Arguing with Daisy was wasted effort. Sam stood up to welcome the new arrivals.

Mariah had indeed brought Valdis. Wielding her walking stick like a cane to keep her weight off her injured ankle, Sam's aunt lurched across the yard.

"Valdis, go home," Daisy cried from behind the hedge.

"You can't stop Death," Valdis called back.

Behind her, Mariah caught Sam's eye and shrugged. It was good to know she wasn't the only one thinking she needed to learn the Lucys' language.

"Monty and Kurt were about to come to blows in the parking lot when I left Dinah's," Mariah whispered, letting Valdis limp ahead on her own. "If only cell phones worked, we might have heard them yelling at the real bastards. But that slimeball Gump apparently wasn't within shouting distance."

"He was in the café earlier with his sales team, remember? What does Gump have to do with anything?" Sam helped Val over the stone foundation.

"Don't know. His name just kept coming up. And he's an asshat who needs to be yelled at. He agitates the universe. And I think he's harming Xavier." Mariah pushed through the hedge with her sack of food.

"How is he harming Xavier?" Sam followed her.

"He just busted him out of rehab."

CHAPTER 30

Late afternoon, June 23

THE SHERIFF THREW A FILE ON WALKER'S DEATH. "WASN'T MUCH OF A cross to set a mountain on fire. It wasn't more than a dead sapling nailed into a dead tree trunk."

Walker flipped open the file and scanned the arson team's report. "If it was Xavier who nailed the sapling. . ." Walker shoved his hand through his hair. He knew a little too much about these people. "He probably only meant to ward off evil spirits with a Christian symbol. It makes no sense that he'd rub that kerosene can free of prints, then incriminate himself carrying it around."

The sheriff shrugged. "The kerosene was poured on the base of the tree in pine debris. The team has no proof your clown ignited it."

Who else would want to burn down the Kennedy's mountain? The Lucys seemed the only likely suspects, but they were tree huggers, not arsonists. At least, that's what he'd thought.

He'd had enough for one day. He needed to get back to Sam before his brain burned out. He strode out to the sheriff's parking lot and almost ignored his phone when it rang. Sam wouldn't be calling it. But his office might. With a sigh, he punched the button.

"Gump had Xavier transferred to a rehab in Vegas," Sofia said curtly into his ear.

"What?" Walker shouted, hurrying toward his car. "Gump? How the hell do you know that?"

"Earlier, I asked one of the nurses to let me know if there was any change in his condition, and she gave me a call."

"Have you located him yet?"

"It's private information. I'd need to lie or hack their computers," Sofia said stiffly.

"We're legal. We don't do things like that," Walker assured her. Looked like his burned-out brain needed another workout. "Unless we have a case against Gump, even the sheriff can't act. Go home. It's late."

"You should, too, dear. Your father wouldn't want you to work yourself to death."

But if he didn't follow up the links to the killers, other people might die. He didn't want one of them to be Sam. If he couldn't talk to Xavier, maybe he could get some sense out of Francois. He sure as hell wouldn't persuade a moneymaker like Alan Gump to even look at him without a warrant and a raft of lawyers.

Walker pulled out his cell phone and the file on Francois and punched in the numbers while he was still near a tower.

"HAVING US BOTH IN THIS PLACE IS WHAT SUSANNAH FEARED MOST, I think," Valdis said unexpectedly, as she settled onto a rock seat and reached for Daisy's sticks and stones.

Sam couldn't leave after that mention of her mother. Walker would just have to wait. She added more of the statues to the outer circle but encouraged her aunt to keep talking. "Do you know how to reach Susannah? Should I let her know I'm here?"

"Mariah, bring me more of those redwood branches," Daisy demanded.

Mariah grimaced and accepted her place of servitude in Daisy's palace. She sent Sam a look that said she wanted to hear all about it later, then climbed out to fetch branches.

"Sue washed her hands of us," Valdis responded in her usual gloomy voice. "She left with no forwarding address and doesn't keep in touch. I have no good idea where she is. This place nearly broke her, broke all of us. You should have stayed away."

"Sam, gather up some of those foundation stones over there." Nibbling at the sandwich Mariah had brought for her, Daisy pointed at the far end of the house. "We need this wall done if you won't leave."

Sam began gathering stones, but at least she was still within listening distance. She looked for a way past her aunt's gloomy prognostications. "She must have been crushed with grief, losing so much in such a short time."

"It had been coming long before that, disaster upon disaster. They should have all left when I did. But Sue stupidly thought she could save your father. They were happy for a while, I suppose." Val snipped wire and wrapped it around the stones, handing the rough form to Daisy to finish. "Of course, as I learned, life in the city wasn't any safer."

Dang, what did she have to do to get past the gloom? Sam looked for a way to carry more stones at once but she only had her pockets. "How did my mother know Jade and Wolf?"

"Sue went to the university for a while. She wanted to write and illustrate children's books. She imagined herself as a modern Dr. Seuss. Jade and Wolf were teachers who encouraged her. She must have kept in touch when she came back here. The house had burned, and we'd lost the land by then, of course, so she and Zach stayed with Cass."

"Do you think she's still writing children's books?" Sam asked cautiously, emptying her pockets in front of Val. Her aunt had never been so loquacious. Maybe she needed familiar territory to feel safe? Or to vent grief.

"Hope so. She was good, and she shouldn't have to sacrifice everything. She sent you away because she loved you, wanted you to be safe, and she was homeless, broke, and just a teenager. Our parents were dead, and I was barely surviving as a waitress. She didn't want to live off your trust fund or Cass. Jade and Wolf were older, already established, desperately wanted children—and promised to live a long way from here and danger. It must have made sense at the time."

"And she didn't want the Kennedys to have this land," Daisy

added, sounding completely coherent for a change. "Your mother gave you away in hopes the Evil One would wither and die, but evil doesn't die," she finished sadly. "He is up there now."

Oh well, almost coherent. "So you had the land back by the time I was born." She'd never quite understood the time line of the disastrous year of her birth.

Val pushed back her veil to sip from her water bottle. In the dying light of the sun, shadows danced on her angular face. "I remember my parents when they were good people, talented, generous, gregarious. My childhood was happy, if a little strange, with so many people wandering in and out of it. I think the intentions of the commune were initially sound. But drugs and jealousy consumed them and blackness descended. The land returned after their souls departed."

That sounded vaguely ominous. Sam wasn't certain she wished to explore this path any longer. "So you and my mother inherited the result of your parents' lawsuit?"

"The vultures lingered," Daisy said. "They had to be dispersed."

Val gestured toward Daisy with her water bottle. "We scattered the ashes and fled to all the corners of the earth. And the land was happy again."

"So twenty-five years ago, your parents died, and my father died, and you and Susannah left, so there was no one left to fight?" Sam suggested as she gathered stones.

"We buried Evil's eggs, but they're still hatching," Daisy said in a voice almost as mournful as Val's.

Yup, the Lucys had their own language. Sam could understand Walker's frustration. "Evil can't be a person if he's hatching eggs. Where did you bury them and how do you know they hatched?"

"Daisy mixes up time periods," Val offered. "The evil in this ground has been here since prehistoric times, if it's in the rock crystals as we suspect. The only thing *we* buried was my parents' artwork, and maybe some others. They were corroding and probably should have been set on fire, but others had been saved, so we'd hoped someday these might be too."

"So that's what we're protecting with the sculptures, artwork?" That almost made sense in its own weird way. Sam carried more of the small army to the outer foundation.

"And ourselves, for now," Val added. "If Evil is back, we have no shield."

Sam hid a sigh of exasperation. "Fighting evil requires identifying the source—and rocks can't be *evil*. Polluted maybe. The Kennedys are not evil just because they're trying to save their property and offer jobs to people who live up here. They may be going about it the wrong way, but being wrong is human, not evil."

"Greed is evil," Valdis said prosaically. "My father's desire to be rich and famous was evil. He drove an entire community to drugs and destruction."

This was an argument she couldn't win. "I need to get home. Walker is expecting me." Sam prepared to leave—until Mariah's distant call intruded like the cry of an eagle high above.

"Green jacket at Bald Rock!"

Sam thought the call emanated from the copse of redwood near the bluff, but she didn't see anyone. *Green jacket*? Xavier? Was Mariah speaking in code?

Looking around, she thought she saw Harvey striding up to the ridge above Bald Rock. And was that Aaron hiking up from the direction of the vortex? Neither of them wore green.

"The battle is nigh," Daisy said prosaically, as if she'd just been waiting for this moment. "Put the rest of the lamassu across that open space." She gestured at her hastily assembled army and a break in the foundation where a door might once have been.

With her sprained ankle, Val wasn't hurrying anywhere. Feeling as if she'd fallen through the rabbit hole, Sam gathered as many of the figurines as possible and contemplated some way of getting the heck out of there. She might want to know about her past, but she was starting to think it was best to leave it to a good psychiatrist.

"Why are we in a hurry?" she demanded, even as she did as told.

"He's here. The only way to fight him is to unite, just as in the old days."

"Who's here?" Sam demanded, not expecting a sensible answer but searching the rocks above for something clearly labeled *Evil*.

"Do we need Mariah?" Val fretted. "She's a powerful force."

"No time. And the eagle flies better free," Daisy said, setting down her wire.

The eagle flies better free? After thinking Mariah's cry had sounded like an eagle, Sam wondered if Daisy was reading her mind.

"Time for the shelter." Daisy used her staff to pull herself up, obviously stiff from so many hours of sitting. "Sam, help Val. I'll open the door."

Confused, Sam obeyed the command to help her aunt. As Daisy shoved aside what had appeared to be a stack of dead brambles, revealing a steel door, Sam didn't know whether to cringe in horror or explore her morbid curiosity. "Is that a bomb shelter?"

"The finest homes had them," Val said dryly, taking Sam's arm and using her stick to stand.

"And by now, they're home for spiders and snakes," Sam said in distaste. "I think I'd rather take my chances in town." She really, really did not want to enter that black hole for reasons known only to two half-mad old women. *Mature* women, she mentally amended. They had to be about the same age as Jade would have been had she lived.

"Hurry," Mariah's voice carried from a greater distance than earlier.

Sam glanced back up the mountain, but she still couldn't see Mariah. She did, however, catch a glimpse of emerald green behind Bald Rock.

Conquering her fear of snakes to help two addled women feel safe inside a bomb shelter made perfect sense in Hillvale. She shot a nervous glance back to the various Lucys gathering in the hills. They couldn't all be crazy, could they?

WALKER DROVE INTO HILLVALE AND SCREECHED TO A HALT BEFORE HE RAN over a wheelchair granny shouting and swinging a cane.

The whole damned parking lot was churning with Nulls and Lucys screaming and swinging at each other. Flabbergasted, Walker sat there for half a minute just making sense of the scene. It was almost good enough for a movie comedy, if it weren't so tragic.

Monty and Kurt had stripped off their fancy suit coats and were jabbing at each other like old-fashioned English boxers. Pasquale, the grocery store owner, was in Dinah's face, shouting and gesticulating.

People Walker had never seen before argued, struggled, and swung at folks he'd only occasionally seen in the diner. The town's whole entire population of 350 had to be out here.

Sam was not.

That's when Walker's observational skills kicked in. All the stores were closed and dark. Mariah wasn't here. Neither were Aaron, Tullah, or any of the people he identified as active Lucys. He parked in the lot, cut off his engine, and warily climbed out. The people here now, the ones not identifiably Null like the Kennedys, were mostly the elderly and infirm, swinging their sticks and shouting the usual incomprehensible gibberish about Evil.

The Nulls were fighting them as well as each other. He couldn't arrest the whole town.

So he aimed for the men he'd counted on to be sensible. Not even bothering to tune into the arguments, Walker strode through the melee.

He blocked a cane blow with his forearm and winced at a kick to his ankle. He was less than happy when he finally reached the Kennedys. He grabbed Kurt by his starched collar and yanked him backward, unbalancing him before the resort manager could swing. Monty's cross blow just missed Kurt's jaw.

"Take different boxing classes next time, will ya?" Walker advised, gripping Monty's right fist and shoving him off before he could swing again. "You know each other's moves before you make them."

Both men glared and appeared on the verge of turning on him. Not having time for a brawl, Walker yanked their arms behind their backs, hard. "Where's Sam? And all her friends?"

Kurt and Monty looked blank, then glanced around. Both muttered the same expletive in the same tone. Walker released them.

"Last I saw, Sam and Mariah were headed up to visit Daisy," Monty said, rubbing his wrist and glancing up the bluff behind the town.

The summer sun hadn't completely set. Golden light illuminated sandstone outcroppings and cast crevasses into shadow.

The border of evergreens prevented any good view of the flat farm land.

Walker's instincts screamed for action, but experience had taught him to go in with all the information available. "What's going on here?" He gestured at the melee, although it appeared as if the fury had gone out of it and now they were just getting their jollies by dodging each other.

Kurt frowned. "Monty and I were arguing. My security guy stepped in. Then Pasquale intervened, and I don't know what happened from there."

"I think they were trying to keep us from blows," Monty said, frowning in the same manner as his brother. "I was pissed that no one had seen the actual deed to the farm. Pasquale took my side. Alonzo took Kurt's."

Idly swinging a frying pan, Dinah stepped in. "Mariah and Valdis took food up to Daisy half an hour or more ago. Mariah said she'd be right back and that Sam was supposed to go straight home and stay there. There are bad auras all over, including yours." She pointed at the Kennedys.

Walker's gut twisted, but he clung to the hope that Sam was waiting for him at her place. Still, with bad news piling up, he had to ask, "By any chance did you see Alan Gump or Xavier Black here today?"

"They locked Xavier up, didn't they?" Kurt asked. "If the law can't keep arsonists—"

Monty interrupted. "Alan was up here earlier with the engineering team. They're probably back in the city by now."

"Gump ain't," Dinah corrected. "He was watching the two of you make fools of yourselves just a bit ago. Looked like he had a bee up his rump."

"While they were arguing over farm deeds?" Walker asked. His brain was adding two and two and a cold chill ran down his spine. "Could Gump hear what they were saying?"

"They were shouting it to the world," Dinah agreed.

Anxiety levels rising, Walker checked the bluff for movement. Was that a glint of steel? He turned to the Kennedys and demanded, "Did Gump ever say anything about negotiating with the owners of the trust?"

"Gump assured us the deed had been *settled*," Kurt shouted. "There should be no negotiating necessary! He was here with the original development team and knew all the details. That's why we hired him."

"Is he the only one on the team who was up here when my father died?" Walker asked pointedly.

"Gump is old enough to have been," Kurt admitted. "I've not met all his salespeople. It's only the engineers who've been up here, and they're all too young to have been part of the original group."

Not proof positive, but enough to raise Walker's hackles. "If you see Gump, hold him. I need to talk to him. I'm going up to check on Sam. Whether you like it or not, you have a murderer on the loose, and Gump is the one who broke your arsonist out of rehab."

Walker strode off, leaving the brothers to act on the information as they thought fit.

Why would *Gump* take poor muddled Xavier out of rehab?

Not until Walker reached Sam's studio and found it empty did his anxiety reach full-fledged fear.

When he turned to find a bruised, bleeding, and jacketless Xavier pointing up the mountain, fear escalated to alarm.

"He'll kill them all, just as he did the others," Xavier said, before collapsing.

CHAPTER 31

Evening, June 23

Before helping Valdis descend into the bowels of hell, Sam cast one last glance over her shoulder. She could swear she saw sunlight glinting off crystals—like gleams off polished swords—all over the cliff face. But if any ephemeral figures were up there holding staffs, they were concealed by shadows in the dying sunlight.

"Don't dally. They'd not be up there unless they've felt Evil walking," Valdis said briskly.

Yea, though I walk through the valley of the shadow of death, I will fear no evil. . . Sam thought, shivering. Staffs detected evil? She hadn't felt it. Hooking the stick over her wrist, she offered her arm for her aunt to lean on as they descended what appeared to be stone stairs into the mountain. This wasn't a properly built concrete bunker, but a cellar only her creatively insane family could concoct, she suspected.

The concrete walls were embedded with crystals that caught what little light came through the open door. Below, Daisy lit a lantern.

No snakes rattled. Sam took a deep breath and relaxed a little.

"Shut the door," Val commanded.

"Against what, nuclear holocaust?" Sam knew better than to expect a rational answer. Reluctantly, she swung the steel door closed.

Amazingly, it didn't dim the light. Crystals, mirrors, and polished metal set in the walls reflected the lantern's gleam. Val grasped a metal rod set in the concrete walls and balancing on her staff, managed the stairs on one foot.

"Evil," she repeated, as usual. "Evil was committed on this land for eons. It seeps into the rocks, flows through the vortex, pollutes the soul. You'll see. Now that you're here, you'll see."

That aroused her curiosity. Sam followed Valdis into the bunker, where Daisy was igniting more lanterns with mechanical lighters.

"Does anyone else know about this place?" Sam asked, glancing at the artwork hanging helter-skelter and stacked against the walls.

"The oldest of us," Val said. "My parents lived here after the bastards burned them out. Their art reflects the evil." She pointed at a painting done in a similar style to the ones Sam had seen at the lodge.

The man with the long, curly blond hair she assumed was her grandfather faced forward in this painting. He was about her age in this self-portrait. A half-naked pregnant woman reclined on a couch in a mirror on the artist's wall—her grandmother?

"Early days," Val barked. "He was a handsome man, and I remember loving the tender look in his expression as he painted my mother. And still it corroded. Look at the eyes. It's always the eyes. His were once a crystal blue, like yours."

Daisy held up a lantern so the sparkling color of what had to be decades-old oil was illuminated.

The beautiful young artist's eyes had turned an evil red.

Sam went from painting to painting. Not all were by the same person. Many were too abstract to discern identity. She thought one rural idyll depicted a man with Kennedy features—her *paternal* grandfather, Geoffrey? His eyes had turned red too.

"The originals didn't have the red?" Sam asked skeptically. "They all corroded in the same way over the years?"

"Only the eyes of the *infected*," Daisy elaborated. "The children are still fine." She pointed at a tableau of two blond children with brilliant blue eyes.

"Me and your mother," Val said curtly. "We escaped. Our mother didn't, although she held out until the last, when she lost everything." She pointed at a small portrait of a plump, blond, graying woman with a pleasant expression—and red-rimmed eyes. Not totally red like the others, but *infected.*

"Now," Daisy commanded urgently, pointing her staff at the door. "The mountain tumbles *now.*"

~

"I'D HOPED WE COULD SETTLE PEACEFULLY THIS TIME," CASS SAID sorrowfully, striding toward the vortex.

"Just tell me what the hell is happening and maybe we still can," Walker urged. "Why is Sam up there? What was Xavier trying to tell me?" He'd radioed for back-up and left the unconscious old man with the nurse Cass had brought in.

He'll kill them all was a clarion warning if he'd ever heard one, but Walker had to know who and how and why. And Cass wasn't talking.

Cass gestured at the mountain. "Xavier knows Evil just as we do. He knows it must be buried. We pray we are strong enough to protect Sam. She is the Earth Mother, the good in all of us."

Disregarding Lucy inanity, Walker focused on the one word to exacerbate terror. "Protect her from *what*?" Locking down his raging fear, he concentrated on the area above the amphitheater that Cass pointed at. Had those glints of light always been there?

"Can't you feel it?" Cass asked in what seemed like despair. "It's a dark cloud forming. The earth is vibrating with fear and rage."

The only vibrating he felt was his *own* fear and rage. "Where is she?" he shouted, giving up on rational discussion.

"We hope she has taken shelter. We tried to warn her not to go." Cass took the path toward the vortex, where half the town seemed to be gathering.

Or just the Lucy half—the ones with Harvey's staffs. Except Harvey wasn't here. Or Sam. Those gathering were of Cass's generation, the older ones who had been beating up Nulls with canes. What wind had blown them *en masse* in this direction?

"You'll be safe with us," Cass said prosaically. "The vortex energy draws out the evil, but it also protects. We can only hope we have the strength to send enough of the good energy to deflect the bad."

This time, when Walker studied the mountain, he thought he saw a glimpse of green, not a natural green but the emerald of Xavier's jacket —the same emerald green that had been on the brochures from eighteen years ago. It made no sense, but Walker gave up on Cass and took off at a run in pursuit of that flash of green.

Cass yelled a warning. He ignored it.

He'd climbed this path following Sam and her stick through the dark last time. This time, there was sufficient daylight to see the trail leading up to the Ingersson farm, Bald Rock, and that flash of green. The question became—did he go after the green that might simply be Xavier's discarded jacket or find Sam?

This job meant making terrible choices that could be the difference between life and death. He wasn't an all-knowing god. He wanted to save Sam—for his own selfish reasons, because he didn't want to lose her and all the good her trusting intelligence had shown him these last days.

But he couldn't always be there to protect her if there was a murderer on the loose, which was where his duty stepped in. If he believed Xavier and Lucy insanity, the entire community was in danger and would continue to be in danger until the killer was caught.

He had to surmount his defensive urge to protect what was his. War raged within him, but he continued racing up the trail toward Bald Rock—and not down to the farm where he hoped to find Sam.

As if to confirm his decision, Harvey stepped out of a shrub-shrouded crevasse. Garbed in his usual black, he was barely visible except for the glinting crystal in his staff.

"Gump." Harvey spat out the name as if it were a bad taste. "He's planting something under Bald Rock. He could be carrying a detonator."

Walker bit back bile and studied the enormous boulder above. "Sam and Valdis?"

"Farm. Daisy has a hiding place. I don't know how safe it is if half a mountain falls on it." Harvey looked pale and grim. "We're tuned to the crystal vibrations. We can divert a partial slide. We can't predict results though."

Diverting a landslide was a particularly high level of crazy to accept. "Is there any reason to believe he planted explosives and not his dear dead mother's diary?"

Harvey lifted a black brow in disbelief.

Walker sighed. Right. Xavier had said a killer was up here. There was no *good* reason for a wealthy city real estate mogul to suddenly be hiking around on Bald Rock—in a green jacket. Walker's gut said he needed a SWAT team. The Lucys apparently felt the same way, except their SWAT team was a little unorthodox.

"I'm going up on Bald Rock," Walker said. "The sheriff's men are up at the lodge. I've radioed them. If the mountain blows, you'll need all the help you can get. Try not to drive off the authorities."

He didn't wait for Harvey's response. Gut instinct said Gump had motive and opportunity for two murders. Xavier's warning might be that of a drug-addled madman, but Walker had learned his lesson. He couldn't ignore whatever voices spoke in the old man's head. Lives might depend on listening.

He wished he'd really listened to Tess, heard her desperation. Maybe he could have prevented tragedy. This time, failure would devastate an entire town.

By the time Walker reached the summit, he could see the stout real estate mogul sliding down from Bald Rock. Gump's feet had just hit the narrow ledge below, the one where they'd laid out Valdis the other night.

Crossing his arms and firmly planting his boots on safe ground, Walker blocked the rock path over the snake's nest.

"Fine evening for a hike," he said, studying the usually elegant businessman.

Gump had discarded his designer suit coat and was wearing what had to be Xavier's green jacket—it was three sizes too small for his portly stature.

The green would be highly visible against the browns of the cliff. If he'd seen it, others had. If anything happened—most people would blame Xavier. Or would have, if Xavier hadn't escaped whatever Gump had done to him.

"Just checking the million-dollar view," Gump said affably, slicking back his glossy blond hair. "Remove a few of those trees and tenants can watch a sunset over the ocean. What brings you up here?"

Only a sociopath could believe he was so slick that Walker would accept this scenario without question. "Xavier," Walker said tersely. "Did you think you could blame your next evil deed on the old man if you set him loose?" Damn, he sounded like the Lucys.

Gump tried to edge past Walker. "I don't know what you're talking about. I have a meeting with the Kennedys, if you'd let me pass."

"The Kennedys know about the deed. They know you have no right to build on this land. Did you think the owners would never come back?"

"I don't know what you're talking about," he said irritably. "I invested everything I had in this land. I've worked hard and mortgaged my life for this development. In a few years, we'll all be rich."

Mortgaged his life maybe, and possibly his soul, but not the land he didn't own. "Want to give me Xavier's jacket? There's something in the pocket he wants back," Walker lied.

He was facing the man who may have cold-bloodedly *killed his father*. Lying wasn't the only sin he'd commit to get the truth. But if there was any chance Gump really was carrying a detonator, the situation needed to be de-escalated pronto.

Gump laughed a little nervously. "Xavier's a nutcase. This is my team jacket from the old days, bit of nostalgia, I guess. Didn't want to ruin the Armani."

Yeah, because it was so cold up here in the ninety-degree sun that he needed a coat.

"The jacket, Gump," Walker insisted, putting a threat into his stance as well as his voice. The sheriff could fire him later. He maintained his most intimidating, arms-crossed, beefcake stance. Pity Sam couldn't see him.

"What is this, some kind of highway robbery over a damned cheap jacket? If you're that desperate—" The older man began shrugging out of the too-tight sleeves. Not even a crow cried as he tugged it off.

A humming chant filled the eerily silent air. A mechanical device tumbled from the coat's pocket—into the snakes' rocky nest below.

CHAPTER 32

EVENING, JUNE 23

"*HERE,*" DAISY SHOUTED, STABBING HER STAFF INTO A CRYSTAL-LINED PIT in the concrete floor as the ground began to rumble. "Connect them here."

Val did the same with her staff, then yanked Sam's in the same direction when she didn't respond fast enough.

All three sticks touched, and Sam almost fell backward from the earth energy surging through the wood. Terrified, she grabbed the staff's grip with both hands and hung on, praying to whatever gods might be watching that she wasn't harnessing a dragon.

A shattering boom shook the bunker. She bit back a shriek as pieces of rotten concrete tumbled from the walls, creating a fog of dust. Glancing fearfully at the ceiling, she didn't see cracks, but the crystals blazed a brighter blue. That's when she noticed their staff crystals glowed weirdly. The effect of concrete dust?

Energy continued surging through the wood, and her stick bucked like a wild horse.

The ground rumbled. What sounded like an avalanche roared in the distance. But it was the power rushing through her hands that frightened her most.

Her aunt and Daisy hummed a high-pitched note that was almost as scary as the thunder outside. But the energy they evoked was positive—she could swear it was as if she were part of a giant magnet pushing back a negative charge.

The rumble rolled closer, lifting the ground they stood on. *Earthquake?*

WALKER WATCHED IN HORROR AS THE DETONATOR FELL FROM GUMP'S pocket and his world exploded. Slammed back against the bluff, he covered his head as the impact blasted Bald Rock into splintered boulders, shooting the massive outcropping into the air.

In the echoing horror that followed, he and Harvey clung to the rumbling mountain as the debris rained down on the already dangerously loose hillside. Rocks and dirt began to slide.

In an instant, an avalanche cascaded straight toward the farm and *Sam.*

She was down there, he knew it, he could feel her terror resonating with his, and it was all he could do not to follow the landslide down.

Take out the enemy first.

Fighting the bile boiling up his gullet, Walker edged along the cliff wall while the ground beneath his feet shook. The wide path didn't crumble. The same couldn't be said of the precarious ledge where Gump perched.

Even as Walker reached for him, the ledge cracked. The sociopath lost his balance—and tumbled into the snakes' nest as it slid downward with half the mountain.

Gump's screams followed him down—a violent end to a violent man.

But Walker had no compassion for evil. His heart and mind roiled in terror for Sam—beautiful golden, laughing Sam, frowning, snarky, intelligent Sam, naked loving understanding Sam—down there, amid the rubble and debris surging relentlessly toward the shrub-covered foundation he assumed had to be the original farmhouse. Where the hell could she be hiding? There was *nothing* to hide behind or stop the tide of destruction.

His heart plunged with the rocks. Paralyzed with helplessness before nature's revenge, he watched Gump's green jacket disappear in a cloud of dust and stone. Once again, he had no control over the shit life threw at him. He hadn't even prized a confession from the bastard, although the detonator and explosives confirmed the man wasn't worth the rocks he'd stood on.

But Sam didn't deserve to die because Walker hadn't been able to stop a lunatic—*again*. He had to find a way down, find Sam. . .

The eerie hum continued in a crescendo, echoing off the bluff face, even as the slide lost momentum on the level ground of the farm. Skidding downward on the loose shale in his quest to find Sam, Walker watched in disbelief as the powerful tide of granite and debris tumbled to a gradual halt.

It formed a barrier of rocks and dirt outside what appeared to be a line of Daisy's peculiar *guardians*. A few smaller stones rolled through an unfinished area of the circle—just as if the tiny stone statues had halted a landslide.

Harvey climbed down to stand beside Walker in silent appreciation of the utter destruction. In the distance, sirens screamed.

"Holy shit," Walker muttered, searching for any sign of movement below. "The sheriff won't believe this."

"If Gump's head wasn't crushed, he'll die of snakebite," Harvey said prosaically. "We could pretend we didn't see him, if that helps."

That jarred Walker from his shock. "If he's alive, I want a confession. But if Sam's down there, I'm going after her first."

"She's there all right. Her energy is almost as powerful as Mariah's," Harvey warned. "She's not going anywhere. This earth is hers. You'd do better to look to yourself."

Walker didn't bother sending him an incredulous glance. Choosing the safest trajectory over the loose stones, he clambered down to the farm. The avalanche had provided a safer angle than the steep bluff.

By the time he reached the bottom, ATVs were roaring up the rutted drive from town. Lucys trekked up from the vortex or off the bluff from various directions where they'd been concealed. It was as if all the spirits on the mountain had materialized and were finding their way to the farm. If he didn't know better, he'd think the Lucys had been hiding in caves with their ancestors.

Praying that Harvey was right and that Sam was safe, Walker hurried downward, hailing the sheriff and Monty on the first ATV in his path. Another deputy and Kurt rode the second. Officialdom and Lucys gathering on the same plain. The sun might implode next.

When he got close enough to be heard, Walker gestured up the rock slide to where the sleeve of an emerald coat could just be seen. "Alan Gump is up there. He had a detonator in his pocket. Watch for the vipers."

The sheriff and his man looked grim and spoke into their radios. No one seemed eager to climb to the rescue.

Walker kept walking. Or limping. The climb had been hard on his bad leg. He didn't stop to investigate Daisy's crazy lamassu farm, but slid over it, trying not to fall on the hill of loose rubble. Inside the circle, Cass was shoving aside shrubbery and tugging on a nearly invisible steel door. A bunker. Of course the crazies would have a bunker, if only for drug storage. Either he was going insane or he was starting to understand their rationale.

Daisy popped out of the concealed door, her frizzy gray hair coated in dust. Ignoring Cass, she strode straight past the gathering Lucys, to her line of lamassu. Walker noticed the gathering Lucys deliberately placed themselves between the door and the Nulls, hiding it from view.

Sam emerged next, with a hopping Valdis on her arm. Walker thought he'd never seen anything more beautiful than Sam's smile as he hobbled up to greet her.

"You're alive," she said, joy lighting her eyes like blue sapphires. Just the sight jump-started his long dead heart.

Someone took Val's arm, leaving Sam's free. In heady relief, Walker gathered Sam against him, offering prayers to this universe of insanity that had returned her to him, hearty and whole. He drank in the wonder of her heart beating against his, of her arms wrapping around him as if she could never let go.

And the adrenalin racing through him like an amphetamine high found a focus. He was almost light-headed with joy as his terror seeped away. That didn't mean a new set of fears didn't take its place, but this was the kind of anxiousness that formed when someone you *loved* was endangered.

"I need you," she whispered, clinging to him as she never had before. "I spent these past hours with you in my every thought. It was almost like having Cass in my head again, but better. I knew you would come."

Walker wanted to jump for joy and carry her away and make love and forget the world. He nibbled her ear and ran his hand down her back and pulled her closer. "I couldn't protect you," he protested, releasing some of the horror of these last moments.

"You don't need to," she told him, hugging him harder. "I am responsible for me."

Sam said that heroically, trying to absolve Walker from his overactive sense of responsibility, but having him in her arms. . . she wanted to weep for joy. "I thought I might never see you again," she murmured, giving in to tears.

Her heroic lawman clutched her tighter, covering any part of her face he could reach with his kisses. "You want to imagine how I felt, watching a mountain tumbling down on you? I'm not sure I could survive your loss."

And there it was—they'd both suffered devastating losses. How did they find the courage to love again? She lifted her face to give him a salty kiss, then murmured, "Then you know how I feel. If we're only given these fleeting moments. . . shouldn't we grab the joy while we can?"

Walker shuddered and rested his cheek on her head. "It's more than just sex, isn't it? That's what scares the crap out of me."

She smiled through her tears. "You can afford to lose a little crap. I want to believe what we feel is real and not just a result of terror, but I'm too shaky to think straight. Give me time."

"I'd give you the stars, if I could." Walker glanced over his shoulder to see if they could get away.

In the dusk, the mob of Lucys was gathering brush and blocking view of the door. The sheriff and the town Nulls were further up the hill, playing with ATVs and shotguns, going after the snakes and climbing up after Gump.

With decision, he shed the need to follow up on the killer. "Gump most likely killed my father for the same reason he blew up the mountain—money. He can go to a hell of his own making."

She nodded in understanding. "We can't help up there. I want you to see something before the Lucys hide it all again."

"I'll gladly follow you anywhere." Walker took Sam's hand, relishing the warmth and life and fearing what lay ahead for his damaged heart. "Just don't ever do that to me again."

"Do what? Stay alive?" she asked, blinking and feigning innocence as she led him down the cold stairs. "Did we have an earthquake?"

"Of the human kind." That's what he liked, maybe loved, about Sam. She might be a starry-eyed Lucy, but she stayed grounded. His heart still hadn't slowed down, but he flicked on his flashlight to see what she wanted him to see. The beam glinted off a crazy construction of mirrors and crystals. Paintings were stacked against walls and hung anywhere that had space.

She briefly leaned into him, letting their mutual relief calm their racing pulses. As if afraid to get too close, she kissed his cheek, then pointed at a gallery of small portraits. "Look, that's Xavier, when he was younger. His eyes are a lovely brown. He must have visited here back when it was a commune."

She'd brought him down to look at an ancient painting? "What am I supposed to see?"

"No red," she said inexplicably, dragging him on. "The small portraits are Lance's style. Daisy probably stole them from his studio. He's not very original, but he's obsessive and a good copyist. Look, doesn't this look like a younger Gump?"

She pointed at an arrogant-looking blond man in his early thirties, with his coat pushed back and his thumbs hooked in his trouser pockets. Even then, he wore expensive suits. There was something peculiar about the expression. Fascinated by the way her mind worked, Walker leaned over and studied it closer. "Why are his eyes red?"

"Evil. He's infected with evil. Most of these paintings down here are portraits of evil. This is Daisy's way of burying them." Sam gestured at the bunker. "Let's go back up before they lock us in."

She grabbed the small portrait of Xavier and took Walker's hand.

To hell with portraits and evil. What was important was Sam's trusting hand in his—and that they were alive to see another day. He didn't want to waste another precious moment without her.

"I'D GIVE YOU THE STARS, IF I COULD."

Sam replayed Walker's words in her head as she showered. She longed for family. She wanted to believe she was the one who could fill the empty place in his heart, make a family with him, build the life they both craved. There hadn't been time enough to grasp what she was feeling, but it was much stronger than sex. She could easily love a man as thoughtful and caring as Walker. But was she twisting his promise to suit her needs?

Exhausted, rattled, and thrilled that Walker had come for her, Sam dreamed an impossible future while scrubbing off a mountain's worth of dust. How could they make a life here, where her only family lived, after what they'd just experienced?

She still couldn't process what had happened. Had Daisy's lamassu actually *stopped* an avalanche? Had the positive energy she'd felt in her staff been real or just her imagination?

Was there a study she could conduct to test physical energy around what everyone called a "spiritual" vortex? What if *ghosts* were part of that spirit energy?

That's how tired her mind was.

When her bathroom door opened and a filthy, disheveled Walker entered, she forgot thinking entirely. He'd been magnificent out there today, with his shirt stripped off, his shoulders and biceps bulging and covered in sweat while he shoveled and hauled with the rescue crews. But inside that muscled body existed an inquiring mind and a huge heart, a heart he was currently protecting from harm after a merciless bruising.

She didn't know if she could heal him, but she welcomed him into the shower with all she had to offer. Until Walker had come along, she'd felt like a lost child. Despite his ridiculous need to protect, he made her realize she was a grown woman capable of accomplishing anything she set her mind on. Her mind wasn't on anything except him right now.

They made passionate, bone-jarring love in the shower, then tumbled between the sheets in sheer exhaustion.

"Did Mr. Gump survive?" Sam asked in a sleepy whisper.

Walker tugged her into his arms. "Not long enough. I couldn't wish that level of agony on anyone. What the rocks didn't crush, the rattlers poisoned. We didn't even try to make sense of his curses, although he seemed to be blaming Xavier and half the world for not doing as told. He wouldn't admit wrong, even at the end."

"Proof he was a self-serving ass, but not that he killed your father," she said, understanding. "I'm sorry. Do you have enough information to lay the case to rest?"

He hugged her closer. "Cass took Xavier in, promising to work her voodoo and see that he stays clean. We're hoping he'll talk. And we're thinking Gump has been threatening Francois about the gun. We're hoping he will speak up. We'll see. But other than details, I have a good idea what happened and why. It's enough."

She nodded against his broad shoulder. She could already hear the distance in his voice. He was thinking of the time ahead, when he returned to his real world. This was the point where she had to make herself vulnerable, strip away the immature Sam, and become the woman he needed.

She kissed his shoulder and tilted her head to kiss his bristly jaw. "I'm not ready to give you up," she murmured. "I don't think what we have is just physical."

He hugged her closer. "That's what I'm afraid of. You make me want to live again—which terrifies me. I should let you walk away, find a better man, but I want to find a way to keep you. I want to see what we can build together. If that's selfish, I won't apologize."

"It's not selfish to follow our dreams, our instincts." She snuggled against him, reassured that she wasn't the only one dreaming here. "As long as we're honest with each other, we can do this one day at a time."

"Come with me to LA then. You won't have to be a waitress. I can take care of you while you decide what you want to do next."

She punched his biceps instead of kissing it. "I can't believe you just said that."

CHAPTER 33

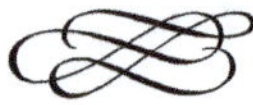

Morning, June 24

Striding into Hillvale the next morning, Walker rubbed his bruised arm and studied the gardens of colorful flowers decorating the boardwalk and every vacant alley. Heavily blooming pink roses had seemingly sprung up overnight, spilling over what had been a broken, faded fence by the town hall. In addition to the playful barrels on the boardwalk, baskets displayed an array of blossoms dangling from the sagging overhangs of several stores.

Sam had turned the tired town from faded gray to a bouquet of vibrant color and fragrance—just as she was bringing *him* back to life. If he believed in magic, he would call her enchanted.

The men waiting inside the town hall were not in the least magical.

Walker had persuaded the sheriff that Xavier and Francois were more likely to talk if they weren't intimidated by badges and uniforms. Monty was there as a witness. He'd brought in more chairs from the lodge, and the two older men had aligned themselves in front of the mayor's desk. Walker pulled the last chair to one side so he could watch faces.

Xavier no longer wore a green jacket. Someone had provided him with a navy blazer that he wore over an open-necked white shirt. Clean-shaven, back straight, with his graying hair trimmed, he almost looked like a lawyer again.

Francois had removed the epaulets from his livery, but his brass buttons still shone with polish. His face was lined and yellowed by years of smoking, and he hadn't done more with his thinning gray hair than tug it into a rubber band at his nape. His brown-stained fingers shook as he reached for a cigarette that wasn't there.

Monty had dressed casually, sporting a short-sleeved shirt—a blue one with a fancy collar and expensive detailing that had been probably been purchased in a Monterey boutique. Kennedys couldn't even do casual properly. The mayor glanced at Walker, waiting for him to lead the discussion.

"All I want is details for my report, gentlemen," Walker said. He wasn't wearing his uniform, but he'd chosen his blue, collared shirt and khakis to give him a measure of authority. He addressed the lawyer first. "We'd like to close the case with no loose ends."

He pulled out his recorder. "If you don't mind, I'd like to record while we talk. Xavier, do you mind if we start with you? I think you've been familiar with Hillvale for as long as Monty and Kurt, am I right?"

The rental agent looked relieved to be able to speak. He hesitated, apparently seeking a starting place. "I came up here with their father during spring breaks, before Geoff married. Hillvale had quite a reputation as a *happening* place." He looked almost startled that he'd said that. "The commune was no more than a group of starving artists, and the farm was dilapidated. We mostly came to do drugs. Ingersson always had a supply."

"How much did you know of Geoffrey Kennedy's desire to acquire more land and create a resort town?" Walker asked, not looking at Monty.

"Everything." Xavier shrugged. "The shops were empty. Rats ran loose. The Ingerssons smoked up anything they earned. By the time I had my law degree, we'd already started buying out people who wanted to leave. Our families had money, and property up here wasn't worth anything then. It was all perfectly legal."

Walker waited, letting the older man gather his thoughts. This many words out of the spaced-out lawyer was a miracle in itself. Cass had done some serious mumbo-jumbo on his head.

He couldn't believe that Cass had magic potions or hypnosis to influence witnesses, but Xavier had changed overnight. Or maybe he'd just dried out. That ought to worry him, but oddly, it didn't. He'd seen what Cass had done to Sam—and what the Lucys had done to an avalanche. He still didn't believe in magic, but there was something at work in Hillvale that he'd never seen in the city. He'd settle for believing in geological energy for now.

"But after a while, Geoff got impatient. He knew Alan Gump from school. Gump persuaded him to partner with his father's Commercial development team and. . ." Xavier wrinkled his forehead. "I'm not sure when it became intense. Geoff hired me to work with his mortgage company. Gump taught us how his family applied aggressive sales pitches. Eventually, they became borderline coercion. We went after the shop owners to borrow and improve their buildings, even though we knew they couldn't pay back the loans." He hesitated, gathering his thoughts.

That Gump had been involved from the start set off alarm bells. "Was Gump invested in this deal in any way at that point?"

Xavier rubbed his head. "Commercial Development invested in Geoff's mortgage company so he could make the original loans, so I guess, yes. His family money was tied up in it just the way Geoff's was. It took a lot of leverage, but we had grandiose ideas."

"And then you went after the biggest piece of land up here, right?" Unfortunately, Walker had seen these kind of investment schemes in his work. Pull one card out of the house of cards, and it crumbled.

Xavier nodded and looked pale. "I arranged a refinance on the Ingersson farm, even though they couldn't prove they had an income, knowing they'd smoke the money and fall behind. Ingersson thought we were friends helping him through a bad time. That's where the greed demon devoured our morals and our souls. We focused on the endgame and didn't care about our friends or their families who lost their homes or stores. We told ourselves that the old shacks needed to be torn down anyway. We were young and ambitious and the world was our oyster, even after Ingersson went bankrupt and sued."

Monty got up and opened a small refrigerator, producing icy

bottles of water that he handed around. This was Monty's father Xavier was talking about. It couldn't be easy hearing this.

"And then six or seven years after the lawsuit was settled, and we had almost acquired all the land we needed, I had a tourist ask me an odd question about the ownership of the farm and some of the lots in town." Xavier quit looking in Walker's direction. "That was nearly two decades ago. The face and name have faded. I was drinking heavily then. I got sloppy drunk and told a few of the guys on the development team. They wore those awful green jackets and everyone hated them."

"The people or the jackets?" Walker asked, hiding the horror building at this tale. Xavier didn't even remember Michael Walker's name, but his father had almost certainly been the tourist asking questions.

"Both," Xavier replied with a snort. "But they were going to make us rich. Alan Gump was Geoff's buddy so I pointed out the snoopy tourist in the bar."

Walker glanced at Monty, who looked pale beneath his tan. But the mayor tightened his jaw and drank from his water bottle without speaking.

Xavier continued, "Talking to Gump was probably the worst decision of my life, but at the time, it was just meaningless bar talk. He said he recognized the inquisitive guy from LA, and he'd have a talk with him. I went back to my office in San Francisco the next day. I had no idea what happened until later, when the sheriff started making inquiries about a missing tourist."

Francois had tensed at the mention of Gump. The chauffeur reached for a cigarette again, then took the bottle of water just to steady his hands.

Intent on telling his tale, Xavier seemed unaware that anyone was in the room. He stared at an ugly piece of abstract art over Monty's head. "The bottom started falling out of our dreams about that time. It's all pretty blurry in my head," Xavier admitted. "The sheriff canvassing the town for a missing tourist was followed by legal beagles from the attorney general's office. Gump and the rest of the green jacket sales team faded away. Geoff died, and I . . . fell apart. When he came back this spring. . . I let him make me believe the glory days were back. I've learned my lesson. Drugs don't make anything better."

He stopped like a mechanical toy whose spring had worn out. He stared blankly at the bottle cupped between his hands.

"Kennedy's death halted the development plans?" Walker asked, disappointed that Xavier knew no more about his father's death. "The plans died with him?"

Xavier shrugged. "Some of the team may have hung around, talking to Carmel, but she was too grief-stricken to care. She sold the mortgage company, and I was too addled to hold onto my job. I'm sorry I can't be more help."

Francois took a swig of water, then spit it on the worn wooden floor. "You let the monsters live to kill and torment again, you pathetic, sanctimonious bag of hot air."

After the chauffeur's burst of venom, Monty Kennedy lost it. "Francois! This is not the time to throw blame. They found *your* finger-print on my mother's gun, the one that killed Juan!"

Walker understood the explosion. Until this moment, Xavier had seemed to convict Gump for murder, if only by innuendo. But Francois had hit the guilt button. Not spineless Xavier, but *Geoffrey Kennedy* had been the one to set the vultures to picking Hillvale's bones. Monty's father had let loose soulless fortune hunters to claim Hillvale, much as the gold diggers had destroyed the Spanish in a different era. And the Spanish had destroyed the natives before that.

Walker gestured for Monty to sit back. "Tell us about Juan and Gump," he said to Francois, offering him a stick of gum.

The chauffeur ripped off the wrapper and chewed to calm himself. "They are murdering turds," Francois finally said.

Monty clenched his hands in an apparent attempt to keep from throttling his mother's toady. Walker had to keep one eye on him while interviewing Francois.

"You saw them kill Michael Walker?" he asked without inflection.

Francois shrugged. "I saw nothing back then. The green-jacket turd told me he needed to change his tire, and I gave him my tools. He brought them back washed. He was wearing his ugly green jacket when he borrowed the tools but not after. He stank of sweat, but I thought nothing of it until I saw him get in a car with matching tires. Who keeps matching tires for a spare? Not in that little Corvette."

Walker's gut twisted, but he pushed on. "Was anyone else with Gump who might have seen him change or not change his tire?"

"Juan," Francois spat. "The blackmailing little worm was everywhere, even back then. I had to give him the watch Mrs. Kennedy gave me for Christmas when he threatened to tell her I was letting kids wash the car and pocketing the extra she paid me to have it done."

Monty raised his eyebrows. "That was an expensive watch. You make that much on car washes?"

Walker figured the blackmail was over more than car washes, but that line of questioning was beside the point. He gestured for Monty to quiet.

"So Juan might have seen Gump using your tools for whatever purpose?" Walker asked.

Francois shrugged. "I saw Juan burn a green coat in the incinerator. It looked muddy, and when I asked him about it, he told me Gump was good for a lot of cash for keeping his mouth shut. I figured I'd look out for chances, but the ugly coats did not come back much after that, not until recently. The snake shed his green skin, but he was still poisonous."

Walker kept his expression neutral, even realizing that Francois offered only circumstantial evidence that Gump had killed his father. But everyone involved was dead, adequately punished for their misdeeds.

What mattered was how justice should be served now.

"And recently?" Walker asked. "What made you take the gun? Were you frightened?"

Francois gestured dismissively. "Me? Not me. It was Mrs. Kennedy. That pig Juan threatened to tell you about how the skeleton died. He said it would look very bad for her and her family. He wanted a pay increase."

Shit. Walker glanced at Monty, who ran his hand over his eyes at this hint that his father may have been involved in murder.

"Your uncle learned from your experience with Juan's blackmail," Walker told the mayor, not opening the path of Kennedy involvement in the skeletal remains. "Presumably, your mother did too?"

Monty nodded understanding. "Juan was all bluff."

"So how did Mrs. Kennedy deal with Juan?" Walker asked, as if they were sitting at a bar carrying on irrelevant bar chat.

Francois rolled the water bottle between his hands. "She got the gun from the vault. She locked it there when the mister died, said she didn't want her boys to have it."

"And then she shot Juan?" Walker asked, allowing a hint of incredulity through.

Francois shook his shaggy head. "No! She is a lady. She would never do such a thing. She just threatened the swine and told him if he ever approached her in such a manner again, she would kill him rather than just fire him. She finally booted the little turd."

Monty raised his eyebrows. "That must have been the night she was in such a rage. She told us she'd fired the wretch, and Kurt argued. Juan was a rat, but he was an observant rat and good at his job."

Walker nodded and directed his question at Francois. "And then she told you to put the gun back in the vault?"

Francois nodded. "She gave me the key and the gun. But Gump was there that night. I saw him having dinner, and I remembered what Juan said about him paying big cash. So when I had a chance, I told him that Juan had been blackmailing Mrs. Kennedy about the skeleton on the property. I didn't know what he knew, but I took a chance, just to see if he'd pay to keep my mouth shut."

Xavier drained his bottle and set the empty on the table. "I remember that night. Kurt had to drive me home because Gump was staying at the lodge and had been drinking. Gump didn't want to take me home as he usually did."

Walker nodded and turned back to Francois. "And then what happened?"

"Gump gave me a hundred, thanked me for letting him know. He asked if he could borrow the gun before I put it back. He said he wanted to threaten Juan into leaving so he didn't bother Mrs. Kennedy again. I thought maybe he was sweet on her."

Monty buried his head in his hands, and Walker sympathized. The mayor had to suck up the knowledge that his family was the reason that a monster had been unleashed on Hillvale. And the second time was his and Kurt's fault. The two of them had sat there that night, discussing plans for a development with a murderer. That was how Monty's father's life had ended—with blood on his soul.

"You didn't think anything of it when Gump returned the gun at midnight and told you to take it to the vault?" Walker asked, sounding like a cynical cop.

"It smelled of gunpowder," Francois said in distaste. "I'd heard the shots earlier, but Bernardo said he'd heard a lion in the woods, and Gump had been shooting at it. I took his money and drove the gun to the vault and didn't think anything more."

"Until morning, when you learned Juan was dead?" Walker asked in disgust.

Francois chomped on his gum hard enough to crack molars and refused to speak.

CHAPTER 34

MORNING, JUNE 24

SAM DELIVERED CASS'S THIRD CUP OF TEA AND STUDIED THE SMALL portrait of Xavier on the booth table, the one she'd rescued from the bunker. The café was filling, as if everyone waited for a verdict from the mayor's office, although Sam couldn't imagine what they expected. Gump was dead. Who would admit to murder once they had a suspect? But she worried about Walker. He needed his ghosts laid to rest.

"The ghosts don't go away," Mariah said, as if reading her mind. She stopped by Cass's booth to deliver one of Dinah's sugary confections. "We either let them haunt us or set them free."

"I thought you set them free," Sam said, not baiting her but genuinely curious.

She wanted to see if she had a future with Walker, but if he had to return to LA, she had to decide how to shape her life. Somewhere along the line, she had quit thinking of returning to teaching. This town was very much part of her plans. She needed to know more about its inhabitants.

"I can only free the lost spirits with no connection to the living.

Walker's father isn't hanging around. He's almost past the veil, which is why it's hard to reach him. It's Walker who needs to let go." Mariah walked away to serve another customer.

Cass ran her fingers over the portrait on the table. "Sometimes, it's *memories* we need to let go. It's hard to tell the difference. Have you let Jade and Wolf go yet?"

Sam shook her head. "I won't forget them. I am what they made me. But if their spirits exist, I don't want them hanging over my head, worrying about me. They deserve to leave this mortal coil for whatever lies ahead."

"Yes, it's easier to accept the memories once a loved one has passed," Cass said. "I loved your father like the child I never had, but I'm hoping he's in a better place. It's the memories of people who still live, the missed chances, the paths not taken, those are harder."

Dinah shouted an order, and Sam left Cass to her thoughts. She wondered if there had once been anything between Cass and Xavier. It seemed hard to believe, but looking at the old portrait, she could tell Xavier had once been a handsome lawyer, and Cass had been a lonely widow.

The news that the meeting in the mayor's office had broken up spread like a ripple in a pond. Heads came up. Eyes turned toward the door. Even Lance was here, ignoring his meal, studying the mural, and listening.

The paintings, the glowing crystals, and the conflicting energies were all part of the mystery surrounding Hillvale, a mystery Sam longed to unravel, along with finding her birth mother. But right now, she just hoped Walker had found the answers he needed.

Xavier was the only one to enter the café. That seemed to be enough for the waiting Lucys. Dinah sent him to sit with Cass and took over his favorite omelet. Mariah brought him his coffee. Valdis slid into the seat with Cass. Chatter died except for the few Nulls who had no idea anything unusual was happening.

"The Evil has one less soul in its possession," Cass told Xavier in a quiet voice that wouldn't normally have carried. The rare stillness gave it weight. "Sam brought you this."

She'd done what? Sam had to drift over to see what she'd been guilty of doing. Cass was simply pushing the portrait toward Xavier, who looked at in puzzlement.

"Maybe it isn't crap," Lance murmured on the other side of her. "The red is gone, isn't it?"

Sam reached over his shoulder to fill his water glass. "Daisy said the eyes had once been red in the painting and now they're not." She didn't know if Lance knew about Daisy's shelter or if she should mention it. "Does the corruption eventually fade?"

"Usually not," Lance said sadly, still gazing at the mural. "Sometimes, we can only cover it up. I'd like to think corruption can be cured."

She wasn't certain they were talking about paintings any longer. She cast a glance at the faded mural and hoped Elaine would be able to come up and look at it soon. "All we can do is hope to make the world a little better place with each day."

Lance snorted. "That's what the peace and love hippies said, and now they're as corrupt as the rest of the world. Maybe I should start believing it's in the soil."

She patted his shoulder. "Or the soul."

In Cass's booth, Xavier was tearfully studying the old portrait. She hoped they were good tears.

He looked up as she refilled his water glass. "I found the heirs to Ghostly Grace's property," he told her, as if this had been the topic of discussion all along. "They want to rent it out."

"The ghost house, the one with the roses?" she asked, trying not to think this was a sign from above. She didn't want to be a superstitious Lucy, but. . .

"We told him to look," Cass said with a hint of dryness. "Miracles do occasionally happen with a little work. Are you staying?"

"I don't know," Sam said honestly. "I want to, I think. But I need more to occupy me than filling water glasses."

Valdis held up hers for filling. "There will be. Now that you've come home, the town has potential. Stay awhile and help us find it."

Sam looked out the plate glass window to her beautiful blooming flowers—and Walker crossing the parking lot. Long and lean and the strongest man she'd ever known, aside from Wolf. Walker had character. Could she give him up for *potential*?

~

Mid-morning, June 24

WALKER ENTERED THE CAFÉ, HOPING FOR A CUP OF COFFEE AND A QUICK word with Sam before heading back down the mountain to talk to the sheriff. But the entire population swiveled to watch him enter. Were they expecting him to report confidential police information?

Of course they were. Ignoring their expectant faces, he walked up to Sam and kissed her cheek. Before he could ask for it, Dinah handed him coffee in a thick paper cup and shooed him out.

"Go, take Sam with you. They can all hold their curiosity like *normal people*." She emphasized the last while glaring at the Lucys.

"Have you taken up mind reading?" he asked her, before tugging Sam outside and around the corner where the entire town population wasn't watching.

Sam wrapped one arm around his waist, so as not to disturb his coffee, and kissed him, not questioning, not demanding, just holding him. She offered him a peace he'd never be able to find in the city. But he had so many obligations. . .

"Are you okay?" she asked.

He sipped his coffee and thought about it. "I think so, yeah. My father knew he was in a dangerous business. It wasn't as risky as police work, but he didn't have to come up here personally. He came anyway. We all make choices."

He could feel her nod against his shoulder, again accepting, not questioning. "Wolf didn't have to be a pilot. Jade didn't have to fly with him. But a bus could have hit them on the road."

They weren't just talking about their parents. He had to let Davy and his guilt go as well. He was human. He couldn't relive what was done.

"We can only take so many precautions," he agreed. "Hillvale has potential," he added tentatively, sounding her out.

She giggled and turned laughing sapphire eyes up to him. "Valdis just said the same."

"Damn, I hate sounding like a Lucy," he muttered, watching her expression. "Are you agreeing with her?"

"Oh, I'm agreeing with *you*, of course," she said, airily waving her hand. "And me," she admitted. "I kind of like it here. Even if it's on the verge of ripping apart, the town grows on you."

"Like fungus, yeah. Monty is aware the town is dangerously divided. He wants to avoid any further violence by holding a referendum to see if they're willing to hire full-time law enforcement. It's not healthy to have to wait half an hour or more for the county to respond." He let that sink in while he sipped his coffee.

Her eyes widened, and he could swear he saw hope in them.

"Xavier just told me Grace's cottage is for rent, the one with all the flowers and roses," she offered, definitely with hope in her voice.

"The one with ghosts?" Walker thought about what they were discussing—life in a town that believed in ghosts.

"Spirits," she corrected with a half smile. "Or maybe I can prove there is some kind of physical energy in the vortex creating illusions, but I definitely want to work with the energy of the earthquake fault. *Potential*."

"I have a corporation to run," he reminded her.

"And I have a mother to find, plus Elaine Lee said she'd be up to look at Dinah's mural, and then I want to experiment on crystals. . ."

He grinned, understanding that this town was as important to her as his career was to him. "I can only do so much from a laptop. We'll have to take this slow. You need to stretch your wings and find your path."

"What, you're not going to keep me in a million-dollar mansion and give me a BMW?" She kissed his cheek and snuggled closer.

"I have a BMW. And a mother. And a raft of employees. And a house I'm dreading returning to. It's complicated."

She laughed. "I have Valdis and Cass and an entire town of ghosts. How complicated do you like it?"

Walker lifted her up and kissed her thoroughly. "Samantha Moon complicated, that's how I like it."

She wrapped her arms around his neck and showed him just how uncomplicated she could be.

ABOUT THE AUTHOR

With several million books in print and *New York Times* and *USA Today's* bestseller lists under her belt, former CPA Patricia Rice is one of romance's hottest authors. Her emotionally-charged contemporary and historical romances have won numerous awards, including the *RT Book Reviews* Reviewers Choice and Career Achievement Awards. Her books have been honored as Romance Writers of America RITA® finalists in the historical, regency and contemporary categories.

A firm believer in happily-ever-after, Patricia Rice is married to her high school sweetheart and has two children. A native of Kentucky and New York, a past resident of North Carolina and Missouri, she currently resides in Southern California, and now does accounting only for herself.

For further information, visit Patricia's network:

http://wordwenches.typepad.com/word_wenches/
http://patricia-rice.tumblr.com/
http://www.patriciarice.com

ALSO BY PATRICIA RICE

The World of Magic:

The Unexpected Magic Series

MAGIC IN THE STARS

WHISPER OF MAGIC

THEORY OF MAGIC

AURA OF MAGIC

CHEMISTRY OF MAGIC

NO PERFECT MAGIC

The Magical Malcolms Series

MERELY MAGIC

MUST BE MAGIC

THE TROUBLE WITH MAGIC

THIS MAGIC MOMENT

MUCH ADO ABOUT MAGIC

MAGIC MAN

The California Malcolms Series

THE LURE OF SONG AND MAGIC

TROUBLE WITH AIR AND MAGIC

THE RISK OF LOVE AND MAGIC

Crystal Magic

SAPPHIRE NIGHTS

TOPAZ DREAMS

Historical Romance:

American Dream Series

MOON DREAMS

REBEL DREAMS

The Rebellious Sons

Wicked Wyckerly

Devilish Montague

Notorious Atherton

Formidable Lord Quentin

The Regency Nobles Series

The Genuine Article

The Marquess

English Heiress

Irish Duchess

Regency Love and Laughter Series

Crossed in Love

Mad Maria's Daughter

Artful Deceptions

All a Woman Wants

Rogues & Desperadoes Series

Lord Rogue

Moonlight and Memories

Shelter from the Storm

Wayward Angel

Denim and Lace

Cheyennes Lady

Too Hard to Handle

Texas Lily

Texas Rose

Texas Tiger

Texas Moon

Mystic Isle Series

Mystic Isle

Mystic Guardian

Mystic Rider

Mystic Warrior

Mysteries:

Family Genius Series

Evil Genius

Undercover Genius

Cyber Genius

Twin Genius

Twisted Genius

Tales of Love and Mystery

Blue Clouds

Garden of Dreams

Nobody's Angel

Volcano

California Girl